Funestine
and Other Adventures
in Romancia

Funestine
and Other Adventures in Romancia

Edited, introduced and translated by
Brian Stableford

A Black Coat Press Book

Visit our website at www.blackcoatpress.com

ISBN 978-1-61227-812-4. First Printing. December 2018. Published by Black Coat Press, an imprint of Hollywood Comics.com, LLC, P.O. Box 17270, Encino, CA 91416. All rights reserved. Except for review purposes, no part of this book may be reproduced or transmitted in any form or by any means, electronic or mechanical, including photocopying, recording, or by any information storage and retrieval system, without permission in writing from the publisher. The stories and characters depicted in this novel are entirely fictional. Printed in the United States of America.

TABLE OF CONTENTS

Introduction

The first three stories in this anthology appeared in 1735 a small volume entitled *Trois nouveaux contes de fées, avec une préface qui n'est pas moins sérieuse*. When Charles Mayer reprinted the three stories in his *Cabinet des fées* in 1786 he identified their author as Catherine de Lintot, who had been previously identified as the author of *Histoire de Mademoiselle de Salens* (1740), but he added to that attribution the remark that the author was now fifty-eight years-old. As that would imply that she had written the collection at the age of seven, either "fifty-eight" must be a misprint or the attribution must be incorrect.[1] That did not prevent many subsequent sources copying the paradoxical claim, although the Bibliothèque Nationale catalogue put a dutiful question mark after the suggested birth date of 1728. Some later sources added a death-date of 1816, although the BN catalogue does not. Joseph de La Porte had previously included Madame de Lintot in his *Histoire littéraire des femme françoises* (1769) as the author of the 1740 novel, but he had not attributed the collection of *contes de fées* to her and he did not offer a date of birth or any other biographical information. The attribution must therefore be reckoned dubious.

The apologetic preface to the 1735 collection, which is not reproduced here, was attributed by some later commentators to the Abbé Antoine-François Prévost, but that is equally

---

[1] It is pure speculation, but might Mayer not have accidentally transposed the numbers and actually meant to say that Madame de Lintot was 85 rather than 58 in 1786? Mayer gives her maiden name as Caillot, although some later citations substitute Cailleau, but that does not make the individual to whom he is referring any easier to identify using presently-available sources.

speculative. If it were correct, however, it would provide a second link to the first of the two long novellas also translated in the present volume, in addition to the fact that it, too, appeared in 1735, and thus helps to provide a valuable insight into the context in which the first three *contes de fées* appeared. Although Abbé Prévost is not named in *Voyage merveilleux du Prince Fan-Férédin dans la Romancie* (tr. as "The Marvelous Voyage of Prince Fan-Férédin in Romancia"), he is a significant presence therein.

Voyage merveilleux du Prince Fan-Férédin dans la Romancie was written by the Jesuit Guillaume-Hyacinthe Bougéant in direct response to a scholarly essay, *De l'usage des romans, où l'on fait voir leur utilité et leur differens caractères, avec une bibliothèque des romans* [On the Usage of Romances, which shows their utility and their different characteristics, with a library of romances], illicitly published in two volumes in 1734, allegedly in Amsterdam, with the by-line "M. le C. Gordon de Percel," although it was actually by Abbé Nicolas Lenglet Du Fresnoy. The second volume constitutes a bibliography of "romances," categorized into different types. Lenglet Du Fresnoy went on to become a significant bibliographer of works on occult science and apparitions as well as further essays on *romans*.

By the term *roman* Lenglet Du Fresnoy clearly meant "romances" rather than "novels" in the modern sense of the term, although the word was already shifting its customary meaning in French and several of the cardinal examples brought into focus by Bougéant, including those by Prévost, would nowadays be seen as early novels, and contrasted with the more fantastic stories that provide the basic material of his parody. Bougéant recognizes the nascent differentiation himself in observing that *Romancie* has already been geographically divided into *Haut Romancie* [Higher Romancia] and *Bas Romancie* [Lower Romancia].

Bougéant's work provides a striking allegory of the situation of fiction in Paris in 1735, symbolizing the world of publishing in one episode as a "city" in which the various annalists of Romancia each have their own street and shop-signs, according to their particular character, in a classification system markedly different from the one employed by Lenglet Du Fresnoy. Bougéant's discriminates *enfileurs* (threaders) from *souffleurs* (blowers—as of soap bubbles), *brodeurs* (embroiderers) and others, including *lanterniers ou faiseurs de lanternes-magiques* (manufacturers of magic lanterns), which last category, includes writers of *contes de fées*, the contemporary scarcity of which is noted, but not explained.

Although two fays are featured among the population of Romancia, the protagonist does not actually get to meet them, even in the somewhat cursory fashion in which he encounters centaurs, hippogriffs and all manner of other fantastic creatures and phenomena. The genre is tacitly regarded as something already consigned to the remoter annals—Bougéant obviously had not had an opportunity to see *Trois nouveaux contes de fées* before writing his own text, and no characters from *contes de fées* obtain the privilege granted to those in several more recent works, who are permitted to take their creators to task for their ill-treatment before a stern imaginary tribunal.

Bougéant judged too soon, however; *contes de fées* were not dead, but had merely been consigned to an enchanted torpor, like his Prince Zazaraph. Not only were several of the collections that had received royal prerogatives in 1697-99, before new contributions to the genre was effectively banned from licit publication, still available and still popular, but they were still influential, about to prompt a new generation of writers to take up their literary quest—particularly the developments pioneered in competition by Madame d'Aulnoy and the Comtesse de Murat—and to carry forward the evolution that they had begun before being cut off in their prime.[2] That

---

[2] Accounts of the curious circumstances of the effective interdiction of the genre after a brief burst of fashionability can be found in several other Black Coat collections, most fully and

renaissance was permitted and provided with a economic context by the paradoxical circumstances eloquently illustrated by
Bougéant's allegory, and it began in the same year as the publication of his own work with the illicit publication of *Trois
nouveaux contes de fées* and an anthology, *Nouveaux contes
de fées allégorique*s, similarly illicit and anonymous, although
the longest story it contained, reprinted separately as *Boca, ou
vertu recompensée* (tr. as "Boca; or Virtue Recompensed")
was eventually attributed to Françoise Le Marchand, who—
according to Joseph de La Porte—paid for the publication.[3]

The two 1735 collections were soon followed by two
longer and more robust, albeit fugitive works, published in
1737, the long novellas *Tecserion*, and *Funestine*. The former
was eventually attributed to Mademoiselle de Lubert, who
went on to publish numerous works of a similar nature, all
issued illicitly, a selection of which, including "Tecserion,"
can be found in the Black Coat Press collection *Princess Cam-
ion*.[4] The latter, which concludes the present anthology, was
attributed to the dramatist Pierre-François Godard de
Beauchamps (1689-1761), whose principal literary work was a
licensed four-volume history of the French theater,
*Recherches sur les théâtres de France depuis 1161 jusqu'à
présent* (1735). Other illicit publications speculatively attributed to him included contributions to the genre of "liber-
tine fiction" that began to flourish in the 1730s—much to
Guillaume-Hyacinthe Bougéant's disapproval—but he was
also part of the *"petite cour"* of the Duchesse du Maine, a
princess of the blood, who might have been peripherally involved in the initial fad for *contes de fées* in the 1690s. The
Duchesse hosted literary salons of her own at the Château de
Sceaux, and is also said to have obliged her courtiers to make

---

most recently in the anthology *The Queen of the Fays*, ISBN
978-1-61227-814-8.
[3] cf the Black Coat Press volume *Florine and Boca* by
Françoise Le Marchand, ISBN 978-1-61227-810-0.
[4] ISBN 978-1-61227-796-7.

up stories for her during frequent periods of insomnia; it is possible that *Funestine* owed its origin to that practice.

It is difficult to give an accurate account of the renaissance of *contes de fées* spearheaded by the two 1735 volumes, not only because all the illicitly-published volumes were necessarily anonymous but because the people involved maintained a careful discretion in their other writings, carefully not revealing what they knew about who had done what, when and why. Fragments of circumstantial evidence suggest, however, that Françoise Le Marchand's salon might well have been the most significant crucible in which the renaissance of the genre was nurtured. The internal evidence of the *Trois nouveaux contes de fées* suggests that their primary influence was the work of Baronne d'Aulnoy and the Comtesse de Murat, which were also the principal influence on the other major writers involved in the renaissance, but if one juxtaposes the work credited to Lintot and Le Marchand with the generic works published over the following decade by such writers as Mademoiselle de Lubert, Madame de Villeneuve and the Comte de Caylus it is tempting to infer that the writers must have been closely aware of one another's endeavors, and consciously working in a common cause, perhaps with a element of tacit competition.

Caylus, in an apologetic preface to the final brace of his *contes de fées*, written in 1760 or thereabouts but not published until 1775,[5] states that he was urged to write his first such tales by members of the "companies" that he frequented in the late 1730s, and although he was careful not to name any names, the probability is that he was referring to Françoise Le Marchand's salon, among others, and implying very strongly that there was a cabal of female writers there consciously recapitulating what Mademoiselle L'Héritier, Mademoiselle de La Force, the Comtesse de Murat and Baronne d'Aulnoy had done forty years earlier. If that is the case, then the author of

---

[5] cf the Black Coat Press collection *The Impossible Enchantment* by the Comte de Caylus, ISBN 978-1-61227-809-4.

11

Trois nouveaux contes de fées was surely a member of that group, and probably one of the most important in providing new exemplars for the others to follow. However, Caylus was also a prominent member of the Duchesse du Maine's petty court, and was undoubtedly acquainted with Beauchamps. Caylus' mother, who was brought up by Madame de Maintenon, had known the Princesses de Conti, and Caylus had known the Duchesse du Maine since they were children; he too might have begun improvising some of his tales in order to help soothe her insomnia.

The first three stories herein translated do not add up a vast body of work by any means, but they are nevertheless remarkable. They show a very marked evolution, each story being more substantial, more complicated, and more imaginatively innovative than its predecessor. Although, to a large extent, they clearly attempt to take up where Baronne d'Aulnoy and the Comtesse de Murat had been forced to leave off, in terms of their imaginative extravagance, their use of metamorphoses and their quirky employment of allegory, they do so in a robust manner that is certainly not merely imitative. In particular, they show a marked further development in the direction of the calculatedly absurd and the surreal. Although it is arguable that the very multiplicity of those trends make the stories rather untidy and imagistically overloaded, there is certainly more virtue in striving to do too much than settling for barely doing enough. The hectic pace and bizarre imagery of "Le Prince Sincer" (tr. as "Prince Sincere") and "Tendrebrun et Constance" (tr. as "Tendrebrun and Constance"), in particular, gives the stories a peculiar charm that might have remained unique had not Beauchamps, Lubert and Caylus taken up the thread, surely deliberately, and with an awareness of those models.

If Madame de Lintot really did write the three stories translated herein, it is perhaps regrettable, in retrospect, that her subsequent publications appear to have been far more conventional and pedestrian, and that she left it to others to carry on what she had started, but it has to be remembered that all the people involved were operating outside the umbrella of law. Bougéant's satire includes a sequence in which new books are likened to ships arriving in port, and notes that although only some of them carry an official seal of approval, the remainder presumably carrying "contraband," it seems to make very little difference to their reception. Indeed, by 1735 the number of illicit publication printed in Paris probably exceeded the number equipped with royal privileges, and the police had already adopted a policy of turning a blind eye to most of them, in order to concentrate their attempts at active suppression on those they considered genuinely pernicious. There is, however, a considerable difference between tacit toleration and safety; any book about which someone in a position of authority cared to make a complaint, on any grounds, was likely to become a target, exposing its printer and author—if they could be identified—to prosecution and severe punishment. It was not a risk that anyone would take without a strong motivation, and as such books could only be sold, so to speak, "under the counter" the possibility of them generating any substantial financial return was remote.

Although Bougéant's satire is a flamboyant fantasy itself, its attitude to the fantastic in fiction—the principal stock-in-trade of his *lanterniers*—is curiously ambiguous. He clearly regrets the decline of Haut Romancie, but for largely nostalgic reasons, regarding it as charming but essentially obsolete. As a satirist, he is naturally unable to take the chimerical seriously, but he is not insensitive to the esthetics of the absurd, as developed by the author of *Trois nouveaux contes de fées*. Indeed, it is arguable that the depiction of the two fays of whom Prince Zazaraph gives a brief account to Prince Fan-Férédin celebrates that esthetic with an appropriate irony. Given the historical point that French fiction, seen in broad panorama, had reached in 1735, Bougéant was undoubtedly right to reserve his most careful attention and his most scathing criticism for *romans* carefully purged of the supernatural, and the trend-setting works of the Abbé Prévost in particular, but whether or not Prévost actually wrote the preface to *Trois nouveaux*

13

contes de fées, there is still a connection between his melo-dramatic but de-supernaturalized fiction and that of the authors of the new wave of *contes de fées* that was about to flourish. Bougéant's careful analysis of the strange formalities of Romancian amour is very clearly reflected in the three tales preceding his satire in the present collection, as well as the novella succeeding it.

It is worth noting in this context that although Bougéant has obvious doubts about the utility and moral value of much recent prose, he has none at all about François Fénelon's *Les Aventures de Télémaque*, (written before 1697; first published 1699; reprinted and much more widely read in 1716) although that work, whose content seemed treasonous to Louis XIV on the part of the tutor to the potential heir to the throne,[6] might have played a key role in bringing fantastic fiction into bad odor with the royal censors. Bougéant clearly considers *Télémaque* to be a towering achievement, and it obviously played a considerable role in inspiring his own endeavor. Although clearly on the side of the angels, therefore—as befits a loyal Jesuit—Bougéant can also be considered as tacit ally of the fays, and perhaps as useful to their cause, in his own fashion, as the heroic author who might or might not have been Madame de Lintot.

As to whether Pierre-François Beauchamps read *Voyage merveilleux du Prince Fan-Férédin dans la Romancie*, we can only speculate, but in spite of their very obvious differences of style and ideology, that work and *Funestine* have a certain amount in common, in their interest in and attitude to the historical development of "romance" and its brief flirtation with *contes de fées*. The allegorical intrusion in *Funestine* in which the renegade fay Imagination describes her love affair with Extreme, the brother of Fabulous, and his betrayal of her amour with the flamboyant Chimera, can be read as a commentary on that episode, and the climax of the story surely has

---

[6] cf the introduction to the aforementioned anthology *The Queen of the Fays*.

La Tyranie des fées détruite (1703 as by "Comtesse D.L.")[7] and the sad fate of the 1690s genre in mind, in providing a much more violent end to that "tyranny." Like Madame d'Aulnoy in her later work, Beauchamps expresses explicit contempt for himself for stooping so low as to write a *conte de fées*, but he is clearly being deliberately disingenuous. He was not to know when he wrote the story that he was in the forefront of an outlaw renaissance, and does not seem to have been tempted to repeat the adventure, but he must surely have been delighted to discover, as time passed, that he had, in fact, been a pioneer of sorts.

Like many of the key works in the under-the-counter generic resurrection, *Funestine* rapidly became scarce, and because it was by a male writer it was not documented by Joseph de La Porte. It was added to Mayer's *Cabinet* slightly belatedly, in volume thirty-one—then intended as the last, although Mayer eventually added another ten in dribs and drabs, as more material was brought to his attention—and within the context of the *Cabinet* it seems decidedly anomalous, although its mock-allegorical pretentions, its deliberate inversions of convention, and its reckless narrative disorder all have notable precedents. It is, however, a remarkable work, exploiting the license for excess tacitly granted by the genre's conventions in a blithely casual and conscientiously idiosyncratic fashion. It is not the only work of the period to extrapolate its licensed disorder to the chaotic brink of surrealism, but it does so more self-consciously than most, and its tongue-in-cheek comments on its own procedure are thought-provoking, all the more so in juxtaposition with Bougéant's commentary and the exemplars provided by the first three stories in the anthology. Although by no means a coherent set, therefore, the materials gathered herein do provide an intriguing kaleidoscopic pattern, and can justly be reckoned to be more than the sum of their parts.

---

[7] tr. as *The Tyranny of the Fays Abolished*, Black Coat Press, ISBN 978-1-61227-792-9.

The translation of the three stories attributed to Madame de Lintot was made from volume 14 of the version of the *Nouveau Cabinet des Fées* reproduced on the Bibliothèque Nationale's *gallica* website, which is the facsimile reprint published in 1978 by Slatkine. The translation of *Voyage merveilleux du Prince Fan-Férédin dans la Romancie* was made from the version contained in volume 26 of Charles Garnier's collection *Voyages imaginaires, songes, visions, et des romans cabalistiques* reproduced on *gallica*. As well as reproducing the author's footnotes from the original, Garnier added a few of his own; I have distinguished the two sets in the translation as "Author's note" or "Editor's note" as appropriate, with additional comments outside the quotation marks; the remainder of the notes are entirely mine. The translation of *Funestine* was made from the version of volume 31 of the *Cabinet des fées* reproduced on *gallica*.

Brian Stableford

THREE *CONTES DE FÉES* ATTRIBUTED TO CATHERINE DE LINTOT

TIMANDRE AND BLEUETTE

In the charming city of Cangam a prince reigned who was given the name of Silent. He was not loved by his subjects, because he spoke very little and only laughed rarely. He was, however, intelligent, he loved to do good and he governed his kingdom with a good deal of generosity, justice and prudence. So many fine qualities did not prevent conspiracies sometimes being formed against his life.

Silent was not unaware of the extent to which he was hated. That hatred caused him a great deal of chagrin, but he hoped that by the force of benefits he might win the hearts of his people; that hope engaged him to appear frequently on a balcony of his palace that overlooked the main square; from there he distributed a considerable quantity of gold and silver.

Once evening, he perceived in the crowd a little old woman, simply dressed, who was holding a basket of herbs on her arm, and who shouted to him: "Sire, do me the favor of buying my herbs; I am so unfortunate that no one wants them, although they're good and I sell them at a better price than others. If Your Majesty has that generosity, he will prevent me from dying of hunger."

Touched by the poverty of the poor woman, the king sent her a purse full of gold; she received it with a joy that is easy to imagine, and begged the man who brought her that money to take her basket of herbs, to give it to the king on her behalf, and to ask him for a brief audience.

"Keep your basket," the courtier said to her, mocking her.

Fatima—that was the good woman's name—was not put off, and she made the same plea to several other officers, but none of them would listen to her. She therefore made the decision to wait at the door of the palace for Silent to come out in order to go to the temple.

When she perceived him, she approached him with a great deal of respect and said to him: "I've come to thank Your Majesty for the favor that he was kind enough to do me and to beg him to order that my herbs be taken to his cabinet. I cannot, Sire, give you a more sensible mark of my gratitude. This basket contains a present worthy of Your Majesty, if what a beautiful lady told me one day is true. She gave me a leaf of sorrel to compensate me for having allowed her to pick a few flowers in my garden. 'Conserve this leaf carefully,' she said to me; it has properties that render it precious. So long as you carry it on your person, no accident will happen to you.'

"I've kept it for a long time, Sire, but, seeing that I could not sell my herbs today, I decided to give it up. I showed it to several people, and explained its virtues to them, offering to give it to them for very little, but I was treated as a madwoman. Chagrined, I threw it in my basket. If Your Majesty is curious to discover it, he will find it easily, because it is larger and longer than the others and there are several characters on it that I could not read."

The king thanked her, and had her given two purses similar to the first. Having the basket of herbs carried to his apartment then, he went back to look for the leaf, which he found without difficulty. Examining it attentively, he remarked that someone had indeed written on it that, by putting the leaf in the left hand, one rendered oneself invisible, and that by placing it over one's heart, one could know the most secret thoughts of those who were nearby.

Silent, wanting to test its virtue, placed it in his hand and then, traversing his apartments, he discovered with an infinite pleasure that no one could see him. Putting it over his heart then, he read in the mind of the captain of his guards that the man had the intention of assassinating him that very evening, in the hope of reigning in his stead.

The king retired to his cabinet, had the traitor and his accomplices arrested, and their punishment followed immediately after they had confessed their crime.

The prince, deeming that he was very fortunate to have such a useful herb, placed it in a little bag of golden cloth, which he always wore thereafter over his heart. By that means, he knew the character of all the people who approached him. He only perceived false hearts delivered to ambition, and slaves of the most shameful avarice.

Frightened to find so many vices among his favorites and courtiers, he wanted to find out whether all his subjects were equally perverted; he found hardly any who were not different from what they appeared to be.

Revolted by reigning over such a depraved people, Silent made the decision to abdicate the throne and to go to end his days in one of his castles, situated in the middle of a beautiful forest, preferring the mildness of a tranquil and solitary life to the tumult of the court and the honors that were rendered to him there.

The queen, his wife, had died a long time ago, and had only left him from his marriage a daughter who had been stolen from her cradle by a huge black dog. Since then, it had not been possible for him to determine what had become of the princess in question, so nothing prevented him from making the decision to retreat. Solitude had charms for him that high society no longer presented; he liked to read and study. Although he was a prince he was a philosopher and a scholar, but he did not have the usual faults thereof; his knowledge did not render him insupportable, like many people; he was devoid of obstinacy and presumption, and not curious to hear his works praised. In sum, he rendered justice to those who spoke or thought better than he did.

As he was getting ready to leave, he saw Abdal, a man of distinction and merit, entering his cabinet. The king had not seen him since he had been wearing the sorrel leaf; the minister had been prevented from appearing but a long and inconvenient malady. Silent, having no doubt that the newcomer was as scantly virtuous as the others, was about to leave without looking at him, but he made the reflection that, prior to his illness he had charged him with a few affairs that interested him particularly, and he asked him for an account of them.

How surprised he was! He saw that Abdal was the only man in the realm who was veritably virtuous. He was so charmed by it that he embraced him, and told him that he merited wearing the crown that he had made the resolution to quit. He begged him to accept it, assuring him that his people would cherish him, because he had all the qualities necessary to make himself loved.

In fact, Abdal was the most amiable of men; he had a noble air, beautiful eyes, a laughing mouth and a gracious smile; the sound of his voice was agreeable, he sang divinely, and knew everything. In sum, he was well made and had an infinite intelligence, but what rendered him accomplished was the generosity of his heart. Compassionate to the suffering of the unfortunate, his greatest pleasure was to help them, and he did it with a good will that charmed those he obliged as much as the pleasure itself. Everyone's joy can therefore by imagined when people learned that Silent had ceded his kingdom to him on retiring.

Abdal had done his best to turn the king away from the decision he had made, and not to reign in his stead, but he had been forced to obey, to the great contentment of the whole kingdom, by which he was adored and respected, along with the beautiful Zemona, his daughter, and the young Timandre, his son.

That prince had a merit equal to his father's he was so handsome and so well made that one could not see him without admiration. One day, when he was in a forest, occupied in reading a book that pleased him while instructing him, he saw a piece of paper fluttering in front of him on which something was written in golden letters; he got up in order to catch it, but as he tried to reach out for it, the paper drew away from him. Timandre ran after it, the paper moved further away, and did the same every time the prince tried to get closer to it.

Timandre, not put off, wanted to see how far the paper would take him; he followed it all day, and found himself at nightfall in a part of the forest that was unfamiliar to him. Then the note came to settle in his hand, and the prince read the following:

> *A charming princess*
> *Feels the strongest love for you;*
> *If you respond to her tenderness,*
> *You will possess her one day.*
> *But if your indifference*
> *Makes her shed any tears,*
> *You can prepare your constancy*
> *For all the greatest woes.*

The prince reread those lines several times, and was not frightened by the threats they contained. He did not doubt that one day, he would love the unknown princess very much. Thus far, he had not loved; no object had appeared to him to be worthy of his attachment. It was not that Zemona did not have a great many beauties in her retinue, but Timandre had always found faults in their mentality or in their humor.

Belise, filled with self-esteem and incessantly occupied with the desire to please, wanted all hearts and only accorded a gracious smile to those who told her that she was beautiful. Celereine, at certain moments, was kind and affectionate, and at others she was disdainful and piquant. Fatma prided herself on being knowledgeable and hardly ever talked about anything but current affairs, was decided about everything, and did not think women intelligent enough to converse with her. Barbane was proud and bored by everything. Felice moved too much when she spoke, and had an expression that was too embarrassed or too pinched. In sum, of all the young women he knew, there was not one that could please him. He imagined that the one of whom the paper spoke must be everything he could desire.

Flattered by that idea, he only thought about the pleasure of seeing her. What annoyed him greatly was that the little piece of paper did not indicate to him where she lived. In that uncertainty he walked on, in the hope of finding some house in the forest where he might be able to learn more about what he wanted to know.

A few moments later he heard a buzz in the air; he looked up, and perceived a little throne of roses and jasmine sustained by a prodigious quantity of bees, which were flying slowly toward him. That spectacle astonished him greatly, but he was even more surprised when he saw the winged troop stop nearby, and one of the insects presented him with a rose-leaf, by which he was instructed to mount the throne without delay and allow himself to be taken to a place where he was awaited impatiently.

Timandre, not making any reflection about the chagrin that he was about to cause the king and queen by his absence, did what any young person devoid of experience would have done. He did not listen to reason, and, abandoning himself to his inclination alone, placed himself in the midst of the jasmines and roses, and saw with an infinite pleasure that his little team cleaved through the air with an incredible velocity.

He resembled an inhabitant of Olympus in that charming carriage; large curly brown tresses fell negligently over the blue and silver gauze coat in which he was clad. Two violet canaries were beside him on a jasmine branch, whistling two-part tunes with an astonishing accuracy; their sounds were so soft and sweet that one could not hear them without experiencing an agreeable emotion.

The prince had never traveled with as much pleasure and such great speed, for his eyes, although very good, could not distinguish the different lands over which they passed. He traversed the air for four hours, and then the insects set down the carriage in a garden so magnificent and so surprising that it appeared to be the abode of the gods. He had never seen anything remotely like it.

The sand in the pathways of the garden was gold and the branches of the trees were transparent, the color of emerald. The leaves, the most beautiful green in the world, never fell. Finally, all the trees were garnished with flowers and fruits that spread an odor so sweet and agreeable that the senses of smell and sight were equally satisfied. Patches of nascent grass were offered on all sides to anyone in quest of mild repose. Thousands of birds were singing in the shady pathways of the wood, in perfect harmony with a charming symphony that could be heard in the heavens.

A continual spring reigned in that beautiful abode; no rain or wind ever made itself felt there; only the zephyr could blow there. Violets, hyacinths, jonquils and many other flowers were the only things that charming place produced. No useless plants were to be seen there and no inconvenient animals; white fallow deer wearing diamond necklaces ran through the woods; in the pathways one saw grouse, pheasants, turtle-doves, peacocks and squirrels; all those animals were tame and docile to the voice of anyone who called to them.

Clear, fresh and pure water emerged from several springs and formed a quantity of little streams that flowed in rock crystal channels, the borders of which were garnished with violets and pansies. Palisades of jasmines, pomegranates and orange blossom were the only walls that forbade entry to that enchanted place. Timandre could not weary of admiring all those beauties, but he was dying of impatience to find the mistress of the charming garden.

When he had been wandering for some time in the beautiful places he saw an ivory caleche passing by drawn by two stags whose antlers were gold, and in the caleche he perceived a young woman more beautiful than Hebe; he was enchanted by her, and tried to place himself in front of the carriage in order to stop it, but the deer were going so rapidly that he soon lost sight of it.

That adventure would have afflicted him if he had had time to think about it, but twelve other caleches of Japanese porcelain, drawn by white unicorns and driven by twelve young women more beautiful than the first caused him such a great astonishment that he was as if paralyzed, unable to pronounce a single word. He repented of his silence, for an instant later he no longer saw any carriages.

He followed the route they had taken rapidly, and advanced all the way to the end of a broad avenue, but when he arrived there he saw neither the caleches or the ladies who had given him so much curiosity; he discovered a canal that seemed to be infinite in length, and on which there were several crystal ships with masts of gold and sails of silver and roseate gauze; all the sailors were clad in silver cloth and carried garlands of flowers that served to attach golden reins to those superb vessels. The prince, surprised by that new spectacle, with reason, stopped and considered that fleet attentively, which was advancing slowly in his direction. A little launch was detached and came to the shore where he was.

A child formed as Amour is depicted emerged therefrom and asked the prince whether he was not curious to know the beauty who reigned in that place. Timandre assured him that he could imagine no greater happiness than that of being able to render his homages to her.

"Enter my boat, then," said the child, with a malicious smile, "and you will not be long without achieving the fulfillment of your desires."

The prince did not have to be begged any longer; he leapt into the launch precipitately, which a gust of wind had soon brought close to the largest of the ships.

He was received there by two young women, who led him over the deck to where the queen was sitting on a throne made of a single amethyst. Four lemon trees in emerald pots formed an arbor above her head, which had the most beautiful effect in the world.

She got up when the prince had arrived nearby and, inviting him to sit down, she asked him whether he believed the lines that he had read in the forest and whether he had been touched by the hope that had been given to him.

"I did not have enough vanity, Madame," he said to her, "to dare to think that such a pleasant fate was destined for me. I believed, however, that I ought not to defer rendering to the amiable princess that had been announced to me. I departed, therefore, with the design of going to offer her my heart and my services. But Madame, your presence has already given birth in this heart to other sentiments that a divinity would not be capable of destroying. I would deem myself the most fortunate of mortals if you would permit me to make them known to you and if you were kind enough to suffer that I send my days admiring you."

"I grant you willingly what you are asking," the queen said to him, "and I am glad to admit that I am the person for whom you are searching. I saw you yesterday in the forest from which my bees removed you; you were pursuing a stag with a great deal of ardor; you appeared to me to be a god, so charming did I find you. I sensed that you alone could make my felicity, so I formed the design to enable you to know what I thought and to attract you to my court; I carried out that design today. My name is Gracious and I am the daughter on the Queen of the Fays. I possess the art of enchantment, as she does, and this place only depends on me.

"This realm is the abode of the Pleasures; one encounters Laughters, Games and Graces everywhere; Chagrins and Ennuis are banished from it forever; I have engaged myself by an inviolable oath to punish them as soon as they appear; see whether you will be capable of preventing them from approaching you, and whether it is possible for you to love me as constantly as I demand. If you promise me a fidelity proof against anything, you will reign in this beautiful place and nothing will trouble the pleasures that are being prepared for you here.

"If my heart, my hand and my crown cannot flatter you, you can return to Abdal's court; I will have you taken back there, although I sense that your going away might make the unhappiness of my life. Make up your mind, but remember that a frightful destiny awaits you if you break your word to me."

Timandre, enchanted by Queen Gracious, swore to her that all the beauties in the world could never make him repent of his attachment to her, and that she would always be the unique object of his amour—an oath that lovers ordinarily make when they commence loving, but which they forget as soon as they are content.

Gracious, satisfied by the assurance that the prince gave her, presented her hand to him, which he kissed with a transport that did not displease the queen. She had a conversation with him that, although very long, only appeared to have lasted a moment.

Timandre found her the most perfect of all women; the most touching graces were distributed over her person; her mind was easy, fine and delicate. She was tall, and her figure was perfect. She had admirable breasts, arms and hands, but a thick veil hid her face and gave the prince a curiosity that he would have liked very much to satisfy; but she told him that it was not yet time for her to show herself to him, that she wanted to hide the shame of the confession that she had made to him to promptly, and that she also wanted to test whether she could be loved as much as she desired, without the aid of her face.

"I want you, my dear Timandre," she added, "to be more touched by my character than my beauty. A beautiful face is striking and very pleasing, but it is like a fresh and beautiful flower that a ray of sunlight a little too ardent fades in a moment; even when it can be protected from the accidents that might spoil it, it cannot avoid the effects that the number of the years inflicts upon it. Don't be chagrined, however; I shall not always wear the veil that afflicts you; I want to test your fidelity, and when I am sure of it, I will render you master of my person, as you are of my heart."

The prince found so much reason in what the queen said that he dared not insist, in spite of the vivacity of his desires.

He had been on the ship for four or five hours when he perceived a palace on the bank of the canal that Gracious told him had been organized to receive him. It was built of diamonds of a surprising size and beauty. The ships came to moor there.

Timandre disembarked with the queen and her retinue in order to enter the superb building; he praised its structure and magnificence more than once. After several eulogies he was taken into a drawing room where there was a table served with the most exquisite dishes. Gracious sat down there beside the prince, with a part of her court. At the end of the meal she played the lute and sang in such a fashion that if Timandre had not been the most amorous of men he would have become so instantly. In spite of the prodigious range of her voice it was soft and perfectly accurate.

A ball followed that magnificent meal, composed of a magnificent youth of both sexes. Gracious danced and danced, always with Timandre. The prince had never experienced such sweet moments.

He spent others during six months that were no less agreeable, for new pleasures were invented every day to prevent him from getting bored. He loved and he was loved; however, his happiness lacked possessing his dear Gracious and the pleasure of seeing in her eyes the tenderness that she testified to him continually.

One evening, when he was walking along the canal bank with her, he implored her to complete his happiness, since she was convinced of the violence and the sincerity of his passion. He pressed her so urgently that she could not refuse him, but his prayer was not granted immediately; the day was set and awaited with an equal impatience by both of the lovers.

When it arrived they gave one another their hands and swore an eternal love in a little temple surrounded by trees and consecrated to sensual pleasure. Amour and Hymen were reconciled at that moment, and were with the two spouses all day; after the ceremony they were taken to an apartment carpeted with jasmine and orange-blossom; two carbuncles placed beside a beautiful bed spread a bright light there, but Gracious ordered her maidservants to take them away. The prince consented to that with difficulty, but in the end, the pleasure that was taken away from him did not prevent him from delivering himself with an inconceivable joy to those he had awaited with so much impatience.

No night have ever seemed so short; he saw the daylight arrive, and imagined that it had commenced its career sooner than usual. He consoled himself, however, in the hope of finally seeing the face of the woman he loved so ardently. He hastened therefore to open the curtains and cast his eyes upon the queen, who was sleeping profoundly.

But great gods, how astonished he was! The person who had inspired so much amour in him had the face of a little she-monkey, which was making grimaces even in sleep that were very pleasant, but which appeared so frightful to Timandre that he was consternated. He went pale and cold, and conceived for the queen an aversion as strong as the amour he had felt had been violent. He repented, but too late, of having engaged in an adventure that had appeared charming, and whose consequences were so deplorable. He swore that if he could get out of it, he would never allow himself to be seduced by appearances again.

"How deceptive they are!" he exclaimed. "Who would have believed that such a beautiful body could have such an ugly head?"

Those words woke the queen. She heard them, and although she had to do herself justice, she was sharply stung by them. All women like to be flattered; the truth only pleases them to the extent that it does not seek to destroy the opinion they have of their beauty. One can therefore imagine the chagrin of Gracious, who had that weakness to a greater extent than any other person of her sex. She looked at the prince and knew the horror that he had for her. What despair for a woman in love, to sense that she only inspires hatred!

Instantly, she formed the design to avenge herself, and executed it without delay. Her wand was by the side of the bed; she picked it up and, touching Timandre, she said to him:

"Ingrate, since I can no longer inspire amour in you, become so different yourself that you can never please anyone whatsoever."

As soon as she had finished speaking, the prince became a pink and blue butterfly. The fay metamorphosed him thus by a sort of injustice, attributing to his inconstancy what she ought only to have imputed to her own deformity. He did not change his way of thinking in changing his form. Gracious left him the memory of what he had been, and expelled him from the palace and the garden of graces.

He drew away from it rapidly in order not to see any longer the monster who had just metamorphosed him, and he flew for several months without knowing where he was going. He was sad and chagrined, and no longer hoped to savor any pleasure, but he dreaded nevertheless that cruel fate might cut the thread of his days; the smallest bird made him tremble.

All human beings resemble one another on that point; it is in vain that they proclaim their woe and the desire for death; there is not one who does not seek to prolong life. Timandre took as much care of his days as if he had been the most fortunate of mortals.

After having flown for a long time he found himself at the entrance to a wood, the trees of which appeared to be several centuries old. He paused to rest there, and after a few moments saw a young woman of sixteen or seventeen pass by, whom nature had ornamented with a beauty so perfect that the mother of the amours could not have surpassed it. A linen dress and a few cornflowers that she had arranged with great care in her hair were her entire adornment. All the charms of which she partook did not appear to render her vain; an air of mildness and modesty gave rise to a prejudice in her favor.

What a difference there is, Timandre said to himself, as he considered her, *between that beautiful young woman and those at Gracious's court! She does not borrow any assistance of artistry in order to please, yet she is capable of setting the entire world ablaze. The others, on the contrary, in spite of the cares that they give themselves, can only have an effect with difficulty, because there is nothing natural about them; their speech and expressions are studied; they affect in their words and actions a liberty that seems to permit everything to those who approach them.*

While making those reflections, the prince perceived that he was following the beautiful person involuntarily, and that a secret penchant was commencing to take possession of his heart. He drew as near to her as possible, and finally came to alight on the flowers of her bouquet.

Bleuette—that was the young woman's name—found the butterfly so familiar and so prettily patterned that she left it where it was. She continued on her way, and shortly thereafter she went into a little house, the furniture of which was simple, clean and of exquisite taste. A garden ornamented with flowers and filled with fruit trees, surrounded by a hawthorn hedge, allowed a glimpse of a meadow irrigated and rendered agreeable by several streams bordered by two rows of willows.

The prince was more enchanted by that rural spot than he had been by the beautiful abode of the queen of the Graces. He perceived in that simple dwelling a little old woman, who appeared as respectable by virtue of her air of mildness and good will as by the number of her years. She was spinning when Bleuette came in, but as soon as she saw her she set her spindle down and held out her arms to her.

"There you are then, my dear daughter," she said to her, embracing her. "What anxiety you have caused me! Please, in future, don't go away for so long. Persons of your age, and as beautiful as you, are often subject to deplorable encounters when a prudent mother does not accompany them."

"I'll take advantage of your advice," said Bleuette, "but I haven't encountered anything dangerous during my walk; only this butterfly offered itself to my eyes, and I want to conserve it for a long time, because it's beautiful, and I imagine that it has no desire to quit me."

She did, in fact, take good care of it, and did not fail to put a large bouquet of flowers beside it every day, in order that it could repose there. Timandre often sighed as he gazed at her, and thought himself very unfortunate in loving her, in being so close to her and only being a butterfly. He had never seen a young woman so lovable and so well brought up.

The old woman, who, appearances suggested, was not of distinguished birth, often astonished the unfortunate prince by her speech and the instruction that she gave to her daughter. She banished therefrom the air of severity of which the majority of mothers make use when they speak to their children. The good woman said that it was necessary to instruct the young while amusing them. She had neither the ill-humor nor the infirmities of old age; a tranquil and contented air was distributed throughout her person; she did not fatigue her daughter with long stories of times past or untimely remonstrations.

One day, when Bleuette was walking in the meadow with her butterfly, she heard Fatima calling her—for it was Fatima that had retired to that solitude; she had bought the little house in which she lived with part of the gold that Silent had given her, and used the rest to live tranquilly with her dear Bleuette—and she ran to the house to find out what she wanted.

"I'm very afflicted, my daughter," the woman said to her. "In trying to take my distaff from this shelf, I knocked over that bottle that you see on the floor. It was filled with a liquid given to me by the same lady that made me a present of the leaf I told you about. A single drop of that liquid can destroy the greatest enchantments."

In order to console her, Bleuette said to her: "You have no malevolent fays for neighbors, why regret that liquid?"

Timandre heard that conversation and had no doubt that, since the liquid had such a great virtue, it could restore him to his original form. He therefore flew immediately to the place where it had spilled, and instantly, a dense smoke rose up in the room. When it had dissipated, the prince found that he was as he had been before his metamorphosis—which is to say, the most lovable of all men.

31

Fatima and Bleuette were very frightened on seeing him appear, and it was with great difficulty that the prince prevented them from running away.

"Have no fear," he said to them, "and deign to listen to me for a moment."

They finally consented to that, and then he told them what had happened to him, his name and his birth.

Fatima expressed the joy she felt at the end of his enchantment, but begged him very honestly not to stay with her any longer and to return to Abdal's court, which was only four leagues away

"Pardon me, Sire, "if I urge you so strongly to depart, but my daughter is young and so are you; I don't doubt her virtue, or yours, but it's always necessary to fear malicious gossip."

The prince dared not contradict her, but he only determined to go away from his other half in the hope of seeing her again soon. "Adieu, sage Fatima," he said to her. "I shall go to find the king, my father, and render a son to him whom he is perhaps no longer expecting to see; but I shall also inform him of to whom he owes the obligation of my return. I shall beg him at the same time to allow me to unite my destiny with that of the charming Bleuette."

Fatima was not flattered by the honor that the prince wanted to bestow on her daughter; she had examples of several great lords who had married persons of obscure birth because they were very amorous, and who had scorned them later. However, she thanked him very politely.

As for Bleuette, she blushed deeply in receiving Timandre's adieu; she felt something for him that she had not yet known, which rendered her eyes more touching than they had been previously. She sighed involuntarily as she watching the prince draw away.

He heard that sigh and, flattering himself that he was the cause of it, he believed himself to be the most fortunate of men. He arrived not long afterwards at the court, and surprised both the king and the queen, who loved him tenderly. There was public rejoicing to celebrate his return; no one received orders for that, the amity alone that people had for the prince caused all labor to cease and obliged the great and the humble to testify the joy that they felt.

Silent, having heard that news, emerged from his solitude expressly to congratulate the king. As he entered the king's apartment he encountered a lady whose appearance and majestic bearing astonished him. After having saluted him, she told him to follow her if he were curious to learn things that would interest him infinitely. Silent obeyed her, and went with her into a clump of trees in Abdal's garden. The lady sat down there and invited him to sit beside her.

She said to him: "I am the fay Favorable.[8] A short time after the death of the queen, your wife, I passed through your estates; I saw you there and I admired the sagacity with which you governed them. I also saw the little Princess Zelima, your daughter; I read in the stars that she would be the most perfect creature in the world if the care of her education were confided to someone capable of it. Touched by seeing hr surrounded by women devoid of virtue and principles, I made the resolution to remove her from their hands.

"In order to do that I took the form of a black dog, and I removed her from her cradle. I gave her the gift of succeeding perfectly in everything that she attempted: she can sing, dance, and play all sorts of instruments as if she had had the most excellent masters. Then I confided her to Fatima she is the woman who gave you a leaf of which I had made her a present, and to which you owe your life. I recommended the princess to her and ordered her at the same time to pass her off as her daughter. I knew her character and had been witness to the grandeur of her soul and the rectitude of her heart on several occasions.

---

[8] The name of this character is subsequently rendered in the original as Secourable [Helpful], and on grounds of frequency it is perhaps the present term that ought to have been altered, but Favorable has a better ring to it.

"Fatima descends from virtuous parents, who were not noble, in truth, but her way of thinking is proof that one can have sentiments of virtue and elevation without being of illustrious birth. She has brought Zelima up with extreme care and has given her an education that responds perfectly to the grandeur of her extraction. She is beautiful and well made; Prince Timandre is extremely amorous for her. He merits her tenderness and your esteem; you cannot do better than to unite them. I am not telling you anything but the truth; I will take you to the princess."

Silent would have taken for a dream everything that the fay said to him if she had not instantly caused an ebony chariot to emerge from the ground, drawn by flame-colored pigeons, in which the king placed himself with her, and which took them to Fatima's house. He recognized Zelima there; she had all the features of the queen, her mother, and also a cornflower on the left foot that she had had since birth and which had caused her to be given the name Bleuette.

Silent made himself known to his lovely daughter and made her a thousand caresses, which she received with a respect full of tenderness. He gave the good Fatima the praise of which she was so worthy, and offered her everything that depended on him.

"I do not want any other recompense," she said to him, "than the pleasure of not being separated from the princess."

He granted her that request, and assured her that he would heap her with benefits; but she was only touched by the permission that he gave her to accompany her dear Bleuette everywhere,

The princess embraced her, and begged her always to conserve the same tenderness for her of which she had given her so much evidence. Fatima was as sensible to her caresses as one can be. She recognized Favorable as the lady who had given her Zelima, the sorrel leaf and the bottle for enchantments.

The four individuals spent a few moments together, and then separated. The fay took Silent back to Abdal's palace and disappeared, saying: "You'll see me again when you least expect it."

He gave her a great many thanks, even when he could no longer see her, and went go to see the king in order to congratulate him on the return of Timandre, whose story Favorable had told him. He told him that he had also found his daughter again, that she was as beautiful as his son was handsome, and that it only depended on him whether they would be united by blood as they were by amity. The king, flattered by that proposition, consented to it with pleasure, but Timandre, who was present and who had already received permission from his father to marry the charming Bleuette, implored him to remember that without her he could not be happy.

Seeing the king embarrassed, Silent took him to one side and told him that Zelima and Bleuette were the same person, but that it was necessary not to tell his son yet, in order to surprise him agreeably.

Abdal, charmed by the news, approached the prince and told him that there was no longer any question of thinking about a young woman whose status was so different from his, and that it was absolutely necessary that he dispose himself to marry Zelima. He went out with Silent as he spoke and ordered the captain of his guards to prevent the prince from leaving his apartment.

The king's speech tendered Timandre furious. He employed all sorts of means to deceive the vigilance of the man guarding him or to corrupt him, but in vain.

On the other hand, Silent sent for the princess and told her that in two days she was to marry an amiable prince, the successor to a great empire. A young woman to whom a young and charming husband is promised usually learns that news without dolor, but Zelima was very afflicted by it. Timandre had made such a strong impression on her heart that she felt that she would never be able to forget him. Not daring to reveal her sentiments to her father, however, she disposed herself to obey hm. It was not without lamenting her destiny more than once in secret, and that of Abdal's son.

"How light he is," she said to her dear Fatima. "Would one have thought on seeing the dolor with which he quit me, that he could forget me with so much facility? Alas, he was less fickle when he was a butterfly. I wish he still were; I would at least have the pleasure of seeing him."

Finally, the day arrived that, in her view, would be the most unfortunate of her life; she was conducted the temple like a victim. Timandre, for his part, went there firmly resolve to assure the person destined for him that he was determined to lose his life rather than give her his hand. He entered, therefore and, traversing the numerous assembly proudly, he approached the princess. She was pale and trembling.

He had no sooner set eyes on her than he recognized her for the person he adored. What joy for him! What a charming surprise or her! He made her know, in a few words, how favorable he found his fate; he thanked Silent and the king, his father, for the trick they had played on him. Then the ceremony took place, which was concluded to the great satisfaction of everyone.

As they were about to leave the temple, a loud thunderclap was heard that made the most determined tremble. The vaults of the superb edifice opened, and a veiled woman appeared mounted on a black chariot of terrible dimensions.[9] She approached the newlyweds and, touching them with a golden wand, said to them: "Too fortunate lovers, receive from my hand the death I give you."

Immediately, Timandre and Zelima fell unconscious, causing all those who witnessed the spectacle to utter cries of dolor. Then the cruel magicienne, taking a dagger from beneath her dress, plunged it into her breast, saying: "And you,

---

[9] The original text has *chat* [cat] rather than *char* [chariot], but it is presumably a misprint, as subsequent reference is made to the *char* on which the newcomer had arrived. Any reader who prefers to interpret both references as feline is at liberty to make the imaginative substitution.

too tender and too unfortunate queen, die, abandon life, since it is devoid of charms for you."

As she finished speaking she rendered the last sigh, and the chariot on which she had arrived carried away her body through the same gap by which it had entered. The spectacle had gripped the entire court with fear; the two kings and the queen had fainted at the sight of the calamity that had just occurred.

An admirable concert of voices and instruments caused them to recover from their weakness. They perceived the vault of the temple open for a second time and allow through a ruby caleche drawn by twelve white eaglets, in which a beautiful lady appeared, clad in a white robe embroidered with diamonds, who was recognized by Silent and Fatima as the fay Favorable.

"Console yourselves, Princes," she said to the two kings. "Your children are not dead; I was watching over their conservation and I prevented the wand of the jealous and fraudulent Gracious from abridging their days. She did not perceive that they are merely torpid, so, her vengeance satisfied and in despair at having lost the person she loved, she has given herself veritable death."

Addressing the two spouses then, she said: "Get up, amiable couple, and live a long sequence of years without ceasing to love one another and without anything ever being able to trouble your felicity."

At that voice, Timandre and Zelima recovered their senses. Cries of joy were heard on all sides, but that joy was changed to sadness when the fay, having made them mount her caleche with Silent, Abdal, Zelima and Fatima, was seen taking them all into the realm of the Graces, where the prince and princess reigned for several centuries, always lovable and always lovers.

Silent and Abdal spent tranquil days there; the latter abandoned his kingdom without difficulty and the latter did not regret his subjects, even though they had loved him sincerely. He had never been able to inspire them with sentiments of justice and piety. He found more satisfaction living as a simple commoner with virtuous people, than he had experienced in reigning over a corrupt people.

Favorable, having rendered them all happy, quit them in order to go and soothe the pains of several other unfortunates.

PRINCE SINCERE

There was once a king in the land of the Zinzolantins who had an extreme passion for silkworms. He spent entire days in his gardens collecting mulberry leaves for their nourishment. The rest of the time he shut himself away in his cabinet in order to watch the little animals toil, and in order to make hanks of the silk that they had spun, not finding anyone else who could do it to his liking. In fact, no one wound silk better than he did; he often gave it to noblemen—the majority of them winders like him who gloried in imitating their sovereign—but what happened? Intelligence and politeness abandoned an abode where they were so scorned; impoliteness took possession of the young, and ennui was the share of the most beautiful women.

In the impossibility of making use of their charms with men who only knew and admired the beauty of their worms and the finesse of their silk, almost all of the latter withdrew to distant provinces. The formed a small court there, not of princes and dukes, or even of marquises—they had experienced too much impertinence and impoliteness from them—but of persons of a less elevated condition who had no less merit for not having any of those titles. Good taste and probity was found among them; they cherished the sciences and enjoyed all pleasures without ever banishing the delicacy that alone makes all charm; in sum, they were men different from those at the court of King Dévideur.[10] The queen was one of the first to retire; she had a fine castle in a forest situated on the edge of the sea, and chose it for her residence.

After having taken her leave of the king, who was not displeased by her departure, she took with her two princesses who were the only fruit of her marriage, and a few of her sub-

---

[10] *Dévideur* is French for "[textile] winder."

jects of whose zeal and affection she was aware. The solitude of the place did not frighten her; she had it embellished and rendered the abode charming, combining there all that nature had of the most beautiful with all that art had of the most perfect. Surrounded by people she loved, she savored a tranquility in the palace that she had never experienced before.

The princesses also found the abode enchanted. They loved music, and the most skillful musicians in the world were found in their retinue. The two young women were as beautiful as they were well made, but they were not equally lovable. The elder, named Aigremine, was proud, envious, vindictive and cruel. The younger was mild, obliging and had no greater pleasure than that of obliging. She had a thousand charms in her intelligence and character that made all those who knew her love her, so she merited the name Aimée. She felt a veritable amity for her sister, although she was not unaware that she was hated in return.

One day, after having endured a thousand reproaches because she did not want to appear negligently clad at a ball where there would be a great many people, Aimée went for a walk on her own in order to dissipate the chagrin and annoyance that her sister had caused her.

Aigremine, for her part, went into the forest in order to imagine a costume that would efface her sister's. Occupied with those thoughts, she walked for a long time, without perceiving the path that she was following. Lassitude finally obliged her to sit down at the foot of an oak tree that provided a shade the sun's rays could not penetrate. Examining the height and girth of the tree, she discovered a little key hidden between the bark and the wood. She took it out, but, unable to imagine what use it could be, tried to put it back in the same place.

After having tried in vain, she inserted it in a small hole that she could see; instantly, the key turned of its own accord and opened a door accommodated in the oak with an infinite artistry. That door hid a stairway. Curious to know where it led, the princess decided to go down it. The first steps seemed very dark, but after having descended a few she saw, with surprise, that the staircase was illuminated by several candles placed in beautiful rock crystal chandeliers.

She continued her descent, and when she had gone down more than three hundred steps, she arrived in a magnificently-furnished apartment. One might think it astonishing, and almost impossible, that a person of her sex would be bold enough to enter an unknown subterrain on her own, but I shall say, because I know, and in order that no one will be astonished by it, that she was wearing on her little finger a ring that her grandmother had given her when she died, in order to preserve her until the age of twenty from dangers of any sort.

Convinced that she had nothing to fear, she advanced as far as a large cabinet, or rather a store-room of rare jewels and precious stones. She stopped in order to examine all those riches, but when her sight was drawn to a bed with silver sheets placed in a kind of alcove she was very astonished to perceive the most handsome young man there ever was. He appeared to be plunged in a profound slumber.

Aigremine approached the bed in order to consider him more closely. That curiosity cost her dear, since, from that moment on, she was no longer mistress of her liberty. Convinced—as all pretty women are—that no one could see her without loving her, she did not hesitate to wake the handsome stranger, with the design of inspiring in him the tenderness that she wanted him to have for her. She therefore made a certain amount of noise, but went into the next room, in order that she could not accuse her of anything.

There she found a piece of paper on which was written:

Only the person who can make herself loved by the ugliest of all mortals will have the power to render the prince who reposes here sensible.

The princess read the piece of paper several times. She flattered herself that her eyes were powerful enough to touch the young prince, and that she could make his conquest without being obliged to go in search of the ugliest of men in order to induce him to amour. Filled with that confidence, she attempted to go back into the cabinet, not doubting that the unknown man would wake up; but a spider-web through which it was impossible to distinguish any object immediately sealed the entrance as she tried to approach it.

"Such a slight obstacle won't prevent me from going through," said Aigremine. She advanced, but, in spite of all her efforts, she could neither lift nor pierce the web.

Astonished by such great resistance, she made the decision to go back up to the forest, to return to the queen and to go in search of the ugly man that it was necessary to render amorous before she could inflame the one she had just seen. She went back through the same apartments, therefore, went back up the stairs and emerged into the forest through the door that she had opened.

Scarcely had she come out than the door closed again without being possible to see where it had opened or to rediscover the little key. She went around the tree several times, but in vain.

Despairing of the adventure, she resumed the path to the castle, and found herself on the sea shore. She perceived the princess, her sister, who was looking attentively at a diamond of surprising size and beauty. A bird had just dropped it on her dress, telling her to conserve it carefully, because it would preserve her from a great danger one day, if she had recourse to it.

Aigremine, enchanted by the beauty of that admirable stone, wanted to take possession of it, but she was prevented from doing so by a little man whom she found behind her, and whose frightful face caused her and Princess Aimée to run away. They both withdrew into the forest.

The little man was three feet high. His flat and very broad head was ornamented by an abundance of red hair; his eyes were sunken and so narrowly open that they would have been indistinguishable without their bright red borders; his nose was long and pointed; his jowls hung down over his chest; and his mouth and chin were garnished with a long and bushy red beard, His deformed body was only sustained by one leg, on which he was posed as if on a pivot, but he was so well equilibrated that the slightest wind made him spin continuously—which is why he only went outside when the air was extremely calm. He could not walk, but he hoped with a marvelous agility, and by making several small leaps he arrived promptly wherever he wanted to go.

Aigremine, having recovered from the fear that the little monster had caused her, approached him, and in a tone full of bitterness she asked him who he was and what could have rendered him bold enough to oppose what she had wanted to do.

"I'm a powerful king," he said to her. "My name is Sincere. Reasons that I cannot tell you drew me away from my estates, and I'm spending my days in the depths of a rock that isn't far from here. I've seen you several times in this beautiful place, and I've noticed the unjust conduct you've often had toward your sister. I've just witnessed the violence you wanted to do her in snatching a diamond that ought to belong to her. The love that I have for justice, combine with an emotion that I dare not declare, engaged me to act on her behalf and prevent you doing her that violence."

The princess listened to that discourse with an extreme impatience; however, she dissimulated that anger because she made the reflection that the man who was talking to her could not possibly be equaled in ugliness by anyone in the world, and that, in consequence, she ought not to neglect anything to please him, since it was written than she could only render the man she loved sensible on that condition. She therefore adopted a mild manner and told him that the quality of king and the unfortunate state to which he appeared to be reduced obliged her to forgive him, that she even desired to be his friend, and that she flattered herself that he would not refuse her amity. Then she begged him to come and see her at the castle, assuring him that the queen, informed of his quality, would doubtless offer him an apartment where he could wait at his ease until fortune ceased to persecute him.

The king thanked her politely, and told her that he was far too well aware of the excess of his ugliness to dare to flatter himself with the amity of a beautiful princess and to go to live in a court, where he knew that deformity of the body is not pardoned. As he said that he made a hop in order to take his leave of her, bowed to her, and retired with a sigh—not without looking at the lovely Aimée, whom the presence of her sister had retained a short distance away.

The latter princess had listened to the conversation of her sister and Sincere; she had been surprised by the appearance of generosity that Aigremine had affected and he invitation she had give him to come to the castle. She judged that the princess had only had that mildness because she wanted to hide some desire for vengeance. The pity that Aimée had for the unfortunate man caused her to make the resolution to warn the king to beware of the apparent caresses that her sister was giving him. She put off the execution of her project until the following day.

That day having arrived, she went out with one of her women and took the path to Sincere's rock. She was some distance away from it when she stopped to listen to a song, the words of which appeared to be addressed to her. The sound of the voice that she heard was so touching, and flattered her ears so much, that she remained where she was for a long time, even after the song had ended.

Cephise—that was the name of the maidservant accompanying her—extracted her from her reverie by drawing her attention to the fact that Sincere was coming toward her. Although she was determined to consider him without fear, she could not look at him without trembling and without turning away immediately.

He perceived that with chagrin, and, saluting her with a great deal of respect, he invited her to enter his rustic palace momentarily in order to rest there. Aimée consented to that, and told him that she had only come out in order to see him and tell him things of an extreme consequence. The king offered her his hand with the best grace possible, led her toward the grotto, and spoke to her in the wittiest fashion in the world. She had never imagined that a man as ugly could express himself with so much grace. Everything he said was pronounced in a tone that pleased the princess so much that she wished more than once that she might have a lover who had as much wit as that unfortunate.

Eventually, she arrived inside the rock; fresh green moss carpeted it; a table made of a fragment of white marble, which nature alone had sculpted, a bed and a few grass seats were the only furniture it contained. A spring from which clear pure water emerged fell from the height of the rock and formed a little stream, the noise of which, combined with that made by two nightingales perched on an orange tree laden with flowers and fruits, appeared more charming to the princess than the finest concerts she had ever heard.

After have sung the praises of that agreeable retreat, she told Sincere the reasons that had engaged her to pay him a visit. The prince, charmed by the interest she was taking in his regard told her all the things most appropriate to express his gratitude; he even let a few escape that made it known that his heart was filled with the most tender amour. Aimée understood them very well, but she pretended not to divine that they were addressed to her. In order to change the subject she told the king about the satisfaction she had had in hearing a charming voice before encountering him, and asking him whether he knew who it was that had sung so well.

"It's a prince who adores you," said Sincere, "and who would offer you his heart, his hand and the crown that he ought one day to wear, if his form did not forbid it," He sighed as he finished speaking.

The princess blushed and, understanding that he was talking about himself, did not question him further, but she became pensive. She quit him shortly thereafter, because she feared that her absence might be perceived.

She took the path to the palace, talking to Cephise about the intelligence that she found in Sincere. "I confess, my dear Cephise," she said to her, "that in spite of his ugliness, I feel for him what I have never felt for anyone. I don't know whether it is amity, but I tremble that it might be something more."

"What, Madame?" said the maid, astonished. "You could love that little monster? Everything about him doesn't horrify you? You could resolve yourself to live with him? The slightest wind makes him spin like a weathervane."

"Oh," said the young Aimée, "he thinks so delicately, and he speaks with so much wit, that I would prefer him to the handsomest men in the world. They almost always have an excessive stupidity; delighted with themselves, they only take pleasure in consulting their mirrors, as much as persons of our sex."

The princess was about to continue her discourse when a squeal she heard prevented her from doing so. Looking down at the ground she was surprised to see a white viper, which was hurling fire from its eyes, and which said to her: "You nearly crushed me, Madame. If I weren't as good as I am, I'd punish you for your stupidity, but I forgive you, on condition that you put me back on the trunk of the chestnut tree that you can see, from which I've just fallen. I'll recognize that service one day, for I'm a fay, but like all my sisters, I'm obliged to quit my natural form one day a week to take one that was given to me by an old sorcerer on which we depend. He punished us in that fashion for having cut off his beard and moustache, which displeased us greatly, one day while he was asleep. I'll resume my ordinary form this evening and you'll have news of me."

Aimée picked it up, trembling, carried it to the tree, and drew away promptly in order not to see the animal any longer, which had frightened her horribly.

She arrived at the castle, and found Aigremine there, who was sending someone on the queen's behalf to invite King Sincere to spend a few days at the palace.

Those orders frightened Aimée at first, because she was aware of her sister's malevolence, but it did not take long for her to be reassured, because one of Aigremine's maidservants confided to her the adventure that the elder princess had had in the forest, which the princess had related to her.

Sincere was surprised by the invitation that the queen had sent him. His first impulse was to refuse politely, but, making the reflection that he would see every day the beautiful princess that he loved, he determined to go, and leapt into a caleche that had been sent for him.

He was awaited at the castle with impatience, but that impatience had various motives. All the ladies were curious to see a man made differently than all others. Finally, he arrived, and received the honors that were due to his rank. Aigremine gave him a very agreeable welcome; she was extraordinarily adorned, and without the beauty of her sister one might have thought that she was the most beautiful woman in the world. In spite of all her cares, however, she had the chagrin of seeing that day, and those that followed, that Sincere was untouched by her charms; his gaze was incessantly turned toward Aimée.

Aigremine's irritation was inconceivable; she had put everything to work in order to please the most frightful of mortals, without being able to succeed. Anything that offends a lady's self-esteem is never pardoned, so she became furious against the prince and the princess. What would she not have given to prevent them seeing one another! But that was not possible, for the king had the liberty to talk to her, and sought opportunities to do so. They presented themselves frequently, and Aimée did not refuse the pleasure of talking to him.

The younger princess was walking one day in one of the paths of the park when she perceived a ball than was rolling very rapidly, and stopped when it was close to her. The ball opened, and a little woman emerged who, suddenly growing, became ten or twelve feet tall.

"I am the fay Farouche," she said to the princess, "to whom you rendered a service not long ago."

Aimée recognized her, because she was emitting fire from her eyes like the white viper she had put in the tree. She saluted her very respectfully.

The fay told her that the amity she had for her had engaged her to ask the princess her mother for her in marriage, for her nephew, King Papillon; that she had just come from the queen's cabinet; that the queen had given her consent; and that in two days the prince would arrive to marry her.

That news, which would have given great pleasure to many princesses, afflicted young Aimée sensibly; she was so troubled by it that she did not have the strength to respond a single word to the fay. Farouche, imagining that it was joy that was preventing her from speaking, kissed her on the forehead, and, bidding her adieu, put herself back in her ball, which went back the way it had come.

Cephise arrived immediately thereafter, coming to tell the princes that the queen wanted to speak to her; she therefore went to see her. Without giving her time to respond, the queen told her to be ready in two days to receive Prince Papillon as her husband.

Aimée threw herself to her knees and begged her to withdraw the promise she had given to Farouche. The queen was inflexible; she feared the power of the fays, and, in the hope that the fay might one day give her evidence of her amity, she told her daughter that she wanted her to obey. The princess dared not respond, and withdrew, very afflicted.

Aigremine, who, at any other time, would have been jealous of the preference that the fay had given her sister, was delighted by it, flattering herself that Sincere, no longer seeing Aimée, might attach himself to her.

Such catastrophic news soon reached the unfortunate king's ears; he fell dangerously ill in consequence.

Meanwhile, the day when the fay's nephew was to be presented arrived. The queen, the princess and the entire court went to meet him. Scarcely were they on the terrace when they saw in the far distance a sort of very bright cloud, which approached at high speed. No one doubted that it was the prince.

It was, in fact, him; he was in a diamond chariot drawn by ten thousand butterflies, all pink. They were attached by golden threads interlaced very artfully; a hundred young lords followed their master in crystal caleches garnished with rubies and emeralds, similarly drawn by butterflies, but those were white.

The king descended and stopped his chariot as soon as he was next to the ladies. He came toward them with all his retinue, in the finest order in the world. He was magnificently dressed, and no man had ever been more powdered and better curled than he appeared at that moment; he must have spent at least three hours on his toilette. The fear he had of deranging his hairstyle caused him to walk very gently, but that did not prevent him from having a very fine appearance; everyone admired and commented on the freshness of his complexion and the whiteness of his hands. There was nothing prettier than his face, with which he appeared to be infatuated himself.

He recognized the princess easily from the description that the fay had given him, and having approached his mistress, he gave her the most studied of reverences. After having presented her his hand, he said to Aimée: "This is not an appropriate place to make a compliment on your beauty; the air is too hot; can one chat at one's ease on a terrace exposed to the ardor of the sun? Let us go inside, and not run the risk of becoming as black as Africans."

Having said that, he set off for the castle; he barely saluted the queen and the other ladies of her retinue. After entering a large drawing room with the princess and those accompanying her, which was prepared to receive him, he threw himself on to a sofa, saying that the heat was stifling him, and, adopting a pinched expression that was not very respectful, he asked the princess to forgive him for not conversing with her; he told her that it was absolutely necessary for him to take a little repose, and that he had to cool down before being able to resolve to talk.

Immediately he took from his pockets several little bottles garnished with diamonds, filled with scented water. He spread some over his hands, and then opened several golden snuff-boxes studded with precious stones. Then he hummed a little tune through his teeth, which he only ended in order to ask the princess whether she found his equipage vey brilliant, and whether the coat, which he had chosen from among two hundred, was to her liking. His conversation fell thereafter upon the amour that several women had had for him.

It can easily be imagined whether such discourse was to the taste of the beautiful Aimée, who preferred intelligence and good sense to anything else, and who was not like others of her sex, whom a magnificent coat, well tailored, and a few other scarcely estimable embellishments touched more force-fully than a good heart and a delicate and natural mind. She easily conceived such a strong dislike for him that she left the room, saying that she felt ill, and retired to her apartment to hide her sadness and her tears.

Although Sincere was very ill, he dragged himself there shortly thereafter in order to ask for her news. The princess sighed on seeing him, and said: "Oh, Prince, why isn't it you for whom the queen has destined me? Can you not tear me away from the one with whom they want to unite me?"

Sincere, transported, took one of her hands, kissed it ten-derly, and said to her: "What! Can it be true, beautiful Aimée, that you would rather live with me than with a prince whose beauty and fine attire are admired by everyone? Made as I am, could I be fortunate enough not to displease you? Reply to me please; your response would make the happiness or the unhap-piness of my life."

"Yes, Sire," she said to him, "I love you. That confes-sion..."

She was about to continue, but Sincere, making a back-ward leap, became tiny—so tiny that in the end, she could no longer see him. A thick smoke appeared in his stead, and when it had dissipated, the princess saw before her a young man as beautiful as the day, whose appearance, simultaneously noble, gentle and intelligent, inspired a certain I-know-not-what that made one love him as soon as one saw him. She looked at him, therefore, with as much admiration as surprise, but she was even more astonished when he said to her with all imaginable graces: "The charming confession that you have just made, Madame, has put an end to my enchantment. I am Sincere, who, under an unpleasant form, has been bold enough to tell you that he adored you.

Aimée recognized him by the sound of his voice, and allowed the joy that she felt on finding him so different from what he had been before to burst forth. She begged him to tell her how such a similar metamorphosis could have taken place.

"I am the king," he said, "of the Isle of Sincerity. I reigned there peacefully, loved by all my subjects. One day, I was hunting with a great deal of ardor a lion that had escaped me several times; I became lost, and found myself in a path where I perceived a woman made as I was a moment ago. I looked at her, and could not help laughing on seeing her spinning on her leg like a top. She perceived that, and, becoming angry, asked me what I was laughing at. Politeness prevented me from making the confession to her, but in the end she pressed me so forcefully that I admitted the effect that the singularity of her figure had had on me. My sincerity displeased her; she frowned.

"She turned three or four somersaults, after which she said to me: 'To punish you for your insolence, I want you to become similar to me. Nothing will be able to return you to our natural state unless you can find a princess who unites intelligence, generosity and beauty, for whom you feel a violent amour, and whom, in spite of your deformity, you can inspire sufficiently to obtain the confession of her tenderness. You can, however, resume your natural form for one hour every day, but only in a subterrain in a forest that belongs to King Dévideur. I also want it to be prohibited for you to relate or misfortune to anyone in the world until you are no longer enchanted.'

"I listened to those threats patiently; I thought they would have no effect; but imagine my dolor when, after that frightful fay—for that is what she was—had blown upon me, I found myself transformed like her, and I saw her draw away from her laughing with all her might. I no longer dared to return to my palace, nor to proclaim my birth, convinced that no one would believe me. The desire I had to recover my original condition determined me to travel in various kingdoms and see various courts, in the hope of finding a princess such as the fay had described to me, but it was in vain.

"I wearied of the search, therefore, and made the resolution to live in some corner of the world distant from all commerce. I chose the rock where you saw me. I had been living there for a year when I had the good fortune of seeing you for the first time; you appeared to me to be a divinity, and I sensed that you were the only one who could inspire amour in me, without daring to hope that I might inspire it in you in my turn, or think that it might be possible or you to become accustomed to seeing me. I sometimes went into the subterrain in the forest to have the satisfaction of finding myself for a few minutes as I am. I was surprised one day to see the princess, your sister, because a talisman forbade entry to all mortals. I pretended to be asleep, in order not to speak to her, and because I sensed that the moment of my transformation was about to arrive. It did, in fact, as soon as she had left the cabinet. I left the subterrain then by a route unknown to anyone but me. She left too, because it was impossible for her to return to the apartment where she had seen me. She had just completed her twentieth year, and her ring only had virtue until she had attained that age.

"That, my dear Aimée, is my story. It only remains or me now to swear an eternal tenderness to you and to beg you to suffer that I make every effort with regard to the queen, your mother, for her to accord you to my amour, and to permit you to come and reign in my estates, where you will find everyone eager to please you."

As he finished speaking, he saw Aigremine and Farouche came in; they had been listening to their conversation. Both of them were furious, the fay because Aimée had disdained her nephew, and Aigremine because Prince Sincere, whom she recognized as the charming man she had seen in the subterrain, was in love with her sister. She allowed her anger to burst forth against the two lovers, but Farouche concluded by dispute by approaching the unfortunate Aimée and, taking her by the curls of hair that were dangling from her coiffure, she flew away with her through the window, without the despairing king being able to raise the slightest obstacle to it.

He went out immediately, in spite of Aigremine, who tried to stop him. Without knowing where he was going, he drew away from the palace, resolved to take no repose until he had recovered his dear princess.

The King of the Butterflies, when he heard the news, started to laugh; he found the story very much to his taste, and returned to his kingdom.

In the meantime, his good aunt was carrying Aimée away as fast as she could. After having traversed several large deserts and sheer rocks she arrived at the foot of an iron tower; at her order the door opened; she made the unfortunate princess enter and took her to a large hall full of snails; she told her, in a bitter tone, that since she did not want to consent to marry King Papillon it was necessary that within a week she had taught those snails to dance, or she would take the form of one of those loathsome animals herself.

After making that threat, Farouche flew away, and the princess allowed tears to flow in abundance, without having the slightest desire to obey her. Let us leave her to weep at her leisure and return to King Sincere.

That prince, after having traversed several countries, found himself in a forest. After he had walked for a few paces he perceived a house made of leaves, and on the doorstep of the house a little old woman who was wearing a pair of spectacles on her nose, which she was using to read a vellum book. He went past her without stopping and without paying any attention to her, and even continued on his way, but she shouted to him to stop, and said to him in a hoarse voice, while shaking her head: "Prince, you're searching in vain; you can't encounter your princess until you've found a shining frog, an extremely ugly woman who is aware of her ugliness and doesn't seek to please, and a man devoid of intelligence who doesn't flatter himself with having some."

The king knew by that fashion of talking that he was dealing with another fay, and he therefore asked her to give him other means to find his charming Aimée, but her only response was to pull a face, with a loud burst of laughter and to go back into her house. He continued on his away, therefore, extremely weary, afflicted and more uncertain than ever of the road to follow,

He had not taken a hundred paces when he encountered another old woman who asked him the cause of his chagrin. He recounted his misfortunes, without forgetting what the fay he had just seen had said to him. He added that he could not flatter himself with the hope of ever seeing his dear Aimée again, if it were true that his happiness depended on finding a shining frog, which appeared to be impossible, although the other two conditions gave him less anxiety.

"Don't flatter yourself," replied the good woman, "they're scarcely more within the rules of possibility. However, you might find all three things by searching for them. But if you haven't discovered them in a year's time, take my advice and abandon yourself to despair; you'll be too unhappy on earth. Go, I can't tell you anymore. Don't let my sister, whom you've just quit, see you here; she's malevolent and you might experience some perfidy in consequence. She's only told you the means of getting your princess out of the place where she is because she's convinced that you can't make use of it."

The prince, who feared enchantments, went away without delay, and traveled the world with the aid of a horse that he had found, very fortunately, when he emerged from the wood.

He searched scrupulously in towns, castles and villages for the ugliest women and the most stupid men; he encountered a great many, but he noticed that all the women, young and old, persisted in their toilettes and even had the hope of pleasing after making some repairs to their faces. He saw many who, with a stick of rouge, a few artfully-placed beauty spots and a great many flowers and ribbons, imagined that someone might find them lovable in spite of their ugliness, and believed that they could compete in charms with the prettiest women. That ordinary effect of self-esteem did not surprise the prince—he knew that all women brought that good opinion of themselves with them in being born—but what astonished him was encountering the same self-esteem just as strongly among men, as well as all the petty foibles that attract so much scorn to the fair sex.

He had always heard it said that men were the most perfect work of nature, and he had believed that discourse without delving too deeply into the matter; but he thought very differently when he had studied those supposedly perfect creatures; he discovered easily that the majority were only occupied with trifles. He saw that some divided their days between their dressing-tables and the gaming table, or, what was worse, in feigning passion, without experiencing any veritable passion. He recognized that others appeared in their companies, not in order to reason there with intelligence and good sense, but only to repeat a few insipid points that they had heard said elsewhere, a few quips taken from a book, and to show off the expensive rings, jewels and all the magnificence of which fortune had made them a present. They mingled with others even more stupid who believed themselves to be very amusing. He saw some who babbled continually without knowing what they were saying and did not perceive that they were causing those who were patient enough to listen to them to yawn; others who thought they were pleasing others by repeating badly stories that they had already told a hundred times before; and others, finally, who did not say a word because they did not know what to say, imagining that their silence was a mark of intelligence.

I would never finish if I listed all the species of fools he encountered—without, however, finding the one he wanted, for there was not one of them who did not think that he had intelligence. The fool, the woman and the frog were so rare that his search obliged him to go twice around the world, but in vain. He therefore lost hope of ever seeing his princess again. Remembering then what the good little woman had advised him to do, he thought that, following her advice, he ought to renounce life, since it no longer had any charms for him.

Those reflections led him to the bank of a river. The opportunity was too good to miss; he threw himself in, resolved to end his days, the woes of which rendered them insupportable to him.

Instead of drowning, however, as he had the design to do, he found himself falling gently. A moment later he found himself on a lawn in the middle of a beautiful garden. He thought at first that it was the illusion of a dream, but, seeing thereafter that he was not asleep, he stood up to see if he could discover anyone in this unknown region.

He walked for a long time in the solitary place; finally, he heard the sound of hunting horns and dogs. A moment later he saw the hunters appear. No surprise ever equaled his; the hunters in question were as many huge frogs mounted on green cats, which were running after a hare; some were dressed as amazons; others had taffeta robes with little bonnets garnished with flowers and feathers; some of them were sounding horns, others shouting to call the dogs. In sum, it was the funniest thing in the world.

The hunt came to a halt at the sight of the prince, and the frogs dismounted from their cats in order to come toward him; they only walked on two feet, making use of the others as we make use of our hands.

When the troop was close to him the one who appeared to be the mistress of all the others, who was wearing a long crimson robe embroidered with pearls and diamonds and whose forehead bore a mark so brilliant that the eyes could not sustain the glare, saluted him with a great deal of grace and said to him:

"Be welcome, Sire; we've been waiting for you for a long time; we're enchanted, and it's you who has to break our enchantment. I haven't always been such as you see me; I was once the queen of this country and all the frogs following me were my subjects; I had an aversion so great to animals of this species that I gave orders for all those in my realm to be the victims of my disgust.

"Nothing was neglected to carry out my orders, but one evening, while out walking, I found one near my apartment. I immediately called for help and ordered that it be put to death; but that was not done with enough diligence; it had time to hide so well that I could never find it again.

"The next day, in the same place, I saw an ugly black woman appear before me who was holding a hazel wand in one hand and a phial full of oil in the other, which she poured over my head, saying to me: 'I am the fay Grenouille, and it's me that you wanted to put to death yesterday. Your orders have exposed me to death a hundred times, and it's time I avenged myself. Become a frog in your turn, you and all your subjects who have obeyed you blindly. I want you to be in that state until a king who needs your help comes here to return you to your original form.'

"Scarcely had she finished speaking than I was transformed as you see. A fay who protected me, but who was not knowledgeable enough in her art to return me to my original state, told me that that power was reserved to you alone; that you would have a white hair in the left eyebrow, of which a skillful magicienne had made you a present at the time of your birth, and that that hair would have the virtue of breaking all enchantments.

"That fay is the one who brought you here; it was her, in the form of a bird, who made a present to Princess Aimée of the diamond that you saw her receive; finally, it was her who took care to give me this shining mark on my forehead, and who will enable you to find a man devoid of intelligence who is not unaware of it, and an ugly young woman who agrees that her ugliness is insupportable. She has brought those two persons here, for fear that the self-esteem that reigns in society might corrupt them, as it has done the rest of mortals, and destroy your hopes by that means.

"You'll find them in a cabin not far from here, but Prince, before going to see them, return us to our original form and suffer that we pluck out the famous hair, in order that you can make use of it in our favor. It will also be necessary for you to deliver your princess."

Sincere did not have to be begged; the hair was pulled out; he took it then and touched all the frogs with it, who immediately became very amiable princes and princesses. The queen and her subjects gave him many thanks. The second little woman that he had found in the wood appeared at the same time, and told him that, in order to recompense him for the service that he had just rendered her friend, she would transport him to where the beautiful Aimée was imprisoned, after he had paid a visit to the stupid man and the ugly woman, who would make him a present of a herb that he would need in future.

He went there in haste, found them as he wished, and received the mysterious herb from them. After quitting them, the good woman picked an apple and changed it into a pretty carriage, which traveled a hundred leagues a minute of its own accord. She climbed aboard with the prince, who found the vehicle charming, but it did not go quickly enough for a lover impatient to see his mistress again. They arrived nevertheless in a very short time at the foot of the tower in which the beautiful Aimée was imprisoned.

Every day the fay gave her tasks that were equally impossible to execute, with the design of having a pretext for tormenting her. I said when she was locked in the prison for the first time that Farouche ordered her to teach a quantity of snails to dance, which were then in a low room, but I did not say how the princess succeeded in such a difficult commission. I shall instruct those who have a desire to know.

At first she only thought about weeping, for seven entire days, without taking the trouble to teach the pupils confided to her, and on the eight day, which was the one on which the fay was due to see her again and to change her into a snail if she had not yet succeeded, she was afflicted again; however, she wanted to try to give the animals a few lessons. She soon saw that she was wasting her time, and, convinced that her misfortune had no resource, she thought seriously about killing herself, for she would rather die than become a snail or marry the King of Butterflies.

With that design she climbed up to the window, in order to throw herself out; but, by an infinite good fortune, she remembered the diamond that she had received from the bird and what the bird had said when it gave it to her. She took it out of her pocket and, while looking at it, said: "Beautiful diamond, if you have the virtue of getting me out of the danger I am in, do not leave me unfortunate and longer."

Scarcely had she pronounced those words than the gem opened and several dancing-masters emerged from it with violins, who made the snails line up, showed them all sorts of dances in an instant, and disappeared thereafter.

That marvel gave great pleasure to the princess. She wiped away her tears, kissed her diamond with a transport of incredible joy and put it away more carefully than she had done before, for fear that Farouche might discover its value and take it away from her.

The malevolent fay arrived a moment later, and asked her with a malign smile whether her pupils were very skillful.

"You can judge for yourself, Madame," said Aimée, in a soft and fearful voice, and opening the room where they were. She began to sing, and immediately, all the little animals danced, and danced so prettily, especially the bourrée, the allemande and the mariée, that Farouche was simultaneously surprised and furious.

Annoyed that the poor princess had succeeded so well, she gave her other tasks that were even more difficult, but she always acquitted them by means of her diamond. That success made the fay so angry than she locked the princess in a large iron cage, and placed it in a courtyard full of ferocious carnivorous animals. She confided it to the guard of two horrible dragons, which made frightful efforts continually to break the cage and devour the princess.

The unfortunate princess had been imprisoned thus for a month when she saw Sincere arrive. She shivered at seeing the danger to which her lover was about to be exposed.

He had opened the door of the courtyard simply by touching it with his herb. He had no sooner seen his dear Aimée in such a cruel situation than he drew his sword in order to slay the dragons, but the good woman shouted to him to stop, and only to throw at them the herb he was holding in his hand. He did that, and the animals immediately fell at his feet, lifeless.

Running to the cage, he touched it with the hair from his eyebrow, and at the same moment he felt himself, the princess and the good fay rise up into the air, where they were surrounded by a cloud, which carried them very rapidly to the Isle of Sincerity.

The king was recognized by all is subjects and received with acclamations of joy that enabled him to see how much he was cherished. Delighted to find himself in company with his charming Aimée, he said the most passionate things in the world to her; she responded with a equal tenderness.

He sent ambassadors to King Dévideur and the queen, his wife, in order to ask for the princess in marriage. They were not on the road for long. They learned that King Dévideur had killed himself with a pistol shot nearly a year ago because he had been unable to succeed in unwinding a tangle of silk that was extremely complicated; that the queen had died of smallpox six months ago, and that Aigremine had poisoned herself on the day she had seen her depart.

That news afflicted Princess Aimée; she wore mourning for her parents for six months. At the end of that time she married King Sincere and sent a long sequence of years with him without experiencing the slightest chagrin.

They loved one another tenderly all their lives. The good woman quit them in order to go and join her friend, Queen

Brillante. The hair from the king's eyebrow was mounted in a golden ring, which he always carried with him, to preserve him from the malice of the fays.

TENDREBRUN AND CONSTANCE

There was once a fay named Vicious. She made her abode on one of the highest mountains in the realm of Pentasila. The number of years had augmented both her ugliness and her malevolence. She was rarely seen to emerge from her castle; what was the point of tiring herself out unnecessarily? Her children, the Vices, served her at the whim of her desire, traveling the world and causing infinite disorder there. Kings and noblemen had been warned always to be on their guard against such monsters, but they had the secret of slipping into the most carefully sealed palaces. All doors opened at the mere sight of Flattery, their beloved sister. The great, especially, and the rich, allowed themselves to be drawn by her sweet insinuations, and Vicious's children obeyed her everywhere.

King Judicious was the only one who closed entry to his estates to them. It would be difficult to express how much he hated that numerous family. In spite of all his precautions, however, one of the little Lies was clever enough to penetrate all the way to his bedroom without being recognized, and lived there for a long time.

One day, the king, who was in front of his mirror having his hair combed, took it into his head to ask his courtiers how old he appeared to be. They all replied with sincerity that he looked to be about forty-five—which was, in fact, the number of his years—but the Lie assured His Majesty that he had the appearance and freshness of a man of forty.

At that speech the king looked at him attentively, recognized him as one of the Vices, and ordered that he be whipped and immediately expelled from the kingdom. Several noblemen spoke in his favor, but were unable to obtain clemency for him.

"The child you can see," the prince said to them, "is a monster to be feared a thousand times more than the cruelest beasts in my forests. He pleases and amuses you because he is small, but he will grow, and if I tolerate him he will soon introduce all his brothers here in spite of me. Let him leave promptly and let him be chastised as he merits."

Judicious was obeyed and the Lie, after having been punished, retired weeping to the home of the fay, to whom he related what had just happened to him. Vicious frowned, took him in her arms, kissed him twice on the forehead and, in order to console him, assured him that in future, he would be covered with such disgraces.

She kept her word, but she swore by the green and blue bonnet that she wore that she would avenge herself on the king and all his race before the end of the day. As she spoke those words she uttered five frightful shrieks, leapt three times over an ardent ember that she kept in a heater full of fire, and spat on a spider-web that she found in a corner of her room; after which she touched the cobweb with her wand, which became a winged toad of monstrous size, wearing a green saddle embroidered with glow-worms

The fay caressed the toad, gave it a cake made with milk, sugar, almonds and caterpillars, and, having told it to wait, went to sit down at her dressing-table; for she was extremely coquettish, although she was more than two thousand years old, and never went out without a great deal of rouge and beauty-spots. She put on a large quantity that day, and coiffed herself and dressed herself like a young woman. All that adornment certainly rendered her even more frightful than she was. Content nevertheless with her appearance, she imagined, like several old women of my acquaintance, that the attire in question prevented anyone from perceiving her wrinkles and her emaciation.

Finally, Vicious mounted her toad, traversed the air with an incredible velocity, and in very little time rendered to the abode of King Judicious.

That prince was in an arbor in his garden, sitting on a little throne of leaves that young Constance, his unique daughter, had taken care to ornament with different flowers. She was at his feet, leaning over the edge of a stream, which formed a sheet of water. She told the king several stories that she had made up in order to amuse him. Her narration was interrupted by a frightful clap of thunder, which almost made her faint, and which tipped Judicious off his throne. Overwhelmed by dolor at the sight of that fall, she tried, in spite of her lack of strength, to run to pick him up, but a frightful darkness spread instantly and prevented her from helping him.

Rendered desperate by that new prodigy, Constance went in all directions, searching in the obscurity and calling out in a voice as sad as it was faint to the person to whom she owed the light of day. Several bursts of laughter that she heard stopped her tremulous steps; then the darkness dissipated and she perceived nearby an old woman, whom she took for one of the three Furies, so horrible did she appear.

It was the malevolent Vicious, who, charmed by all the woes that she was commencing to make felt, was laughing with all her might. She ceased laughing, however, seeing that the young princess wanted to go away, in order no longer to see her, and to try again to find the king. She seized her by the arm and, touching her with her wand, said: "Don't look for your father; he's in my power. Only prepare yourself to suffer the torments that my hatred is getting ready."

With those words she took a pinch of red powder, which she threw into the air, pronouncing a few words, and immediately, a rain of fire fell that consumed the entire realm of the unfortunate Judicious.

Turning then to Constance, she said: "You've just seen the fashion in which I've avenged myself on everything that belongs to you. Now I'm going to make you experience how I treat people who dare to displease me. Then she made her toad hop over the princess's head. The animal let three drops of a black liquid fall, which immediately metamorphosed her into a crayfish. In that form she conserved the memory of what she had been, but she lost the use of speech. Then the fay tapped the ground with her wand and caused a frightful abyss to appear, into which she precipitated the unfortunate Constance.

The princess fell for a week, with great rapidity, into that frightful gulf, of which she could not find the bottom. At the end of that time, she realized that she was in a pool, which appeared to her to be immense. She sensed that she was swimming there and living as if she had spent her entire life in that element. However, she did not eat anything, for fear of being caught by a fisherman's hook. The smallest fish that she saw or heard made her tremble, because she imagined that it was some animal come to devour her.

One evening, when the aquatic troop was sleeping tranquilly, Constance became bolder, and resolved, by courtesy of a beautiful moonlight, to go for a swim on the surface of the water. The first thing that was offered to her sight was a young man of about twenty-two lying under foliage that the brilliant night star illuminated perfectly. He appeared to be overwhelmed by sadness and ennui, and seemed quite indifferent to the officious cares that Zephyr was rendering him by blowing softly in the air and displacing slightly from his cheeks long thick curls of hair that were falling negligently over his shoulders. His reverie no longer permitted him to take any pleasure in the soft concerts of nightingales that were striving close by to make the echoes repeat their melodious sounds. In sum, nothing seemed capable of distracting his thoughts.

The princess stopped in order to consider him, and found a thousand charms in him that obliged her to sigh several times, and made her sense more than she had done before the misfortune of being a crayfish. She swam nearby for a long time without him noticing her, but in the end, she made so many jumps in the water that he looked in her direction. She perceived that, but for the moment, the dread she had of being caught and put on the fire did not present her approaching him, in such a fashion that he could easily have caught her with his hand.

The young man was the son of a great Tartar Emperor. Vicious had abducted him from his father's court. For two years the fay had kept him imprisoned in that frightful abode. How hard she had tried to make him love her! All her artifices were futile; the hatred that the prince had conceived for her was invincible; he could not look at her without horror. Vicious soon discerned his sentiments; that might have put an end to his life; she would have sacrificed him to her rage and her chagrin if the violence of her passion had not calmed a fraction of the fury by which she was agitated.

The prince was named Tendrebrun. He was tall and well built, and all his features were agreeable; he had an air of majesty and the politeness of the noblest society attracted all hearts to him. In sum, he had been born with a great penchant for amour, and when he wanted to please, he pleased.

The indolent life that he led in the fay's abode bored him infinitely; he was retained there by an enchantment that all his courage was unable to overcome; he had the liberty to stroll in the gardens of the palace, but he usually only made use of it when night had deployed its wings, because he dreaded encountering Vicious or someone from her retinue. The edge of the pool where Constance was confined was the place he almost always chose to repose and to think about means he might employ to get out of his prison.

He had already been savoring the agreeable coolness of the night for some time when he saw the crayfish, which, as I have said, was looking at him very attentively. He thought at first that it was dead, but, after picking up a little twig, he touched it, and knew that it was not. Astonished by the fact that it did not appear to want to escape, and that its eyes were attached to him in a particular fashion, he considered it attentively. Then, picking it up, he heard it sigh; after that, he had no doubt that it was some unfortunate person whose metamorphosis was the work of Vicious. He voiced that idea, and noticed that it made all the signs that a crayfish can employ to make him understand that he was not mistaken. He therefore carried it rapidly to his apartment, put it in a golden bowl full of water, which he found in his cabinet, and threw himself on his bed.

Curiosity soon came to trouble the mildness of the repose that he had begun to enjoy, however. The memory of his prisoner snatched him from the arms of sleep; he ran to the cabinet, visited his crayfish, and gave it a piece of biscuit. Having perceived that it ate it with pleasure, he felt sorry for it again and promised to keep it company as often as he could.

Sometimes, he looked at it and thought he remarked something in its eyes so tender and so touching that he could not help uttering imprecations against the person who had reduced it to that state.

One day, when he assured her that no one was interested in her misfortunes as much as he was, she emerged from the water, took a pen and a sheet of paper that he had left on the table, and, making use of her paw, wrote her name and the causes of her metamorphosis. She thanked Tendrebrun for the care he had taken of her and implored him not to abandon her, and to be careful that the fay did not discover her.

The prince, charmed by what she had just done, swore that he would rather lose his life than suffer that the slightest harm be done to her; in order to reassure her, he told her that Vicious ought to be away from her palace for a month.

From that day on he was more assiduous toward her; he read her several amusing stories in order to relieve her boredom, and he anticipated her in everything that might give her pleasure. Constance listened to him with an infinite satisfaction, and although amour made further progress in her heart every day, she refrained nevertheless from letting him know the extent to which she was smitten with his charms. Such a confession appeared to her to be shameful, and she did not hope that Tendrebrun would ever fall in love with a crayfish. Those thoughts caused her so much pain that she made the resolution one evening to allow herself to die of starvation.

She therefore stopped eating. The prince perceived that, and asked her the reason, but she refused to tell him, which gave him a great deal of chagrin. He imagined that perhaps she did not like what he gave her, and that she would rather eat fish. With a view to making sure, he took a line and went straight to the pool.

A small fish was caught on his hook; he took it with al diligence to his dear crayfish and threw it into the bowl, imploring her to eat it; but the fish was no sooner there than it agitated the water and troubled it in such a fashion that the prince could no longer see anything.

A moment later the water calmed down and became clear. Tendrebrun saw his crayfish again, but instead of the small fish he saw a little old man, whose cheerful and agreeable expression reassured those his sudden appearance might have frightened.

"Have no fear, Prince," he said to the son of the Tartar Emperor. "My name is Beneficent; the fay who is retaining you was irritated against me because I had removed a young princess that she had taken to the court of a king, one of my neighbors, in order to give her in marriage to a monster, one of his friends. She changed me into a small fish, because her power is far greater than mine, and told me as she threw me into the pool where you caught me that I would remain there until someone fished me out. I've been there for three hundred years. I owe you my liberty and I want to render you happy."

As he was speaking he took a little golden box from his pocket, and a flame-colored bird emerged from the box.

"This bird," he said to the prince, "will take you in a short time to wherever you wish, provided that you hold on to the tip of its wing without ever letting go. That's not all I can do for you. This crayfish is a charming princess in whom you have inspired a great deal of tenderness. I want to return her original form; you can take her with you by letting her hold on to the other wing of the bird.

Having said that, the old man took the crayfish and cut off its head, to the great astonishment of the prince, who was preparing to make him the sharpest reproaches, but he was prevented from doing so by a loud noise that he heard.

It was Vicious, who was arriving home sooner than she was expected. The fay remarked the disturbance of the prince and the bird that he was already holding in his hands. She quivered with rage on seeing that the animal would have stolen her lover a moment later. She snatched it from his hands furiously, therefore, and crushed it, searching in all directions to see whether the person who had made him a present of it might be; but he had disappeared, and her search was futile.

Tendrebrun, in despair, said to the fay everything he could imagine of the most insulting, but she only heard a part of his reproaches, because she went out, in order to go and augment the prince's enchantment.

The latter was no sooner alone than he ran to the unfortunate crayfish, whose head the old man had cut off. Scarcely had he touched it, however, than the chamber appeared to be ablaze and he found himself in the midst of flames. Immediately thinking of saving himself, he left the crayfish in order to look for the window or the door. The fire dissipated as he was about to go out, and he perceived that it had not done him any harm. Seeing then that he had been alarmed unnecessarily, he searched for the crayfish, in the hope that some new prodigy might have brought it back to life.

After a futile search, he had no doubt that it had been consumed by the flames, a misfortune for which he blamed the fay. He felt a dolor so sharp in consequence that, scarcely able to sustain himself, he collapsed on a sofa, which fortunately happened to be behind him, and lay there for a long time, his eyes looking at the floor, without making the slightest movement.

Finally, he perceived something moving at his feet, which appeared to him to be extremely bright. Having leaned over to see what it might be, he was greatly surprised to see a tiny young woman about the size of a large pin, all of whose features were charming. She was wearing a dress of white gauze, sown with tiny carbuncles, and he discovered on her head a spray of feathers garnished with precious stones.

Astonished by that new prodigy, Tendrebrun picked her up very delicately, placed her on the table in order to consider her more easily, and found her so beautiful that he gave no further thought to the crayfish he had just lost. Instantly, he felt for that admirable little person a passion so violent that he thought he was going mad, on making the reflection that he would never be able to do anything but gaze at her, since she was so small, and it was impossible for him to unite himself with her by means of bonds stronger than those of amity.

Those thoughts would have rendered him even unhappier than he had been before if he had had time to deliver himself to them, but the beauty with whom he was occupied, gazing at him with eyes capable of inflaming the least tender hearts, said to him in a voice as soft as it was charming:

"Prince the old man you saw had just returned me to my original form. A moment ago I was a happy crayfish, since, in that for, you had the generosity to take care of me and I lacked nothing. Presently, I'm an unfortunate princess, devoid of parents, devoid of support and devoid of a realm, only too content, however, to be able to assure you of the gratitude that I shall have all my life for the services that you have rendered me.

"What! It's you, beautiful Constance, that I had the good fortune of conserving here for a few days?" Tendrebrun said to her. "It's you whom I was regretting so deeply a moment ago, and who, if I can believe Beneficent, will suffer without difficulty that I adore you for as long as I live? How can it be that the old man's knife has not caused you to perish, and that you have escaped the flames that surrounded you on all sides?"

"Everything the magician did was necessary to disenchant me," she told him. "He was the one who made the fire appear that alarmed you so much. He took me at the instant you abandoned me, and, touching me with a coral wand, he returned my natural form, at a reduced stature. He also gave me this crystal egg, telling me that as soon as you have touched it with a branch of jasmine that you will find on the ground at the entrance to the garden, you and I will no longer be in the power of the fay."

Constance then gave the mysterious egg to the prince, and implored him to go in search immediately of the jasmine that would set them free. Before obeying her, however, he wanted to tell her how much he loved her, and to let her know how desperate he was in seeing her so tiny.

"I'll become taller," the young princess said, smiling. "The worthy old man assured me that within an hour, I'll be as tall as I was before the fay turned me into a crayfish. So don't worry, but don't delay, and run to search for the jasmine that alone can get us out of here."

The prince, full of pleasure and hope, was about to follow that advice when Vicious suddenly came back into the room and forbade him to go out. The princess, seeing her cruel enemy, ran to hide, but fell off the table-top, albeit without injuring herself.

Tendrebrun, wanting to pick her up without the fay perceiving it, forgot that he was holding the crystal egg and dropped it, with the consequence that it shattered into a thousand pieces. To complete the misfortune, Vicious advanced so promptly that he did not have time to put Constance in his pocket, and the poor princess found herself directly underneath the dress of her mortal enemy.

The prince trembled, seeing that the fay might crush her by making the slightest movement, but fortunately, she remained in the same place. In one of her hands she held a gilded vellum book, and in the other an ebony wand, with which she tapped him on the shoulder.

"Don't think of escaping me, ingrate," she said. "I've just rendered the charms that retain you close to me so powerful that all the powers of Hell couldn't break them. Resolve, therefore, to see me incessantly by your side to torment you if you don't accept immediately the heart and the hand that I still want to offer you; on the contrary, imagine all that might make the happiness of a mortal, and be assured of enjoying it is you respond to my desires. Speak quickly, and remember that your response will decide the good or ill fortune of your days. I'll give you a quarter of an hour to make up your mind."

The prince, to whom the discourse and threats of the fay caused scant anxiety, was only occupied with what he could see. His eyes were attached to her dress, because he perceived that it was stirring, and had no doubt that it was the unfortunate Constance who was visibly growing. The excess of his dolor was unimaginable when he thought that his lovely princess was soon about to appear before the fay, and would then be exposed to new punishments. How he repented amusing himself talking about the amour that she caused him; he ought instead to have run after the jasmine branch that was so necessary to them—but regrets were futile; the moment when he was about to lose the princess had arrived.

She was growing so prodigiously and so rapidly that Vicious finally sensed her, and her head suddenly emerged from the split in her skirt.

"Aha!" she said, extremely surprised. "What does this mean? How, little creature, have you dared to come so close to me? Does the fellow who gave you back your original form think that I'm not sufficiently powerful to take it away from you again, and that you can show yourself to my eyes with impunity? I'll prove the contrary to him."

"Stop, cruel woman!" said the prince, hastily. "Don't maltreat a princess who has experienced your fury excessively."

"And what interest do you have in her?" she replied, in a tone that made Constance feel faint and the prince go pale. "How do you know her and what renders you so sensible to her?"

"Only the pity that I have for the unfortunate," said Tendrebrun, who dared not confess the truth.

But the fay turned her head, and, showing her long black teeth as she muttered a few words, opened her book, and discovered everything that had happened between the two lovers.

That knowledge put her into such great wrath that it made the earth tremble. Her first impulse was to kill them, but, changing her resolution, she uttered a screech similar to that of an owl, and spun for a quarter of an hour without stopping, holding the prince by the hair without him being able to make use of his strength to extract himself from her frightful hands. Then a frightful griffin appeared and an enormous bat, which asked her what her orders were. She showed them the prince and the princess.

"Take them," she said. "Go away, and do your duty."

She was obeyed, and both of them took directly opposite routes with their prey.

The griffin, charged with the prince, traversed a number of countries, and after having traveled through the air for three hours descended at nightfall in the middle of a wood, where Tendrebrun imagined that he was about to be devoured. The animal having placed him on the ground gently, however, flew away without touching him.

The obscurity was so great that the prince did not know whether he ought to go forwards, backwards, or stay where he was. After having remained irresolute for a few moments, however, he made the decision to walk, groping, awaiting all the catastrophic events that might happen to him.

He had only taken a few paces when he perceived a light, which seemed very distant as yet. He walked for more than a quarter of an hour in order to reach it. Finally, he found himself next to a castle whose windows were illuminated.

He examined the building, but he was extremely surprised when he realized that it was that of the emperor, his father. Suspecting that it was a dream, he advanced as far as the door of the guard-room with an agitation that did not leave him the liberty of speech. The first people who saw him uttered cries of joy and ran to his father's apartment to tell him the good news.

That prince, curbed by the weight of years, was lying on several piles of cushions, of golden cloth embroidered with pearls, and lending a very mediocre attention to a concert of voices and instruments that some of his women were performing. When he saw the men enter who had come to tell him that

Tendrebrun was in the palace, and perceived that dear son in person, whose loss had been so sensible to him, the joy that the two individuals felt is imaginable, if one knows the tender emotions of nature. I shall not describe them, therefore; I shall simply say that no prince had ever found his father and his subjects again with more pleasure than Tendrebrun felt.

The emperor was very old; he obliged his son to take the reins of the empire, finding him more capable of governing than he was himself.

The prince took charge, reluctantly, of the care of a state that had been rather neglected for some years. The splendor of his crown and the pleasure of reigning over a numerous people did not prevent him from thinking about Constance. He sighed continually and regretted the moments that he had spent with her.

How lovable she is, he sometimes said to himself. *What tenderness, grace, delicacy and intelligence are assembled in that divine person! What would I not sacrifice to find her again? Alas, perhaps the Fate has already cut the thread of her beautiful days; or, if she is still alive, it is doubtless only to experience the further furies of the malevolent Vicious. Are you thinking about me in your misfortunes, charming princess? Do you remember that Tendrebrun will never cease to love you, and that he will put everything to work to deliver you from your troubles? Yes, you must be convinced of that, you must believe that my dolor will soon put me in the grave if I do not see you again promptly.*

It was thus that he conversed with himself in thinking about young Constance; he imagined the methods of Vicious very often; he could not understand how he had escaped from her hands, or why she had sent him back to his estates without doing him any harm, although he had experienced until then such violent marks of her amour and her anger. He was far away from her, but he was still fearful of her fury and malevolence.

That dread, combined with his passion, troubled the tranquility of his days infinitely. Unable to live overwhelmed by so many anxieties, he resolved to go to the island of Tintarinos in order to ask Beneficent for news of Constance and obtain from him some talisman that might preserve him from the fay's enchantments.

Having confided his design to the emperor he had a ship equipped, charged it with rich presents, and left the court accompanied by a dozen of the youngest and bravest lords of the empire.

The god of winds, impelling his vessel rapidly, soon allowed him to perceive the tip of the island he was seeking, but when he was only a short distance away, the sky darkened and was covered with thick cloud. The sea changed color and the waves swelled, colliding with one another with such a great impetuosity that the prince's ship could not continue its route and ran aground on a sandbank, on which they would all have perished if the sea had not calmed down some time thereafter.

The air then became as tranquil as the waves. The clouds dissipated, and permitted the prince to run his eyes over the vast empire of Neptune, by which he was surrounded, to see if he could discover any ship.

He had not been looking for long when he saw something shiny appear, albeit a long distance away, which came towards him at a prodigious speed. When the object was within visual range, he saw that it was a mother-of-pearl boat, in the middle of which was a rose-bush that served it as a mast; the leaves were large enough to serve as sails. Eight tritons and eight sirens, who were conducting it, brought it very close to Tendrebrun.

Then one of the sirens spoke to him, saying; "Prince, we have been sent here by young Bounty, our mistress, to tell you that she is waiting for you on her island. She is the daughter of Beneficent, and is only occupied, following his example, with the care of rendering mortals happy. The art of faerie, which she possesses, has informed her of your misfortunes. Touched by the troubles you are suffering, she wants to deliver you from them by giving you the talisman of which you were going in search on the island of Tintarinos. Here is a bracelet that we have brought on her behalf; never take it off; it will return to you the lovely princess from whom you are separated. It is to our mistress that you owe your liberty and your return to Tartary, in spite of the efforts of the wicked Vicious. Hasten, then, to go and thank her for all that she has done for you.

The prince, delighted to have found such a fortunate adventure at the time he least expected it, climbed into the boat without delay, with all his retinue. After having sailed for six minutes, at the most, he landed on the island where he was awaited.

It was only planted with rose-bushes and jasmines, which formed long covered pathways; the flowers of those trees, mingled with the green leaves, produced a charming effect. Verdant grass, dotted with little pink and white flowers, covered the ground. In fact, any other color than the ones I have just mentioned, was banished from the island. That is why the prince had no sooner disembarked from the boat than he saw the blue and gold coat that he was wearing change into another, of pink gauze embroidered with emeralds and diamonds.

A sheep with a fleece of silver thread and horns of diamond presented itself o serve as his guide. It conducted him, making several bounds over the grass, to an arbor where Tendrebrun saw a hundred young women of an admirable beauty. They were surrounding a young woman of about sixteen years, who surpassed them in grace and beauty. She was lying negligently on a bed of jasmine on the edge of a crystal basin where several swans were swimming. Palisades and a vault of flowers prevented the god of the day from spreading too much light in that agreeable enclosure.

The sheep went to lie down next to its beautiful mistress, and the prince, realizing that she was the daughter of the old man of Tintarinos of whom mention had been made, expressed his gratitude to her with as much respect as intelligence. The young fay received it with a mildness and grace that he had only found previously in Constance.

She asked him whether he had the bracelet, and recommended that he never remove it from his arm, because as long as it was there, the fay Vicious and others would not be able to do him any harm. Then, presenting her hand to him, she got up and led him into a labyrinth ornamented with very well-wrought ivory statues. After having traversed the labyrinth, she led him over a terrace that overlooked the sea shore to a crystal castle, which the prince admired for a long time. She told him that he could rest there for a few days, and promised to transport him thereafter to his dear Constance.

The fay warned the prince not to go out of the apartment that he chose in the palace, during the time he spent on the island, once midnight had chimed. "If you go out," she said, "and if you even open the windows between then and four o'clock in the morning, misfortunes will overtake you from which I will not be able to protect you. In the meantime, I am obliged to quit my palace and go to visit my father."

Tendrebrun assured her that he would follow her advice exactly, and consented without difficulty to remain in that beautiful abode for as long as the sun took to travel the celestial vault three times.

The first day was spent savoring all the pleasures that a powerful fay can procure, and talking about the daughter of Judicious. He was astonished by the attention that Bounty had in talking to him about the person he loved, although it is true that it was always him who commenced the conversation. However, making the reflection that it was lacking in prudence, and even politeness to repeat the same thing so often and continually to exaggerate the amour one has for someone else before a person as charming as the fay, he gradually corrected himself, and his discourse was soon no longer filled with the impatience he had to see his princess again. On the contrary, he often said that he wished that he might be away from her for longer than he had said, in order to discover the effect that absence would produce in his heart. Then, remaining silent for a few moments, he kept his eyes attached to Bounty, sighed, no longer able to sustain the tenderness of her gaze without experiencing a disturbance that was not usual for him.

He eventually perceived that Constance no longer reigned over his soul, and that the beautiful fay occupied it uniquely. He no longer thought about anything, therefore, except making his passion known to her. At first he allowed his eyes and his sighs to speak, and he became sad and pensive. The fay perceived that, and proposed to him that he leave, in order to rediscover the person who was causing his languor; but Tendrebrun threw himself at her feet, took one of her hands, which he kissed with transport, and implored her not to send him away from her, to suffer that he adore her and that he might wear her chains all his life.

Bounty seemed astonished by that declaration, and blushed extremely, but assured him nevertheless that she would not refuse his request, because his inclination responded to the desire she had to content him. But she said at the same time that he could only remain with her on condition of marrying her the same day, because she had sworn an inviolable oath not to permit any man to love her who was not her husband, or to allow him to stay on her island for longer than a brief interval.

That condition pleased the prince extremely; he assured her that he accepted it with all the joy imaginable, and pressed her not to defer his happiness. As she quit him she promised to go and augment her charms, if possible, by donning a costume even more elegant.

She came back after an absence of an hour, and, everything having been prepared for the ceremony, their marriage was concluded. Nymphs came to rejoice with them, by means of their dances and songs, for such a beautiful union. They all had garlands of flowers, with which they enchained the two spouses. Several of them also married young lords in the prince's retinue. Fauns and satyrs made the woods resound with their instruments and celebrated the happy day with games and fêtes that they invented. In sum, everything on the island that breathed was animated by pleasures, except for the unfortunate Constance, whom hazard had caused to encounter it.

She was still in the power of the bat; that monster, after having take her away from Vicious's palace, had traveled over the four continents of the world with her, pretending to be unable to find the realm to which the malevolent fay had ordered it to take her. They had been traveling for a month when they passed over the Isle of Roses. The bat stopped then, and asked Constance whether she wanted to rest for a few moments. The princess, fatigued by the journey, consented to that gladly, and the night-bird descended slowly to deposit her behind an arbor where Tendrebrun and Bounty were swearing an eternal amour.

What a spectacle for a lover! What despair did she not feel on seeing the infidel prince make a thousand caresses and say a hundred things each more passionate than the last to a young person that she found only too lovable. She thought twenty times of standing up in order to go and heap Tendrebrun with the reproaches that he merited, but, making the reflection that she would only cause, at the most, a little shame and that she would only receive from him a few excuses full of indifference, which would be a further triumph for her rival, she preferred to constrain herself and enclose within herself the mortal dolor that the change caused her.

She contented herself, therefore, with letting a torrent of tears flow from her beautiful eyes, and begged the bat to continue its voyage and to remove her promptly from a place so fatal to her repose. The latter, charged with the will of Vicious, was as malevolent as its mistress. Seeing the extreme affliction of the princess, therefore, it wanted to augment it, by telling her about the facility with which the Tartar prince had forgotten her and the pleasures that he had savored since he had been with his new bride.

Constance made no reply, silently charging his perjury with ingratitude and treason. *How perfidious he is*, she said to herself, *but in spite of that, how lovable he is! How much amour I have just seen in his eyes! Gods, can it be that he has ceased so promptly to love me and that I am deprived forever of his tenderness? Amour, it is you who is presently causing my greatest misfortune: you are taking away all that I love, to give it to another. At least render me my indifference. But alas, I sense that it is no longer in my power to recover it, or to extinguish the fire that I feel in my soul, and that fate is condemning me to eternal dolor.*

That was what the princess was thinking. When the bat had consented to depart, it stopped after a few hours of flight and told her that she had arrived in the realm of Indolent, to whom Vicious had sent her in order to marry him that same day, and it was taking her down to the palace that the king had prepared or her—which it did, immediately. It put her in the hands of several women destined to serve her and flew away, after having gone to Indolent's apartment in order to give him the fay's compliments and inform him of the arrival of Constance.

That prince received the news with joy, for he had a great desire to get married. He was tall, young and well made, but he had no head, and, in consequence, he could do nothing for himself. The Vices, to whom he had given free entry to his kingdom, reigned there with more authority than him.

All those monsters had taken such firm possession of all his subjects that the unfortunate king dared not do anything without their advice. Debauchery and ignorance extended their empire over the men of war and the persons of the highest status; injustice and interest made the magistrates act; hypocrisy and avarice were followed secretly by the dervishes and other ministers of altars, and gallantry by the female sex.

In sum, all of Vicious's children had their courtiers, and commanded, independently of all that, the men and women of the realm, without fear that Indolent would have anything to say about it. So the complaisance the king had for the Vices procured him the amity of their mother. That fay had made him a present, a few days before the arrival of the daughter of Judicious of a beautiful polished head, which replaced—in appearance, at least—the one that nature had refused him. That head was attached to the shoulders, and, by means of a few springs, made all the necessary movements. At first he had a little difficulty in wearing it, but he became accustomed to it.

It might be difficult to imagine how he could see, hear and talk; I shall explain. He had a mouth in a dimple in his neck, an ear in the left hand and an eye in the right. I agree that the arrangement had its inconveniences, but in sum, a fay who had wanted to avenge herself on his mother, the queen, had placed them in that fashion when she became pregnant with the unfortunate prince. As for a nose, she had not given him one because it appeared to her that it was unnecessary, so he could not smell anything.

The prince, formed in that fashion, had no doubt that Constance would consent joyfully to marry him. He therefore went to visit her, and proclaimed that to her the day would not pass without her being his wife.

She was in a beautiful apartment; gold and silver gleamed there in abundance, but her eyes, although full of tears, spread an even greater splendor there than all the riches put together.

Indolent approached her, and, in order to see her more clearly, put his right hand near her face. He was delighted to find her so beautiful, and paid her a compliment on her beauty that he had spent two days learning by heart, and which had been found for him in a new book. Then he gave her his hand in order to conduct her to the temple, where she would, he said, receive her crown and be united with him. But the princess push him away gently, assuring him that she would never accept the honor that he wanted to do her and begging him to permit her, on the contrary, to retire to one of the temples in the city where a number of young women were enclosed, consecrated to the service of the gods.

That response astonished the king so much that he did not say anything for several moments. Recovering slightly from his surprise, he tried by mans of his pleas to make her resolve to what he desired, but, everything he said being futile, he got carried away in such a fashion that his head, which was not attached very well, fell to the floor and revealed to the

princess a species of monster that appeared to her to be frightful.

The accident augmented the prince's anger; he said a
thousand offensive things, and warned her that he would only
give her a week to decide to marry him, after which he promised to put her to death if she were obstinate in refusing him.
Going out then, he left the unhappy Constance unintimidated
by his threats, still occupied with the infidelity of the ingrate
she loved.

The week passed without her reflecting even once on the
fate that was in preparation for her. No sooner had the time
had expired than Indolent came to visit her, in order to discover whether her sentiments were in conformity with those he
had; but, having found them opposed to his own, he ordered
immediately that she be taken to the black forest.

That forest was thus named because it was never illuminated by the sun's bright rays. Thick fogs reigned there from
the commencement of the year to the end. A continuous cold
wind made itself felt there violently, and blew with such force
that it shook the largest trees in the forest, which were only
charged with yellow and faded leaves. The cries of barn owls
and long-eared owls and the howls of ferocious beasts with
which it was filed were heard in all directions. A wall a hundred feet high surrounded it on all sides and prevented anyone
from getting out of it. In sum, one could not find a more
frightful abode.

However, the exceedingly unfortunate Constance was
imprisoned there, and found herself less unhappy there than in
the palace she had just quit, because the most somber and deserted places seemed more appropriate to hide her dolor.

As soon as she found herself in the sad place, she expected to become the prey imminently of some of the wolves
or wild boars that she saw running all around her; and although she had no appetite or life, she felt gripped by horror
and dread in thinking that she was about to be devoured. Directing her tremulous footsteps toward the places that seemed
to her to be the least accessible, therefore, she went to hide

there, in order to avoid encountering cruel animals, and to wait there for a milder death that dolor and weakness could not fail to procure for her.

Incessantly agitated by those various thoughts, she saw a lion of enormous size coming toward her, the fierce and proud appearance of which left her no hope. At that sight, she started running at top speed; but the furious animal, more skillful in running than the young princess, caught up with her promptly and, seizing her by the dress, caused her to fall unconscious on a pile of dry leaves that the wind had assembled.

The lion in question, less cruel than Constance had imagined, did not do her any harm. On the contrary, touched by the state she was in, it promptly went to fetch water in its mouth and spat it out over the face of the dying princess.

That aid brought her round. She opened her beautiful eyes, and seemed astonished to see the light again and to perceive nearby the lion she had feared so much, which was licking her hands and washing them with its tears.

"What a prodigy!" she exclaimed. "I've found humanity among ferocious animals, and I only encountered cruelty among humans. Why has this lion not taken away my life? My misfortunes would be over and I would not have the chagrin of thinking at this moment that the ingrate I adore has forgotten the oath that he swore to love me eternally, and is enchanted by the pleasures that he is savoring with my rival."

As she finished speaking she allowed a great quantity of tears to flow, and would doubtless have made a few resolutions fatal to her days if the lion had not moderated her dolor somewhat by means of its caresses and attentions.

Sensible to what it was doing in order to calm her, she stroked it, in spite of her chagrin, and even thanked it, as if she were certain that it had understood her. Two frightful bears that she saw passing by terminated her discourse and caused her to forget the desire that she had had to die. She therefore got up in order to run away again, without thinking that she had a defender beside her stronger than those animals. Seeing her design, however, the lion, which was still lying beside her, tugged her gently by the dress and made her sit on its back. Then, immediately rising to its feet with a surprising lightness, it ran through the forest.

The princess, feeling herself carried away, was uncertain of her fate, and did not know whether she ought to feel dread or hope. She was finally informed. The lion took her to the foot of a rock, which the sea beat with its waves. It was the only place that was not surrounded by walls, because it was inaccessible. The lion placed her on the sand gently, and then went to look for oysters and other shellfish, which it presented to her very politely. She ate some, and drank, with pleasure, water from a spring that was not far away, which the lion had collected in a large shell.

After that light meal, which would not have displeased the princess in a less unfortunate situation, the lion pushed her into a cavity in the rock, and, having followed her in, it closed the entrance with a large stone.

In spite of the marks of amity that Constance had received from the animal, she trembled when she found herself alone with it in that obscure lair. It was vast and only received daylight through a few cracks that time had made. Several piles of dry leaves seemed to have been piled up to serve as a seat and a bed; in fact, they had been gathered there with that design. The cavern was her defender's, who had only taken her there to defend her during the night from the animals of which the forest was full.

Seeing that the daylight had almost faded away, and observing that the lion was not seeking to do her any harm, the princess understood its intention and sat down on the leaves— not in order to go to sleep; her mind was too agitated, but in order to recover somewhat from the fatigues she had endured. The sad master of the place lay down beside her and spent a part of the night sighing, kissing her hands from time to time

The princess, who could not sleep, reflected on all everything that had just happened to her, unable to divine the reason for the animal's sadness, or why it was treating her with so much kindness. She spent two thirds of the night in those re-flections.

Finally, she fell asleep, and only woke up at daybreak. She was surprised not to see the lion beside her and got up to see whether it was in some other place in the rock, but her efforts were futile; she could not find it. Anxious that it might have quit her, she found the stone disturbed and went outside to see whether it was on the sea shore. She went there, but without discovering anything.

Alarmed to have lost her companion, she was about to go back into the cavern to hide from the animals she feared when she perceived a man among the trees, who was defending him-self with a sturdy staff against a monstrous boar. That specta-cle frightened her, but did not cause her to run way. She had no doubt that it was some unfortunate condemned, like her, to end his days in the forest. She hoped that he would be victori-ous over the boar and that he might be able to get her out of this horrible place. She therefore waited some distance away for the battle to end. It did not take long; the boar received several blows on the head, delivered so vigorously, that it soon fell dead. That was not, however, without having wounded its valiant enemy, who immediately leaned against a tree, only able to sustain himself with difficulty because of the quantity of blood he had lost.

Seeing him in that state, Constance thought she could not refuse him help without lacking humanity. She therefore ran to him with the design of helping him to staunch the blood.

Gods! What became of her, as she approached, when she recognized Tendrebrun. He was pale, sad and dying, and no less charming for that. What did she not experience on seeing the danger he was in? She forgot all her anger and asked him, in a tremulous voice, with tears in her eyes, whether he still recognized her, and whether he wanted to accept the feeble service that she could offer him.

The prince stared at her, and, without replying a single word, drew away so promptly, in spite of his lack of strength, that he was soon lost to sight. Her despair, after that astonishing behavior, is imaginable.

"How he flees me!" she cried. "The sight of me horrifies him more than the most cruel beasts, than death itself. Unfortunate as I am, can I still resolve to live after so much scorn? No, let us run to death, since it alone can terminate my pains."

As she finished speaking she turned her steps back toward the sea, and threw herself into it without hesitation. She would have found death there if the lion, returning to its cavern, had not perceived her and immediately thrown itself in after her, in order to rescue her.

That prompt rescue was necessary; an instant later and the beautiful days would have ended. The lion prolonged them by means of its cares, so well that she recovered her senses. Carrying her into its cavern then, it laid her down on the bed of leaves, started a fire with stones that it struck together, lit a few tree branches with it that it went to fetch, and which it lay on the dry leaves, and warmed up the unfortunate princess.

She was about to reproach it for the pity that had engaged it to help her when she heard a voice, which said to her: "Find the door that is here if you want to find the end of your troubles."

That oracle rendered her strength and appeared to give great pleasure to the lion.

They both searched the extent of the rock for that door, therefore, even advancing into places so dark that they feared getting absolutely lost.

Hazard finally enabled Constance to encounter the door so much desired. She stumbled and tried to lean against the rock, and placed her hands precisely on the door, which opened instantly under the thrust she had provided.

She alerted the lion to the discovery, and climbed a stairway within it that was presented to her. It was less dark than the interior of the rock. After having climbed about ten thousand steps they arrived on a green lawn, which occupied the entire summit of the crag.

It was so prodigiously high that the tallest trees in the forest seemed no more than a foot in height.

It was only possible to reach that lawn by way of the stairway that Constance had discovered. She did not have time to examine the summit because she perceived a young woman attached to a stake by thick iron chains, who was making every effort to prevent a steel box poised on a feeble pivot at the very edge of the rock from falling into the precipice.

The lovely young woman had a tranquil, mild and modest physiognomy. Virtuous people could not have seen her without experiencing an infinite esteem and respect for her, so she inspired a good deal in the princess, who, touched by her situation, ran toward her in order to make efforts to set her free. She advanced, therefore, with that design, in company with her faithful companion, but they had scarcely reached the unfortunate woman when her chains fell and she stood up— without, however, quitting her box.

Looking at the princess then, with an air of recognition and majesty, she said: "For a long time, beautiful Constance, I have been lamenting your fate, and have desired to see you in this place. Don't be surprised; several centuries ago I read in the book of destinies that you would one day render me the power that I lost an infinite time ago. Although I appear young to you, I have seen an infinite number of centuries go by, and I am the one who enabled my voice to pass through the rock in order to advise you to seek the door through which you have just passed in coming here.

"My name is Virtue; I once reigned in the world and I was loved and adored by sovereigns and their subjects. No one envied my empire except Vicious, who, jealous of the happiness that I procured for mortals, spread all the weaknesses in the human heart and gave birth to all the vices. She took advantage of my absence and employed the time of a voyage I was making to a country unknown to anyone but me. In the end, the Vices expelled me when I returned, and took away the splendid radiance by which I was surrounded. Since them I have been misunderstood, and generally abandoned. There was no king who wanted to lend me his support; that completed my doom, because I cannot reign over any people if I am not cherished by their princes.

"Not content with having made me lose my authority, Vicious brought me to this rock, where she chained me, in order to prevent me from troubling her new domination. Her superior strength does not, however, prevent me from quitting my chains for two days every year, during which I travel all over the world, visiting those who have not forgotten me. I have often traveled without finding a single person who still remembers my name.

"Once, however, in passing through your father's estates, I saw him and found that he had the sentiments for me that I desired. I perceived with pleasure the aversion that he had for Vicious and her children: since that time I limited my excursions to his realm and I visited him every year. In the year when you came into the world I witnessed your birth, in the form of an old woman, and I gave you all the gifts that might render you perfect.

"I consulted the destinies in order to know what would happen to you; I discovered that a great many misfortunes were reserved for you, but I read then that you would overcome them and that destiny had chosen you to restore my initial splendor—in sum, that you were to extract me from the undignified slavery that I was in. Content with that knowledge, I returned to my mountain; since that time I have continued to see you without making myself known and without showing myself.

"One day, when I was coming here to resume my chains, I saw Vicious arrive in a chariot of fire; she stopped it close to me and, showing me the box you see, she told me that it contained one of my most faithful friends, who was about to be precipitated at that moment into the depths of the sea. The malevolent fay then placed the box that she had in her chariot on the tip of the rock, and went away, convinced that it would not take long to fall. Fortunately, I've had enough strength to retain it until now. I've tried several times to open that prison, but in vain. Now that I'm free, I'm going to deliver the unfortunate friend. Only interest yourself in me, beautiful princess, and you shall soon see the effect of my power."

The lovely Virtue then pronounced a few words; the box opened, and allowed her and Constance to see King Judicious, chained by the midriff. What a surprise it was for the king to see the light again, and to rediscover a daughter whose loss he had mourned! What a joy it was for that charming daughter to see again a father who had cost her so many tears! Finally, what a pleasure it was for Virtue to make the happiness of those virtuous individuals! It is easy to imagine the contentment of all three, and one ought not to think that a long time passed before Judicious was completely liberated.

He gave Constance a hundred caresses, as well as his friend, and told them that he had been imprisoned in the box ever since he had been abducted from the gardens of his place; that he would have died of despair and hunger if the malevolent Vicious, who wanted to prolong his suffering, had not made him drink a liquid that had preserved his life in spite of him.

Constance was so penetrated by joy that she could not speak; she contented herself with taking his hands, kissing them and bathing them with her tears.

The lion, who had been a tranquil witness thus far to what was happening, approached the king and kissed his robe respectfully. Turning then toward Virtue, it looked at her in a fashion that seemed to be asking whether he was to be the only unfortunate one.

That person, who could do anything, read his thoughts and said to him: "It is just, amiable prince, that I also compensate you for having conserved the sentiments that I inspired in you." Immediately placing her hand on his forehead, she pronounced these words in a soft and gracious voice: "Resume your natural form, never to quit it again."

Then the lion disappeared, and allowed to be seen in its stead the son of the Tartar Emperor.

After having thanked his benefactress in a few words, which marked his keen gratitude, he ran to throw himself at the feet of the princess, in order to obtain a pardon that, he said, she could not refuse him without injustice and cruelty.

Constance, seeing him so close to her and seeing him tender and charming again, felt an extraordinary emotion. Her first impulse was to tell him that she had forgotten everything, since he still loved her, but what she had seen him do with Bounty and the last mark of indifference that he had given her in the forest returned to her mind so forcefully, that she resolved not to forgive him

Turning her eyes away from him, she told him that he ought not to think about her any longer, that she never wanted to see him again, and that he had offended her too deeply for him to be able to hope to occupy in future the place that he had had for a long time in her heart.

Seeing the despair that that response caused the prince, Virtue addressed the daughter of Judicious and said to her: "Cease, beautiful Constance, to drive a lover who adores you to despair. Believe that he only loves, and has only ever loved, you. Only deign to listen to him, and you will be convinced of it."

After having denied herself that briefly, the princess consented to it, and the prince, charmed that she was permitting him to justify himself, told her how he had found himself in the palace of his father, the Emperor, after having been taken away from her, and made her a sincere confession of all the woes that he had suffered since the cruel moment when he had been distanced from her.

The time that he employed in expressing his pains and his love for the princess interrupted the thread of his narrative somewhat, and gave Virtue the time necessary to inform the king briefly about the adventures of his daughter. After that account, Tendrebrun continued, in the following fashion:

"The sojourn I spent on the Isle of Roses will no longer appear to you to be a crime, my dear Constance, when I have told you that I was forced to land there and remain there by the enchantments of Vicious, who, in the form of a young and beautiful person named Bounty, offered me her help in order to take me to you, with the sole design of attracting me to her by means of deceptive charms. She could not retain me otherwise; she therefore had me given a bracelet, which, she said, would protect me from all sorts of misfortunes as long as I had it on my arm; but it was, in fact, a powerful talisman that inspired in a short time a violent passion for the person who had composed it, and which prevented me from discovering her faults. I soon felt its effects, since I became the most passionate of men in the fay's presence. I forgot you in spite of myself, and put all my felicity into pleasing my greatest enemy. I did not imagine that anything could be found more perfect than her. I would have remained in that error for a long time but for what happened to me one night when I could not sleep.

"I heard a sound of voices in the gardens, which did not seem to me to be ordinary, and I saw such a large quantity of torches passing the windows of my apartment that, curious to know what it could be, I got up and went to my window without thinking about the prohibitions that had been imposed on me.

"I had no sooner opened it than I perceived in the air and in the pathways of the wood an infinite number of frightful monsters, some of which were carrying lanterns and the others torches, and they were all heading for the arbor where I had seen Bounty for the first time.

"That surprising spectacle caused me to make the resolution to slip close to that enclosure in order to see what would become of those frightful figures. I left my room quietly and traversed the wood by way of the darkest places. I soon repented of having followed those dense routes because, as I tried to move aside a few tree branches that coed my route, they hooked on to that fatal bracelet. It fell off, and I could not find it again in the darkness.

"That loss, which I thought considerable, afflicted me greatly, but it could not prevent me from continuing on my way. I finally arrived at the enclosure, where I was gripped by fear on seeing Vicious surrounded by that troop of monsters.

"They were her children, the Vices. My first impulse was to flee, but, far from following it, I made the decision to listen to what the members of that horrible company were saying. I heard Vicious recounting to her sons that it had been a long time since she had made use of all the artifices of which she was making use in order to deceive me, and telling them how she had composed the mysterious bracelet that had made her appear so beautiful to my eyes. I learned then that the reason she had forbidden me to open my windows during four hours of the night was because she feared that I might see all the Vices arriving for the audience she was obliged to give them during that interval. In sum, I heard enough to know how I had been deceived and the unfortunate state to which I had been reduced.

"I thought about you, then, beautiful princess; the idea of your charms presented itself to my imagination, and rendered me the most miserable of all mortals. Overwhelmed by a thousand different thoughts, I perceived that the assembly was about to finish, and I returned to my apartment, determined to pretend that I had not discovered anything, in order to find an opportunity to escape and to travel the earth in order to search for you.

"As daylight had not yet appeared I went to bed in order to dream there at my ease, but as I undressed I found the bracelet that I had lost; it had hooked on to one of the buckles of my gaiters. I was very glad to have it in my hands in order to convince myself of the effect that it produced.

"Night had no sooner given way to day than I saw the false Bounty arrive, accompanied by a numerous retinue. The sight of her would have inflamed me as usual, if I had not removed instantly the powerful charm that deceived me. Scarcely was it unfastened from my arm than all those beauties disappeared and allowed me to see in their stead the hideous face of the cruel Vicious and all her daughters.

"In spite of the efforts that I made to constrain myself to caress the fay, she perceived the change in me; it made her suspicious. She stared at me, and, seeing me nonplussed, she wanted to see whether I was still wearing the bracelet.

"Not having found it, she trembled and rose into the air to a height of six feet, after which she touched me with her wand, changed me into a lion and swore that she was going to invoke all the infernal powers in order to hate me as much as she had loved me. She added that I ought to expect to feel the cruelest effects of her hatred. Then she sent me to her friend King Indolent, in order that he could make me combat several animals of my species on his birthday, which he ordinarily celebrated with similar fêtes.

"She ordered him to enclose me in the black forest after I had served as a spectacle for his subjects, and I learned before my departure that when I was in that forest I would resume my natural form for one hour every day, in order not to be in a state to defend myself against the animals that inhabit it. However many wounds I might receive I would not lose my life, because she wanted me to live for a long time in order to have the pleasures of prolong my suffering. While I was a man I would not have the liberty of talking and I would be forced to flee the sight of any person of either sex.

"The sentence was carried out. I fought twelve lions in the presence of Indolent's entire court; you were a witness, reluctantly, to that frightful spectacle. I had the joy of seeing you there, and the mortal displeasure of not being able to tell you about my misfortunes. Then I was taken to the black forest. There I discovered the cavern that served you as a retreat and made it my habitation.

"A few days later I encountered you. On seeing you, I experienced an incredible joy, but it was not of long duration because I could not make myself known to you, and, in spite of all the cares I took to enable to you avoid death, you were exposed to a thousand dangers.

"Those thoughts caused me a great deal of sadness and made me shed tears, which you noticed. Several times I heard you say things that proved to me that you still loved me. I saw with extreme satisfaction the dolor you experienced when you had seen me wounded by the boar. I have never sensed the malevolence of Vicious more sharply than when I was forced to draw away from you at a time when you were offering me your help with so much generosity.

"In sum, until now I have been the most unfortunate of men. It is you, divine Constance, who can render me the most fortunate. Do not delay, then, and let me read in your eyes that I still possess your heart entirely; I flatter myself that the king, your father, touched by my troubles, will not disapprove of you."

Judicious immediately spoke, assuring him that he would not raise any objection if his daughter wanted to give him her heart and her hand.

Constance, seeing that her lover was faithful, promised to love him as long as she lived. That assurance compensated him for all that he had suffered. Virtue told the king that it was necessary to unite those lovable individuals immediately, but that, as the place where they were as inappropriate to such a beautiful celebration, she was going to take them to the Tranquil Isle, which was a thousand times more charming than the Isle of Roses; nothing would trouble their felicity there.

As she finished speaking they saw a magnificent chariot appear carried on a shining cloud, which came to settle at their feet. She made the princes and the princess climb into it, and took her place with them. They were all carried into the air and taken to the island that was to be their abode.

That island was a land of delights; nothing was lacking there. The beauty of the gardens, arbors and waters surpassed anything that they had seen thus far. Palaces of flowers, diamonds and crystal were built in different places The Fountain of Youth flowed in that beautiful place. Virtue made Judicious drink from it, and the prince became again what he had been in his early youth.

Tendrebrun, who still conserved a veritable amity for his father, begged the amiable sovereign to permit him to drink that marvelous water too. She wanted to take charge of that personally; she departed immediately, and returned with him two hours later.

The good emperor blessed the day a hundred times that had enabled him to find his dear son again; he gave Constance a thousand caresses, as well as her father, and urged them both to render his son happy. He drank the water of youth and recovered the strength and the features that the great number of years had taken away from him.

Those illustrious individuals reposed for two or three days, in order to recover from the fatigues they had endured, after which the two lovers were taken to the temple of Hymen, where they swore an eternal love to one another joyfully.

Virtue rendered them immortal, as well as their fathers, and promised always to dwell with them. There were charming fêtes for an infinite time. The inhabitants of the island were delighted with the princes and the princess that Virtue had given them. They were all subjects of that divine daughter, and had always loved her; that is what had brought them to assemble in that beautiful abode.

After the first days of the happy marriage, Virtue proposed to the two spouses to accompany them in the voyage they wanted to make in the world. They consented to that with pleasure and departed, each mounted on a white eagle.

First they went to the Isle of Roses where Vicious had made her abode, but they no longer found her there. She had returned to her mountain. They therefore took the road there, and found her boiling in a huge cauldron a quantity of spiders and vipers with quicksilver, in order to make a spell that she wanted to use that same evening. She uttered a frightful screech when she perceived Constance and Tendrebrun and trembled on seeing the person who was accompanying hem.

Her design then was to flee and hide, but Virtue said to her: "Remain attached to this mountain until the end of centuries, and stay there without it being permitted for you to do the slightest harm. That is what I order you to do to punish you for all the crimes you have committed; but I want you to give me the little box that you keep in your pocket."

The malevolent fay, finding herself powerless against her enemy, was obliged to obey; she therefore gave her the box and remained chained next to her cauldron, without being able to move.

Virtue knocked her down, tore up all her magic books and left her in that horrible place uttering howls that could be heard for at least a league around. Then she opened the box, and showed the prince and princess the little magician of the island of Tintarinos, whom the malevolent Vicious had imprisoned there some time ago.

Beneficent, charmed to find himself among friends again, made them a thousand amities and begged Virtue to permit him to follow her everywhere. She consented to that with pleasure, and traveled with that amiable company through several realms, which she found governed by Vices. She could have expelled them if she had wanted to do so, but the people of whom they had rendered themselves the masters were so wicked and corrupt that she resolved to punish them for not having followed her by leaving them under the domination of those monsters.

She renounced thereafter the empire that she had once had over the earth, and only formed the design to make a voyage from time to time to remove the small number of men and women who had an extreme aversion to the Vices in order to transport them to her island—which she has executed until the present day, and that is why there are so few virtuous people to be found in the world.

After having traveled all over the world, she returned to the Tranquil Isle with the prince, the princess and Beneficent. Their return caused extreme joy to the Emperor, the king and all the inhabitants of the beautiful country. Constance augmented that joy a short time afterwards by bringing into the world a charming princess, who was subsequently as perfect as those who gave her life.

The happiness of all those individuals has not deteriorated since; they live content in that unknown land, because they refuse entry to the children of Vicious. Only Virtue makes their felicity; they love her and respect her, and never ceases to say that those she protects and who do not abandon her are fortunate.

GUILLAUME-HYACINTHE BOUGÉANT:
THE MARVELOUS VOYAGE OF PRINCE FAN-FÉRÉDIN TO ROMANCIA

I. The Departure of Fan-Férédin for Romancia

I could, following a sufficiently common custom, begin this story with an account of my youth and all the cares that my mother, Queen Fan-Férédine, took in my education; she was the most virtuous princess in the world, and, without vanity, I have sometimes heard it said that by the sagacity of her education she was able to render me, in no time, one of the most accomplished princes that had ever been seen. I am even persuaded that the story, full of fine maxims for the education of young princes, would figure quite well in this work; but as my design is less to talk about myself as to recount the admirable things that I have seen, I believe I ought to omit that detail and every other circumstance unnecessary to my project.

Queen Fan-Férédine did not like romances much, but having read by chance in I know not what work,[11] composed by an author of respectable character, that nothing is more appropriate to form the hearts and minds of young persons, she felt obliged by conscience to make me read as many romances as I could, in order to inspire in me as soon as possible a love of virtue and honor, a horror of vice, flight from passions and an appetite for the true, the great, the solid and everything that is most estimable.

---

[11] Author's note: "*De l'usage des romans.*" [i.e., *De l'usage des romans, où l'on fait voir leur utilité et leur differens caractères, avec une bibliothèque des romans* by Nicolas Lenglet Du Fresnoy, as detailed in the introduction.]

In fact, as I was, it is said, born with fortunate disposi-tions, I soon felt the fruits of such a praiseworthy education. Agitated my a thousand unknown movements, my heart full of fine sentiments and my mind filled with great ideas, I began to be disgusted by everything that surrounded me.

What a difference there is, I thought, *between what I see and hear and what I read in romances! I see here everyone occupied with objects if interest, fortune, establishment or frivolous pleasures. No singular adventures, no heroic enter-prises. A lover, if one can believe him, goes straight to the denouement without the embarrassment of any preliminaries. What a way to behave! Why was it necessary for me to be born in a climate where fine sentiments are so unfamiliar?*

But why, I added, *should I condemn myself to spend my days sadly in a land where heroic virtues are not esteemed? I reign here, it is true, but what satisfaction is there for a great heart to reign over barbarians? Let us abandon their vulgarity and go in search of a glorious establishment in the marvelous land of romances, where even the proletariat is made up of heroes.*

Such were the thoughts that came to my mind, and I did not take long to put them into execution. After having equipped myself secretly with everything necessary for my voyage, I departed by moonlight one beautiful night, in order to attempt, by traveling, the discovery that I was meditating.

I traversed many plains, passed over many mountains, encountered castles and cities without number on my route, but, only finding everywhere lands similar to those I already knew and people who had nothing singular about them, I final-ly began to find the length of my search tedious. I sought in vain for information and news of the land of Romances; some people replied that they did not even known the name; other told me that they had, in truth, heard mention of it, but that they did not know in what part of the world it was situated. The only thing that sustained my courage in the length and difficulty of the enterprise was the reflection that, after all, it was necessary for Romancia to be somewhere, and that it could not be a chimera.

For in the end, I said, *if that country did not really exist, it would be necessary to treat as ridiculous visions and puerile fables everything that one reads in romances. What an illusion! Is it imaginable that so many otherwise reasonable people, who love that reading, and so many intelligent people, would employ their talents composing such works?*

In spite of those reflections, however, I confess that I was sometimes on the point of repenting of my enterprise, and it would not have taken much for me to make the resolution to turn back. *But no,* I said to myself, yet again, *after having done so much, it would be shameful to retreat. How do I know whether I might not be nearing the goal so much desired?*

I was, in fact, nearing it without knowing it, and this is how it happened, by virtue of a bizarre accident that might have cost me my life anywhere else.

After having been climbing the great mountains of Troximania for some hours, with a great deal of difficulty, I finally arrived at their summit, leading my horse by the bridle. There I suddenly felt the earth give way beneath my feet; in fact, my horse slid down one side of the mountain and I fell on the other, without knowing what became of me from that moment until I found myself at the bottom of a frightful precipice, surrounded on all sides by terrible crags. It is evident that some good genius sustained me in my fall in order to prevent me from perishing, and I would have perceived it then if I had had all the knowledge that I acquired subsequently, but the thought did not occur to me and I attributed to a fortunate hazard what was in fact a particular protection of some fay, favorable genius or one of the petty divinities that flutter around the land of Romances in greater numbers than the butterflies of spring in our countryside.

It is, however, not difficult to understand that in the situation in which I found myself, after having looked upwards to contemplate he enormous height from which I had fallen, and having envisaged the horror of my surroundings, that I abandoned myself to the saddest reflections.

Poor Fan-Férédin, what will become of you in this horrible solitude? How will you get out of this profound lair? You're going to die...

Yes, how many touching things I said, how eloquently I complained of destiny, and, by virtue of the right I have acquired in the land of Romances of making moral reflections, I would like people to learn in good time, by my example, to respect the supreme decrees that regulate my fate, and never complain about the events that seem to them to be the most contrary to their desires.

However, the approaching night redoubled my anxiety and I hastened to take advantage of what little daylight and strength remained to me to get out of the abyss that I was in, if I could. It was in vain that I would have tried to gain the heights; they were too sheer. It only remained for me to seek in the depths for an issue that might lead me to some inhabited place, or at least a habitable one.

No vestige of a path was offered to my sight. Doubtless I was the first man who had ever descended into that precipice. I was thus reduced to making a route for myself, and, in fact, I did that so well, climbing and leaping from rock to rock, sometimes hanging on to brushwood, sometimes falling backwards or forwards, that after having covered some ground in that fashion, I arrived at a place that was more open and more spacious.

The first object that struck my sight was a kind of cemetery, a charnel-house or a heap of bones of a singular kind. There were horns of all forms, huge hooked talons, the dried skins of winged dragons, and long beaks of birds of every species. I remembered immediately what I had read in romances about griffins, centaurs, hippogriffs, flying dragons, harpies, satyrs and other similar animals, and I began to flatter myself that I was not far from the land for which I was searching.

What confirmed me in that idea was that, a moment later, I saw a centaur emerging from the opening of a lair, which came straight to the place I was observing and threw down the large carcass of a hippogriff, after which he withdrew and plunged back into the lair from which he had emerged.

Although I was perfectly familiar with centaurs by virtue of the reading I had done, and, in any case, am not lacking in courage, I confess that that first sight caused me some emotion. I even hid behind a rock in order to observe the centaur until he had retired. Recovering my spirits then, however, and arming myself with resolution, I said to myself: *What do I have to fear from that centaur? I have read in all romances that the centaurs are the best folk in the world. Far from being enemies of humans, they are always disposed to lend them service and to tell them a thousand curious secrets, as witness the centaur Chiron. Perhaps this one might carry me to the land of Romances; at least it won't refuse to get me out of this horrible place.*

Immediately, I marched toward the lair, and, stopping at the entrance, I called loudly: "Charitable centaur, if your heart can be touched by pity, be sensible to the misfortune of a prince who implores your generosity. It is Prince Fan-Férédin who is appealing to you."

But I called and shouted in vain; no one appeared.

Full of anxiety and secret fear, I went into the cavern, and I saw that it was a subterranean road, which plunged a long way under the mountain. What should I do? I could not think of anything other than following the centaur, judging that it was impossible that I would not encounter him, or that I would soon make myself heard to him.

But should I confess my weakness here or not? Is it necessary to speak or be silent? This is one of those difficult situations in which I have often seen the heroes of romances who are recounting their adventures, the embarrassment of which one can only know by experiencing it oneself.

In sum, as I have remarked that, all things considered, those gentlemen always decide to confess with a good grace, I too shall confess. Scarcely had I taken a hundred steps in that profound tunnel, still following the rock that served as a wall, gripped by the horror of finding myself in such a frightful place, without knowing how I was going to get out, than I let myself collapse weakly, almost devoid of consciousness. I retained sufficient, however, to remember that in a very similar situation the celebrated Cleveland had had the wit to go to sleep, and finding the expedient rather good, I did not hesitate to imitate him.[12]

After such a confession, however, it is only just that I compensate myself by means of something that does honor to my courage. Soon afterwards, therefore, I got up, and, considering that it was either necessary to resolve myself to perishing in the profound darkness of the bowels of the earth or find a means of getting out of it, I decided to continue my route as far as it could take me.

Imagine a man walking without light in a narrow tunnel in the earth, perhaps two leagues deep, often obliged to crawl or fold himself up, to slither like a snake through tight passages, only able to advance by groping with his hand and testing the ground with his foot. Such was my situation; it would doubtless be difficult to imagine a more frightful one. The memory of that adventure still fills me with so much horror that I shall cut the story short.

What I cannot help saying, however, is that I have never recognized better than I did then the verity that I have seen in all romances, that one is never closer to obtaining what one

---

[12] This is the first of numerous references in the text to *Le Philosophe anglais, ou Histoire de Monsieur Cleveland, fils naturel de Cromwell*, by Antoine-François Prévost, whose first four volumes were published in 1731. Bougéant could not know in 1735 that Prévost would eventually add a further three in 1738-9, although he would have been aware of an apocryphal fifth volume, by an unknown hand, published in 1734, which contains attacks on the Jesuits—which, as a Jesuit himself, Bougéant would naturally have resented, and might have assumed, erroneously, to be Prévost's work.

desires than at the moment when one appears to be most distant from it. That is what happened to me.

After having traveled for a long time in the fashion that I have just described, I thought that I was beginning to perceive a feeble light. I could scarcely convince myself of it at first, and I attributed it to an effect of my anxious and troubled imagination. However, I soon perceived that the light was gradually augmented, and I no longer had any doubt of it when I realized that I was beginning to distinguish objects. What joy I felt at that moment! My entire body quivered with it, and I do not know words capable of expressing it. I still do not understand how that sudden transition from an extreme sadness to such a great excess of joy did not cause me a dangerous revolution.

At any rate, seeing that the light was still increasing, and judging that the exit I was seeking could not be far away, I increased my pace—or, rather, I ran, urgently, in order to get there. In fact, I found it, and I saw...how can I put it? Yes, I saw the most astonishing, the most admirable, the most charming things that one can see.

In a word, I saw the land of Romances. That is what I shall relate in the next chapter.

II. The entry of Prince Fan-Férédin to Romancia. A description of the natural history of the land.

Most voyagers like to boast about the beauty of the lands they have traveled, and as the simple truth dos not furnish them with enough of the marvelous, they are obliged to have recourse to fiction. For myself, far from wanting to exaggerate, I would like, on the contrary, to be able to dissimulate a part of the marvels that I saw, in the fear that people might suspect the sincerity of my account. Having made the reflection, though, that it is not permissible to suppress the truth in order to avoid the suspicion of lying, I shall generously make the decision appropriate to every sincere historian, which is to recount the facts with the most exact verity, without any party interest, exaggeration or disguise. I foresee that strong minds will be obstinate in their incredulity, but their very incredulity will take the place of punishment, while reasonable minds will have the satisfaction of learning a thousand curious things that they did not know. I shall therefore resume the continuation of my story.

Scarcely had I arrived at the exit from the subterranean tunnel than, casting my eyes over the vast country that was offered to my gaze, I was struck by an astonishment that I can only compare to the admiration that a man born blind would have on opening his eyes for the first time. The comparison is all the more just because all the objects seemed new to me, such that I had never seen anything similar. There were, in truth, woods, rivers and springs; I could distinguish meadows, hills and orchards; but all those things were so different from the things that we call by the same names in this land that one can honestly say that we only have the name and the shadow of them.

The first reflection that came to mind was to think that there many countries that we do not know under the earth; that appeared to me to be an important observation for geography and physics; but it is true that, drawn by curiosity and admiration for the objects that were offered to my eyes, I did not linger long over those philosophical reflections. I entered into the country without having any clear idea of where to direct my steps, feeling equally attracted on all sides by new beauties, scarcely giving myself the time to consider any in particular.

I finally decided to follow a charming river that snaked across the plain. The river was bordered by the most beautiful, the brightest and softest grass imaginable, embellished by a thousand flowers of various species. It irrigated a meadow of admirable beauty, the herbs and flowers of which perfumed the air with an exquisite odor, and if, in places, it appeared to double back, it is doubtless because it had a sensible regret in quitting such a beautiful place.

The meadowland was ornamented, throughout its extent, by delightful clumps of bushes, spaced out in a way apt to please the eyes; and, as if nature sometimes liked to imitate art, as art is always pleased to imitate nature, I perceived in some places regular designs formed by grass, flowers and small trees that made charming flower gardens; but the river itself seemed to exhaust all my admiration. The water was clearer and more transparent than crystal. As soon as one lent an ear to it, one could hear the waves moaning tenderly; that soft murmur combined with the melodious song of swans, which are very common there, and make a very touching music.

Instead of sand, mother-of-pearl could be seen shining on the river bed, and a thousand precious stones; an infinite number of gilded, silvery, azure and crimson fish could be distinguished without dutifully in the bosom of the waters, which, to render the spectacle even more agreeable, were amusing themselves playing a thousand pleasant games.

"It's a pity, though," I murmured, "that one can't pass from one bank to the other in order to enjoy both sides of the river equally."

Would you believe it?—undoubtedly, for I have many other marvels to recount—no sooner had I pronounced those words than I perceived beneath my feet a very neat little boat. Thanks to my reading, I knew the usage of that boat too well to hesitate for a moment. I descended into it, in fact, and in a moment I was carried to the other bank of the river. Let the incredulous dare, after that, to make use of nasty quibbles against facts so undeniable! What will finish confounding them is that, considering a certain stretch of the river and finding that it was appropriate to make a bridge there, I was astonished to see one completed at that moment, in such a way that nothing more convenient has ever been seen.

I continued my route, however, and I can say without exaggeration that I encountered new objects of admiration at every step. Among others, I perceived a place in the meadowland that seemed to me to be a little more cultivated. I was curious enough to approach it, and I found a spring. The water seemed to me to be so pure and beautiful that, not doubting that it was excellent, I wanted to taste it; but what did I feel, instantly, within myself! What ardor, what transports, what unknown emotions, what fires!

Those fires had, in truth, something very mild about them, and it seemed to me that I found pleasure in them, but they were, at the same time, so vivid and so unquiet that, no longer in possession of myself, falling alternately into the liveliest agitation and the most profound reverie, I marched across the meadowland without knowing exactly where I was going.

I encountered in that fashion a second spring, and I know not what impulse made me drink from it as well. Scarcely had I swallowed a few drops, however, than I found myself utterly changed. It seemed that my heart was enveloped by a black vapor and my mind covered by a dark cloud. I felt furious transports and confused emotions of hated and aversion for all the objects that presented themselves.

That change opened my eyes. I recalled what I had read about springs of love and hatred, and did not doubt that it was those from which I had just drunk. Then, remembering that I had also read that the lake of indifference ought not to be far away from the two springs in question, I hastened to search for it, and having encountered it—for in that land one always finds what one is seeking—I had only drunk a few drops therefrom in the hollow of my hand when, instantly returned to myself, I felt a mild and tranquil calm succeed the disturbance that had agitated me.

I shall say nothing about the singular plants that I observed. It is sufficiently well known that the land in question is covered with them. It is only in Romancia that the famous herb moly is found, and the celebrated lotus. Even the plants that we know, which are also found in that land, have a virtue so admirable that one cannot say that they are the same plants, and I cannot in that regard help admiring the simplicity of the unfortunate knight of La Mancha, who thought he could compose with the herbs of his homeland a balm similar to that of Fierabras; for it is true that we have plants of the same name, but they are far from having the same virtue.

It is for that reason that amorous philters, enchanted beverages, charms and all the spells that our magicians attempt to compose with magic herbs do not succeed, because we only have plants devoid of strength and virtue, and I imagine that the reason why we no longer see the marvelous wands, the surprising rings, the talismans, the powders and a thousand other curiosities that operate so many prodigious effects is because we do not have in this land the veritable materials of which they need to be composed.

But what I ought not to forget is the admirable bounty of the climate. I have never understood while reading romances how the princes and the princesses, the heroes and the heroines, and even their domestics and their retinues pass their entire lives without ever mentioning drinking or eating. For after all, I thought, one might be amorous, passionate, avid for glory and a hero from head to toe, but one must still sometimes be subject to a need as pressing as hunger.

I have changed my mind, however, since I have respired the air of Romancia. To begin with, it is the purest, the most serene, the healthiest and the most invariable air that one can breathe. Also, no one has ever heard it said that any hero was inconvenienced by rain, wind or snow, or that he caught a cold in the nocturnal calm while lamenting his amorous torments in the moonlight. But that air has one singular property above all, which is that it can take the place of nourishment for those who breathe it. The consequence of that is one can undertake the longest voyage there, through the most uninhabited deserts, without going to the trouble of making any provision for oneself, or even for one's horses.

Here is another thing that struck me extremely. Our rocks in all the lands here are so hard and of such great sensibility that one can talk to them for an entire year about the most touching things in the world, and they will not even listen. But the rocks are very different in Romancia. I encountered a considerable accumulation of them in my path, and as my curiosity led me to observe everything, I approached them in order to consider them at closer range. I even tried to feel some of them with my hand, but imagine my astonishment to find them so tender that they yielded to the effort of my hand like grass or silk.

I confess that that phenomenon seemed so strange to me that I uttered an exclamation of astonishment, and I would never had understood it if it had not been explained to me subsequently. It was because the previous day, one of the most unfortunate and most eloquent lovers in the land had come to relate his torments to those rocks, and his story was so touching, his tone so dolorous and pitiable, that the rocks had been unable to resist it, in spite of their natural hardness. Some had split from top to bottom, others had allowed themselves to melt like wax, and the hardest had been softened and tenderized to the point that I have just described.

If the rocks of Romancia are so sensitive, it is easy to judge what the complaisance of echoes must be there for those who speak to them. There is nothing as amiable or so docile. They repeat anything one wants. If you sing, they sing; if you lament, they lament with you. They do not even wait for you to finish speaking in order to respond, and rather than let a poor lover speak alone, they will converse with him for an entire day.

It is one of the great resources that one has in the land in question that, when one has no one to whom to confide one's secret troubles, one only has to go and find an echo—especially if it is a female echo—and one is set up for as long as one wants.

III. A continuation of the previous chapter.

The trees of Romancia are, in general, quite similar to ours, but there are certain important remarks to make about them. In addition to the fact that their foliage is always a beautiful green, their shade delightful and their fruits much better than ours, it is only in Romancia that one finds trees so rare and precious that some bear golden branches and others golden apples. It is true, however, that it is rare to encounter them, and it is even more difficult to approach them and pick their fruit, because they are all guarded by dragons or terrible giants, the mere sight of which imports fear into the most intrepid souls.

One flatters oneself in vain that their vigilance can be deceived; their eyes are always open and they do not know the sweetness of slumber. On the other hand, to attempt to force a way past them is to risk certain death, with the consequence that it is necessary to renounce ever picking such precious fruit unless one is favored by some special protection; then, nothing is easier. A little herb that one carries on one's person, a mirror that one shows to the dragon or giant, a wand with which one touches them, a beverage that one presents to them, or the slightest charm, puts them to sleep, after which it is easy to cut off their heads and thus put oneself in possession of all the treasures of which they are the guardians.

I ought, however, to did that this is only according to the reports of others, for, as those trees are very rare, I did not find any in my path and I had no interest in going to search for them.

One thing I have seen, however, which can be regarded as certain, is the liking that the trees in that land have for music. This is something that happened to me and caused me great surprise at the time.

One day, when I had abandoned myself to sleep in a charming grove of young chestnut trees, I was astonished when I awoke to find myself exposed to the ardors of the sun and entirely uncovered, without my being able to imagine what had become of the trees that had been lending me shade a little while before. On looking round, however, I perceived them, already some distance away, moving as if in cadence toward a small plan, where a excellent lute-player was attracting them to him by means of the harmonious sounds of his instrument. A few rocks had joined their company, with all the lions, tigers and bears in the region. It was one of the spectacles that gave me the greatest pleasure throughout my voyage.

As for what I have heard a celebrated historian relate, that trees have a very intelligible language with which to converse together when a gentle breeze agitates the extremity of their branches, I listened carefully in the various forests that I saw, but either that observation must have escaped me or the fact is not true, all the more so as that historian is not always exact in his narrations.[13]

It is not so with regard to those who have asserted that trees serve as abodes for rural divinities, for it is an undeniable fact to which I have often been witness. Nothing is more commonplace, in fact, in the evening, when the moon begins to illuminate the shadows of the night, than to see all the oaks suddenly open up in order to allow the dryads who spend the day therein to emerge from their bosom, and then to open again at daybreak in order to receive them, after they have danced in the fields with the naiads. As it is easy to distinguish the inhabited trees from those that are not, they are extremely respected, and no mortal is bold enough to touch them. If some reckless individual dares to strike one, blood is immediately seen to flow therefrom in abundance, but his impiety will soon be punished.

Fauns, like dryads, also have their trees and there are marks to distinguish them. That gives rise, on occasion, to very pleasant games. On returning from dancing, a young faun might take possession of a dryad's tree. The dryad arrives and knocks on her tree in order to make it open. Who goes there? The place is taken. It's is necessary to improvise. The dryad defends herself, escapes and runs to seize in her turn the abode of another dryad. The latter comes and makes a racket, during which the faun emerges quietly and comes up behind her to

---

[13] Author's note: "Cyrano de Bergerac." As a Jesuit, Bougéant might well have disapproved of Cyrano's ardent championship in *L'Autre monde* of the Copernican model of the solar system, rather than the Aristotelian one favored by the Church. There are some things to which one ought not to lend faith, even momentarily, if one is devout.

surprise her. But she son perceives him and flees. The faun runs after her, and while he is running the first dryad goes back to her tree. The one being pursued reaches another if she can, but eventually, there is a last to arrive who pays for all the others, and the game finishes thus. It is to that little amusement that we owe the game known as four corners.

In any case, it is only for a few moments that these divinities can be permitted to dislodge themselves thus, for they are obliged by the laws of their natural condition to live and die with their trees, without being able to be separated from them except by death. It is necessary not to believe, however, that they really die; their death only consists of passing into another form when the tree finally perishes of old age or by virtue of some accident. One can thus distinguish the old divinities from the younger ones, and even recognize by the disposition of the tree that of the divinity that inhabits it—which is to say, whether she is happy or not.

Among others, an aspen was pointed out to me that was inhabited by one of the wisest and most virtuous fauns of his species. It was even said that he had rather amiable qualities, but after having lived in indifference for a long time he had the misfortune to fall in love, and for several years he had only felt the torments of amour without ever experiencing the pleasure. Chagrin and despair had finally overcome his courage and his reason. He languished without hope of living very long, or rather, if anything could still please him, it was the hope of soon dying, and that was perceptible in the pallor of the tree's leaves, the dryness of its branches and its crown, which was already beginning to be deprived of verdure.

As I continued walking, I encountered a few streams of milk and honey. They are quite common in that land, and as I had often heard mention of them, I was not very astonished. I did not know, however, what the source of those charming streams could be, and I had the pleasure of seeing it with my own eyes. It is because, in Romancia, the cows and goats produce milk so abundantly that they render it continually by themselves, without taking the trouble to be milked, with the consequence that as soon as there are a dozen or so gathered together, they form a rather considerable stream in no time. The bees attach themselves to a tree in order to make their honey there, and make such a prodigious quantity of it that the drops fall incessantly, forming a stream.

That gave me occasion to consider more closely the live-stock that was grazing in the meadows. I can assure you that it is worth the trouble, and you will believe me easily since I saw in that country, in fact, all kinds of animals that are not seen here. The herds were separated in accordance with their different species into different parks.

To begin with, I considered a stud-farm of horses, and I remarked three kinds of them.

Firstly, there were horses quite similar to ours, but of an incomparable beauty. They were all so lively and ardent that their breath seemed fiery, and what astonished me most of all is that their agility was so surprising that they could run through a field of wheat without breaking a single stalk. Also, they were not engendered in accordance with the ordinary laws of nature. They had no other father than the zephyr; in order to perpetuate the race it was only necessary to expose the mares to a gentle wind and they were immediately in foal. It is doubtless greatly to be wished that we had similar stud-farms in our lands, but they have only ever been seen in Libya. I noticed there, above all, one mare of an admirable beauty. She was known as the tinkling mare because a great many little golden bells were hung from her mane, which, in the judgment of connoisseurs of harmony, produced a very beautiful music.

The second species was that of pegasi—which is to say, winged horses that fly through the air as lightly as our swallows. Everyone knows that only one has appeared in our hemisphere, in the time of Bellerophon, but they are quite common in Romancia.

The third species is that of the beautiful white unicorns that have a long horn in the middle of the forehead. They are highly esteemed in the land, although they are not rare there.

Near the park of horses I saw one of griffins and hippo-griffs. Those animals are terrible in appearance and one cannot consider without a certain apprehension their terrible claws, their hooked beak, their huge wings and their lion's tail, but they are, in fact, the most docile of animals and very easy to domesticate. Once one of them has been tamed, one can do anything with it that one wishes. They are admirably conven-ient for hitching to carriages, and cover a lot of ground in a short time.

As regards centaurs, people once wanted to put them in parks like horses and griffins, because they certainly had a lot of the equine about them, but they would not consent to it, claiming that they were no less human, and as it was, in fact, difficult to decide whether they were humans or horses, the matter remained undecided; in the meantime they were given the liberty to travel the countryside in accordance with their will, and to live in their own manner

The park of hircocervi and chimeras appeared to me to be one of the most curious to see. All those monsters were contained in individual dwellings in the form of cages, which allowed their full height and form to be seen, and formed a kind of menagerie that was very diverting, on the one hand, because of the bizarre assortment of animals combined, and terrible, on the other, because of the monstrous and menacing form of those wild beasts.

Wide canals had been dug to either side of that menager-ie, but quite different from one another, because one was full of bright and lively fire, which was maintained continuously with great care in order to lodge and nourish a company of salamanders. The other was filled with beautiful clear and transparent water; it was the dwelling of two or three bands of sirens that were lodged there, as if in a prison, to punish them for the frightful debauchery in which they had engaged a quantity of heroes by means of the charm of their voices. In addition to the retreat to which they were condemned they had been forbidden to sing for some years except for a few pieces of the opera of H***,[14] because it was judged that there was no risk of anyone being seduced by it; but they found the song so primitive that they preferred to keep quiet, with the result that they were, in fact, as mute as fish.

In addition to those two canals there was also a rather deep well, which served as a dwelling for basilisks, but I refrained from presenting myself at the opening of the well in order not to risk being killed by the murderous gaze of those monsters.

I passed from there to a quarter where I perceived sheep. I had never seen any so amiable, but I obtained a singular pleasure, above all, in remembering the charming scene that was offered to my eyes. Everyone knows that nothing is more abject or disgusting in our lands than shepherds and shepherdesses, and, never having seen others, I was convinced that everything I had read about those elsewhere, especially those living on the banks of the Lignon, was only playful and pure fiction. It was me who was deluding myself.

No, nothing is as gallant and amiable as the shepherds of Romancia.[15] Their attire is always extremely clean, simple but in good taste, scantily laden with adornments but elegant and well-matched to the stature and the figure. All their crooks are decorated with ribbons, the color of which is never chosen at random, for it must always mark the sentiments and dispositions of their heart, and I never saw one that was not also charged with ingenious and very gallant figures.

Although the shepherdesses are ignorant of the usage of rouge, ceruse, beauty spots and all borrowed attractions, that is because the natural gleam and vivacity of their complexion surpass anything that artistry can lend to charms. The only adornment of their heads consists of a few new flowers,

---

[14] By far the most prolific composer of operas with this initial in the early 1730s was Georg Friedrich Handel.

[15] Author's note: "*Roman de l'Astrée.*" [i.e. Honoré d'Urfé's classic pastoral prose epic *L'Astrée* (1607-27; tr. as *Astraea*), set on the banks of the River Lignon.]

which, mingled with the curls of their hair, have an effect a thousand times more charming than pearls or diamonds. But what completes rendering them the most amiable women in the world is the touching and natural grace with which they are all provided.

Whether they are lively or more tranquil in humor, whether they are singing or dancing, smiling or sad, asleep or awake, they do everything with so much grace and gentility that there is no heart so insensible that it is not moved thereby. Amiable candor and innocent simplicity are virtues that never quit them. They are ignorant even of the names of dissimulation, perfidy and infidelity, and of the dangerous artifices that jealousy or coquetry put to work.

The shepherd who lives among them is the most fortunate of men; if he is in love, he is sure of being beloved; his tenderness is repaid with tenderness, and his constancy with fidelity. The shepherd who is not in love and who cherishes his indifference has no fear of being seduced by the deceptive wiles of a perfidious or flighty coquette. Amour and simplicity is their motto, and the Golden Age recommences every day for them.

What is most admirable about them is that with the innocent simplicity that makes their character, the shepherds and shepherdesses, like those of the Lignon, combine all the most sought-after refinements of the most delicate amour and the most sensitive of hearts; but it is unusual for them ever to make use of them except to the profit of amour itself. Sitting in the shade of verdant boscage, or on the edge of a clear stream, one always sees them agreeably occupied in singing their amours and making the echoes of the valleys resound to the music of their flutes and reed pipes. The birds never fail to mingle their tender songs with it, and the streams join in as well with their soft murmur.

The flocks sense the felicity of their masters and one always sees the sheep and the lambs bounding in the meadows without the wolves daring to cause them the slightest alarm. Furthermore, those happy shepherds never think of the bonds of matrimony. They put all their satisfaction into receiving a few tender marks of amity from their virtuous and chaste shepherdesses, and until death they constantly prefer the hope of possession to the insipid mildness of possession itself.

I confess that, touched by a spectacle so cheerful and so gracious, I was tempted to take up a basket and a crook immediately and settle down in such a beautiful abode, in order to spend the rest of my days in peace and innocence and to savor the sweetness of tranquil repose forever. I am not even the first person for whom that thought has come to mind, on merely reading about the perfect rewards that innocent simplicity can find on the edge of springs, in the meadows, the woods and the forests, but, making the reflection that I would always be the master of choosing that kind of life whenever I wanted, and that I still had a vast country to travel, I continued my route.

On the way I noticed a few bulls without horns, because they had been removed in order to make horns of plenty; I saw other bulls that had horns and hooves of bronze, cows of admirable beauty that descended from the famous Io, several Amaltheian goats, Cerberuses, or large three-headed dogs, booted cats and green monkeys. Above all, a little further on, I saw, in a little lake, a frightful hydra with seven heads, each of which opened a terrible mouth armed with trenchant and venomous teeth. As I did not have Hercules's club or any enchanted sword, I refrained from approaching it, and even hastened to draw away.

That finally gave me the opportunity to encounter the inhabitants of the land.

IV. The Inhabitants of Romancia

I was surprised only to have encountered animals thus far, except for the shepherds and shepherdesses that I have mentioned. I knew that, in general, the Romancians are great travelers, but I could not imagine that the country was absolutely deserted. Finally, looking into the distance in all directions, I perceived a place that seemed to me to be densely populated. It was, in fact, a promenade, where a considerable number of the inhabitants of both sexes had the custom of going to take the air.

I headed in that direction, and I had the pleasure, on the way, of verifying for myself something that I had always had difficulty believing: that flowers are born under the footfalls of beautiful women; for I remarked on the ground several traces of flowers still fresh, that ended at the edge of the promenade and surely had no other origin. The specific place where the beauties were walking was covered with them, and in Romancia no other secret is known for having the most beautiful flowers in gardens and flower-beds in all seasons.

I found everyone divided into various parties of four, three or two, as many men as women, and several who were walking alone slightly apart. As I did not know anyone I thought I ought to follow the last example, in order to examine the countenance and manners of the Romancians before approaching one of them.

The first observation I made was that of not perceiving any children or old people. There are, in fact, none in the whole of Romancia, and the reason will soon become clear. The entire nation, in consequence, consists of a brilliant, healthy, vigorous, fresh youth, the most beautiful in the world. That proposition is so exactly true that one cannot, without injustice, make the slightest comparison in that regard. The French, for example, are reputed to be a reasonably good-looking nation, but if one examines them closely, one finds many ill-made people among them, and nothing is more common than seeing people who are entirely deformed. One also sees faces there so disagreeable, with mouths too small, noses too long, mouths too wide and chins too sharp.

Now, that is what one never sees in Romancia; it is, however, true, that a small race of extremely ugly men and women has been conserved there throughout the ages in order to serve as a contrast when the occasion arrives, in accordance with the need of writers. Apart from the fact that their number is very small, however that is a race as foreign to Romancia as negroes are to Europe, and it is very unusual to encounter a woman there who does not have a perfectly beautiful figure; a slightly elongated nose or slightly small eyes are regarded there a monstrous.

Everyone, as many men as women, and especially the latter, have extremely regular facial features. It is there that the whiteness of the forehead effaces that of alabaster, that the arches of eyebrows dispute perfection with the rainbow; it is there that ebony and snow, lilies and roses, coral and pearls, gold and silver, sometimes all mixed together and sometimes separately, collaborate in forming the most beautiful heads and the most beautiful faces that one can imagine; all the ladies there have, above all, eyes of an admirable beauty; they know that somewhere in the country there are others as beautiful, but they are rare, because they are brilliant stars whose glare dazzles, suns from which a thousand streaks of flame depart that set all hearts ablaze; at the sight of them one sees cold indifference melt like ice exposed to the ardor of the sun; Amour makes his dwelling there in order to launch his arrows more surely, and no shot ever misses. Oh, what heart can resist them? There is no defense against them; sooner or later it is necessary to yield and surrender with a good grace to such powerful conquerors.

What completes making the inhabitants of Romancia the most beautiful women one can see, however, is that in addition to all those features of beauty they all have a delicate air, a noble physiognomy, something both majestic and gracious, proud and gentle, pen and reserved; something charming, mysteriously engaging, a cast of the visage so attractive, a certain charm in the mannerisms, a certain grace in speech, a smile so soft, charms that are indescribable, a thousand things that are inexpressible—in a word, a thousand I-know-not-what that enchant you I know-not-how.

That is, however, not all, for, as if nature delighted in exhausting all her gifts to make the inhabitants of Romancia at the expense of all the rest of the human race, one sees combined with so many natural advantages all the perfections of body and mind that can be desired; they all dance admirably well; they sing delightfully; they play instruments with the greatest perfection; they have an infinite skill in all bodily exercises; if there is a joust, they win all the prizes; if there is a combat, they always emerge victorious. One can judge in consequence how much greater an advantage there is being born a citizen of Romancia than in being born a prince, a duke or, at one time, a Roman citizen.

I confess that it was not without an extreme confusion that I saw myself, at first, in the midst of a people so well made, for, although I am not deformed, I render myself the justice of thinking that, compared with so many good looking people, I must have appeared a disgraceful specimen of humanity. That thought struck me so forcefully that, in the dread of being an object of ridicule, I retired to an isolated spot in order to hide from the eyes of passers-by.

There, as I deplored the discomfort of my situation, my reflections bore me naturally to take a small mirror out of my pocket in order to look at myself. What was my astonishment to find myself changed to the point of no longer recognizing myself! My hair, which had been almost red, was the most beautiful blond; my forehead was broader, my eyes, having become keen and brilliant, were no longer sunken; my nose, which had been too elevated, was reduced to a just proportion; my overly large mouth had narrowed; my overly flat chin had rounded out; my entire physiognomy was charming.

I understood immediately that it was to the local atmosphere that I owed such a fortunate change, but I had the weakness...shall I confess it? Will my readers pardon me...? No matter, it is necessary to admit it; it ill behooves a Romancian writer not to be sincere, and I have promised to be... I admit, then, that I was transported by joy to find myself so handsome and well-made.

Does beauty, a trivial advantage, merit human esteem? No, undoubtedly. But at the time, those reflections did not come to mind. I could not weary of looking at myself and admiring myself. I studied a thousand agreeable facial expressions in my mirror; I was smug, and, flattering myself that I would soon make some important conquest. I hastened to join the companies of men and women that I had left.

I joined several in succession, with all the liberty that I knew that the laws of the land permitted, and I stayed in the place for some time in order to familiarize myself with their mores, their mentality, their manners and their character. All that detail is so curious that the readers will doubtless be glad to be informed of it.

One does not see as much wit shine anywhere as in Romancian conversations, but it is not so much the wit that one admires therein as the sentiments and the fashion of their expression; for, as amour is the subject of all their conversations and they like to talk about it a great deal, they find turns of phrase so long and so varied to express something that we would say in four words, that a entire day would never be sufficient for them and they would be obliged to postpone some until the following day. They have, above all, such a talent for, so to speak, decomposing and anatomizing all the thoughts of the mind and all the sentiments of the heart that one is tempted to compare them to lace whose network is wrought with extreme delicacy.

How different human tastes are! What we treat here, by virtue of our barbarity, as verbiage and gibberish is what shines there, and is held in highest esteem in Romancian conversations—among others, the tirades of minute reflections on everything happens inside an amorous, anxious, uncertain, suspicious, jealous or satisfied heart. All that, expressed at length, with the for and the against, the yes and the no, the empty and the full, the clear and the obscure, makes a discourse that enchants; there are a thousand petty trivia, each of which is almost nothing, but all those trivia, all those tiny things, when placed end-to-end, have a marvelous effect.

It is true that it is necessary to know the language of the country, as I shall soon explain; otherwise, many beauties and shafts of wit would escape you, but once one possesses it, one savors an infinite satisfaction therein—that, at least, is my opinion; the reader may think otherwise if he judges it appropriate, for it is necessary, so it is said, not to dispute tastes.

I shall pass lightly over the nourishment of the Romancians; it is very simple, as I have said elsewhere, and, in fact, when one is in love, and even more so when one is beloved, what need does one have to eat and drink? Nor I shall say any more about their attire; it is ordinarily rather negligent, for the reason that in Romancia, scrupulous attire never adds anything to a person's charms; it is, on the contrary, always natural charms that heighten clothing.

A few princesses in that country, however have a rather singular privilege, which is that of dressing as men and traveling the world thus for years, mingling with cavaliers and soldiers, in taverns and the most dangerous places, without shocking decency. Those sorts of disguises were once highly esteemed, in fact, especially if a damsel in the attire of a cavalier, happened to encounter a lover dressed as a damsel, which made a event so singular, so novel and so ingeniously imagined that it never failed to be applauded.

What readers will doubtless be glad to know, however, is the character of the Romancian people

There was a certain mischief in the man who first represented the god of love as a child, for it seems that he wanted to insinuate by that means that amour is merely puerility and that lovers resemble children. But who can be persuaded of that, when it is so well proven by the testimony of so many grave authors that, of all the passions, amour is the most beautiful and the most heroic, to the point that, for a long time, all the heroes of the theater, and even those of opera, do not seem to have known any other passion except for its form? One can judge it even better by the character of the inhabitants of Romancia, who are the most perfect of lovers.

These are the principal traits that I shall report, merely to sketch the portrait.

They have a talent for occupying themselves very seriously for an entire day, or a entire month, if necessary, with the smallest bagatelle; they weep copiously for the slightest thing; an indifferent gaze or an equivocal word makes them dissolve in tears. That is because they are, in fact, extremely delicate and sensitive; the majority are, simultaneously, so anxious that they do not know themselves what they desire or what they lack; they want and they do not want; one can assure them of something twenty times over in vain. Should they believe what they have been told? Should they be afflicted or rejoice? Are they satisfied or not? That is what they never know.

Excessively jealous, if anyone speaks to their princess or if, by some mischance, she casts a glance at someone, all their tenderness turns to fury; adieu all assurances and all oaths; adieu letters, notes, bracelets, portraits; everything is forgotten on either side, torn up, smashed; they no longer want to see one another, they do not even want to hear mention of one another…unless, an opportunity presents itself, and by the greatest good fortune in the world, one never fails to turn up. What to do then? It is necessary to enlighten one another; and once the enlightenment is complete, it is necessary to patch things up; at every reconciliation there are always little expenses; the princess takes them on her account, and there is peace made, until further adventure.

But there is something more dangerous in that regard; that is when one of the two is maliciously obstinate in concealing from the other the subject of a secret discontentment, as the overly credulous and taciturn Fanny sometimes does, from her overly melancholy and somber lover.[16] That always gives rise to the most tragic adventures; it is true that without that, the sad hero would have difficulty in reaching the fifth volume, but is that not paying too dearly for the advantage of having one volume more?

I could add here several other features of the Romancian character: that they are naturally pensive and distracted; that they are overly fond of swearing, and that oaths cost them

---

[16] Author's note: "*Cleveland.*"

nothing; that they forget them rather easily when they have obtained what they desire; and other similar features. As I have much more to say, however, I shall not extend myself further on this subject. Also, it is necessary that I relate the marvelous encounter I had in the forest of adventures.

V. Encounter and awakening of Prince Zazaraph, great paladin of Dondindandia, with the dictionary of the Romancian language.

Although it was not difficult to recognize by my manners and my language that I was a newcomer to the land, all the people I met and with whom I conversed, apparently too occupied with their particular affairs, hardly ever thought of offering me any assistance, even though they were otherwise very polite. Finally, a handsome young man who might perhaps have been importuned by my presence, addressing me in speech, asked me whether I had passed through the forest of adventures.

"No," I said to him. "I don't even know where it is."

"Well," he said, "you'll be wasting your time here until you've gone through it. As you're newly arrived, it's only just to inform you. That forest is called the forest of adventures because one never passes through it without encountering one, and as this land is the land of adventures, it's necessary that newcomers, as soon as they arrive, pass through the forest, in order then to be naturalized in Romancia. It isn't far from here, and by following that little path to the right you'll encounter it."

I thanked the person who had given me such important advice as best I could, and, having set forth, I soon arrived at the forest.

As I entered it I heard a great racket above my head, even more disagreeable than that made by a flock of frightened magpies flying from tree to tree in order give one another the alarm. I saw immediately what species of bird it was that was making the noise: they were harpies. Everyone knows that those bird-women are great talkers, and they are no less glut-tonous.[17] Just then they were hurling themselves furiously at a table and seizing the meat with which it was laden. Although I was not carrying any provisions, I nevertheless put myself on guard, sword in hand. I knew that that was the best means of warding them off; but I did not receive any insult, and I es-caped with enduring the frightful infection with which they poison the air around them.

A little further on I found innumerable parrots, which were speaking all languages with an admirable facility, blue-birds, white blackbirds, flame-colored crows, phoenixes and a quantity of other birds that are only ever seen in that land; but that spectacle did not make me pause for long, because an unexpected object attracted my gaze.

I perceived a knight lying under a large tree, who ap-peared to be profoundly asleep. I approached him immediate-ly, and after having contemplated his face for a while, which had something noble and amiable about it, and his stature, which was very fine, I deliberated as to whether I ought to wake him, in order to ask for clarifications of which I had need, but I judged that it would be more honest to wait for him to wake up.

I did, in fact wait for quite a long time, but finally, fol-lowing the movements of my impatience, I approached him. I took his hand, called to him, and even shook him, but it was all in vain.

I did not know what to think about such an extraordinary slumber, and, imagining that the unfortunate knight might have fallen into a lethargy, I applied to his nose and temples a divine water that I was carrying on me. I had the chagrin, however, of seeing my remedy fail. In the end, I remembered that in Romancia the plants have astonishing virtues. Immedi-ately, I collected a few of them, which appeared to me to be the most singular, and in order to try their effect I rubbed the face of the sleeping knight with them. The first did not suc-

---

[17] Author's note: "Virgil, *Aeneid*, Book III."

ceed, but having collected some of another species, scarcely had I made him smell them than he woke up instantly with a great sneeze, which make the forest resound and put all the birds in the vicinity to flight.

"Generous Prince Fan-Férédin," he said—calling me by name, which astonished me greatly—"what do I not owe you for the service you have just rendered me? You have woken me up, and in three days I shall possess the adorable Anemone. It's necessary," he added, "that I tell you my story, in order that you will understand all the obligation that I have to you.

"My name is Prince Zazaraph. Nearly ten years ago, by the death of my father, whose unique heir I was, I became the great paladin of Dondindandia. I had the good fortune of making myself loved by the Dondindandians, my subjects, whom I governed more as a father than a sovereign, for it is true that every day of my reign was marked by some new benefit. They pressed me to marry some princess in order to fix the succession of my estates within my house.

"I consented to that, but I wanted a perfect princess and I could not find one, although Dondindandian women are reputed elsewhere to be the most beautiful. One had beautiful eyes, beautiful eyebrows, a shapely nose, a complexion of lilies and roses, a lovely mouth and a charming smile, but one could be absolutely sure that her chin was a little too long. Another had everything capable of charming in her bearing, her figure and her facial features, and even had beautiful hands, but her fingers did not seem sufficiently rounded. Finally, another seemed to unite everything in her person, with all the aspects of beauty, all the most touching graces and everything the mind has of charms; I was so smitten with her that no one doubted that she would soon fix my choice; I believed so myself for some time and congratulated myself for having encountered a princess as amiable and so perfect. By the greatest good fortune in the world, however, I noticed one day that her ears weren't small enough. It was necessary to detach myself from her.

"Despairing of ever finding what I was seeking, I consulted a sage greatly renowned by the knowledge he had acquired by long study. 'No,' he told me, 'don't hope to find any perfect beauty in your estates or neighboring kingdoms; they are only seen in Romancia, and if anything in that land can make a choice difficult it's that all the princesses there are so perfectly beautiful that one does not know which one to prefer; it's your heart that will determine it. Depart, then, and bring back as soon as possible a princess worthy of you and your crown.'

"As for the route that it was necessary to take to find Romancia, he assured me that there was none that was fixed and regulated, that it was sufficient to set forth, and by continuing to travel, everyone eventually arrived there, some by sea and others by land, and a few even via the moon and the stars.

"I therefore undertook the journey, and after having traveled through many lands I finally arrived several years ago in it, without being able to say how; all that I have been able to learn since I have been living in the country is that one enters it, it is said, though the portal of amour, and leaves it by means of that of marriage. What completed my happiness, however, is that scarcely had I arrived when I encountered in Princess Anemone everything that can be imagined of beauty, charm, allure, attraction, perfection and much else.

"After all the preliminaries that are absolutely necessary in this land, I had the good fortune to please her and to be loved by her. All that remained was the matter of uniting ourselves by the eternal bonds, but that ceremony requires preliminaries of infinite length here and I could not obtain a dispensation of any of them. It would take too long to tell you what they are, and once you have been here for a while you will know them well enough, because they all resemble one another.

"Finally, I came to endure the final proof. It was written in the continuation of my adventures that a rival jealous of my happiness would find a means, with the help of an enchanter, to put me into a profound slumber, and that he would take advantage of it to abduct the beautiful Anemone; that I would continue to sleep for a year, only able to be woken up by Prince Fan-Férédin, to whom it was reserved to disenchant me; that three days after my awakening, the beautiful Anemone, delivered from her odious kidnapper, who would perish, would reappear to my eyes more beautiful and more lovable than ever, without having lost anything in such suspect hands of what might render her dear to me; that I would nevertheless have a few suspicions; that the suspicions would be followed by a quarrel, the quarrel by a clarification, and the clarification by a reconciliation, after which no obstacles would any longer oppose my happiness.

"I am, therefore, sure of seeing my beautiful princess again in three days. We shall depart immediately for Dondindandia; and it is to you, Prince, that I have such great obligations."

I was extremely satisfied by Prince Zazaraph's story, and to have found someone who could give me the instruction that I would inevitably need in an unknown country. After having testified to him how charmed I was to have had the opportunity to be of service to him, and explained to him how the desire to see beautiful things had brought me to Romancia, I let him glimpse the embarrassment I was in of finding someone who wanted to take the trouble to serve as my guide and enlighten me as to what I might not know about a land of which I had no other knowledge that that provided by books.

"Can you believe," he said, obligingly, "that, after the service you have just rendered me, I could leave that care to anyone other than me? No, no," he added, embracing me with a tender expression by which I was touched, "I shall not quit you. In any case, have I anything better to do in the three days that I need to wait for the beautiful Anemone? Three days ought to be sufficient for you to know all of Romancia without going to the trouble of traveling it in its entirety, because one sees the same things everywhere."

I accepted such obliging offers without hesitation, and we conversed thus for some time in the forest. During that conversation, he had no difficulty perceiving that I did not know the language of the country, and I confessed to him ingenuously that in the conversations I had had with a few Romancians they had said many things that I had not understood.

"That ought not to astonish you," he told me, "for although all languages are spoken in Romancia—Arabic, Greek, Indian, Chinese and all modern languages—it is nevertheless true that there is a particular fashion of speaking them that one learns here. For instance, what would you call a person whom you loved and by whom you are loved? You would simply call her your mistress. Well, that word is not understood here. It is necessary to say *the object I adore, the beauty whose irons I wear, the sovereign of my soul, the lady of my thoughts, the unique goal to which my desires tend, the divinity I serve, the light of my life*, or *the one for whom I live and breathe*. There is, as you see, a lot of choice."

"That's true," I said, "but what must I do in order to learn that language, which I have never spoken?"

"Don't worry about it," he replied. "It's a very limited language, and with the help of a little dictionary that I've made for my own usage I'll have you talking a Romancian purer than Cyrus and Cleopatra."[18]

In fact, after we had sat down at the foot of a huge odorous cedar, Prince Zazaraph showed me a little book, neatly bound and as big as a pocket almanac, all written in his own hand, in which he claimed to have assembled all the phrases and words of the Romancian language, with the rules that it was necessary to observe in order to speak it well. He made me scan it attentively, and in less than no time I knew the entire language. I could reproduce the entire dictionary here, but

---

[18] The references are to the central characters of *Artamène, ou le grand Cyrus* (1649-53), by Mademoiselle de Scudéry, the great best-seller of its era, and *Cléopâtre* (1648; abridged version 1667) by Gauthier de Costes, seigneur de la Calprenède, the author of numerous tragedies and tragicomedies.

I think it will suffice to report a few of the principal rules and the most remarkable phrases, just to give an idea of it, because it would be futile to try to speak Romancian here; for that, it is necessary to go to the land itself.

Above all, there are two essential rules. The first is to express nothing simply, but always with exaggeration, imagery, metaphor or allegory. Following that rule, you must refrain carefully from saying "I love." That signifies nothing. It is necessary to say "I burn with love," or "A secret fire is devouring me," or "I languish night and day," or "A sweet languor is consuming me." If a woman is beautiful, she "effaces everything that nature has of the most beautiful," or "she is the masterpiece of the gods," or "it is impossible to see her without loving her," or "she is the goddess of beauty," or "the mother of graces" or "she charms all eyes and enchains all hearts," or "one might take her for Venus herself, and Amour would make that mistake."

The second rule consists of never saying a word without one or several epithets. It would be ridiculous for instance, to say amour, indifference, or regret; it is necessary to say tender and passionate amour, cold and tranquil indifference, and mortal and burning regret. Sighs are ardent, dolor bitter and profound, beauty ravishing, hope sweet, disdain proud and scorn insulting. The more epithets there are in a phrase, the more beautiful and truly Romancian it is.

As for the words that compose the language, they are very few in number, and that is what facilitates Romancian intelligence. Here are almost all of the nouns: love, hate, transports, desires, sighs, alarms, hope, pleasures, pride, beauty, cruelty, ingratitude, perfidy, jealousy, dying, languishing, happiness, enjoyment, despair, heart, sentiments, charms, attractions, allures, enchantment, delight, dolor, regret, life death, felicity, disgrace, destiny, fortune, barbarity, cares, tenderness, tears, prayers, oaths, grass, verdure, night, day, streams, meadows, image, reverie and dreams.

Those are almost all of the nouns in the Romancian language; it is only necessary to add, as I have said, various epithets such as sweet, tender, charming, admirable, delightful, horrible, furious, frightful, mortal, sensitive, dolorous, profound sharp, ardent, sincere, perfidious, fortunate or tranquil, and, above all, the expressions that are the most convenient of all: inexpressible, unimaginable, indescribable, beyond representation, surpassing all expression, beyond words and unthinkable.

With that little collection one would be able to compile a folio volume in the Romancian language. There is, however, one observation to be made, and that it that it is necessary to try only to combine words with suitable epithets, because if someone for example, were to say "my dear and delightful sadness,"[19] that would be a ridiculous and ill-assorted expression.

VI. On High and Low Romancia

The various reflections that we made on the Romancian language gave Prince Zazaraph the opportunity to inform me of an item of geography that I did not know, which is that there was a High and a Low Romancia.

"Here," he told me, "we are in High Romancia, and it is easy to distinguish from the Low on by virtue of all the marvels with which it is filled, and which you must have noticed in coming here; instead of which Low Romancia is similar to all the other countries of the world. For example, in Low Romancia a meadow is a meadow and a stream is only a steam, but in High Romancia a meadow is essentially covered in flowers, or at least with beautiful grass, and a stream never fails to roll silvery or crystal waters over little pebbles, in order to make a soft murmur that lulls lovers to sleep or wakes up the birds. But perhaps you'll easily learn to make that distinction."

"It's true," I said, "for everything I see and hear only excites my curiosity more."

---

[19] Author's note: "*Cleveland.*"

"I can easily understand that," he said, "and I even fear that you might be secretly holding it against me that I've delayed you for so long in this forest, where one sees nothing new, instead of taking you to some habitation. Let's get up, then, and continue our conversation while walking."

He continued: "Once, Romancia was a very limited country, so only a few habitants were received there, all chosen from among the most celebrated princes and heroes. Everyone remembers the names and adventures of the first inhabitants of Romancia, including Arthur and the knights of the Round Table, Palmerin of Oliva, Palmerin of England, Primaleon of Greece, Perceforest, Amadis, Roland, Melusine and several others whose names I don't recall. Nothing is as brilliant as their history. One saw them signaled by a thousand unusual exploits, pell-mell with genii, fays, enchanters, giants, endriagues, monsters, always fighting, never vanquished. Heaven and earth were interested in their success, continually lavishing the greatest miracles upon them, which made Romancia the most beautiful country in the world.

"But such great splendor could not fail to attract many foreigners to the land, among others Pharamond, Cleopatra, Cassandra, Cyrus, Polexandre: great personalities, in truth, but who, not being, so to speak, *our* heroes like the former, and only by imitation, remained far below their models. However, as they had a truly extraordinary valor and virtue, they were given a place in High Romancia.

"Things degenerated much further subsequently, for the vilest individuals were received in Romancia: adventurers, valets, professional vagabonds, women of low life. Only a few zealous romancers made efforts to reestablished the glory and the marvelous sublimity of times past; from there came the heroes and princes of Faerie, those of the *Thousand-and-One Nights*, *Chinese Tales* and many similar ones; but one saw in their history marvels mingled with so many puerile, common and vulgar things that no one knew how to classify them.

"Eventually, in order to avoid confusion, the decision was made to divide Romancia into High and Low. The former is the abode of princes and celebrated heroes; the later has been abandoned to subjects of the second order: travelers, adventurers, men and women of mediocre virtue. It is even necessary to confess, to the shame of the human race, that High Romancia has been almost deserted for a long time, as you have been able to perceive in what you have seen, while Low Romancia is more and more populated every day. Thus, the fays and the genii, seeing themselves abandoned and almost unemployed, have mostly made the decision to go away, some into imaginary spaces, others into the land of dreams. That is why you no longer see Romancia ornamented, as it once was, with an infinity of crystal castles, silver towers, fortresses of bronze and enchanted palaces."

"How sorry I am, I said, interrupting him, "not to be able to witness such a beautiful spectacle!"

"It would be very easy for me," he said, "to enable you to see two castles of that kind not far from here, if you and I were sufficiently weary of our liberty to consent to lose it. A league from here, to the right, there is one inhabited by the fay Camalouca.[20] Nothing is as brilliant and magnificent as the apartments, galleries and halls that compose that palace, but nothing is as dangerous as approaching it.

"For three hundred paces all around it the fay has formed a kind of invisible vortex, which whirls away all though who have the misfortune or the fatal curiosity to enter it. Borne away to the courtyard of the castle, they are instantly engulfed in great crystal vases full of water, and the moment they enter into one, the fay blows a huge bubble of air at their back, which attaches itself to them and, by virtue of its lightness, holds them suspended in the water, where they only spin, rise and fall incessantly. They can be seen through the crystal, and that assemblage of various figures makes a bizarre assortment, by which the wicked fay is amused; for one sees ladies and

---

[20] A name apparently derived from the Spanish phrase *cama loca* [crazy bed], referring to a sensory disorientation associated with drunkenness.

lords pell-mell with pontiffs and priestesses, animals of very sort, grotesque monsters and a thousand different forms that are continually blurred and mingled. It is on that model that those long tubes of water full of little enamel figurines are made in Europe.

"The other palace, which is to the left, is the abode of the fay Curiaca; she is the most dangerous individual in all Romancia. As she has many charms, nothing is easier for her than captivating the hearts of all those who see her, and she takes a malign pleasure in it. Then she takes them for a walk in her gardens, on the edge of a fountain or a canal, and there, when they least expects it, she metamorphoses them into birds, which she constrains by an effect of her magic power to keep their long beaks in the water continuously, leaving them in that ridiculous attitude for entire years. That is all the fruit that one obtains from the cares one has rendered her, and that is also the origin of the proverb of keeping someone's beak in the water.[21]

My readers have too much good taste not to sense that these stories are extremely agreeable and there is, in consequence, no need to tell them that they gave me a great deal of pleasure; I hope that they will find as much in reading the next chapter.

VII. On a thousand curious things and the malady of yawning.

We saw a rider mounted on a kind of black griffin coming toward us on the road we were on. His seemed sad, pensive and distracted, but as soon as he had perceived us he turned his mount and, taking a side road, he soon disappeared from our view.

---

[21] In the early 18th century the French expression *tenir le bec en l'eau à quelqu'un* [keeping someone's beak in the water] meant keeping someone waiting. This fay is clearly modeled on Circe.

"Who is that misanthrope?" I asked Prince Zazaraph. "I didn't know there were any of that species in Romancia."

"There are, however, several of them," he replied, "as witness poor Cardenio,[22] who frightening the shepherds so much in the mountains of Sierra Morena. That one is named Sonotraspio. How I pity him! Warned about the dangers of an amorous passion, he lived as an indifferent philosopher, even laughing about the weakness of lovers. But Amour was keeping an arrow for him that his philosophy could not ward off. He finally fell in love, and he fell in love with Tigrine, whose heart was engaged to another and so made him understand that he had nothing for which to hope.

"He understood that so well, in fact, that in order to strangle an unfortunate amour at birth, he wanted to take the only course that remained to him, which was to go away from the object that had captivated him. 'But no,' Tigrine said to him, 'your cares give me pleasure, your services are useful to me; if you love me, I demand that you do not flee me.' To an order to absolute she added a few slight favors, which completed robbing the unfortunate lover of any hope of liberty. It was not possible for him to see Tigrine without loving her; it was not permitted to him to avoid her; but he had nothing for which to hope: what a situation!

"He resolved himself to it, however, with a courage that gave as much evidence of the firmness of his soul as the excess of his passion. He flattered himself that he could at least extract occasionally from the hands of the cruel woman the few slight favors that she had already accorded him. He succeeded in that, in fact, even beyond his hopes, and, limiting all his desires and all his happiness to that, he dragged his chain with a sort of satisfaction, but that slight and apparent happiness did not last long.

"While Sonotraspio, always modest and respectful, strove to persuade himself that he was fortunate enough, an unjust caprice persuaded Tigrine that he was too fortunate.

---

[22] Author's note: "*Don Quixote*, part I, chapter 23."

'It's over,' she said to him. 'Don't hope for any more from me; your passion importunes me, your cares have become indifferent to me. Go away; I consent to that, and even advise you to do it.'

"Gods, what was Sonotraspio's astonishment! A sudden thunderclap causes less consternation to timid women surprised by a storm in vast open country. He doubted it for some time; he thought he had misheard, but his doubt did not last long. Tigrine explained it, and did so with all imaginable harshness. Then, penetrated by dolor and with despair panted in his eyes, he said: 'You're permitting me to flee you, then? It's high time, cruel woman, after...' His sobs did not permit him to finish, and Tigrine even drew away in order not to hear him.

"Neither tears, nor the most tender prayers could bend her, or even persuade her to grant the unhappy fellow, for one last time, some mark of kindness. On the contrary, she only seemed more arrogant and disdainful. In the end, the unfortunate Sonotraspio, overwhelmed by chagrin and dolor, abandoned everything that hope can inspire in an unjustly maltreated lover. In vain he strove to recall the sage lessons of philosophy. Continually occupied with his woe, one sees him, in order to distract himself, sometimes seeking solitude and sometimes dissipation, running like an insensate all over Romancia. He detests the day when he saw Tigrine for the first time; he strives to forget her; he would like to hate her; but nothing succeeds for him; the wound is too profound, and there is reason to fear that it will never heal."

"In truth," I said to Prince Zazaraph, "poor Sonotraspio moves me to pity; I would like Tigrine either never to have granted him anything, or not to have refused him a few slight favors one last time; it would not need many similar examples to discredit Romancia."

"You're right," he said, "for one would be tempted to regard all the inhabitants as mad; but that is an effect of the injustice and ignorance of men, for it is true that, only consulting reason and the maxims of wisdom, it is necessary to tax as folly and pitiable aberration the entire series of fine sentiments and reciprocal procedures of two lovers. But if, on the one hand, one refers to our annalists, whose authority is all the greater because several of them are of respectable character, and on the other, one judges by the sublime fashion in which they are able to embellish the passions that seem least sensate in themselves, one would have a much more advantageous idea of the heroes of Romancia."

Here I interrupted the great paladin. "What do I see?" I said to him. "After the tragic, is it not the comic that is presenting itself to us? What, I pray you, are those bands of cockchafers, locusts or huge ants that I see traversing the forest like an army on the march? What kind of insects are they?"

"Insects!" replied Prince Zazaraph, laughing. "Please, treat more honestly a species that is nothing less than human. Have you never heard mention of Lilliputians?[23] There they are. Those poor little runts of human nature have established themselves in Romancia and seemed initially to be thriving here, but the air of the country is doubtless contrary to them; they have never been able to multiply here, and, desperate at seeing their race becoming extinct, they have finally made the decision to go and settle elsewhere. Be careful, in passing by, not to trample any underfoot, for that's the only danger one runs in encountering them.

"It's not the same with the Brobdingnagians, however. Those monstrous giants, by a bizarre coincidence, settled in Romancia at the same time as the Liliputians, and like them, they have been obliged to seek another dwelling. The entire country could not suffice for their subsistence, but woe betide anyone who found themselves in their passage. The ravages are indescribable that those frightful colossi made all along

---

[23] Author's note: "*Voyage de Gulliver*." The first French edition of *Voyages du capitaine Lemuel Gulliver en divers pays éloignés* appeared in 1730, allegedly printed in The Hague, but it does not contain the full text, which had not yet been published in its entirety in England.

their route, crushing castles underfoot as we crush a clod of earth and breaking all the trees in forests as elephants break ears of wheat as they cross fields. No one really knows the reasons that led both species to establish themselves in Romancia, having no other merit to distinguish them than a laughable smallness or a horrific gigantic size, so people see them leave without trying to retain them, and all that can be said about it is that it wasn't worth making such a long voyage to learn what everyone already knew, that there is no point of absolute grandeur in the word, and that tall or short stature makes no difference to human nature ."

"In that regard," I said to Prince Zazaraph, "haven't I heard it said that the animals can talk in this realm?"

"Nothing is more true," he told me. "It used to be quite common in the times of Aesop, Phaedrus and a Frenchman named La Fontaine, who had the secret of making them talk, as well as and better than human beings. But it seems that, losing their taste for that usage, they have, so to speak, lost the power of speech, especially since another Frenchman named L. M***[24] has taken it into his head to make them speak an unnatural and forced language that it is sometimes difficult to understand; he allows a few loquacious individuals to be found among them, however, who talk as much and more than one could wish, and very recently, a mole has rendered itself ridiculous by its extravagant babble, although some have claimed that it was only copying another."[25]

While Prince Zazaraph was conversing with me thus, a desire gripped me to yawn so prodigiously that it was necessary, in spite of my efforts, to yield to the natural impulse.

---

[24] Antoine Houdar de La Motte, a member of the Académie published his *Fables nouvelles* in 1727, in spite of having been blind for many years: he was presumably related to François de la Motte, Baron d'Aulnoy, and was a correspondent of the Duchesse du Maine.

[25] Author's note: "*Tanzaï*, part 2." [i.e., *Tanzaï et Néadamé* (1734) by Crébillon fils].

"Aha!" he said, laughing. "You've already caught the local malady, that's lucky. Please don't constrain yourself; no one here will hold it against you; in Romancia it's an inevitable affliction for anyone who spends any time here, like seasickness for those making a first voyage over that element."

As Prince Zazaraph finished speaking, he started yawning immeasurably himself, which did not prevent me laughing in my turn.

"I can see, I said, "that the malady is indeed quite common in Romancia, but I don't understand how one can be subject to it in a land filled with so many marvels."

"That's also what embarrasses physicists in trying to explain the phenomenon, all the more so as it's observed that it's precisely in the places where there are the most marvels heaped on top of one another—in the Peruvian province,[26] for example—that people yawn the most. Physicians, for their part, still cannot find any remedy for the ailment than a change of air. It's necessary, however, that I enable you to see beforehand one of our amorous woods, for that's almost the only singular thing that remains to be seen in this region."

VIII. Amorous woods.

As we were already out of the forest, we directed our steps toward a charming wood in the plain; it was one of the amorous woods that the prince had just mentioned, and many similar ones have been planted in all parts of Romancia for the convenience of lovers, just as one sees them at intervals in a well-maintained terrain to serve as a refuge and retreat for game. Such woods are almost all planted with odorous myrtles, orange trees, pomegranates and young palm trees, which interlace their branches amorously to form agreeable arbors; they are admirably well pierced with various paths, which

---

[26] Author's note: "*Contes péruviens.*" [i.e. *Les Mille et une heure: Contes péruviens* (1734) by Thomas-Simon Gueullette.]

form stars, goose-feet and labyrinths, and various compart-
ments are contrived in the clumps of bushes, the ground of
which is covered with lush grass strewn with violets and other
wild flowers. The palisades are rose-bushes, jasmines, honey-
suckle or other flowering shrubs, and each one has its fountain, its spring or its little waterfall.

It is unnecessary to ask whether, in these delightful
groves, zephyrs refresh lovers with the gentle breath of their
sighs, or whether the birds make the boscage resound with
their amorous songs. Everything is alive, everything respires,
everything is animate and everything makes love in these amorous woods. How could it be otherwise, when one sees
amours perching in the trees like parrots, incessantly occupied
in launching a thousand flaming arrows, which set the very air
ablaze? Oh, how tender, lively and passionate the conversations there are! How many sighs are uttered there, how many
desires formed, how many pleasures savored!

"Don't believe, however," Prince Zazaraph said, "that
people stroll at random in the various quarters of the wood.
Every clump of bushes has its particular purpose, in such a
way that one can distinguish the grove of happy lovers from
that of the discontented, the grove of jealous suspicions from
that of quarrels, that of reconciliations from various similar
ones.

"There was a time when the inhabitants, uninformed of
the laws and ancient customs, also wanted to establish groves
of enjoyment in amorous woods, but such a dangerous innova-
tion was zealously opposed, and it was proven by the testimony of the Romancian annals that there was nothing more contrary to the interests of Romancia, because enjoyment extin-
guishes desire and passion, which are the sinews of good government here."

"But what are those people doing that I see over there," I
asked, "some standing and others sitting under that large elm
tree?"

"They are people waiting for their companions in order
to go into the wood," he replied. "That elm has been planted

expressly to serve as a meeting-place. Those who arrive first wait there for the others, and as there are always a few who wait in vain that was the origin of the saying: 'wait for me under the elm.'

"In any case," he added, "we can approach the groves if you wish in order to see what is happening there and hear what people are saying."

"What!" I said "Things are done here with such scant secrecy?"

"Of course," he said. "How else could the authors that pose the Romancian annals know in such detail all the most private conversations of two lovers, down to the last syllable?"

"You're right," I said, "and you've explained there something that I've never understood. But even so, I don't understand how writers—those of *Cyrus* or *Cléopatre* for instance—can write such long sequences of discourse without losing a single word."

"That's because you don't know how it's done," Prince Zazaraph replied. "But let's go into this grove, which is that of declarations; you can judge the others by this one alone, and you'll understand that mystery. Do you see those four large writing-pads attracted to the entrance to the grove? They're four different models of declarations of amour, containing the requests and the responses, and if there are only four of them it's because no one has yet been able to invent a fifth—for, to say it in passing, our annals are usually quite well-written, but they rarely have the imagination known as invention, which enables them to find something that no one has said before them; that's why they all copy one another.

"Now, to get back to the writing-pads, all the lovers who enter this grove in order to declare their amour to one another, never fail to take one of the four models, which they recite immediately. The annalist only has to observe which of the four models is being employed and he knows the whole of the conversation at a stroke. It's the same with the other groves, including that of sighs, the number of which is regulated, in order that the annalist doesn't make a ridiculous blunder contrary to the verity of the story, by making a princess sigh four times who only ought to have sighed three."

"If that's the case," I said, "there's no need to listen to what all the couples are saying whom I can see distributed in the wood."

"That's true," he replied, "for if you only take the trouble to read the notices that are suspended, in small numbers, at the entrance to each grove, you'll know everything that has ever been said there in the last thousand years; and it's necessary to say that if that doesn't make a eulogy to the intelligence of the Romancian annalists, it's at least very convenient for them and for us, for the history of Romancia is considerably abridged by that means."

In spite of that, the desire gripped me to listen for a moment to what was being said in the nearby groves. I went into one with Prince Zazaraph, but I noticed that, indeed, everything that was being said was nothing but repetition of what I had already read in romances, and the yawns possessed me again with so much force that I thought they would never end.

Prince Zazaraph was afraid that I might eventually be inconvenienced by that, and in order to ward off the danger he proposed a change of air to me.

"In any case," he added, "you have nothing in particular to see here any longer, and everything you don't yet know about Romancia is to be found elsewhere, in all the other regions as well as this one. You can inform yourself equally of everything that merits your curiosity, except for differences that I'll point out to you when it's worth the trouble."

I accepted the proposal immediately, and in order to make our journey we each climbed on to a huge saddled and bridled grasshopper; those mounts, gentler but less rapid than hippogriffs, scarcely make two or three leagues per jump, with the consequence that they only cover two or three hundred leagues a day, but that is sufficient when one is not in a hurry.

In that regard, I ought to recount how people travel in Romancia.

IX. Vehicles and Voyages

There is a country in the world that is said to be the most convenient for travel because one finds highways everywhere and good inns, but it appears that those who believe that have never traveled in Romancia. I shall not mention, however, the admirable comfort of ancient vehicles, when an enchanted boat came to pick you up from the sea-shore, ornamented with red flames and a flame-colored flag, to take you in less than two hours more than half way around the world, or when one had only to mount the rump of a centaur or the back of a griffin that would transport you in an instant beyond the Caspian Sea, into the grottoes of Mount Caucasus, in order to rescue a princess abducted by the giant Coxigrus,[27] who wanted to force her to suffer horrible caresses. As the heroes of today are not of the same stripe as those of old, it has been necessary to change the old methods, and only to send them overland, or in a good ship, and those ships no longer know the ocean.

Nevertheless, all the advantages and charms that it has been possible to preserve from the old method of traveling have been retained; it is only necessary, before setting out on campaign, to be given Romancian letters in due form. For example, two men leave Peking to go to Ispahan, or Paris to go to Madrid; one, on departure, has take good Romancian letters of exchange; the other, unfortunately, has not. What happens?

One will simply make his journey, perhaps going all around the world, without the slightest adventure happening to him; it will always be necessary for him to dine at inns at his own expense, only too glad to have found one; he will be wet, fatigued, muddy, ill, ready to die without aid; he will only find companies of ridiculous or tedious individuals; not a single beauty will fall in love with him, and he will not have the

---

[27] This name is derived from *coquecigrue*, a word coined by Rabelais in *Gargantua* to describe an imaginary compound animal, and which was subsequently adopted as a term for any fanciful chimera

slightest singular encounter that he can recount on his return; in brief, he will come back as he went.

Instead of which a prince, the son of the Caliph Scha-Schild-Ro-Cam-Full, a Knight of the White Rose, or a Marquis de Rochenoire, once equipped with good Romancian letters, encounters the most singular things in the world at every step. Wherever he lodges, he will turn the heads of all the ladies and princesses in the vicinity; he is a true firebrand of amour, who will cause a general conflagration everywhere. Of rain or bad weather there is never any question. His Sedan chair breaks sometimes, and sometimes he gets lost in a wood far from the highway, although the guide who has lost him knows full well what he is doing; it is at exactly the right moment to rescue, at his choice, either a cavalier attacked by assassins or a young woman who finds herself about to be torn apart by a wild boar in the course of a hunt; he is immediately conducted to a castle that is not far away, and from all that he proceeds to new adventures.

At any rate, although he takes care to conceal his real name, in order that ill-advised people mistake him for an adventurer, because of the virtue of his Romancian letters he is welcomed everywhere, caressed and pampered like a divinity; even princes want to see him; he has no sooner said four words to them than he enters into their intimate confidence, and nothing important happens of which he is not a part. In a word, I find that fashion of traveling so agreeable and so reliable that I cannot understand how anyone can resolve to leave home, even if he only has four or five leagues to travel, without furnishing himself with Romancian letters.

One can even take another very advantageous precaution, which is to take with one, on the faith of voyagers, a good list of princes and lords with whom one can lodge, at their example, in the various places where one wants to travel, for in Romancia there are several of those lists printed for the convenience of travelers, and I will gladly give a specimen here, according to a celebrated traveler.[28]

Here goes. If, for example, you go to Spain, you will infallibly be well-received:

In Madrid, by the Count of Ribaguora, a grandee of Spain aged forty-five who has very good manners, receives good company at his home and likes horses, dogs and the French; or at the home of the Duke of Los Grabos, the former governor of Peru, where he amassed immense wealth of which he loves to do the honors, and who has the convenience that, as soon as he sees a good-looking foreigner whose name is the Chevalier de Roquefort or the Comte de Belle-Forêt, he acquires such an amity for him that he can no longer do without him.

In Toledo, in the home of the Marquis de Tordesillas, who is extremely amiable and whose two daughters are the most beautiful young women in Span, the object of the tender prayers of all the most brilliant Spanish nobility, although a young foreigner who can present himself to them with good grace cannot fail to capture the heart of one of them, especially Doña Diana, who is the more amiable; however, if it is necessary for the intrigue to finish because the young traveler has business elsewhere, Doña Diana will die of the plague or in some other, more honest, fashion, if any can be imagined.

In Saragossa, in the home of Don Felix Cartijo, a gentleman who has had a few adventures, which he will recount immediately in order to serve as an episode in the story of the voyage, and as there inevitably other people in his house who

---

[28] Author's note: "*Aventures d'un homme de qualité* and several other romances." The named romance is by Abbé Prévost; its first four volumes were published in 1728, and he added a further three in 1731, the last of which contained a section published separately as *Histoire du chevalier des Grieux et de Manon Lescaut*, which became his most celebrated work, usually known simply as *Manon Lescaut*.

will also narrate theirs, that will gradually furnish the material for a volume of the right size,

That little specimen suffices to give some idea of the aforementioned lists, and there is no need to extend it further. But one thing about which it is necessary to warn voyagers, and, in general, all Romancian heroes, is that they must have a good memory, in order to remember all those with whom, since the beginning, they have had some particular liaison, or who have commenced the story of their adventures without being able to finish it; for it would be extremely indecent of them to forget those people and not to make any further mention of them. A voyager might say that his has left them in China or the depths of Tartary, but it is necessary that he go to find them or that they come to find him, even if it is at the extremities of Japan; in brief, it is necessary to have them fall from the clouds rather than lack them. The Turks, in particular, are religious in regard to that article, and I know one of them who, in order to rejoin his man, made the journey from Amasie to Holland expressly.[29] I have been as scrupulous as that myself, in that, having lost my horse, as you have seen, on the eve of my entry to Romancia, I did not fail to find it again on my emergence from the country, as you will see in due course.

There is, however, one means of getting rid of promptly of the importunate individuals who intervene in a story and with whom one does not know what to do, and that is to kill them immediately or let them die of disease. To tell the truth, though, that expedient is odious, and one is bound to disapprove of voyagers who cause too many people to die inhumanely.

With regard to memory, however, I perceive that I am only talking about myself and forgetting that I had a companion who ought have shared with me the story that I have just told. I beg my reader' pardon and I will repair my fault in the next chapter. It is, however, as well to warn you that we

---

[29] Author's note: "*Aventures d'un homme de qualité*."

Romancian writers knew nothing about the beautiful rules that Lucian and so many others have given for the writing of history, for the reason that we have a special privilege to write anything that comes to mind without taking the trouble of what are generally called order, planning, method, precision or plausibility, neither that which ought to follow nor that which ought to precede, inasmuch as we always have the date of events at our disposal, in order to advance it or recede it as we please; that causes me to admire the precaution that one of our modern annalists has taken of putting at the head of his history a reasoned preface,[30] in order to justify very seriously the facts that he reports, as if one did not know that in the capacity of a Romancian annalist he has the right to say the most implausible things without being criticized for it.

X. On the thirty-six preliminary formalities that ought to precede proposals of marriage.

While the great paladin of Dondindandia and I were traveling by air, well-mounted on or giant grasshoppers, he asked me whether I had the design of choosing some beautiful princess of Romancia in order to make her my wife.

"Of course," I said, "and that was part of the reason that prompted me to make the voyage."

"I suspected as much," he said, "all the more so as it would be difficult for you to see all the beauties with whom the land is populated without your heart declaring itself for one of them. But dispose yourself to be patient and don't waste time, for the treaty is long between the day when one begins to love and the one when one marries."

"It's true," I told him, "that the delays have sometimes made me impatient in the adventures of Théagène,[31] Cyrus,

---

[30] Author's note: "*Cleveland.*"

[31] In the prose romance *Les Amours de Theagene et Charicle* (1626), preceded by a 1623 dramatic version, based on the Greek romance *Aethiopica* by Heliodorus of Emesa, which

Cleopatra and several others. But can't I abridge the formalities…?"

"So," the replied, "you'd only like it to be one chapter of the *Thousand-and-One Nights* or *Chinese Tales*? No, Prince, people of our condition, above all, ought to do things in accordance with the great rules, and pass through all the ranks of the amorous militia. It is, however, sometimes permitted to abridge the time. But since we're on the subject, it's appropriate to give you advance notice of the principal laws that it's necessary to observe in this matter. Those are what are known as the preliminary formalities. There are some who estimate that there are thirty-six of them, or more, but I'll explain them to you without bothering to count them.

"You understand, of course, that it's necessary to commence by falling in love. Now, that is very pleasant, for one is sometimes in love for an entire year without knowing it, and it's not unknown for a man not even to suspect it. If his gaze has paused on a person, it is without design, and if he finds her extremely amiable, his sentiments are limited to esteem and admiration; at the most, he believes that he only has amity for her. It's true that he desires to see her often and that he has particular attentions for her, and that he is not sorry to perceive that she has for him, but in his opinion all that signifies nothing; it's only a commerce of politeness, a liaison, an ordinary inclination into which amour doesn't enter.

"Finally, however, he says to himself: 'What's happened to me lately? I perceive that my slumber is disturbed; it seems to me that I'm becoming distracted and melancholy. I'm losing my usual joviality. What once pleased me is beginning to bore me, what I liked the most now appears insipid.' 'Perhaps you're ill,' someone says to him who in unfamiliar with Romancian usages. 'No,' he replies, 'it's something else.'

---

was said to be Jean Racine's favorite book. In Bougéant's day the story was more familiar via the 1695 opera *Théagène et Chariclée* by Henri Desmarets.

He's right, for those are precisely the first formalities of amorous pursuit.

"At first, he is astonished. 'Me, in love?' he says. 'Me, who has never loved anyone! Me, who has braved all the arrows of Amour! Me, who, until now, has seen all beauties with impunity!' But no matter how hard he tries to hide it from himself, his sighs give him away; anxiety, dread, hope and transports put him on the right track. It's necessary to admit it with a good grace, and he finally admits it."

"It seems to me however," I said to Prince Zazaraph, "that I've seen many heroes who don't take as long to be aware of their condition, and suddenly fall madly in love at the first sight of a princess."

"That's true," he said, "and it's even the most Romancian manner, but after all, they gain nothing by it, for it's still necessary, unless they obtain a special dispensation, for them to wait at least a year before making known the secret fire that is consuming them. In any case, it's necessary not to forget another essential formality, which is that it's necessary for the beauty who has triumphed over the hero's indifference to have a distinguished name. For if, unfortunately, she is called Beatrix, Lisette or Colombine, that would disfigure the whole of a romance, whereas, when she is called Rosalinde, Julie, Hyacinthe or Florimonde, those fine names, always accompanied by suitable epithets, have a marvelous effect.

"Another formality, which embellishes a story infinitely, is when the amorous hero, far from being able to flatter himself that he will ever possess the object he adores, in view of the disproportion of his condition, dare not even make his declaration to the beautiful eyes that have enchained his liberty—although it's true that he is, in fact, very highly-born, and the legitimate heir of a great kingdom, as will be verified when the time comes. It's certain, too, that the princess adores him in the depths of her heart, and secretly curses the eminent rank that takes away the hope of ever marrying such a perfect knight; but on the one hand, the knight is unaware of his birth, and the princess, who is also unaware of it, cannot listen with decorum even if he has the audacity to explain himself. Now, that makes an admirable situation, which furnishes material for the most beautiful sentiments, so our annalists have turned it over and over in a hundred different fashions.

"You see, then," the great paladin continued," that the formalities take much longer than you think, but that's only the beginning. The great difficulty consists of declaring one's passion. For how do you do it? Are you going to say frankly to a beautiful woman that you find her charming, adorable, that you love her with the most tender and respectful amour, and that you would believe yourself the most fortunate of men to be able to possess her for the rest of your days? Refrain carefully from doing that; it would cause her to die of chagrin, and she would not pardon you as long as she lived.

"It is, of course, necessary to make her understand it; but it is necessary to do so with so much precaution and so gently that she almost doesn't perceive it. It's necessary that she divine it, or, at the most, that she has a slight suspicion of it. The language of the eyes is admirable for that, when one makes use of it and takes one's time. For example, the beauty is at her window or on her balcony, where she is taking the air. Prowl around without seeming to be doing anything, and when you're within range, favor her with a respectful bow, accompanied by a glance that is half-vivid and half-dying. You'll see that you'll only have to do that ten or a dozen times before she begins to suspect something, for it is necessary not to think that beauties are unintelligent. The majority understand very well what is said to them, and often even what is not said to them, and, of a hundred glances in their direction, they will not lose a single syllable."

"But," I said in my turn, "to that first means could one not add a second, which is that of serenades sung during the night under the windows of the object of one's desire?"

"What's that you say?" replied the prince, smiling. "The object of one's desires! Very good, you're beginning to form a fine style. Continue, please."

"I was saying that I believed that a concert of voices and instruments under the windows of the beauty whose chains one bears appears to me to be a rather good expedient for insinuating melodiously the tender sentiments that one has for her."

"It's true," he retorted, "but the expedient is scarcely to my taste, because it is subject to too many inconveniences. Firstly, it's necessary to let the whole quarter know that Amour is on campaign, which redoubles the vigilance of fathers and mothers, duennas and spies. Secondly, it's only necessary to spoil the fête for a jealous brute who arrives in the middle of the music to strike you with a sword-thrust, often without you even being able to see the blow coming. I know that you'll kill your man—that's the rule—but it can cause a great embarrassment even so. The affair blows up; the dead man always belongs to a powerful and accredited family; he's usually an only son. It's necessary to hide and flee. During a long absence, many misfortunes can occur. In a word, I tremble every time I see a lover delivering nocturnal serenades to his beauty. The slightest misfortune one has to fear is only getting out of it with a dangerous wound."

"Admit, though, that when one has been run through by a sword and one isn't in danger of dying therefrom, that it's a great boon to know that the beauty for whom one has exposed oneself to danger seems touched by such a great misfortune."

"You're right," replied Prince Zazaraph, "there is no balm in the world that has such a prompt virtue, and in that case, I'll answer for the wounded man soon being on his feet. But once again, that means appears to me to hazardous, and there are simpler ones. A letter, for example, four well-turned lines, can be a marvelous aid. One slips the note adroitly into the pocket of the beautiful Julie, or drops it at her feet, as if by mistake, in order to excite her curiosity; or, if one can't do otherwise, one has it given to her by an assiduous person.

"Once that step is taken, it's necessary to count the affair as well under way. The lover is nevertheless anxious about the success of his note. Has she read it? Has she thrown it away?

What sentiment has she experienced in reading it? That is because he is still inexperienced, for it's true, in general, that there are beauties too reserved, who sometime have difficulty in receiving and reading a letter, but the reserve on that occasion would be entirely out of place, and it would even be ridiculous not to respond favorably to the note, which gives the lover great hope, for that is one of the most indispensable formalities in the preliminaries about which we're talking, and I've never seen it lacking.

"It is then, finally," the prince continued, "that one begins to breathe. It is then that Amour commences to appear the most amiable and the most charming god on Olympus. How many thanks, prayers and offerings on makes him then! But it is necessary that he continue his work. It's not enough that the charming Clorine or the adorable Florise has allowed it to be known that she is not insensible; it's necessary that the amorous comte or marquis has the assurance of it from her own mouth. But will he be able to sustain such an excess of joy? No, he'll faint. What am I saying? He'd die of it, if it were permitted to him to die so soon. But as that would be against the rules, it's necessary that he be content to fall at the feet of the ultimate beauty, speechless and so transported that all he can do is to stick his lips to the beautiful hand of the light of his life.

"Oh, Prince Fan-Férédin," added the great paladin, "What a pity it is that such a sweet moment is only a moment! But one has striven in vain thus far to find a means of prolonging it; all the astrologers in the world have given up on it, and what is saddest of all is that the moment is unique, and a second cannot be found that resembles it perfectly. So, in truth, a reasonable lover ought to leave it at that, and that would be very honest of him—but are there any reasonable lovers? They always lack something.

"After a first conversation, one wants to have a second, after the second, one wants a third, and in the meantime, the hours seem like years. Fortunate is the man who can obtain a portrait. But in default of the portrait, one at least obtains what one can; even if it's only a ribbon, or a scarf, one is the happiest man in the world; until then, one has only felt torments, languor, martyrdom, dread, suspicion, alarm, tears and despairs, and now one finally sees the joyous band arrive of transports, sweetness, calm, satisfaction, rivers of joy in which one swims as in open water, and inexpressible delights.

"Let no one take it into his head then to go and offer a lover the throne of Persia or the empire of Trebizond, on condition of abandoning the sovereign of his soul. He would not exchange his fate for the most brilliant fortune. He would prefer such sweet slavery to the most beautiful crown in the world."

XI. On great proofs, and a singular resemblance that will make the reader suspect the denouement of this story.

"I cannot admire enough," I said to Prince Zazaraph, "the talent that you have for bringing things together and abridging them. What you have just told me in a few words, I have seen in twenty different romances, but it occupies entire volumes there."

"It isn't that I have a talent for abridging," he replied, "but that the majority of romances are all made on the same model, and that their authors have a talent for stretching out events and stories so much that they make a volume out what would only furnish four pages to a writer who does not understand as they do the art of diffuse prolixity. Take note, however, that I have only spoken to you as yet of preliminary formalities, and that before arriving at the conclusion of the marriage, a long road still remains to travel. For, just as, in a labyrinth, one knows very well where one came in, but one does not know where one will get it, those who embark on the stormy sea of amour know full well where they started, but they do not know where, how or when they will arrive in port.

"Two young people love one another like two turtle-doves. They seem made for one another. They will die if they are separated: a barbaric destiny! It's necessary...but no, it isn't destiny that it's necessary to hold to account, it is the laws of Romancia, established for all time by the founders of the nation: severe laws, which forbid, under penalty of perpetual banishment, proceeding with the conjugal union of two young people who adore one another before they have passed through the great profs prescribed by the ordinance."

"Undoubtedly," I said then to the Dondindandian prince, "I have seen in romances what you call great proofs, but I'd be very glad to know them more distinctly, to learn from you on what that law is founded, and whether it is indispensable."

"If you have read the adventures of the pious Aeneas," he said, "you must have remarked that, but for the hatred that Juno bore him, his entire story would have concluded in the first book, for he would have arrived safely in Italy, would have married the Latin princess, and that would have been the *Aeneid* finished. But his historian had cleverly imagined giving him Juno for an enemy; that implacable goddess raised a thousand hindrances in his journey, which were a long sequence of extraordinary events, and provided material for a great story.

"It is on that model that our annalists established the law of great proofs. For want of the Neptune, Ulysses and Juno of the *Aeneid*, they found enemy fays and enchanters, whose powerful hatreds and continual persecutions provided scope for heroes to signal their courage by a thousand unusual exploits, and as neither valor nor human strength could resist such terrible proofs, they were careful also to give them the protection of some good fay or some powerful genius, as Ulysses and Aeneas had the protection, one of Minerva and the other of Destiny. From that it is easy to judge that in Romancia, the law in question must be indispensable, and in fact it is, to such an extent that the sons of kings and the greatest princes are those it spares the least."

"What is it necessary to think, then," I retorted, "of the majority of modern heroes, for whom one does not see either divinities or genii acting, either as friends or enemies?"

"They are bourgeois heroes," he said, "who have neither the nobility nor the elevation that is inseparable from the idea of a Romancian hero. But they are nonetheless subject, like the others, to the law of proofs. A lover, for example, believes he is within reach of the moment that will render him happy, the parents on both sides consenting to the marriage. Not at all. A richer and more powerful suitor appears, who brings parents to bear on his side. What is to be done? It is necessary either to fight or to abduct the beauty. If he fights, he will surely kill his man, but what will become of him? That is raw material for adventures for several years. If he abducts his beauty, it's necessary for him to consign her to some relative capable if hiding her, and that he hide himself as well in order to escape searches. All that takes time, but here comes the tragic.

"One evening, the beauty is getting some fresh air on the sea shore with a relative; an Algerian tartan arrives, which she mistakes for a local vessel; there is an abrupt landing; the two Christian beauties are seized and taken to be sold to their dey. What a proof for a lover! He does not know to what country the dear object of his thought has been transported, nor what treatment she has been subjected to. What a situation! It will be even worse if, while the corsair sets sail for Africa, it is attacked and captured by a Christian vessel, whose commandant is the rival of the unfortunate lover. That is enough to make one die a thousand times of rage and dolor, but fortunately, Romanians have extremely durable lives.

"Let us suppose that the charming Isabelle arrives in Algiers; she is presented to the dey, who falls in love with her, to the extent of forgetting all the other beauties in his seraglio. She tries hard to resist his passion, and puts up the finest defense in the world; the dey, annoyed by her tears and wearied by her resistance, finally decides to use all his power. The appointed day arrives, and he does as he says..."

"Oh, Prince!" I cried, then. "How terrible that proof is! I tremble at it."

"No, no," he replied, "reassure yourself; in Romancia, a remedy is found for everything. The lover has conducted his research so well that he has discovered the place where his dear friend is a captive, and he does not fail to arrive at the point in question on the eve of the fatal day. Disguised as a gardener's boy, he gets into the garden of the seraglio. He finds a means of making a signal and slips a note. Isabelle, transported by joy, prepares to take advantage of the night in order to escape with him. A silken ladder, curtains attached to the window, a rope with a basket, what do I know? On these occasions one finds a thousand expedients, which never fail to succeed.

"Oh what a fine racket the dey makes the following day in the seraglio! How many eunuchs' heads fall under the furious Achmet's scimitar! But the two lovers, letting him exhale all his fury at his leisure, will have found a little boat waiting for them in the port, and they are already far away. In any case, don't think that those adventures are very singular, for, if you have dipped into the Romancian annals, you will have found that there is nothing more commonplace.

"Would you like another specimen?" he added. "The amorous cavalier has a secret rendezvous with his beauty in the garden at night, but in all honor, in a somber clump of bushes, where the moonlight will be dangerous. The little door to the garden has been left ajar. Now, the brother or the father of the princess, wanting by chance to enter by the little door and finding it open, suspects something. The rest is easily divinable: great fuss, attack, defense, torches are bought; the cavalier only fights as he retreats, but what can he do? It is a necessity; and it is a capital rule that the father or brother of the woman he adores will impale himself on the sword of the unfortunate cavalier. Judge how many years it will take to settle such an adventure.

"It is necessary in the meantime to go and serve in Flanders or in Hungary. Another inconvenience, for in Flanders he is thought to have been killed in a battle, and the desolate Leonore, after having torn out all her hair for six months, finally makes some decision fatal to her lover. In Hungary he is taken prisoner and sent as a slave to Turkey in order to work in a garden there or to clean the apartments..."

"I confess to you, Prince," I said to the great paladin, "that of all the profs, that last one is the one I like the best, for I've noticed that of all the men who leave Romancia in order to be slaves in Turkey or Algiers, there is not one who does not make his fortune."

"That is true," he replied, "but note also that before departing there is not one who does not take the precaution of learning to dance well, of having a beautiful voice, playing instruments perfectly and being amiable and handsome. That is all of his success. The slave is shown to the favorite sultana in order to cheer her up; the slave is such an admirable man and all sultanas have such tender hearts that in less than no time there is an intrigue ready made and a poor sultan disrespected. The condition would please them sufficiently if it could last, but there is no means; the laws of Romancia are extremely severe on that matter; it is necessary that the sultan, warned or not, enters the seraglio and threatens to kill everyone. What a hubbub!

"It is, however, only noise. He has been heard coming. The sultana, fearing for her life, finds the means to flee with the charming Bezibezu—that's the name of the slave—and they are already far away. In four days the beautiful Moroccan arrives in Marseille or Barcelona and presents herself for baptism the next day. The only thing that displeases me about that adventure is that the laws dictate that the casket of gems that the beautiful Mooress has brought with her has to be thrown into the sea, which reduces her to beggary."

"Those proofs," I said in my turn, "appear to me to be not very agreeable, but I've seen others that are even more so. What would you say, for example, about a poor lover who, on the eve of marrying the woman he loves, sees the princess abducted by unknown individuals and transported to an unknown location, without him being able to learn the slightest news of her after a thousand researches? You'll confess to me that that's one of the situations most favorable to tragic sentiments and fine despairs."

"Oh, dear Prince," cried Prince Zazaraph, "of what memories are you reminding me? I have endured that cruel proof, and you can ask all the echoes of our forests how much it has cost me in dolorous regrets, pathetic sobs and touching *alas*es. Yes, I would have killed myself a thousand times if the precaution had not been taken, as is usual on such occasions, of taking away my sword, dagger, pistols and other mortal instruments. It was to avoid the deadly effects of such despair that, after the last abduction of my process, I was condemned to a long sleep, because it was not thought that I could sustain without dying a second proof of that nature."

"You would at least have been able," I said to him, "in such sad circumstances, to equip yourself with a portrait of your princess, or a few petty items of furniture that she had employed. That is an infinite resource, for I knew a cavalier called the Marquis de Rosemont,[32] who, having found a means even to have a few of the defunct Doña Diana's chemises, stockings and skirts , spent a lot of time putting them on his body, contemplating them and kissing them one after another with an inexpressible tenderness."

"It's true," the prince replied, "that I also found consolation in contemplating and kissing the portrait of the adorable Anemone a thousand times a day."

At the same time, the prince took out the portrait and showed it to me. Gods, what was my astonishment!

Friend reader, I have not prepared you at all for this incident, but it is true that at the time, I was not expecting it myself, so your surprise will be no greater than mine. I believed that I recognized the portrait of my sister, the infanta Fan Férédine. It is true that she appeared to be extraordinarily embellished, but in sum, they were her features and her entire physiognomy, with the consequence that I would not have

---

[32] Author's note: "*Aventures d'un homme de qualité.*"

hesitated for a moment to believe that it was her, it I had not seen the impossibility clearly.

I was absolutely sure that on departing for Romancia I lad left my sister the infanta at the court of Fan Férédia with my mother, Queen Fan-Férédine. In any case, my sister had never been called Princess Anemone. Thus, I thought I ought to regard that resemblance quite simply as an effect of chance. I could not help, however, telling the great paladin about the thought that had come to my mind at the sight of the portrait.

"That's admirable," he replied, "for at that very moment, observing you more closely myself, I thought I perceived in you striking features of resemblance with the brother of my princess; so, if she resembles your sister, I can assure you that you resemble her brother very closely, except that you are better looking, and have a nobler and more amiable air."

"Oh, given that," I said to him, "I'm tempted to believe that there is enchantment in this, or some hidden mystery, for I also find, on looking at you closely, that you resemble so closely a young man of my acquaintance who is in love with my sister that I could easily have mistaken you for him if you were not incomparably more handsome, better built physically and a great paladin as well, whereas he is a simple cavalier. But," I said, interrupting the conversation, "it seems to me that I perceive a kind of city or grand habitation two or three leagues away."

"Yes," he said, "that's where we're going to stay. You'll see curious things there."

XII. On the workers, trades and manufactures of Romancia.

We arrived, therefore, at the entrance to a long and magnificent avenue planted with orange trees pomegranates and myrtles, mingled with charming flowering bushes. There we descended from our grasshoppers, which took their leave of us, and we advanced, following the avenue all the way to the habitation.

"The place we're about to enter," Prince Zazaraph told me, "isn't a city, properly speaking, since there are only workers and shops here, but you'll doubtless find satisfaction in exploring its various quarters, and it's an object worthy of the curiosity of newcomers."

"Oh!" I said. "Of what species are they, these workers?"

"You're going to see for yourself," he replied, "but I want to give you a general idea beforehand. As all those who inhabit Romancia always find themselves provided with all that is necessary for their subsistence, without them even taking the trouble to think about it, you ought to deduce that the workers of the land don't amuse themselves making cloth, canvas, furniture, bread or flour. Their occupation is much milder, and there are different kinds of them: threaders, blowers, embroiderers, menders, illuminators, makers of magic lanterns, exhibitors of curiosities and a few others."

"You're naming métiers there," I said, "of which I can't quite see the usage in this land."

"I'll explain them to you," he retorted. "What we call threaders here are workers who were once quite common. Such people assemble twenty or thirty trivia from various places, which they have the skill of aggregating and stitching together, and that's their work done.

"Blowers, by contrast, only take one of those petty trivia, but they have the art of inflating it, stretching it by blowing into it, rather like children with soap bubbles, with the result that they make something large out of material that is almost nothing in itself. As you can imagine, those things aren't very solid, but they amuse idle minds nevertheless. Women and children, especially, love to see those little bubbles floating in the air. But it's true that they only have a momentary splendor, and one doesn't remember them the next day.

"The work of embroiderers is another kind. They import a few rare and curious morsels from some foreign land, which they ornament with an embroidery of flowing design, which leaves almost nothing of the backcloth visible.

"Menders are less ingenious. Their entire art consists of giving an appearance of newness to things that are already old and worn; it is, however, that species of workers that is in greatest number today.

"True painters are very rare here, but in recompense we have admirable illuminators who are employed in illuminating with the most brilliant colors the portraits, figures or scenes of the imagination. It is necessary not to ask the people for accurate portraits or depictions of the real; that is not their métier; but no one understands like them the art of charging a scene with red and white, rather like German dolls, and the only thing for which one can reproach them is that all their portraits are alike.

"Lanterners, or makers of magic lanterns, are also workers held in highly esteem. They are so called because the products they make resemble kinds of magic lanterns in which one sees the most incredible things in the world: towers of bronze, columns of diamond, rivers of fire, chariots hitched to birds or fish, and monstrous giants.

"Exhibitors of curiosities do work of a rather amusing kind. It's a mass of various curious things that hey import from far places. That's why they were given their name. When the material with which they work is too ingrate in itself they find the art of augmenting and ornamenting their tableau with various more interesting objects, which they present one after another, such as the map of London, the court of Portugal, the government of Venice and the temples of Rome, much as an exhibitor of curiosities enables you to see in his box the city of Constantinople, the Empress of Russia, the court of Peking and the port of Amsterdam.

"Those," said Prince Zazaraph, "are almost all the different species of workers who labor in this land; but let's go into their habitation in order to see them at closer range, for I'm sure that the sight will amuse you."

In fact, I was charmed by the neatness and admirable order that I saw in the distribution of the shops. The different species of workers are divided into different streets, and each street is formed by little shops arranged in rows to either side, adjacent to one another, similar to the celebrated fairs of Europe; that makes a very agreeable spectacle, and, if one wishes, a very amusing promenade. I particularly admired the variety and singularity of the signs, and even remember a few, like the Blue Beard, the Amorous Cat, the Seven-League Boots, the Talking Portrait, the Good Little Mouse, the Green Serpent, the Unfortunate Neapolitan and a few others of the same stripe.[33]

All the workers are, in addition, extremely polite and obliging, in order to attract the curious and merchants into their establishments, and there is nothing that they would not do to make their merchandise shine. If they can be believed, their work is always admirable, singular and curious. This, says one, is the fruit of a long and painful labor. This, says another, is a precious residue of a worker who left a great reputation when he died. This, says a third, is an imitation of a Chinese or Indian work, much sought-after. For myself, says a seemingly disinterested merchant, I had no desire to communicate my work, but, my friends and persons of good taste having seen it, pressed me so hard to share it with the public that I was unable to rest their solicitations. They accompany these discourses with manners so honest and polished that one can scarcely help buying something, at the hazard of paying dear for poor merchandise, as often happens.

Hazard having taken us first to the threaders' quarter, I was curious to explore a few of the shops with Prince Zazaraph, for it would require an entire year to explore them all. I admired veritably the skill with which I saw those workers stitching together a thousand petty trifles. A very thin thread sufficed for that, and their skill consists of making the thread last until the end without breaking, for if it has to be renewed, or another added, the work no longer has the same value.

---

[33] The descriptions of these "signs" are a slight variant of the motifs well-known tales by Perrault and Madame d'Aulnoy.

The shop that seemed to me to have the most customers had for its sign The Thousand-and-One Nights. The worker, it is said, is one of the most celebrated in the quarter. As his sign has had success, a few others workers have not failed to imitate it, in the hope of succeeding equally. One has taken The Thousand-and-One Days, another The Thousand-and-One Hours, another The Thousand-an-One Quarter-Hours. Their thread is, in fact, almost the same, but they could not have been as lucky as the first in the choice of trifles. I also noticed a few more distinguished signs, like the Breton Evenings, Evenings in Thessaly, Chinese Tales, etc. But those workers, it is said, have more fecundity than strength of imagination. Too feeble to undertake a work on a single subject, they only have resource is multitude, like a man who, not having enough cloth to make a suit, composes it from various assorted pieces, a medley that only ever does the worker mediocre honor.

The quarter of blowers has been almost deserted for some time, because few workers are found who have sufficient breath to furnish that labor. It seems that Cyrus was their favorite sign; at least, several have appropriated it, and each one has returned it in his fashion. A few of those gentlemen, finding that the prince as a subject appropriate to bring customers into their shop, have obliged him, without consulting his inclination, to travel the world as an adventurer, in order to bring back curious materials from foreign lands appropriate to be put to work.[34] It has not been decided whether he came back a better man, but one cannot doubt that after such long journeys he needed to spend some time in retreat, and he was fortunate to find a new master, a intelligent and charitable man, who took the poor prince into his home uniquely to enable him to take a rest.[35]

---

[34] Editor's note: "*Voyages de Cyrus*." The text cited, by Andrew Michel Ramsay, was published in 1727.

[35] Editor's note: "*Repos de Cyrus*." The text cited, by Jacques Perinetti, was published in 1732.

"Some time ago," Prince Zazaraph told me, "one of those rare and sublime geniuses appeared in this quarter, of the kind that nature scarcely produces once every hundred years. He conceived that the work that you see these workers doing might be of some help in forming the heart and mind of young princes, if it were done well and handled with art and wisdom. He set out to give his model of it. His sign was The Prince of Ithaca.[36] This place, which, as you can see has been consecrated to him, out of respect to his memory, as the place where he worked. It is true that he made a masterpiece that one cannot weary of reading, in which he found the art of mingling together everything there is of the most cheerful and the most gracious, with all that wisdom and religion have of the most perfect and sublime. It is that work which ought to serve today as the model for all workers, and some have, indeed, striven to imitate it, but one is reduced to praising their efforts while always being obliged to pity their weakness."

In the same quarter, the prince pointed out to me a few shops that were somewhat accredited. I remember two of them in particular. The first had Prince Sethos for a sign, and, to judge the prince by his portrait, he was a man of intelligence, who could only be reproached for too strong an application to the study of antiquity. The second was occupied by a female worker of a delicate and solid mind who had acquired a considerable reputation in a short time. Her sign was the Court of

---

[36] Editor's note: "*Télémaque*." *Les Aventures de Télémaque*, by François Fénelon was written as a didactic aid while he was tutor to the Dauphin's son, the Duc de Bourgogne, in 1689-97, but it outraged Louis XIV, who construed it, correctly, as a philosophical assault on absolute monarchy; although a few copies were printed in 1699, it was not until it was reissued posthumously—the author and the king both died in 1715— that it was widely read, becoming enormously popular and hailed as a classic, in spite of its lack of a royal prerogative to license its publication.

Philippe Auguste,[37] and the haste of the public to purchase her works having already emptied the shop, she as working on a new one that was awaited with impatience.

I did not find anything in the street of embroiderers that struck me very forcefully. "These workers," Prince Zazaraph told me, "having insufficient talent to create something new themselves, earn their living enlivening things already known, which appear too simple in themselves. Thus, they work on a foreign foundation, and they have the art of charging it so abundantly with their embroidery that once can no longer distinguish the backcloth from that which is only the ornamentation, but it is rather rare for their work to make a fortune. Here is a shop which has the sign Don Carlos, the worker of which is esteemed, but here is another, whose worker had not had as much success in the design to amuse, although his sign promises historic amusements."

"What!" I said to the prince. "Do I not see there the worker from foreign climes known as P.L.? What is he doing here?"[38]

"What he does," he replied. "He figures very well among our embroiderers and is now one of the most accredited. It's true that he seemed at first to want to establish himself in the land of History, and did indeed set up shop there, but he found that it suited him better to make frequent excursions to Romancia; he did that so often that one never knows to which country his works belong, and I believe one can say, in truth, that it is mixed merchandise.

"But I forgot," he added, "to draw your attention to one of our most beautiful shops." He pointed it out to me. "There

---

[37] Editor's note: "*Anecdotes de la cour de Philippe Auguste.*" The cited text, published in 1733, is by Marguerite de Lussan. A veiled reference had been made earlier to her *Veillées de Thessalie* [Evenings in Thessaly] (1735).

[38] Possibly Philibert Le Roux, author of *Histoire du père La Chaize: jésuite et confesseur du roi Louis XIV* (1719), who had been forced to flee France in the 1690s.

it is. It has for a sign, as you see, The Princess of Cleves,[39] and the worker enjoys, justly, a great reputation for never having lost sight, in an extremely delicate work, of the rules of duty and the most austere decorum."

From there we passed into the quarter of menders. They are, as I said, the least esteemed workers in Romancia. What merit is there, in fact, in adapting for a Frenchman, for example, a work made for an Englishman or a Spaniard, or in reducing for a supposedly modern taste works made for an antique taste? So it is rather rare that such works make any reputation for their authors. It is not for that reason, however, that their quarter is almost deserted; that is the fault of the Romancian police, to fix everyone within the bounds of his métier. All the workers dabble in mending, with the result there is hardly one who, in the merchandise he presents to you as new had not mingled a few old morsels, which he had dressed up and recycled in his own fashion; it is for that reason that menders in title do hardly any business, and it is precisely the same for the illuminators. Everyone dabbles in their métier, including the workers in the land of History.

The lanterners, or makers of magic lanterns, amused us for some time. Those workers have an extremely fecund imagination; he never fail to regulate it by means of common sense and plausibility, for there is no invention so bizarre that they cannot discover and execute it, or appear to execute it, with a surprising facility. Ask them for flying chariots, silver palaces, arms which render one invulnerable, secrets for knowing anything whatsoever and everything that is said for a thousand leagues around, charms for making oneself loved, statues that come to life, instant bridges, ships or gardens, giants, animals that talk, mountains of gold, silver and precious stones— nothing costs them anything, with the consequence that in the blink of an eye, their shop is full of marvels. It is true that when one considers their works at close range, it is easy to

---

[39] *La Princesse de Clèves* (1678), attributed to Madame de La Fayette.

166

perceive that they are only trinkets, which have nothing solid or estimable, and I could not help testifying to Prince Zazaraph that I could not understand how those workers were able to find buyers for such merchandise, but he corrected my error.

"If the merchants of Europe," he said, "who set out displays of dolls, whistles. Little windmills, little bells, grotesque figurines and a thousand similar trinkets that are bought for children earn their living by means of that commerce, why don't you want these to be as fortunate? For you can see that their shops and their merchandise resemble one another perfectly. It can even be observed that the majority of people who occupy themselves with Romancian handiwork are idle and slack minds who want to be amused, like children, because they do not have the strength to occupy themselves with their own thoughts or give sufficient application to the thoughts of others. Propose to them something to meditate, an argument to fathom, or even a reflection to make and you overload them, you bore them, like children to whom a lesson for study is proposed, instead of which a series of pretty toys that are passed incessantly before their eyes diverts them and amuses them without fatiguing them.

"That is what determines the large sales of this merchandise; the workers can scarcely furnish enough of it, and as soon as a new magic lantern appears, or a new toy, it is snatched from their hands. It's necessary, however, to admit one thing, which is that as soon as the initial curiosity is satisfied, the same thing happens to those work as toys that are abandoned or broken, they are left neglected in an apartment, without anyone thinking of conserving them, and their usual fate is eventually to be thrown out pell-mell with the rubbish.

"We have now arrived," Prince Zazaraph went on, "in the quarter of exhibitors of curiosities. Their shops are rather fine, as you can see, and even quite rich. It's also true that they don't lack customers, but in spite of that, they are not highly considered, because they only work as subalterns, in accordance with what other workers order from them: sometimes the plan of a city, sometimes a portrait, a description, a battle, a tourney, or some singular event to fill the lacunae in their work or to fatten them."

While we were considering the various curiosities with which the shops of that quarter were garnished, however, we were distracted by a comical troupe of clowns and street performers of every sort, who came into the main square in order to enact a comedy of sorts. The spectacle amused me and I found wit in the invention and execution of the play. A certain Ragotin[40] played one of the principal roles in it with someone named Rancune, and he never appeared on stage without making the spectators laugh heartily, as much by his ridiculous and comical appearance as by the pleasantries he pronounced. The entire play seemed to me to be the work of an intelligent man, and I was told that he author had made even better ones.

That spectacle was followed by a short play entitled "Le Diable boiteux,"[41] which also obtained a great deal of applause. It was in one act, apparently because it did not require more, for I dare say that the author would not have embellished it in wanting to stretch it out. Another play by the same author was promised for the following day, entitled "Gil Blas de Santillane" but I heard the people standing next to me saying that although it had wit and some go things in it, it was not as good as the first.

Finally, I saw a surly masquerade appear, composed of people disguised as vagabonds and adventurers, whom I heard named as Lazarille de Tormes, Dom Guzman d'Alfarache, the

---

[40] Author's note: "*Roman comique.*" [i.e., *Ragotin ou roman comique* (1684), a comedy by Champmeslé (Charles Chevillet)]

[41] Presumably the 1707 comedy by Florent Carton Dancourt, although the subsequent reference to *Gil Blas* suggests that Bougéant is under the impression that it was by Alain-René Lesage, the author of the novel of the same title, published in the same year.

adventurer Buscon and other similar names.[42] Prince Zazaraph warned me, however, that only the populace and people of poor taste usually remained for that final performance.

I did, in fact, remark that all the honest people were retiring, and I did the same with my faithful interpreter. That was not without difficulty, however, for while we were retiring a multitude of other masks arrived, who were named as he blue band, and had at their head a Gargantua, a Robert the Devil, Pierre de Provence, Richard sans peur, and other heroes of the same stripe. We had difficulty piercing the crowd in order to escape from such bad company.

"Let's go to the port," the prince said to me. "We'll surely see a few ships arriving there, and the spectacle is always rather curious. I also have a great interest in not being far away from it, since, as you know, I'm waiting for Princess Anemone, who ought to arrive very soon."

"I want to accompany you there," I replied, "And I sense that it's no longer in my power to separate myself from you; but please, explain to me beforehand what that singular building is that I perceive in that public square."

"That," the replied, "is the building in which the archives of Romancia[43] are kept. A rather poor work, as you can see. The portal, which is as large as the body of the building , is merely a bizarre assembly in which one sees neither method nor principles, and which offends common sense, so it has revolted all sensate minds. The body of the building is scarcely any better; it's a mass of stones piled on top of one another without order or liaison; but one should not, after all, expect anything better on the part of the entrepreneur. He's a man who was once held up as a great worker in the land of History; until then he had given a lesson to all the others and was erect-

---

[42] The references are characters borrowed from works of Spanish picaresque fiction who were frequently adapted into broad farces by traveling performers.
[43] Author's note: "*Bibliothèque des Romans*." i.e. Lenglet Du Fresnoy's bibliography.

ed as censor general; but boasting having succeeded poorly he threw himself in despair into Romancia, where he has been unable to find any other means of subsistence than representing himself as an architect. It is on that footing that he was employed to construct the building in question, but you can see by its execution that the pretended architect is only a mediocre mason."

"O gods" I cried at that moment, "What a frightful vapor! Great paladin, what pestilence is thus?"

"Ah!" he said. "Let's flee as quickly as possible and escape the infection."

We ran, in fact, and when we were far enough away, the prince said to me: "I had forgotten that it is necessary to avoid the street along which we just passed, unless one wants to risk being corrupted." He added: "It is a young magic lanterner who has caused that infection. His name is Tancrebsai.[44] He is the son of a father celebrated for fine works, who has not blushed to embrace the métier of lanterner, and because he is young and inexperienced, in wanting to make a new composition in order to paint his magic lantern, he made a drug so stinking that it was necessary to close his laboratory, and after he had been put in quarantine he was forbidden to work in that genre again.

"But we're nearing the port," he said, then, "And I believe I can already see a few ships arriving. Let's get nearer in order to study them at closer age and watch the disembarkation."

---

[44] Editor's note: "*Tanzaï.*" Bougéant has fused the partial title with the first two syllables of the author's name. Bougéant could not know that Crébillon *fils*, who had landed in prison briefly after publishing *Tanzaï et Neadame*, was to go on to create an even greater scandal when he published the libidinous *Le Sopha* (1742).

XIII. The arrival of a great fleet.
Judgment of the newly disembarked.

Scarcely had we arrived when we saw the port fill up with a large number of vessels that were hastening to enter it. Some were equipped with passports,[45] others did not have them because they were doubtless carrying contraband, but they were not inspected very closely, and I saw them entering pell-mell with almost no attention paid to that difference, provided that they were not carrying anything pernicious.

They were of all sizes, large and small. They were all distinguished by their flags, like the vessels of Europe, and above all by their devices and different names. I have difficulty remembering them all. There were The Four Facardins, Fleur d'Épine, the Mogul Tales, Tartar Tales, Madame de Barnevelt, the Constancy of True Loves, Aurora and Phoebus and several others, which made a very varied spectacle.

"Alas," said Prince Zazaraph, "I don't see my dear Anemone yet, but a pleasant presentiment still makes me hope that she will arrive soon, and this delay at least leaves me the leisure to give you some clarifications of what you see."

"This beautiful fleet," I said to him, "fills me with admiration and I doubt that the Greek fleet that came to snatch Helen from the arms of the amorous Paris was finer. But I don't know what to think about another spectacle that I can see in preparation at the entrance to the port. What does that grave matron intend to do whom I see affecting the air of a magistrate and sitting down in a tribunal of sorts, accompanied by men and women who seem to be taking the place of assessors or counselors?"

"It is, indeed," he replied, "a genuine tribunal, and perhaps the most enlightened and mot equitable of all tribunals.

---

[45] Author's note: "Privileges." Bougéant's book had a royal privilege enabling its licit publication; the work by Lenglet Du Fresnoy that clearly inspired it, and to which it is in part a satirical reply, did not.

This is its function. We have ship's captains here who under-take long-haul voyages in order to enable our heroes and hero-ines to travel the world. They choose those who suit them, and they are allowed to direct their journeys as they please. Some are long and others shorter; some goes eastwards and some westwards; but in the end, it is necessary to return and give an account of their voyage. Now, that account is always very rigorous. The judge who sees you is incorruptible, and her council, made up of men and women, is very enlightened. It is not impossible to impose upon it for a time, but it soon recov-ers from its error and reforms its judgment itself."

"I'm charmed," I said, "that at least Romancia renders justice to women by admitting them to the public council, for it is shameful that they are excluded from it in all the other countries in the world. But explain to me, please, in what the judgments of this tribunal consist."

"They consist," he replied, "in that all the captains are obliged on their return to present themselves of the President of the Council to render an account of what has happened to them. She listens to them, and after their report, she punishes them or rewards them in accordance with the good or bad conduct they have maintained in the course of their voyage. If they have conducted and governed their company with art and sagacity, they are given one of the leading ranks in Romancia. If, on the contrary, they have given their passengers a disa-greeable, tedious or excessively dangerous voyage, if they have caused them to be shipwrecked, if they have treated them with too much rigor—in brief, if they have given them just cause for complaint—the judge punishes them and condemns some to prison and others to banishment, or to some more rigorous penalty."

That procedure seemed sufficiently curious to me to mer-it seeing it for myself, and I asked Prince Zazaraph to ap-proach the tribunal with me in order to witness what was hap-pening as the disembarkation of the newcomers.

It might be difficult to believe, but it is true that among the large number of vessels that were arriving in the port, it was difficult to find a captain who merited some recompense. Some had only followed routes already traced by those who had preceded them without daring to attempt a new one. Others had caused a frightful confusion throughout the equipage by virtue of the large number of people they had taken on to their vessels. Others had only taken their passengers into un-cultivated and arid lands, where they had suffered a great deal from famine and tedium.

Some had exhausted the patience and courage of their people by virtue of too long a sequence of annoying adven-tures; others had only occupied them with puerile and extrava-gant things, with the consequence that having heard their nar-ration, the council, far from giving them any recompense, de-liberated as to whether they merited punishment more for hav-ing wasted so much time and having caused others to waste it. It was, however, concluded by a majority vote that the scant consideration and puerility in which they were condemned to send the rest of their days would take the place of punishment.

A captain named L. D. F*** endured in that regard a long trial. His heroine, whose name escapes me, complained bitterly to the council that without any regard to the propriety of her sex, had made her run around for a infinite time, always dressed s a man, without ever wanting to permit her to don female attire until the moment when she was about to arrive in port.[46] She added that her captain, without any necessity and out of pure malevolence, had abused that ridiculous disguise, sometimes to oblige her to fight cavaliers, sometimes to put her in utterly indecent situations and to take her into the most

---

[46] Editor's note: "*Madame Barnevelt*, by Abbé Desfontaines." The anonymously-published *Mémoires de Madame de Barne-veldt* (1732) is not by Abbé Pierre Desfontaines, and it is sur-prising that Garnier thought that it might be; it is nowadays attributed Jean Du Castre d'Auvigny. The intended signifi-cance of the initials cited by Bougéant is unclear, but it is quite possible that he believed that *Madame Barnevelt* was by Lenglet Du Fresnoy.

suspect places, where her honor had been in peril a thousand times over.

The heroine's complaint appeared so just to begin with and so well-founded, that she excited all minds against the captain, and he was about to be condemned unanimously when one of the oldest counselors came to his defense. He represented to the council that, considering things in themselves, it was true that L. D. F*** merited punishment for having made an honest heroine undergo such a dangerous and indecent voyage, but that her disguises, dangerous and indecent as they were, having always been tolerated in Romancia, as was easily proven by the most ancient annals, they ought not to be held against the captain so much as against those who had given such bad examples; that in consequence, his advice was that they ought to be content to admonish the captain seriously, not to follow again a practice so little in conformity with the laws of decency. However, in order to put the honor of Romancian princesses in security, it was necessary to make a new regulation, which abrogated the ancient tolerance, and forbade all captains from now on to give their heroines attire other than that of their own sex, unless they were forced to do so by some indispensable necessity.

That opinion seemed so reasonable that everyone yielded to it, with the result that the captain got away with a fright.

One of his colleagues was not so fortunate. Scarcely had he returned from his first voyage than he had undertaken a second, and then a third, with the result that, thus far, he had escaped the pursuits of his accusers and the sentence of the council. But he was finally held to account at the end of his third volume and was obliged to appear. First they wanted to enquire as to why he had meddled in the employment of captain, which was ill-suited to his profession, but he justified himself as best he could by citing he examples of a few celebrated captains who had previously exercised the same profession as him. It was not the same for the other major points of the accusation.

A man of quality[47] named the Marquis de **** spoke first, and among other grievances he accused the captain; firstly, of having deceived him, in that he had been obliged to embark in order to run the risks of a second navigation after he had promised to leave him in peace in solitude as soon as the first volume as finished; secondly, of having shamefully degraded him, by only giving him in his second voyage the employment of a tedious pedagogue after having made him play the role of a man of quality in the first; and thirdly, of having overloaded him in both voyages with the most calamitous misfortunes, the detail of which made him shiver. To these here principal accusations, the man of quality added a few other minor ones, to which no one paid much attention. The captain not having been able to respond to the former, however, he was judged guilty and convicted of breach of faith, but sentence was postponed until the other accusers had been heard.

It was a woman who presented herself next, who gave her name as Manon Lescaut.[48] What a woman! I have never seen anyone so wide awake, and I would not have believed that a man of the character of **** could take charge of the conduct of such a princess. I cannot remember the full detail of the complaints but the gist of them was to accuse her captain of having taken her out of the obscurity in which she was living, to which she had justly condemned herself in order to hide the aberration of her conduct, in order to set her on the stage in broad daylight and make her travel the world frantically, defying all the laws of modesty and decency.

The second complaint was followed by a third at least as heated, but much more interesting because of the touching scene to which it gave rise.

---

[47] Editor's note: "*Mémoires d'un homme de qualité* by Abbé Prévost."

[48] Editor's note: "*Hist. du, ch. des Grieux et de Manon l'Escot* by the same author."

The two companions were the famous Cleveland and the sad Fanny.[49] They made the most melancholy couple that has perhaps ever been seen. Sadness was panted n their faces; they could scarcely raise their eyes. Profound sighs preceded, accompanied and followed all their words, and to tell the truth, it was difficult to understand the story of all the misfortunes that their captain had made hem endure in the course of their voyage, without taking part in the just resentment that they caused to erupt against him.

"Barbarian!" cried Cleveland. "What have I done to you to overwhelm me thus with the cruelest misfortunes without having given me a moment's relaxation in the entire curse of my life? Was the sad situation to which an unfortunate birth had reduced me not enough? Were you not satisfied by having given me such a savage education in a frightful cavern? Did you have to take me out of it in order to render me a victim of fortune and assemble over my head all the disasters, all the contradictions and all the frustrations of human life?

"Yes, Mesdames et Messieurs," he added, addressing his judges, "count all the murders, all the baleful deaths, the black deeds, the treasons, the frightful dangers and all the tragic events with which he blackened the course of my adventures, and you will have difficulty comprehending how I was able to survive so many misfortunes and how the story could even have been sustained.

"If, in the catastrophes into which he plunged me he had at least followed the ordinary rules! But has anyone ever heard mention of a tempest like the one he made us endure in passing from England to France? Who has ever seen a lover like Madame Lallin combine so many contrary qualities, malice with goodness of heart, extravagance with reason, the most violent passion with the moderation of simple amity? What is the sense of that ridiculous passion, which he made me conceive at an age already mature, at a time when my heart was devoured by a thousand chagrins? By what right did he make

---

[49] Editor's note: "*Cleveland* by the same."

me speak like a man who only has vague religious principles without any determined worship? Oh, how many other objects of complaint I could add here! But no, I want to forgive him; I even consent to forget the cruel proof to which he put my constancy in having my dear daughter and the unfortunate Madame Roding burned before my eyes and devoured by savages. I only watch myself to one last outrage, which brought a culmination of all his maltreatments. He rendered my wife, my dear Fanny…Gods, can one believe it? Can I say it? Yes, he rendered her infidel."

As he finished speaking, the unfortunate Cleveland, overcome by grief, no longer able to sustain himself, was obliged to sit down. The entire assembly, deeply moved by his just complaints, gazed at him compassionately, while Fanny rose to her feet excitedly, and attracted the attention of the judges and the spectators. The crime of infidelity for which her husband had just reproached her had cut her to the quick. "Ingrate!" she said to him, with an expression of anger and pride, sustained by the modest assurance that innocence inspires. "Direct your complaints against our captain; I will share the accusation with you, since I have shared your misfortunes; but do not dare to accuse him at the expense of my virtue. He was able to render Fanny unfortunate, but he has never rendered me infidel. It is you, ingrate, who has not blushed to prefer an odious rival to me, and Heaven doubtless permitted that to punish me for having loved you too much."

"What, Madame!" cried Cleveland, with a great deal of emotion. "Dare you deny that you abandoned me to follow the perfidious Gélin?"

"It's true," she replied. "I wanted to allow you to renew in liberty your former amours with Madame Lallin; but know that, although Gélin aided me in my flight, his passion for me never had reason to applaud itself for the service he rendered me."

"Me, Madame Lallin!" cried Cleveland, with astonishment.

"Me. Gélin!" retorted Fanny, indignantly.

"What a fable!" said one,
"What imagination!" said the other.
"You're mistaken, Madame!"
"You're in error, Monsieur!"
"God is my witness!"
"I swear by the Gods!"
"Oh, I only loved you too much!"
"Alas, I sense only too well that I love you still."
"What! Can that be possible?"
"Nothing is more true."
"You've always loved me, then?"
"You've always been faithful to me, then?"
"Let's make peace."
"Let's embrace."
"Oh, my dear Fanny!"
"Oh, my dear Cleveland!"

They did, in fact, set one another ablaze with a thousand transports of tenderness

The little children in the party looked at one another, which was a spectacle at least as touching as the coronation of Inès de Castro.[50] Thus, after a momentary explanation, the long quarrel of the two tender spouses ended. But the captain appeared no less culpable for that. No one understood how he had been harsh enough to deliver to despair for entire years, by the cruel persuasion into which he had put them both that they had each been betrayed, without wanting to afford them a momentary clarification.

He alleged for his defense that he had needed that expedient to prolong his voyage, to which views of profit engaged him to give greater extent. No one listened to him, and the council, on the basis of the report and all the defenses on both sides, condemned the aforesaid D. P*** to perpetual banishment from all the lands of Romancia, with a prohibition ever

---

[50] Legend reports that the corpse of Inès de Castro (1325-1355), the lover of Peter I of Portugal, was publicly crowned by him when he belatedly recognized her as his wife.

to return.[51] The sentence was carried out immediately, and it is said that the poor exile wanted to take refuge in the land of History, where he had a few acquaintances, and where he hoped to have better luck.

Scarcely had that affair concluded than the arrival of the Malabar princesses was announced to the assembly. That name excited curiosity. People hastened to make way for them, but as soon as they had begun to explain themselves everyone looked at one another in astonishment, wondering what they were trying to say. It was an allegorical, metaphorical, enigmatic language of which no one understood a word. They even disguised their names under puerile anagrams. They spoke one after another without order and without method, affecting a philosophical tone and an enthusiastic emphasis in order to say extravagant things. It was nevertheless possible to perceive through the insensate obscurities several scandalous impieties and maxims of irreligion that revolted the entire assembly against the ridiculous princesses. A general cry went up to have them expelled. They were banished in perpetuity, and the vessel that had bought them was burned publicly. Fortunately for the captain, he had been in hiding since his arrival, for he would doubtless have been condemned to an exemplary punishment; but he found a means of avoiding all research and thus escaped the punishment he merited.[52]

---

[51] Editor's note: "Abbé Prévost became a Benedictine." In fact, Prévost was a Benedictine before writing his novels, but had fallen out with the order temporarily. He was, indeed, reconciled with his superiors in 1734, but that did not prevent him from continuing to write prolifically, albeit less scandalously.

[52] *Les Princesses Malabares, ou Le Célibat philosophique* [The Malabar Princesses; or, The Philosophical Bachelor] (1734) is a satirical Oriental fantasy speculatively attributed at the time to various authors, including Lenglet Du Fresnoy, but nowadays reckoned to be most probably the work of Pierre de Longue.

XIV. The arrival of Princess Anemone.
Prince Fan-Férédin falls in love
with Princess Rosebelle.

While everyone was occupied with the spectacle of these various scenes, the great paladin Zazaraph, who was distracted by his amour and his impatience, darted glances continually toward the entrance to the port. He was sure that Princess Anemone could not fail to arrive imminently; and, in fact, he finally discovered the ship that was bringing her.

"There she is!" he cried, transported by joy. "It's Princess Anemone herself. I recognize the ship that is carrying her, and the sweet stirring that I sense in my soul leaves me in no doubt of it."

Prince Zazaraph immediately ran to welcome the princess when she descended from the vessel, and I accompanied him.

But how can I recount everything that happened in that meeting? It would be the subject of an entire volume, and anyone who has read a few romances will understand that better than I could represent it. Transports, sharp impatience, tender gazes, inexpressible joys, inconceivable satisfaction, reciprocal testimonies of affection, even tears—al that was put to work and placed appropriately. Then it was necessary to recount everything that had happened during a long absence. The great paladin did not take long to tell his story, having nothing to say except that he had slept for an entire year by virtue of an enchantment, but Princess Anemone's story was much longer.

Prince Gulifax had entered her home one evening, weapon in hand, and had abducted her while she was beginning to undress in order to go to bed, without even given her the leisure to put on her nightcap. She wept, cried and charged her abductor with insults in vain; it was necessary to depart and embark. She was no sooner in the ship than she found herself distanced from her dear Dondindandian prince and in the power of the perfidious Gulifax, who had the insolence to talk to her about amour. She fainted more than twenty times, twenty times she would have thrown herself into the sea had she not been prevented from doing so.

In sum, no other resource remained to her but tears and sobs, a feeble defense against a brutal corsair, so Princess Anemone passed lightly over that chapter in order to continue the remainder of her story, and she did it so well that I remarked Prince Zazaraph, at certain points in the story, testifying some anxiety.

She reported, therefore, that the gods, protectors of oppressed innocence, had delivered her miraculously from the tyranny of her cruel kidnapper. A prince full of valor and generosity had attacked and captured Gulifax's ship; the latter had perished in the combat. As her liberator was bringing her back, however, a frightful tempest had engulfed the vessel in the waves. She had saved herself on a plank and had been cast up on the shore more than half-dead After having brought her round, fishermen had introduced her to their prince, who had fallen in love with her, but, always intractable on that chapter, although the prince was handsome and well-built, she had not wanted to listen to him.

Here, however, I noticed that Prince Zazaraph made another grimace, and it was even worse when she added that she had subsequently passed successively into the power of three or four other princes. The paladin Zazaraph could not stand it any longer. It was written in the order of his adventures that after the return of the beautiful Anemone he had to quarrel with her, and that did not fail to happen. His anxiety regarding the perilous proofs to which the virtue of his princess had been put caused him to ask, stupidly, a few imprudent questions.

The princess blushed, went pale, shed tears and appeared offended to a point where one might have thought that she would never pardon him, but as it was also written that the reconciliation would follow soon after, a few equivocal oaths on the one side and the thousand pardons demanded on the other, with tears, settled the matter, and the virtue of the princess was recognized as having been proof against all adventures and above all suspicion.

It only remained to finish the romance by means of a solemn marriage, but it was necessary for that to leave Romancia, where it is not permitted to marry, and Prince Zazaraph made arrangements to do that.

I confess, moreover, that I did not pay much attention to the detail of Princess Anemone's adventures. While she was telling her story, my mind and heart were occupied with a more interesting object. At the rumor of his arrival, Princess Rosebelle, the sister of the great paladin, who had been linked in narrow amity with Anemone, ran to see her and embrace her. That was the fatal moment that Amour had destined to bring me under his law.

To see Princess Rosebelle, to admire her, to love her and to adore her were, for me, the same thing, and all that only took a moment; so I convinced myself that nothing as lovable had ever appeared on the earth. She was a small composite of perfections, the most complete imaginable, in which one saw youth, beauty, graces, intelligence, joviality and vivacity disputing the advantage.

Throughout Princess Anemone's story, I could not do anything but make my eyes speak, and they were understood. I even thought I perceived in Rosebelle's a certain favorable disposition, but as soon as the beautiful Anemone and Prince Zazaraph had finished their clarifications and I was at liberty to speak, I was no longer master of my transports. Forgetting all the laws of Romancia, of which the prince had informed me, I threw myself recklessly at the feet of the charming Rosebelle in order to declare the passion with which I was burning for her.

I have discovered since that Rosebelle was not annoyed, in the depths of her soul, by such an abrupt declaration, but it nevertheless neglected all the customary ceremonies.

As for the spectators, after a moment of surprise that my action caused them, they all looked at one another, smiling, and as Princess Rosebelle did not say anything, her brother spoke.

"Oh, Prince," he said, obliging me to get up, "how quick you are! What would become of Romancia if such vivacities were tolerated?"

"Eh! What will become of me," I retorted, with enthusiasm, "if the adorable Rosebelle is not favorable to my prayers, and if you, Prince, who can dispose of her, refuse to make me happy? I know all the respect that the laws of Romancia merit, and the preliminary formalities of which you have informed me, but in sum, can I not obtain a dispensation of them, or at least abridge them, for I sense strongly that the violence of my amour will not permit me to sustain that extension without dying?"

"I have already told you, Prince," he great paladin replied, "that it is unprecedented, since the foundation of the Romancian nation, for any hero to dispense with the formalities and proofs ordered by the laws, but it is true that it is not impossible to obtain from the public council that the time can be abridged. I flatter myself that I can obtain that favor for you, in favor of the great examples of constancy that Princess Anemone and I have just given to Romancia in the rude and long proofs that we have endured. It is, in addition, an opportunity for me to acquit myself toward you for the service you have rendered me, and also to bind ourselves narrowly together. I am only awaiting the consent of the princess, my sister to work efficaciously for that."

At those words, a lovely blush that covered the fact of the princess made her appear even more beautiful in my eyes. I trembled while awaiting her response.

"My brother," she said, "it is for you to dispose of me, and since it is necessary to confess it, I would not be sorry if it were in favor of Prince Fan-Férédin."

Gods! What were my transports! I was no longer in possession of myself. I don't know what I became. I wept with joy. I moistened Rosebelle's beautiful hand with my tears; I tried to speak, but I could only stammer; my amour choked me, and I believe that I experienced in a quarter of an hour the value of more than fifteen of the preliminary formalities that I have mentioned—so that counted in my favor when the great paladin asked for the time of formalities and proofs to be abridged for me. He had some difficulty in obtaining it regardless, but he had acquired such great credit in Romancia and a reputation so splendid that he could not be refused anything. He was even granted the favor in its entirety; all that was asked of me was three days to accomplish all the formalities and all the proofs, after which I would be permitted to depart with the great paladin, in order to go to Dondindandia to complete our union.

Here you might imagine that three days would not have been enough for me to do all the things that often furnish material for several volumes, but I can assure you that I still had time to spare, so true is it that our Romancian authors have an admirable talent for inflating and elongating their works. As I was already very advanced with regard to the formalities, I finished all the others on the first day, and on the two following days I underwent all my proofs.

I began by dueling a rival, and I killed him. That was done in an hour. It is true that I received a serious wound, but with a little Romancian balm I was back on my feet in half an hour and in a state to signal myself the same day in a great naval battle that was fought near the port; I don't really remember why.

I performed prodigies of valor. I leapt on to an enemy ship with a valor worthy of a better fate, but having not been followed I was captured, and was already being taken into captivity while my enemies were making their descent on land when, in my despair, I thought of setting fire to the ship. It was consumed in a moment, and, after throwing myself into the sea, I was fortunate enough to reach the shore and to defend myself against those enemies I found here. I made a horrible carnage, after which I returned to my dear Rosebelle.

Alas, I no longer found her there; as the enemies were retreating they had captured her, along with many other prisoners. What despair! It was almost nightfall, and I embarked immediately in a simple fishing boat with a small number of determined men, and by favor of the darkness I reached the enemy fleet without being recognized.

I had no doubt that my princess must be on the admiral's flagship, and that vessel as identifiable among the others because of its beacons. I approached it quietly. Immediately acquiring the uniform of an enemy sailor I climbed aboard without encountering any obstacle and, passing myself off as a crewman I informed myself adroitly of what had become of Princess Rosebelle.

I discovered that she was in a cabin where the captain had just left her, prey to mortal dolors. I went in and had myself recognized by her, making her a sign at the same time to follow me on to the deck under the pretext of getting some air momentarily. She followed me, and scarcely was she there than, taking her in my arms, I leapt into the sea with her.

Here you might believe that both of us ought to have perished. Not at all; I took advantage of an admirable stratagem that I had learned in *Cleveland*. I had ordered my men to extend a large, taut net alongside the vessel, and to draw it in as soon as they heard me fall. I was obeyed exactly; we were scarcely in the water for two minutes. My men pulled Rosebelle and me out, and we got away with vomiting a little salt water we had swallowed. Meanwhile, our fall had been heard aboard the enemy ship, but no one could imagine what it was—not, at least, until we were already far away.

We arrived in the port at daybreak and I flattered myself that we would be welcomed with public acclamations, but what was my astonishment when I saw myself laden with chains and taken to prison! I was accused of intelligence with the enemy, and the foundation of the accusation was the boldness with which I had leapt on to an enemy ship and mingled among them without receiving any wound—and it was added that it was, as the price of that treason that Princess Rosebelle had been returned to me.

If I had had time to abandon myself to regrets and dolors, that would have been a fine opportunity, but I did not have a moment to lose; I hastened to accomplish in summary all the dolorous ceremonial appropriate to such occasions, and scarcely had I arrived in prison than better-informed judges returned me to liberty, even heaping me with eulogies and thanks.

I still had nearly an entire day left and, in consequence, half the work still to do. I nearly had too much. There was a magnificent tourney, to which I was invited. I was sure of carrying off the prize, in accordance with the laws of Romancia, and did not fail to do so. It was a rich bracelet, which the victor had to give, as the rule dictated, to the lady of his thoughts. Now, as the princesses had judged it appropriate that day to attend the tourney in masks, I made the worst blunder one can imagine. I went to present my bracelet to Princess Rigriche, whom I mistook for the adorable object of my prayers.

It is unnecessary to ask whether Princess Rigriche was satisfied with my present. She became immensely arrogant; she stood up, swollen with pride and made all the most agreeable little gestures she could invent immediately, after which, unmasking, as was customary, she enabled me to see a face so ugly that, honestly believing that she was wearing two masks, I waited for her to take off the second, and I was about to ask her to do so when I recognized my mistake, by virtue of a slight sound nearby.

Princess Rosebelle had fallen in a faint. She was carried to her apartment unconscious and devoid of sentiment. A cruel situation! I foresaw all the consequences of that catastrophic adventure. *What will my dear Rosebelle think?* I said to myself. Alas, I could see only too clearly what she already thought. What would her brother think? What would become of me? All those reflections, which I made in an instant, seized me so sharply that I fell unconscious in my turn, overwhelmed by dolor.

People hastened to help me, and as time was precious, I recovered my senses. I opened my eyes, and what did I see?

Princess Rigriche holding me in her arms, calling me "my dear prince," with the action of a person ardently interested in my conservation, and doubtless regarding me as her lover. I confess that I shivered, and of all my proofs, I believe that was the moment in which I suffered the most. I quit her abruptly in order to run to Princes Rosebelle,

A new adventure: the great paladin Zazaraph came to meet me and claimed that I must reckon with him for the scorn that I had shown his sister.

"Me, scorn for Princess Rosebelle!" I said to him, utterly transported. "Oh, I adore her! The gods are my witnesses..." But it was futile. The affair, he said, had exploded; the insult was too sensible. In a word, he had already drawn his sword, and he was threatening to dishonor me if I did not defend myself.

What could I do? One of the singular resources that are only found in Romancia got me out of difficulty. It was forbidden for princes to settle their quarrels on the solemn day of a tourney. The magistrates sent us an order, under pain of degradation, to postpone our combat until the following day. That was all that I wanted, in the hope that I would have disabused Rosebelle and obtained a pardon for my scorn. In fact, I went to find her and justified myself so well, with all the marks of a passion so tender and so veritable, that I perceived that she was very glad to find me innocent. The reconciliation was soon made. The great paladin entered into it for his part, and I believed that all my ordeals were concluded, when Princess Rigriche came to add a very embarrassing scene to them.

She was a stout little person, as lively as anyone who had ever been seen. I was doubtless the first lover who had ever rendered homage to her attractions, and perhaps she did not hope to find a second. She seized the opportunity, as they say, by the hair. At any rate, with wrath and jealousy painted in her eyes, outraged by the fashion in which I had quit her to run to see Princess Rosebelle, she came to find me herself, as a conquest that belonged to her, or a slave escaped from her chain.

She began with very sharp reproaches, to which I made no response. Her reproaches softened gradually to the extent of calling me fickle boy, and enabled me to hope for a facile pardon; but there was an augmentation of embarrassment on my part, and all that I could do was to mumble between my teeth an inept compliment that she did not hear.

Meanwhile, Rosebelle was smiling maliciously, and Prince Zazaraph was showing less restraint. Rigriche perceived that, and, seeing that I was showing no disposition to repair my fault, her sweet talk was soon succeeded by such atrocious insults that I had no other recourse than to surrender the place to her. She retired in her turn, her heart swollen with chagrin, but as I did not have any remedy for that, we had no difficulty forgetting that comical scene in order to make our preparations to depart together the following day.

I expressed some anxiety in that regard because I had no equipage, but the prince assured me that I ought not to worry about it, because it was the custom in Romancia to furnish the princes who had lived here, gratuitously, with everything necessary to them on such occasions, and that I would have reason to be satisfied.

In fact, when we got up with the dawn the following day, we found equipages all ready, such as only Romancia can furnish.

Conclusion
and a lamentable catastrophe.

Oh, to what strange vicissitudes are human things subject! The great paladin and I were two great princes, famous heroes, mounted on two superb palfreys. Golden bridles and saddles and horse-blankets heightened the magnificence of our train. The harness of our equipage was no less rich. Gold, silver and precious stones glittered everywhere. All our officers were remarkable above all for their good looks, and would even have been admired if the advantage given to us by our noble and gracious air had not attracted all gazes to us.

We were riding to either side of a magnificent caleche, the richness of which effaced everything imaginable of the most beautiful. Four golden columns around which wound an emerald vine, the grapes of which were rubies and sapphires, supported the imperial, and the imperial itself was so beautiful that it put the firmament to shame. In the depths of that fine carriage our two princesses shone, at least as much as two of the most beautiful stars in the sky; the splendor of their beauty, heightened by an expression of satisfaction that animated their beautiful eyes, dazzled the world.

No assemblage of men and women so complete in perfections great and small, had ever been seen. The acclamations of people accompanied us everywhere. We found all roads strewn with flowers, the air perfumed with exquisite odors, and musical choirs at intervals that sang the praises of our exploits and the beauty of our princesses.

Finally, already having covered a considerable distance, I believed that I was on the point of arriving at the terminus when a fatal instant stole a perfect happiness from me; but in order to understand that cruel event fully it is necessary to take the matter forward and warn the readers that I am about to change tone.

In the depths of Languedoc there is a gentleman named Monsieur de la Brosse, who, retired to his land, combines rural amusements with that of reading, which he loves passionately. Although he knows enough to prefer good books to bad ones, he nevertheless reads a few romances, less by virtue of the esteem in which he holds them than because he likes to read all books. That gentleman has a sister who has just married a gentleman of the neighborhood named Monsieur des Mottes, and in order to make a double alliance, Monsieur de la Brosse married Monsieur des Mottes' sister at the same time.

While that double marriage was being negotiated, and when it was still on the eve of conclusion, Monsieur de la Brosse, having his head filled with a long sequence of romances that he had read recently, dreamed in a long and profound slumber the entire story that you have just read. After being metamorphosed into Prince Fan-Férédin, he made Monsieur des Mottes into the great paladin Zazaraph. He changed his sister to Princess Anemone, his mistress into Princess Rosebelle, and composed the entre sequence of adventures that has just been narrated.

Now that gentleman, previously Prince Fan-Férédin, is me, not to displease you, and judge, in consequence, how astonished I was, on waking up, to find myself Monsieur de la Brosse again!

I remained so struck by the loss that I had suffered, that all day, I could not think about anything else, and when Monsieur des Mottes came to see me in the morning I said to him: "Oh, Prince Zazaraph, now much the two of us have lost! Have you seen Princess Anemone? What do you think of the folly of Rigriche? Oh, the beautiful diamonds! How I regret that bracelet! Shall we soon arrive in Dondindandia?"

It is easy to imagine that such words astonished Monsieur des Mottes strangely, and I saw the moment coming when he was about to believe that my head had turned, when a loud burst of laughter I emitted reassured him. He started to laugh himself as he asked me for an explanation of what I had just said.

"No," I replied, "it's a long story that I only want to narrate before a complete audience. We're all due to dine together today; after dinner I'll regale you with the story of my adventures, and even yours, which you don't know."

I kept my word, and my story, or my dream, gave them all such a great pleasure that since then, in order to conserve a little debris of my former fortune, we often call one another, in jest, Princes Fan-Férédin and Zazaraph, and Princesses Anemone and Rosebelle. Furthermore, I have been asked to put my story in writing. Friend reader, you have just read it. I hope that it has given you pleasure.

PIERRE-FRANÇOIS GODARD DE BEAUCHAMPS: *FUNESTINE*

PART ONE

Funestine, Princess of Australia,[53] came into the world under the most malign constellation. The fays who presided over her birth were all old or malevolent; they only endowed her with hateful qualities. Earthquakes and phenomena in the sky all seconded their ill humor; an aurora borealis made distinctly legible in luminous letters so large that they were visible in the four continents of the world the terrible words: *All monsters are not in Africa.*

The king, her father, was so frightened by her ugliness and the consequences it might have that, not wanting to give the queen the chagrin of raising a creature so deformed, he had her exposed to the beasts in his menagerie. The panthers and tigers of our continent are lambs by comparison with Australian animals; if, by misfortune, a single one escaped from its cage it devastated twenty leagues of the country in a quarter of an hour. The king of Sweden has killed fewer Muscovites than the humans one such creature devours in a single meal. At the sight of the prey thrown to them, they recoiled in fear.

---

[53] This is not the large island nowadays known by that name, which was still largely unmapped in 1737, its partially-explored coasts being known as "New Holland." This "Australia" is the imaginary Terra Australis [austral continent] hypothesized by several geographers trying to add additional symmetry to distribution of land on the world map as it was conceived prior to 1700.

The following year, the queen, who was told that her first child had been stillborn, gave birth to a second. She was beautiful, compared to her sister, but she had neither grace nor gentility; she was one of those human creatures who vegetate, and of whom one speaks neither good nor ill, very similar to a quantity of others you find every day at spectacles or the Tuileries.

The genius Clair-obscur was traveling through the air. He was surprised to read the celestial inscription. By virtue of a curiosity fortunate for Funestine, he wanted to see what species the newborn monster was. The young princess, lying on the ground, uttered horrible screams that drew him to the menagerie. He has said since that at the sight of an object so hideous he was tempted to flee. An impulse of compassion stopped him.

That genius was a benevolent fellow accustomed to doing good, a habit that in more difficult to give up than that of doing harm, because one finds more pleasure in it, according to modern philosophers who claim to know the heart and dabble in giving it over-refined metaphysical definitions. He put Funestine in a flap of his robe and carried her to his palace twenty thousand leagues from Australia; he confided her to nurses and governesses, who were on the point of strangling her more than once, so disgusting and ill-tempered was she. After three months she had teeth and fingernails, of which she made use in order to bite and scratch.

A son had just been born to Clair-obscur as beautiful as Funestine was ugly; as he was formed by the blood of a mortal woman, and the wives of genii influence the nature and destiny of their children, the little prince was submissive to all the eventualities of the human species, subject to death, and condemned, in spite of his ambition, only to reign over two thirds of the earth: a miserable share, of which he complained subsequently with as much bitterness as the son of Philip of Macedon did in his time.

By virtue of a caprice for which he would have had difficulty giving a reason, he genius took it into his head that he would one day unite Funestine and Formosa—that was the name of his son. He refrained from communicating such a bizarre project to anyone—they would have mocked His Elementary Majesty—but in secret he took all the measures that might enable it to succeed, or render it less ridiculous. Such is the empire of reason over all creatures that the most eccentric and despotic in their determinations strive to give them an appearance of justice. The insensate prince who said: "Let them hate me as long they fear me," explained his thought poorly; he wanted to be feared and approved.

Formosa's mother took charge of his education; she had a brother, a great philosopher, who had initiated her since her childhood in the most profound mysteries of the Cabala; she had made use during her pregnancy of the enlightenment she had acquired to prevent the fays from witnessing the birth of her son; they were very offended by that, but they had missed the opportunity to do him harm, and could not do anything about it.

Both of them applied themselves entirely to equipping the young prince with a character worthy of the great destiny that awaited him, but, seeing that success only responded in a mediocre fashion to their cares, they had recourse to a remedy, which might have succeeded in spite of all the obstacles, if, by virtue of a fatality common to all things down here, the poorly-extended tenderness of that new Thetis had not destroyed it, or at last rendered all its efficacy futile: a fine subject of moralizing for some reflective mind.[54]

In the western part of Mount Caucasus there is a vast cavern where the children of the earth had assembled when they formed the project of scaling the heavens and expelling the gods therefrom. In the depths of that cavern a river had its source, the water of which, more transparent and stronger than

---

[54] Thetis was the mother of Achilles, whose attempt to render him invulnerable by sipping him in a magical stream was flawed in the matter of his heel.

that of Barbades,[55] had the virtue of dissipating al human weakness. It was necessary to roll there for eight successive days over a sharp sand, which, insinuating itself into all the capacity of the body formed new blood and new flesh: a dolorous proof, but infallible.

In the course of an obscure night, the queen, holding Formosa on her knees, climbed with her brother, the prince, into a chariot drawn by aerial tortoises, as rapid as terrestrial ones are slow. Already, all the ceremonies, scrupulously observed, promised a fortunate result. Already, the brother and sister were flattering themselves, one with having a nephew and the other a son, who would be the ornament and delight of the universe. In fact, the prince had sustained the fatal bath for seven days, and had emerged more handsome, more vigorous and almost perfect. The gods, who laugh at the vain hopes of mortals, were waiting for the eighth.

Everything seemed to be complete when Formosa uttered piercing screams with which the grotto and the mountain resounded in the distance. His alarmed mother ran to him, her brother made vain efforts to retain her; drawn by a superior force, she leapt into the river; she found her son with closed eyes and motionless; she moaned, she tore her hair, she thought he was dead; in order to make sure of it she put her hand to his heart at the very moment when the last two vices that were concentrated there were about to emerge. Her action arrested their flight; nothing was capable subsequently of expelling them entirely.

Only too happy to carry her dear prince away in good health, she paid little attention to what was lacking in her work; she was even blind enough to think that those two vices, which were one day to disfigure the excellence of his other qualities, were apparent perfections, or, at least, that they were

---

[55] *Eau de Barbades* [i.e., Barbados] was an alternative name for water mixed with lemon juice, although it was also sometimes applied to an alcoholized concoction reputed for its medicinal qualities.

redeemed by so many virtues that they would escape the most clear-sighted eyes. How many mothers resemble her!

It will be divined without difficulty that I am talking about pride and the love of praise, monsters that seem opposed, but which are maintained and augmented by the contradiction that ought to destroy them. How can the scorn that one has for people be reconciled with the passionate desire to be praised by them? Anyone who does not understand that can serve as an example of it.

Formosa's beauty was proportionate to his age; it became more ravishing from day to day. His penetration and his vivacity left nothing for the masters who instructed him to do except instruct themselves by means of his questions or his replies. Was he doing his exercises? Skill, grace and strength flowed around him? So many marvels were not made either for his happiness or that of the human race; his pride increased with his talents; it was soon limitless; his most outrageous flatterers could not dissimulate its excess.

Not to ask anything of him was to lack respect for him; to have recourse to his protection was to render oneself importunate. Perhaps he was more tractable when one praised him? No. Although he loved praises immeasurably, by virtue of an inconceivable eccentricity, the finest and most delicate revolved him; they appeared to him to be vulgar, insipid and unworthy of him. Disconcerted poets, believing that, if he was insensitive to their incense, he would be flattered by their satires, composed specimens of every kind, against everyone. Few were fortunate enough not to follow the torrent. The prince, even more just than superb, had the most extravagant beaten with rods, and he sent the rest to work in the mines with one eye fewer.

More accessible toward foreigners, he constrained himself in order to gain them, without compensating them when he became their master. With regard to his subjects, he regarded them as slaves born to obey, to whom he was granting mercy by not taking away their lives, even unjustly. That scorn was not limited to men. The female sex was also its object.

The most charming, the most virtuous and the most respectable women were, he said, public pestilences against whom one could not be too much on one's guard; his heart did not speak in their favor; his wit, aided by his memory, furnished the most piquant and bitter darts against them.

The good Clair-obscur, astonished by the character of his son, learned with chagrin that the queen was the innocent cause of it; he punished her as if she were culpable, and repudiated her. He made Formosa a few remonstrations, which were poorly received. Not wanting to embitter him, he let him live in accordance with his whim. Perhaps he flattered himself that time would soften such an arrogant humor; perhaps he even regarded it as the kind of noble pride that, in the opinion of princes, is a sublime sentiment and the most glorious prerogative of their birth and rank.

Formosa was only sixteen years old when he was seen to dispose himself for the conquest the world, with all the more ardor because he wanted to punish people for having penetrated his faults and having dared to talk about them. It is true that, after his conquests, when age had made room for reflection, he had frequent changes of mind, which humiliated him, and then tried to make people forget, by means of his benefits, his clemency and his justice, the harshness of his original mores; he experienced more than once, dolorously, that it is easier to alienate the human heart than to regain it, but I am anticipating the order of events too much. I shall return to Funestine.

She was increasing in ugliness and indocility. People wondered what would become of such a monster. Only the genius, to the great astonishment of his entire court, loved her, and continually redoubled his cares and his tenderness for her. He could read the future, albeit in a confused manner, and seeing, or believing, what would happen one day, he became firmer in his designs.

In order to accustom Formosa to the sight of Funestine, he sometimes made them come to one another's apartments.

Fruitless attempts: the young prince uttered loud cries and fled, weeping. For her part, the princess only strove to approach him in order to pinch him or tear out his hair. Such a marked antipathy put Clair-obscur in despair, but he did his best to dissimulate it.

A further incident gave him even more pain; he perceived that the queen, his wife, whom he then loved passionately, suffered his attentions for Funestine impatiently, and that, imagining that she was the fruit of some secret intrigue, she sought to avenge herself for an unknown rival on the object that reminded her incessantly of her husband's infidelity. From secret murmurs she progressed to overt complaints, and threats soon succeeded the complaints.

He discovered and dissipated several conspiracies, the last of which was the most dangerous. The princess, who was only flattered by bizarre things, only regarded as pleasures things that were not pleasant for anyone else. A great lake bathed the walls of the palace, which was often agitated. Ordinarily, she chose to go out on it when the waves were elevated with the greatest violence. The slaves who crewed the boat were bribed. By whom? No one knows; the queen's brother was accused of it, but he was too clever to take his measures so poorly. The little vessel was pierced in several places, and was soon ready to sink.

Funestine saw with transports of rage that even her women, intimidated by the danger, preferred a certain death, by throwing themselves into the waves, to the shipwreck that might not happen. The boat, almost submerged, wandered freely between step rocks; the roar of irritated winds and the sound of the thunder that covered her with sulfur and flames; the horror of the darkness, rendered more frightful by pale flashes of lightning; even the death of which she was about to be the prey, augmented her fury but did not frighten her, although she had scarcely entered hr tenth year.

In Clair-obscur's cabinet there was a marvelous mirror, to which its maker, prevented by death, had not been able to put the final touches. That mirror, although imperfect, presented to the eyes an image of everything that was happening on earth; in truth, one could not distinguish ether the places nor the persons, but the genius substituted for that by means of a great familiarity with the world rather by the strength of his intellect. He saw someone on the point of shipwreck who was confronting the danger with an intrepid eye.

Always occupied with Funestine, he flew to her apartment; he searched for her, asking in vain for information from her women, who hid, weeping, and kept silent. He no longer doubted that it was the dear object of his complaisance that was about to lose her life. He send to her aid the lightest of zephyrs, who, redoubling his agility in order to please him, found the princess unconscious, lying on a plank, the boat having broken against a reef. He snatched her from the death that was already seizing her, and carried her on his wings into the Palace of Eventualities.

That palace was the work of Clair-obscur; he had built it for Funestine as soon as he had perceived that she was putting his entire court into combustion. At the extremity of his estates there was a desert island about seven hundred and thirty-five leagues in circumference. In order to render it inaccessible he raised all around it an immense volume of water, which, condensed and hardened, appeared to the sight to be a mountain bristling with blocks of ice. He had only left a single passage defended by two fortresses, which served as entrance and exit to a harbor, the broad and comfortable basin of which could contain two thousand ships of a hundred cannons.

Having done that, he ordered the subaltern genii who recognized him as their sovereign to transport there from all parts of the world what was needed to render it agreeable and fertile. They obeyed, and that is why the different cantons of the world lack today things of which they were despoiled then.

Astonished nature saw forests and meadows grow in the most arid places and the most frightful precipices change into delightful countryside terminated by valleys that flatter the sight, cut by streams that are the ornament and wealth of the places they irrigate. Majestic rivers that never overflow are

198

covered with vessels that bring abundance everywhere; neither hail nor frost ever destroy inopportunely the imminent hope of the avid laborer; the seasons are only felt there in their charms, with no devouring chill or excessive heat. The atmosphere, always serene and always temperate, is not subject there to those sudden and annoying variations that cause storms and desolation. Overwhelming languors and sharp maladies are banished therefrom, and death is a term unknown there; no one there would ever cease to live if they did not get it into their heads after a few centuries that there is a more voluptuous life than the one they are abandoning. The priests of the land have no recourse to pious artifices to add savor to their dogmas; the truth guides them, rendering them persuasive; they are disinterested and love one another.

The center of the island was chosen to construct the admirable edifice of which I shall strive to give an idea. The description I shall give, after an irreproachable voyager, might perhaps appear to be above plausibility, but I beg the reader not to think that there is nothing beyond what he can comprehend or imagine. Accustomed only to see little things enclosed within the narrow confines of an education proportionate to the feebleness of our enlightenment, we treat as imposture and chimera everything that does not fall under our senses, much as, an Arab author says, a mite that had never seen an elephant might judge by its own smallness that there can be no mass of flesh in the universe so heavy and so intelligent.

A long and specious avenue, a fine and perpetually green lawn planted with four rows of cedars, led to a vast esplanade paved with Oriental jasper, around which was a balustrade of onyx agate; beneath, two broad canals lined with porphyry offered to the eyes birds of every species and fish of every size; facing it, nine courtyards rose up one after another, forming a perspective of which the vestibule of the palace was the viewpoint.

The first was entered via a bronze grille gilded with molded gold, posed on an alabaster bas-relief. It was flanked at the four corners by large pavilions in white marble, the roofs of which were laminated lead gilded at the back. In the wings, of the same marble and the same architecture, there were two large guard-rooms on the ground floor, with rooms for the soldiers and the serving officers above; the foremost received pay of a one-ounce diamond and two marcs of gold per day, the others in proportion. All were nourished and maintained in arms, garments and underclothes. That guard, comprised of four thousand men, was renewed every year; those who were ruined by gambling or other expenses were expelled ignominiously; the thrifty were placed in the exchequer or the fortresses; they had the choice.

The second, higher than the first but of almost identical form, was in lapis lazuli; it served as guardrooms to six thousand men, who were not subsidized. It was thought that it would be insulting to gentlemen such as they were, or said they were, to give hem wages; they were recompensed— which is to say that after two years, those who wished to retire could do so freely; they were given the most advantageous certificates, twenty thousand gold pieces, a bushel of diamonds and a well beaten plot of land; the chiefs had governments, principalities and as many wives as they wanted, chosen from the most illustrious families on the island, to whom a dowry of a million sultanins was given.

In the third, clad in turquoises and topazes, artfully embedded, were the palace stables, in which twelve thousand horses were nourished that only served for squires and pages. The princess only ever went out in a chariot harnessed to white unicorns or lynxes; she was seen to go hunting once mounted on a sable marten, and was so discontented with its speed that she had it killed in front of her.

Inside was a marvelous stucco, the secret of which has been lost, the whiteness of which nothing could tarnish. The ceiling, painted in fresco by the best masters, represented hunts, tourneys or cavalry battles. The parquets, pillars, paneling and racks and mangers were in sandalwood; the bridles, saddles and harness were enriched with precious stones, the hooves were gold, the shovels, forks and curry-combs silver, and the halters braided from gold and silk. Outside there were granite drinking-troughs and superb apartments for the squires and pages; the horses, Turkish, Arab, Danish, Neapolitan or Persian, had been the stock of races celebrated in history, of which some people still conserve the offspring.

The fourth, of coral charged with leaves of fine gold, served for subaltern officers, all clad in scarlet coats embroidered in silver, and so well-disciplined that they were only permitted to communicate with one another by means of signs.

The fifth, of Corinthian bronze, of a workmanship superior to the material, although it was the most precious in the world, was distributed in several chambers where justice was rendered in the most pompous apparel. Affectionate merchants did not overload it by half with pointless baubles; publishers avid for profit did not stun passers-by with the gaudy title of a conceited novelette to which a hungry author had just given birth. The barristers, incredibly, kept silent in the middle of the day. As the trials only lasted a minute and the inhabitants of the island were enemies of all quibbling, the judges only assembled every five years. Do not imagine however, that those judges were less busy; they ornamented themselves, they invented fashions and they cut out paper shapes.

In the sixth, the simplest of all, although it was green campan marble, were the aviaries, whose trellises were emeralds and sapphires.

The seventh, of mother-of-pearl encrusted with rubies, was for the princess's maids of honor and chambermaids; there were five hundred of the former, each of whom had a staff composed of four hundred domestics, and thirteen thousand of the latter, each of whom was served by three mutes and three black eunuchs.

It was in the eighth, of aventurine, that the various oratories of the palace were. In the principal chapel, represented in the figure of a rhinoceros sixteen feet tall, carved from a single lodestone, was Xisquinima, the tutelary god of the island; in the others there were twelve hundred one-cubit pagodas, each made of a single diamond.

The ninth, separated from the other eight by a solid gold balustrade, each baluster of which was a genius clad like a Swiss royal guard, was the courtyard of the palace proper; the pavement was a mosaic of all sorts of precious stones in which Clair-obscur had traced the history of all times in hieroglyphs. The most curious was a singular figure; considered from a certain direction it represented a goat with the feet of a mule, the head of a screech-owl and the maw of a famished mastiff that even bit the hands that fed it; seen from another point of view it was a Japanese bonze holding a cock in one hand and a brazier on the other, from which thick smoke was emerging.

Twelve amethyst pillars sustained a vast hall of rock crystal, the doors and windows of which were carbuncles. That hall opened over two long enfilades of the same crystal, furnished with even more taste than luxury. To the right was Funestine's apartment, composed of twenty rooms on the same floor, all fitted with mirrors of a single piece and similarly separated by diamond borders. To the left were her bathrooms; as she liked odors, the tubs and the furniture were ambergris.

I ought not to forget the library, richer by the quality than the number of books that composed it, although there were nearly three hundred thousand. There were found the originals of the works that were to be made by Aulnoy, Murat, Durand and so many others,[56] who were given subsequently to the

---

[56] The reference to Catherine Durand Bédacier (1670-1736) in association with Aulnoy and Murat is a trifle surprising, as she was best known as the author of works in the genre of salacious fake memoirs. She did however, interpolate one *conte de fées*, "La Fée Lubantine," in *Le Comtesse de Mortane* (1700) and two more in *Les Petits soupers de l'été de l'année 1699, ou Galantes aventures, avec L'Origine des fées* (1702, allegedly in Amsterdam): "Le Prodige d'amour" and "L'Origine des fées," which not only includes an account of the origin of the fays, as the offspring of Jupiter and a nymph, but also "explains" their apparent disappearance from the world.

ridicule of imitating them; one saw the portraits of all the authors, those I have named being crowned by rays of light, and those whose names I have kept silent by bats' wings.

The historiographer Albupipargarnos, from whose journal I have faithfully extracted what I have just reported, continues thus:

"With regard to the gardens, they appeared to me to be so marvelous, so surprising and so far above the palace that, intoxicated with admiration, I did not even imagine that they could be described. I shall not say a word about the fountain of liquid pearls of the most beautiful water in the world, which rounded out in falling into a basin of old Japanese porcelain. I saw three hundred vessels laden with it without the source weakening or diminishing.

"Those gardens still subsisted in the times of Cyrus, who walked there several times with Araspes. I am not astonished that the author of his voyages made no mention of them; he was too much an enemy of the marvelous to talk about them, but I am surprised that they escaped the sublime Sethos."[57]

When she awoke, Funestine darted distracted and scornful glances in all directions; scarcely touched by the marvels that surrounded her, she contented herself with asking coldly whether the palace in which she found herself was hers, and whether all the people she saw where there to obey her. Her principal maid of honor, clad in a long cape of hummingbird plumes, dropped to her knees and responded, stammering, that she was the absolute mistress of their lives, that she could dispose of them at her whim like toys and dolls; that Clair-obscur

---

Beauchamps had probably read a 1733 reprint of the latter volume, and seems to have taken some inspiration from it.

[57] Sethos, an Egyptian pharaoh mentioned by Herodotus, is the eponymous protagonist of a 1731 pseudohistorical romance with Masonic influences by Jean Terrasson, sometimes cited as a source for Mozart's *Magic Flute*. He is mentioned in passing in Bougéant's account of Romancia.

had not only given her the palace and all the treasures it contained, but also...

She was about to make a long speech, when the princess, who did not like them, made her shut up.

"Dress me; I want to go for a walk."

The person responsible for putting on her slippers could not find them, and no one dared trespass on the rights of her charge. The impatient Funestine leapt out of bed barefoot and made an immodest glissade; other ceremonial followed, equally impertinent, to put a little lavender eau-de-vie on a slight scratch she had made on her elbow. Then she was begged humbly to choose between twenty combing-robes that were displayed to her sight one after another.

"Give me the first that comes to hand," she said, angrily, "and get on with it."

Then she was brought a dressing-table, the same one that the Graces had made for Venus. She tipped it over, adding with a peevish expression that she did not want her hair done and that they were very bold not to wait for her orders. She went into a gallery in which several seamstresses were embroidering some upholstery; she thought it in detestable taste, expelled them and had the fabric thrown on the fire.

When she had descended into the gardens, and odor of lemon trees and bergamot, delectable for anyone else, threw her into a fury. She summoned he gardener.

"Wretch!" she said to him, "do you want to make me expire?" Have those trees, which I detest, uprooted immediately and put pots of tuberoses in their place."

The simple fellow, not very skillful in his art, not knowing anything of the character of Funestine, represented to her modestly that the odor of tuberoses was even stronger than that of lemon trees, and that it would go to Her Highness's head with even more violence. It would have been better for him to obey than to reply. "I believe," she said, "that you're resisting me. Imprison this old dotard, whose physiognomy displeases me."

She made other changes so bizarre, and gave orders so strange, that if the hour for the midday meal had not ended the promenade, she would have turned everything upside-down. Her retinue, although forewarned about her humor by Clair-obscur, were nevertheless frightened by it.

She passed abruptly through a crowd of courtiers at whom she did not deign to glance, went into the dining room and threw herself precipitately into an armchair placed at a table laden with golden vessels, the work of the Germain of his time.[58] Her napkin barely unfolded, she uncovered the first dish that came to hand, lifted the lid of a second, of a third, and successively of all those she could reach, but, only finding millet, she cried: "What! Am I being mocked, or do you take me for a canary?"

The maître-d'hôtel of the quarter, taking off his head a large hat of almond-bark covered with little bells, an attribute of his responsibility, prostrated himself and said: "Very indulgent, very tranquil and very virtuous sovereign, your humble servants are attentive to their duties, and the sentiments of respectful admiration that Your Highness's divine qualities inspire in them are too intimately engraved in the depths of their hearts to dare even to imagine the criminal idea of displeasing you. The genius Clair-obscur, wanting this palace to be a fecund source of delights for you, has taken care to remove therefrom anything that might wound your delicacy, and, fearing that the odor or sight of a kitchen might give you some pain, he has banished that disagreeable apparatus; but, his tenderness for you rendering him ingenious, he has communicated to these seeds, humble in appearance, the virtue of becoming the most delicate dishes and he most appropriate to flatter your taste. May the great, the terrible Xisiquinima punish me before your eyes if I impose anything whatsoever upon Your Highness. Millet, change into meringues, tartlets and blancmange."

---

[58] The reference is to the Rococo silversmith Thomas Germain (1673-1748)

Funestine liked those things very much, but, annoyed by the noise made by the little bells and piqued to the quick because she had not divined the mystery that had just been explained to her, she threw her napkin in the face of the speaker and ran to hide in the most remote corner of her apartment.

The rest of the day was employed in calming her down. Hunger, more persuasive than the most eloquent discourse, made her listen to reason. She supped without sulking and without getting carried away. For the first time in her life she seemed to have some pleasure. She found the metamorphosis of the millet so amusing that she could not weary of renewing it. Never before had so many tartlets and meringues been seen together, nor have they since, and never had she eaten so many of them. Her physician came to trouble her joy with the grave but unwelcome observation that the excess of the best things is harmful. She was extreme in her passions, but she loved herself, and the fear of an indigestion was capable of containing her. She distributed to her pages personally four hundred bowls of blancmange and left the table.

After supper she played quinze. She lost with an ill grace, paid up with an even worse grace, and went to bed in a very bad mood.

Surrounded by the most beautiful young women, she was not at all jealous of them because, having no idea of ugliness or beauty, when she looked at herself in a mirror, finding herself unique of her species, the good opinion she had of herself made her believe that all those who did not resemble her were monsters, and that for her alone, lavished with charms, nature had exhausted her treasures. How many Funestines does one see every day who, content with themselves, display with complaisance a grotesque face, where Callot would have found models more bizarre that those that remain to us of him?

The time was approaching when her illusion was to be dissipated. If only it were permitted to me to reveal the future, which is revealed to me at present!—but the god that enlightens me forbids me to communicate his favors. Let us obey his movements, and only inform curious mortals by degrees of the profundity and economy of his designs.

In the palace there was a certain little man named Quart-d'heure, half-courtier, half-clown, and above all, a prolific teller of tales, which he embellished with all the insipid affectations that passed through his head. The women were mad for him, as they are for everything that amuses them; he was in love with Imaé, a young Circassian whom Funestine loved then as much as she was capable of loving—which is to say that she treated her less harshly than her companions. She was one of those privileged creatures whom the gods in their leisure, sometimes take it upon themselves to render accomplished.

Quart-d'heure, wanting amour to serve his ambition, made so many intrigues that Funestine learned his name and wanted to hear him. He was sought, he arrived, he was introduced into the princess's cabinet.

"It's claimed," she said, "that you tell tales agreeably. Commence without preamble, so that I can judge."

Quart-d'heure, after a profound bow, which he made with a good enough grace took a seat, for one never tells tales standing up, unless one wants to send one's listeners to sleep, and commenced in this way:

"Somewhere in the world there is a kingdom once known by the name of Ulages and now that of Facner,[59] a country which, by virtue of its own wealth, could surpass all the others, but which, because of the industry of its inhabitants, takes its commerce to the extremities of the earth. The race of people that occupy it descends from the bellicose peoples whose valor was so deadly to the world's tyrants. They are accused of inconstancy, but that can only be, at the most, in their fashions. Thirteen hundred years of obedience to their

---

[59] The author or editor—probably the latter—inserts a footnote here in the *Cabinet des fées* version of the story decoding the anagrams as "Gaules" [Gaul] and "France."

kings show well enough that they do not like change in essential matters. They are brave, lively and intelligent. Perhaps they have in their hearts a seed of superiority that makes itself too clearly felt to their neighbors. What renders them the object of their envy is also that of their imitation. They are only jealous of themselves; a spirit of criticism and refinement, as harmful to the arts as to letters, has taken possession of the nation. The man who does most harm to others is the one who finds the most partisans and protectors.

"If I were not a subject of Your Highness, I would like to be the monarch who governs that happy people. He is a young prince with whom no one finds fault because he has none.[60] Virtuous by temperament and by religion, vice is banished from his court because it is banished from his heart, and the example of the master is a living law that is observed of its own accord. He has just concluded gloriously a war that he only undertook in order to secure peace. Unexpected successes have crowned his moderation and rendered him the heart and esteem of his enemies, who supposed foolishly that a long repose had enervated the courage of his soldiers and destroyed the sagacity of his ministers."

"Is he married?" asked Funestine, interrupting Quart-d'heure.

"Yes, Madame," he said, but his unique son, the amour and hope of his empire, is almost the same age as Your Highness."

"Why doesn't he come to see me?" she continued. "I doubt that he has a palace as beautiful as mine; I'd give him half of it, and enough treasure to subjugate one day all the nations that do not obey his father. Continue."

---

[60] Louis XV was twenty-seven years old in 1737, and the country was effectively being governed by his chief Minister Cardinal de Fleury. Fleury's diplomacy had recently enabled the concluded the War of the Polish Succession, to which the description refers in passing.

"I have said nothing to Your Highness about the ladies of Facner; she will know them via the continuation of my discourse. Princess Blanche-incarnate,[61] who is the heroine of my story, was scarcely out of childhood when, a victim of politics, she was obliged to quit her fatherland in order to go to make the happiness of a foreign realm. I ought, Madame, to give you an idea of her, in order to enable you to understand the felicity of the prince for whom she was destined."

Quart-d'heure, carried away by his passion, gazed tenderly at Imaé, who was present, and whom he believed he could describe without Funestine perceiving it. After a moment of silence, he went on:

"At fourteen years of age, her figure had a delicacy and an elegance that left nothing to be desired. An enchanting softness that tempered the vivacity of two large dark eyes, whose gleam bore trouble and admiration into hearts; a complexion of lilies and roses, sheltered from the most stubborn insomnia; a nose fashioned by the Graces; a mouth, the work of the same Graces, which only opened to allow a glimpse of admirable teeth and to say witty and obliging things, whose charm was augmented by a flattering smile; breasts, arms hands..."

Unfortunately, that portrait had too much similarity to Imaé and too little to Funestine.

"She was ugly, then, this Blanche-incarnate," she interrupted, emotionally, "since she resembles my slave so closely?"

"Pardon me, Madame," said he storyteller, stupidly, "she was the most beautiful person in the world."

"And you dare to tell me that!" she added, directing a furious gaze at him.

---

[61] The French "incarnate" does not mean the same as the English word it resembles perfectly, but rather "incarnadine" or rose-red. The princess Quart-d'heure is describing is probably Elisabeth of France, the sister of Louis XIV, who was married on the same day as her brother to Philip IV of Spain.

He sensed all his imprudence then, and, fearing for his life and that of his mistress, he had recourse to tears. They did not touch Funestine at all, who had them locked up separately in an obscure prison.

The unfortunate princess, delivered to the most bitter reflections, could not sustain the weight of her dolor, and abandoned herself to the most frightful despair. "It's true, then," she cried, striking herself in the fact and rolling on the ground. "It's true, then, that I'm ugly! I'm ugly, and I know it! I'm no longer astonished by the horror that I inspire in all those who see me. Their distracted and timid gazes ought to have told me that. Cruel gods! Is it necessary that I confess that it is just? Is it necessary that, unsatisfied by my ugliness, which is your work, you make me sense all its deformity? Enjoy your hated; Funestine is crushed by it. What am I saying? It is mistaken, that barbaric hatred; it only serves to redouble mine for you."

Then, chancing to cast her eyes upon the mirrors of her apartment, she saw herself; she shuddered; she was no longer mistress of her transports; she broke them into a thousand pieces. Calmed in appearance by their destruction, and no longer finding any object on which she could exercise her fury, she went in search of the slumber that flees far from her burning eyelids, a mollification that she could not find, and for which, perhaps, she could no longer hope.

The next day she summoned her women; they entered tremulously, and all received an absolute order never to show themselves before her.

"I no longer want," she said to them, "to be served by anyone except my squires and my pages; inform them of my will and leave me."

Clair-obscur read in his mirror what was happening in the Palace of Eventualities; he came to it, repaired the disorder and went to see Funestine. He found her in the stupid dolor that succeeds great agitations.

At the sight of the genius, her tears and sobs recommenced with more violence. He exhausted all his rhetoric in vain consolations and even more futile advice; she was incapable of hearing anything. Weary of inveighing against the gods, who even refused her death, she addressed the genius and demanded the torture of Quart-d'heure and Imaé. More embittered than humiliated by his refusal, she reproached him for being the fatal author of all her disgrace, and shut her eyes in order not to see him.

It would not have taken much for him, annoyed in his turn by the waste of his eloquence and the injustice of the little Megaera, to destroy the palace from top to bottom and to take her back instantly to Australia. The goodness of his heart made him change his design; he knew that one almost always repents of precipitate resolutions, and that it is necessary not to resort to extreme remedies until all the others have been employed. By dint of meditating on the most efficacious, an idea occurred to him that flattered him so much that, regarding it as infallible, he wasted no time realizing it.

At the commencement of the world he had loved a young person as charming as she was ambitious; more touched by the power of the genius than sensible to his tenderness, she had only appeared to respond to the latter in order to draw upon the former. In one of those unexpected moments when the mind of a coquette employs the language of the heart adroitly she had said to him: "I love you, and the confession of my weakness costs you nothing but the desire to triumph over it. I want in vain to occupy entirely the good fortune of pleasing you; two equally vexing ideas trouble me and agitate me. I fear your inconstancy, because I dread the end of my charms; I lament your lack of delicacy, if one can lament something one adores. You can reassure your lover, you can render her happy, and you're waiting for me to beg you!"

Clair-obscur, clever as he was, or believed himself to be, was less so than his mistress; he swore to her by the Deluge—a sacred oath among the genii—that he loved her madly and was ready to give her whatever proofs of it she might demand.

"Well," she said, without giving him time for reflection, "make me a fay; you can see by that request that I am thinking more about you than about myself; your felicity will be the prize of the gift you accord me. Sure of my heart you will be of my beauty."

The genius, taken for a dupe, did with a good grace what he could not refuse; he only put one tiny mental restriction on it, the effect of which she did not think of anticipating. When one obtains more than one hopes for, one only looks at things from the flattering side. A short time later she gave birth to a little fay who was the mother, grandmother and great-grandmother of another, and from that emerged the innumerable immortals who have made so many marvels of good and evil in the world.

Clair-obscur, by virtue of the reservation I mentioned, was the master of taking away or conserving the immortality of fays that he had granted to them in the person of his mistress. They were unaware of that privilege; he had forgotten it himself; it had not been used because, until then, they had rarely strayed from the gratitude that they owed him. He remembered it, and, not doubting that the hope or dread that he promised himself to employ appropriately would dispose them to collaborating in changing Funestine, he resolved to summon them.

I can hear at his point three or four of those transcendent connoisseurs whom nothing escapes and who set the tone in the alcoves of those precious imbeciles of whom they are the oracles, making an objection that they believe to be without reply. "What is the point," they will cry, on reading this passage, "of the idle author of this insipid tale making his simpleton of a genius have recourse to the fays? Whoever can give mortality can de-uglify a mortal."

Gently, Messieurs. What tells you that one is as facile as the other? What have I told you myself? That Clair-Obscur had power. I stopped at that; I have not said that he was a god, at least not a god of the *Iliad*. You know full well that you have not leafed through the book of destinies. Go on, my negligence will furnish a vaster material for your criticisms; exercise it at your ease; I permit you to laugh, but I don't promise you to be exact. Are you content? No you're not. You're seeking less to harm the work than the author. Your malignity will not find its reckoning with me; there is nothing suspect in my allegories, nothing that is susceptible to sinister applications, and nothing in my portraits that can wound religion or the delicacy of the great men I respect. Calumnies, I do not fear you.

At any rate, he ordered the fays, under penalty of incurring his indignation, to render the same day to the Palace of Eventualities. They were all together at the time, because nothing was happening in the world at that moment requiring their attention: no queen ready to give birth, and, in consequence, no prince or princess to endow with good or bad qualities.

They suspected the reason for which he was summoning them. Annoyed by such an imperious and precipitate citation, they would have liked not to obey; that was their first idea; but, unable to dispense with it, they came, after having sworn mutually not to grant anything to the pleas or threats of the genius.

"If we had been consulted," they said, as they traversed the courtyards, which they criticized one after another, "this edifice wouldn't be so ridiculous. To make something great, it isn't sufficient to lavish gold and precious stones; it requires understanding. What a confused mass of conflicting beauties! What heavy architecture! What dull distribution!" All of that was untrue, but they were annoyed. "Let's destroy this shocking building right away and precipitate its ruins to the bottom of the sea. It will only take a moment for us to build a new one, which will make our tyrant sense that our taste responds to our power."

They were about to set to work when Clair-obscur, informed of their arrival, made them enter the council. The master of ceremonies, dressed in a chameleon-skin simarrre, opened a large register, called them all by their names and attributes, and placed each one according to rank. It was perceived that two of the most powerful and most moderate were missing. As they did not reside in the empire of the others, who had neglected to inform them, Clair-obscur did not say a word; he even counted so weakly on the compliance of the remainder that he was glad to have a resource in reserve in the amity of those two, a measure of prudence that subsequent events justified.

For half an hour there as a formidable hum similar to that made by bees emerging from their hives. The ushers cried in vain for silence; it could not be imposed on the talkers, who only ceased when they were weary of babbling.

The genius, more vehement than Demosthenes and more diffuse than Cicero, said to them: "I am not complaining that, doubtless irritated against Funestine's mother, you avenged your grievances on her daughter; you did not know when she was born that I destined her for my son Formosa. I am only complaining that the knowledge of my designs for that princess had no effect on your hatred, and that, until now, you have not distributed to her any of the favorable gifts that you lavish elsewhere without choice and without measure. I have no doubt that the step to which I am lowering myself today will cause you to think again. It is in your interest and that of your glory not to discontent a sovereign to whom you have the most essential obligations, a sovereign who wants to maintain under the title of a favor what he could demand as a duty. Do not oblige me, by your ingratitude or your obstinacy, to repent of my benefits.

"Let those among you who have not contributed to the ugliness and defects of Funestine work to efface them. Out of condescension to the others I do not want to force them to destroy their work. I will add more; I pardon them in favor of good intentions. Judge all my generosity by such an affectionate discourse. I am requesting, I am not ordering; weigh that term, sense all its force and let us separate as good friends."

At those words, a general stir rose up in the assembly, which the genius saw as a bad augury. A bitter and precious fay marked by a hand gesture that she wanted to speak, and they fell silent in order to listen.

"We have been assembled," she said, "with great noise. What has been the end result of the trouble we have taken to abandon our hearths? Reproaches and threats. And, going further than that, it is demanded that we account for the usage we make of our power: an unprecedented enterprise, of which today furnishes the first example. We are free. That could be our unique response. But in order that we cannot be accused of acting by caprice in the dispensation of our authority, let us enter into detail and refute, article by article, the unmeasured discourse that has just been made to us.

"The princess is ugly, and she is hateful, of which we are the cause. Could she not be both, without us? Let us agree, however, that we are gripped by hatred for her. What appears to Clair-obscur to be an injustice is an effect of our sagacity. We know that beauty carries trouble and despair everywhere. We have preserved a thousand unfortunates from a premature death. Formosa ought to marry her, so we are obliged to work a miracle in order to render her worthy of him. Perhaps she is only too worthy. Does this father, so prejudiced in favor of his son, not know that he is to be the terror of the world, and our most mortal enemy? Does he know us poorly enough to imagine that dread of displeasing him will force us to seek his good graces? Let him learn that, unshakable in our aversions and our amities, they are as immortal as we are.

"However," she added, addressing the genius, "to show you that we are capable of generosity, when no one tries to constrain us, we will offer to serve your tenderness for Formosa by procuring him a beautiful wife, since you want so much for him to have one. Funestine has a sister, we will exhaust our power to render her accomplished. Don't expect anything more. The effort we are willing to make is great enough for no other to be demanded. See..."

"No," Clair-obscur interrupted, inflamed with anger, "No, I will not change my arrangements; this will receive the law, when I can give it. Believe me, do not abuse my mild-ness, even once..."

He did not want to finish, out of the goodness of his heart, but insulting laughter stirred his bile. "I sense that I am becoming annoyed," he continued. "Beware of that; I warn you that my anger might have terrible consequences. I will accord you another two minutes; take advantage of them to make a more reasonable resolution. After that, I shall no long-er listen to anything."

"There is no need for a longer deliberation," retorted a young hothead, gesturing with her fan. "You don't want to change your ideas, we don't want to change ours; and to show you how unsusceptible we are to dread or inconstancy, I de-clare to you in the name of my companions that Funestine will remain ugly, because you wish her to cease to be, and because Rêveuse, her sister, in whom you are not interested, is already the most beautiful person in the world. The sentence that I have just pronounced is irrevocable."

The fay was not unaware that there was a means of em-bellishing the body and soul of Funestine, but she had the mal-ice not to mention it. She even flattered herself that she had the time to raise an invincible obstacle to it.

That impertinent harangue was universally applauded. Clair-obscur made a response to it that the tumultuous assem-bly did not expect.

"Well," he cried, beside himself. "Since persuasion can-not soften the inflexibility of your hatred, it is necessary to have recourse to vengeance. Tremble, ingrates, the lighting is about to depart. I have gratified you with the precious gift of immortality; I am depriving you of it. Get out of my sight, enjoy your foolish independence and the pleasure of doing harm; it will not be for long; I consecrate you to death and all the fear that it inspires."

The assembly broke up and the fays returned home, more satisfied with having stood up to the genius than alarmed by threats that they regarded less as an effect of his power as an expression of vain resentment. The death of a few dissipated the error of the others, but their entire destruction was reserved for Formosa.

Clair-obscur, mortified by the lack of success of his enterprise, departed without seeing Funestine again. What could he have said to her? A movement of curiosity made him take the route to Australia.

He found the court in the first transports of admiration, and of the jealousy caused by the change that had just taken place in the person of Rêveuse. He saw her, and could not resist so many charms; he reminded himself that her marvelous beauty was a present from his enemies, but he found her no less beautiful and no less seductive for that.

The genius, as you have been able to observe, had scarcely more intelligence than common sense. Amour destroys one and does not augment the other. He immediately wanted to reveal his passion, but timidity closed his mouth; gazes and sighs were no use to him, Rêveuse did not perceive them. It took him two days to embolden himself. Finally, he spoke, without being interrupted, but without obtaining a response. The nonchalant princess was profoundly thoughtful, embroidering a muff. He exhausted all the fine sentiments that he had seen in modern brochures. The words of tenderness, confidence, rigor, scorn and despair were out of place and confused. Rêveuse, who did not understand that language at all, looked at him distractedly, replied evasively, and smiled, without knowing the price of a smile.

Let us leave him to forget himself with Rêveuse and return to the Palace of Eventualities.

Funestine, informed of what had happened between the fays and Clair-obscur, was irritated by it, but anger soon gave way to indignation; from day to day she seemed less agitated, less bitter and less furious. There were certain moments when one might have thought that she was no longer sensitive to her ugliness.

That calm was not an effort of reason but a consequence of exhaustion. The most excessive dolors have their term; they weaken of their own accord and become supportable. Consult fortunate people, examine what is happening in their hearts; when good fortune intoxicates them, they shudder at the very idea of its inconstancy; they could not support it without dying. Has it abandoned them? They lament, it is true, but they do not die. Time acts upon them in an imperceptible manner, futile regrets are less frequent, they cease, the sensibility dissipates, or turns to other objects. The least firm eventually adapt to their condition, however frightful it might be.

Such was the situation with Funestine, when a new genre of persecution reawakened her impatience and ill humor. The little fay who had been the last to speak in the council took it into her head, in order to clarify her doubts, to assume the form of a fly. Stubbornly attached to the sad princess she flew, without giving her any respite, over her hands, her breasts or her face, the day passed chasing it away and seeing it return. By night, hidden in her curtains, she frightened her with baleful dreams, the horror of which did not vanish when she awoke. Did she try to go back to sleep? An importunate buzzing forced her to abandon her bed, and pursued her into all the corners of her room: a torture that can only seem light to those who have never experienced it.

My readers will doubtless reproach me for letting her languish for too long; touched by the excess of her woes, they want to see an end to them; let us satisfy their impatience, since it has not been possible for me to prevent it. I beg them, however, to permit me a small digression, which is necessary to me, in order to commence my second part.

PART TWO

People complain every day about the large number of futile books that inundate the city and the provinces, and they have reason to complain of them. What do they contain, for the most part? Elongated trivia in several parts, vague ideas, hackneyed intrigues in which imagination is lacking as well as judgment, the reading of which has nothing to compensate the time that one wastes in perusing them. The instructive is neglected for the agreeable. What happens in consequence? People remain ignorant, and become bored. The authors are less to blame than general taste. Some are only bagatelles, which might be capable of being excellent things; but they want to be read, perhaps they also want to live.

A serious work is scarcely known except to its author; only frivolities are in fashion; the fair sex loves them and devours them, fops learn them and repeat them, magistrates study them, soldiers relax with them, philosophers...I am ashamed to say that philosophers amuse themselves with them. I have been dragged away by the torrent, I am writing a tale of fays. I am publishing it, only expecting to be criticized, and being the first to criticize myself. Let's get back to it.

Toward the forty-ninth degree of south latitude there is a delightful country called Thyas.[62] There, in a palace built on a hill, the two fays I mentioned above make their abode. One is Virtue, the other Imagination; united by the charming bonds of amity, they spend their days loving one another and telling one another so.

Virtue combines with a flattering and intelligent physiognomy mildness of character and solidity of sentiment; one is

---

[62] The term *thyas* is found in Virgil's *Aeneid*—a text cited elsewhere in Funestine; it is not a place name but is used as a label of a bacchanal.

prejudiced in her favor at first sight. One adores her, and never ceases to adore her, when one knows her. Too modest to take advantage of the thousand brilliant qualities that strike everyone, she appears to be unaware of them.

The goodness of her heart, which is never belied, equals or surpasses the justice and extent of her intellect; sensible, but courageous, she was able early in life to fortify herself against all the foibles of her sex; unshakable in the most overwhelming trials, fortune can do nothing against her. Her friends admire her but dare not praise her; their interests are dear to her, their pleasures are her own. Such is Virtue; I am mistaken, I have only sketched her portrait.

Imagination has in her favor the brilliant exterior that dazzles; one does not approach her without emotion or gaze at her without danger; she causes one to experience all the power of something strange. The melodious sounds of her voice pass rapidly from the ears to the heart of those who hear them. Generous and compassionate, she does not wait to be solicited; to be unfortunate is to have a right to her benefits. If she relates the most trivial anecdote, trivia acquire consequence in her mouth; she attaches as much as she amuses, the fortunate terms that alone can render her thought present themselves and arrange themselves of their own accord.

Anyone who judges her without examining her would believe her to be in love with the impossible; it is true that her vivacity bears her to the marvelous, but reason always brings her back to the simple. Beautiful, without making use of her beauty, the amour that never quits her stops in her eyes, their eloquence is deceptive; her heart is not in half of the desires to which they give birth. But what she possesses eminently is the rare talent of imitation; she transforms herself in those she imitates; one sees them, and they are transformed themselves; she only ever makes use of them in bagatelles; far from wounding anyone, the originals recognize themselves, laughing, in their copies.

During one of those delightful summer nights that are preferable to the glare of the most beautiful day, the two of them were walking together on a terrace planted with orange trees, below which the most beautiful river in the world meanders. Virtue stopped and looked at her without speaking.

"What are you thinking about?" her friend asked her.

"I'm admiring," she replied, "the accidents of light that the moon's rays produce; the effect appears admirable to me. You know that I love objects of that sort, and occupy myself with them pleasurably."

"Is there not a danger," said Imagination, "of pausing on it for too long? One passes from one idea to another, one goes further than one would wish, and often, when one returns to oneself, one is surprised to find oneself less sensible to the things one sees than to those one does not see."

"I don't know," said Virtue, "what danger there is in the sight of a river; we're a long way from it. If I were in a boat, I'd be timid; I confess that the calm that reigns wouldn't reassure me, but..."

"It renders you pensive," Imagination went on, "and that's a great deal."

"You're making an unjust war on me," said Virtue. "Why are you reproaching me for an imaginary reverie? Do you suspect me...?"

"No," Imagination continued again, "I don't suspect you of weakness; but I can't hide from you that I've being doing violence to my curiosity for a long time; I'm dying to know the depths of your heart. Your merit has obtained a thousand admirers, does none of them appear to you to be worthy of the slightest return? Perhaps you are sensible without crime; whatever your choice might be, it shouldn't make you blush. Speak; I'm only seeking to inform myself in order to approve. Name your conqueror, and you'll make two people happy at once, your friend and your lover."

"I know," said Virtue, "that there are engagements one can make without offending one's duty; I know that here are some that duty authorizes and justifies; but I am not in that circumstance. People believe me to be severe, and perhaps, in fact, I am. Men hardly ever deliver themselves to amour when they do not see the hope of its consequence. Cares have been rendered to me; to whom can they not be rendered? A constancy has sometimes been sworn to me proof against all the obstacles I could expose to it. People seek to deceive me, or to deceive themselves. The most urgent retreat did not surprise me; I was too indifferent, too guarded against men to regret their homages. They did not interest either my heart or my self-esteem. But you, charming Imagination, object of the worship and the prayers of everything that respires, how many things you would be able to tell me if your confidence equaled my amity!"

"You are going to see," she replied, embracing her, "that I am more sincere, or less reasonable, than you. There are few genii who have not sighed for me; born lively and curious, I receive them with complaisance, but without mystery. I sometimes had ten or twelve in my chamber; it was Madame d'Ussé's aviary.[63] I took advantage of their talents and knowledge; my mind was enlightened without any cost to my heart. Mistress then of my sentiments, I treated those rivals with an equality that suspended their anxiety and their jealousy; the pleasure of seeing me, the fear of being deprived of me by an indiscreet outburst, maintained between them an apparent union, the sincerity of which I did not take the trouble to fathom. That kind of life had its charms, but it had its voids. I abandoned it, without thinking that I would ever regret it; I was deluding myself and I soon repented of my inconstancy, and without you, amiable Virtue, I would still be repenting it.

"At my father's court there was a young woman named Novelty. I made her acquaintance; sympathy spared us the

---

[63] The reference is to Anne-Théodore-Françoise de Carvoisin, Marquise d'Ussé, nowadays remembered as a correspondent of Voltaire. The philosopher spent time at the Château d'Ussé, of which she was the chatelaine in 1737, and which nowadays claims to be the château that inspired Perrault's "La Belle au bois dormant."

care of studying one another; we liked one another as soon as we saw one another, and we became inseparable. We agreed to confide to one another without reserve all the ideas that passed through our heads. The most singular and the most bizarre appeared to us to be the most amusing, and, so to speak, the only ones that could amuse us. Novelty, ever ingenious, always occupied with the desire to please me, seemed to reproduce herself continually. What fire! What sallies! What projects! She was a Proteus that took on a thousand different forms.

"She had a friend about whom she told me so many good things that I did not give her any repose until she had brought her to me. Fabulous—that was her name—was as keen to meet me as I was to meet her, and she responded to my eagerness. I see her come into my room; I fly to meet her, I caress her, I admire her, I felicitate her. Novelty has not flattered her; she possesses that which is most seductive in the art of invention and speaking well; the Graces preside over all her discourse; one cannot weary of hearing her; the most incredible fictions take on an air of plausibility in her hands that verity itself sometimes lacks.

"The joyful commerce of these two charming girls made me forget all my suitors; they wanted to complain; I did not listen to them. The most just reproaches weary us when they touch the pleasures that we are savoring, Amour..."

Suddenly interrupting herself, she became pensive. Then, resuming speaking, she cried: "No, Funestine, you shall not always be unfortunate! The rigor of your fate moves me to compassion, and the hatred of your enemies revolts me." Addressing Virtue, surprised by that sudden emphasis, she continued: "Would you like to help me in performing an action worthy of you and of me? Let us go and extract the Princess of Australia from her misfortunes and imperfections. I'll tell you her story on the way, your help will answer to me for the success of my ideas."

Virtue, who never let an opportunity to be useful to the unfortunate escape, seized with pleasure the one that presented itself. They both climbed into a chariot made from a silkworm cocoon, drawn by two sea-eagles, and departed.

While they were traveling to the Palace of Eventualities, Rêveuse, importuned by Clair-obscur, finally emerged from her lethargy, but it was to say to him, naively, that she did not want either to love or to be loved. The genius, who did not believe her, expanded himself in further protestations; she imposed silence on him with an arrogance by which he was disconcerted. Her indolence was only apparent; when some passion moved her, she was no longer the same person; one discovered that she had a great deal of intelligence and a great deal of firmness. Ashamed of such a misplaced passion, he felt all the ridicule of it, and went home, in order to bid adieu to his son, whom he found occupied with his preparations. He witnessed the review of his troops, out of complaisance, for he was no warrior; they were not numerous, but were brisk and well-disciplined.

"Prince," he said to Formosa, when everything was disposed for his departure, "you are going to serve as a model for all those who, in centuries to come, want to establish themselves as conquerors; you will reign over the greater part of the world; let your good will win you the hearts of those you have subjugated by the might of your arms."

"I shall profit from the counsel of moderation with which you honor me," Formosa replied.

"I have been thinking," Clair-obscur added, "about the perils that menace your days; reassure my alarmed tenderness, and receive these arms; they are proof against cannon and lightning."

"What!" retorted the prince, indignant at the weakness of the genius. "You're trembling for me, as the Sun trembled for Phaeton? What do we have in common? I render thanks to the gods for having an immortal father, but I'm glad not to be immortal myself. Keep your baleful presents. What is the value of a life that one exposes with impunity? It's necessary to know that one might die at any moment in order to confront death with honor. I only want to owe my success to my courage and the value of my soldiers. 'In vanquishing without peril one triumphs without glory.'"[64]

To that dart of erudition Clair-obscur had nothing to say. He embraced his son; they separated; he followed him with his eyes, and lost him in the distance.

After Formosa's departure, Clair-obscur ran to consult his mirror; he only found objects therein so blurred that, in spite of his vast penetration, he imagined that he was reading an enigma from the *Mercure de France*.

What troubled him more than anything else was the sight of two young women descending to his favorite isle. His tenderness for Funestine made him fear that they might be fays profiting from his absence to harm her or abduct her. Discouraged by so many obstacles that he had been unable to overcome, he no longer knew what to do.

The idea of Imagination and Virtue caused hope to be reborn in his heart. Without losing any time, he flew to their palace, learned that they had departed for the Palace of Eventualities and followed them at top speed. He was the fastest genius in the world, and he arrived in time to lend them a hand in descending from their chariot. Out of breath from his race, he told them that he no longer had any doubt about Funestine's happiness, since they appeared to be interested in it. They replied that they would do their best to contribute to it, but that it was necessary to take measures in order to succeed.

The genius, who was not fortunate in councils, would have preferred not to run the risk of that one. Imagination spoke first; she took responsibility for the mind of the princess. Virtue took charge of her heart, but she said that she needed to be aided in that by Docility.

"Docility!" interjected Clair-obscur. "I've often heard mention of her but I've never seen her. Young people fear her,

---

[64] The quotation is from Pierre Corneille's tragicomedy *Le Cid* (1636)

men are scornful of her, and I believe that she's no longer in the world."

"It's up to me to find her," she continued. "I'm offering to go in search of her."

"And I offer to accompany you," said the genius. "You might have to go a long way, and one gets bored traveling alone."

The fay refused politely and advised him to build a little house during her absence, in which Funestine, less distracted by the diversity of objects, would be more capable of attention and meditation. He appreciated the wisdom of that suggestion so much that he had a simple building built by new architects, so comfortable that there was nothing about it to criticize.

Virtue took the route to the hyperborean regions. Docility lived there among a few illustrious unfortunates who, presuming nothing of themselves, sustained without murmuring the reversal of their fortune and the injustice of their persecutors.

As she passed over a cabin she saw a young man of modest and tranquil appearance, who was cultivating vegetables that his industry had preserved from the rigors of the climate. She assumed the form of an old man and approached him.

"My son," she said to him, "I'm looking for Docility, is she not with you?"

"Alas," replied the solitary, "for some time she was all the consolation of my life, but I've lost her, and I no longer hope that she might return."

"Why did she quit you?" Virtue asked.

"By my own fault," added the young man, holding back his tears, "but you doubtless need repose, my father. This," he continued, indicating his cabin, "is the only palace I can offer you; honor it with your presence and deign to receive a frugal meal, such as my present fortune permits."

Virtue followed him; she ate, or seemed to eat, the fruits that he presented to her in a rush basket, while she admired the arrangement and neatness of his cell, where everything reflected the tidy mind of the master. He was surprised by the mildness and majesty of his guest; he looked at him, sighing, was moved, and was no longer in a state to resist his heart.

Virtue noticed his disturbance and said to him: "You're not made for the kind of life you're leading; everything about you announces an education worthy of a high birth; an unmerited disgrace has doubtless led you to this solitude; you believed that you would shelter yourself here from the malice of perfidious men. Were you not mistaken? Does not this precipitate retreat contain as much chagrin as reason? Don't disguise your woes from me; perhaps I'll be fortunate enough to alleviate your bitterness."

Whatever disguise Virtue adopts, her power is always the same; on feels its effect by virtue of the confidence it inspires.

The young man replied: "I was born in the realm of Camor; Ulibec is my name; I descend from the first sovereigns who reigned in India, an advantage too frivolous to glorify me. A new man, sustained by crime and fortune, took possession of the throne of my ancestors; they were constrained to seek refuge in a foreign land. Their subjects have groaned under tyranny for four centuries without being able to liberate themselves. My father, in conformity with his estate, came to establish himself in Camor. The king, the father of the present one, sustained for several years an unsuccessful war against his neighbors, lost three battles and suffered other disgraces more catastrophic, had opened his devastated provinces to his enemies. Emboldened by their success and his misfortunes, they threatened to lay siege to his capital. My father found the means to disunite them, beat them separately, and forced them to consent to peace.

"One of the foremost responsibilities of the realm was the price of his services; he raised me with a view to replacing him one day, and was only occupied with rendering me worthy of it. My brother-in-law Ufebor[65] was four years older than me; that difference did not enter into our sentiments; I had loved him since my childhood; he responded to my amity, and I was all the more flattered by that because I believed him to be sincere. My sister was amiable; she augmented by her mildness the pleasure of a union that seemed unbreakable.

"Such beautiful appearances had nothing solid; my father died too soon for her and for me; we felt that loss in its full extent; we gave him tears and regrets of which nothing could stem the source; the gods had determined the end of our happiness. Ufebor, in order to extract me from my dejection, made me think about my fortune; he told me that I ought to solicit my father's position. At that cherished name my tears flowed more abundantly. 'I'm only twenty years old,' I replied, 'That position requires detailed knowledge; it requires experience; I don't feel capable of fulfilling its duties; don't expose me to a refusal that might close entry to other favors if I have enough virtues to merit one of them one day.'

"He made me ashamed of a sentiment in which, he said, there was more mistrust than true modesty. He added that he would work, in spite of me, to sustain the honor of my house. Innocence is not suspicious; I confided my interests to him. He had friends, he knew the king. He asked for the position for himself, obtained it, and crowned his bad faith with a further perfidy. 'The king,' he told me, 'thought you to young; he has given me your charge until you are old enough to exercise it. More satisfied to render it to you, my dear Ulibec, than to possess it, I shall press him to accept my resignation in your favor as soon as possible.'

"Seduced by that false sincerity, I lived tranquilly; my friends said sometimes that Ufebor was deceiving me; I loved him, I was prejudiced, I did not believe them. I finally opened

---

[65] The *Cabinet des fées* text has a footnote decoding the anagram as "Fourbe" [untrustworthy]. Ulibec is difficult to decipher but might be modified from an abbreviated anagram of *équilibré* [well-balanced]

my eyes, but it was too late. He had as much intelligence as ambition; his charge put him in a position to speak to the king frequently; he knew his weaknesses and was able to profit from them. His favor and his credit became immense. He reigned under his master's name; there were murmurs everywhere about such rapid fortune; I was the only one who still rejoiced in it. I did not take long to repent of the good opinion I had of his sagacity.

"Under the pretext of being overwhelmed by the weight of his affairs he only gave me an audience, so to speak, in public; I could no longer speak to him except in the crowd of courtiers that surrounded him. Such is their character that they detest favorites as a matter of taste but adore them by reason of interest. The king, who had seen me at first with kindness, only received me any longer with coldness. All that alarmed me; I confided my anxieties to my sister; she soothed them without approving them. 'Calm yourself, my brother,' she said to me. 'My husband loves you; he's incapable of abandoning you or betraying you; you'll reproach yourself one day for having condemned him on vain appearances.' Her amity rendered her persuasive; I sacrificed my suspicions to her.

"The foremost dignity in the realm having fallen vacant, Ufebor combined it with his other titles. The opportunity seemed favorable to me; I spoke to him. 'You'll soon have your charge' he said to me, dryly. 'I permit you to request it of the king,' I sensed all the bitterness of such a measured expression, but I did not have time to respond to him; he went into his cabinet and the door was forbidden to me. I returned home troubled and shocked, but less afflicted by the loss of my fortune than my brother-in-law's ingratitude.

"Scarcely had I returned than I was told that my charge had just been given to someone else. I was prepared for that eventuality. I was not for a note that was handed to me a moment later; it only contained these few words: 'You are suspect; there are designs on your liberty, perhaps your life; hasten to put both in safety.' The advice came from a hand too dear not to be taken. I was innocent, but one never is with kings when they want to find us culpable. To spare that of Camor an injustice, I gathered up the sad debris of my heritage and came to hide in this desert. I spent two years here in a calm that filled my heart. Docility did not abandon me; aided by her presence, sustained by her advice, I found that true happiness consists in rendering oneself master of one's desires and reflections.

"Docility believed my constancy to be above events; she informed me of the causes of my disgrace and told me about the further crimes and the fall of Ufebor during my absence. I had supported his treason; I had forgiven him, because I was the only object of it; I was no longer capable of containing myself when I knew that others had been his victims; I forgot myself to the extent of murmuring against the gods; I fell into discouragement. Docility made vain efforts to bring me back, but I no longer listened to her; she became insupportable to me; I forced her to quit me, and I only found myself less unhappy when her presence no longer constrained my tears or my plaints."

Virtue knew the human heart too well to aggravate Ulibec with severe reproaches. She spared his weakness, flattered his dolor, and only criticized its excess. When one makes an invalid love the remedies one gives him, one advances the cure. In sum, she acted with so much dexterity on the mind of her host that she engaged him to continue his story.

"I adored Algée, the sister of the King of Camor; she is beautiful and virtuous; dispense me with going into further detail, it would plunge me back into my first aberration. I only appreciated the impression that she had made on me when I was no longer in a state to efface it. My defeat was too glorious to seek to combat it further. How timid amour is in a heart that is commencing to sense it! Everything appears to be an obstacle; everything arrests it; it mistrusts itself, it fears displeasing; it wants to extinguish its fires, and augments them by the constraint it imposes on them; it is obstinate in hiding a secret that it is burning to reveal. Rarely does hope prevail over respect. I avoided the princess, I dared not look at her or speak to her; I languished; I was dying.

"My circumspection had a success that I did not expect. Algée was surprised by it; she deduced the reason for it; she made a crime of her penetration; she wanted to punish me for it but did not have the strength; I kept quiet, I was respectful; was that offending her? Fortunate without knowing it, I observed myself with so much exactitude that, at the time when I was the most passionate, I passed for the most indifferent man in the court. My passion increased in silence; the princess enjoyed her triumph without risk to her glory. A year passed in that way; fortune was jealous of my happiness, if it is a happiness to love without hope.

"Cimure, the King of Ichionie, an amiable prince of whom much was hoped, had just succeeded his father; his realm was no close to that of Camor that their kings were continually at war in order to extend them or conserve their limits. Cimure, whose rights appeared the more apparent, wanted to terminate a quarrel that was incessantly renewed; he requested Algée, offering in favor of that marriage to desist in his pretentions and to abide by what was decided in the council of Camor. A proposition so advantageous could not find any contradiction. Algée, treated by her brother as queen of Ichionie, received the compliments of the whole court. The universal joy became for me the subject of the cruelest sadness and despair, but the interest of my amour was the less strong; I rejoiced sincerely in a marriage that would render me unfortunate because I believed that it would enable the happiness of the princess I adored.

"One evening, I was in the garden of the palace; Algée was walking there with one of her maids. The sound of her voice extracted me from the profound reverie in which I was plunged. I lent an ear involuntarily. I did not know that I was the subject of a conversation that I ought never to have heard. 'Yes,' she said, 'I shall depart without Ulibec knowing that I regret him; leave me the consolation of imagining that I'm mistaken about his sentiments; I need his indifference to expel

231

him from my heart; don't remind me of anything that might maintain a weakness over which I'm ready to triumph. I owe it to my repose and my glory. Let's go.' she continued, 'it's time to retire.' I saw her go back into her apartment, and I remained in a disturbance that did not permit me to determine whether I ought to praise or complain of fortune.

"Ufebor had only made a semblance of approving of the marriage of the Princess of Camor in order to deceive his master and the King of Ichionie. Blinded by ambition and seduced by amour, he meditated the most horrible perfidy. He commenced by forming difficulties that delayed Algée's departure; he quibbled over every article of the treaty, which he had agreed the day before. It was only possible for him to do that by making unreasonable propositions that he even would have been sorry to obtain. Cimure became impatient; his complaints were ignored, and it came to an open rupture; troops were raised; there was a battle; nothing was decided.

"I confess that, less submissive to my destiny since I knew that I was not hated, I sought out the King of Ichionie in order to dispute Algée with him; that was a lover's extravagance. He was then as unhappy as me. I met him; we commenced a combat that might perhaps only have finished with the death of one or other of us. Heavy cavalry surrounded me. Cimure, persuaded that I had only attacked him by virtue of a sentiment of glory, generously took me out of their hands and sent me back.

"My disgrace followed that evolution closely. Ufebor had betrayed me, my presence reproached him for his crime; one hates those one persecutes unjustly. Perhaps, enlightened by amour, he had even penetrated my sentiments for Algée. Whatever the cause of his malice was, he told the King of Camor, with a feigned mildness, that he was in despair at accusing me, but that a faithful minister listened neither to blood nor amity when it was a matter of the life of his sovereign. 'Ulibec,' he added, 'forgetting what he owes you and what he owes to himself, is conspiring with your enemies against your person.'

"Then he produced letters that I was supposed to have written to Cimure, containing a conspiracy so detailed that that feeble prince, who only saw through his favorite's eyes, believed that he recognized my handwriting and condemned me without hearing me. His tenderness for his sister saved me from the shame of torture; he had hidden nothing from her and he told her about my crime. Algée dared not justify me, but, convinced of my innocence, she wrote me the note I mentioned to you.

"A few days later, Ufebor repudiated his wife, under the pretext that she was the sister of an outlaw; she was relegated to the mountains of Camor among primitive people; she lived there deprived of everything, without any help save what she found in the charity of those barbarians, more humane than her husband.

"The success of so many crimes was only an encouragement to the last. Ufebor had loved Algée for a long time. Too clever to declare himself inappropriately, he had hidden his passion under the deceitful appearances of attachment and respect. The princess was the refuge of unfortunates; she saw with pleasure that at the first word she said in their favor, Ufebor hastened to put an end to their troubles; she did not know that his apparent virtues were real crimes. He only changed his conduct when he believed that he could count on the measures he had taken. What horrible measures they were!

"The King of Camor had scarcely entered his fortieth year, but pleasures, luxury and idleness had aged him prematurely. Enclosed in his palace, he languished in the arms of his mistresses. His body and mind were weakening every day. Ufebor, profiting from his lack of application, had rendered himself master of all the affairs of the realm, but by virtue of a refined politics he affected to fatigue him with the boring detail of the slightest minutiae. 'How one has to complain of being king,' he said one day to his favorite, 'if one can only reign at the expense of his repose! Deliver me of a weight that is crushing me and driving me to despair. I have put all my authority in your hands, I am ready also to give you my crown. I want you,' he continued, 'in order to cement the rights that I am ceding to you, to share those of my sister. Reign together, and henceforth, both of you, only see me in order to talk to me about fêtes or amusements,'

"He refused so many favors with a feigned modesty, but the king told him that he wanted to be obeyed for the last time, and signed orders to assemble the estates, who alone could authorize his abdication and name a successor.

"Assured in that direction, Ufebor no longer doubted the success of his enterprise. All his master's subjects were his creatures. It was then that, ceasing to constrain himself with Algée, he had the boldness to speak of amour. Indignant at his insolence, she replied to him with a haughtiness capable of disconcerting anyone but Ufebor, who, naturally proud and believing himself to be sovereign already, said without emotion that she could choose between the throne and exile.

"A discourse so extraordinary gave birth to suspicions that she wanted to fathom. The greatest crimes are the least impenetrable; their execution requires confiding in too many people for the secret not to be exposed. A mysterious gesture, a word let slip or a simple step all serve to betray them, and interest or remorse almost always creates infidels Algée learned the danger that threatened her; she ran to the king, who refused to see her. Her courage did not abandon her at such a delicate conjuncture; her virtue had made her friends, her prudence put them to work.

"The estates were opened. The king came to support his favorite, the princess followed him. He said in a few words that, his health no longer permitting him to apply himself to the government of his realm, he would abdicate the crown in favor of Ufebor, on condition that she married Ufebor and ruled conjointly with him. Ufebor, taking the floor, opposed his master's speech weakly. The princess, speaking in her turn, begged the king not to abandon people by whom he was adored. 'You can,' she said, 'obtain relief from skillful and virtuous men who will only have your glory and the god of your subjects in view. With regard to Ufebor, he has made a culpable usage of your favor for too long; it is time to unveil his artifices and punish his crimes.'

"Ufebor quivered with anger; he stood up and tried to interrupt. The silence and indignation of the assembly astonished him; he read his defeat even in the eyes of his friends. He was troubled, and went pale; he trembled, and that coward, who had aspired two days earlier to the hand of Algée, embraced her knees in order to beg for the mercy of his life. Justice had closed her soul to pity. He was accused, convicted of the most odious crimes, stripped of his charges and thrown into the depths of the sea.

"The imbecile King of Camor, witness to an event so unexpected, marked neither surprise nor sadness. The crown was offered to his sister; she refused to accept it, but she took care to establish councils to decide great affairs, and to reform the abuses that had been introduced under a violent minister. Her moderation was admired; she was heaped with praise; the estates separated.

"That," Ulibec continued, "is what Docility told me, "And that, my father, is where my deplorable story concludes, Algée is happy; it is a consolation for me to know that, but I sense that, in spite of my innocence, she will never recall me; she has doubtless married Cimure; she knows that I adore her, but she will be the victim of her scruples. I shall not see her again. Die, unfortunate Ulibec, there is no longer Algée for you."

Docility had only quit him to test him; she came back. Virtue was charmed by her return, and begged her not to abandon him again.

While the two immortals were occupied in consoling him, they heard a courier asking loudly for the cabin of Ulibec, to whom, he said, he had to render a letter from the Queen of Camor,

"From Algée!" cried Ulibec. "Gods! Is she still thinking of me?"

"Yes, Sire," said the courier, presenting him, on his knees, with papers that he took from his bosom. They contained the following:

Algée, Queen of Camor, to the virtuous Ulibec.

Justice is the first duty of sovereigns; I render it to your innocence; come back, Ulibec; your persecutors are dead. Algée reigns; you know that she loves merit and Virtue.

All that a tender and passionate soul can experience of delight and rapture, Ulibec felt on reading that letter. "Algée has not forgotten me," he said, with transport. "Algée loves virtue. What do I not owe you, my father? You have saved mine from shipwreck; without you, I would no longer be worthy to appear before the Queen of Camor."

Suddenly, by virtue of a return of suspicion ordinary to those who love, he fell back into his first anxieties, he doubted his good fortune, he feared that of Cimure.

"Please," he said to the courier, "tell me what Algée is doing; I am informed of everything that preceded the assembly of the states; commence our story with the disgrace of Ufebor."

The man, whom the queen had ordered to hide nothing from Ulibec, satisfied him in these terms:

"After the discovery and the punishment of Ufebor's crimes, calm and order was reestablished in all parts of the realm. The princess, who had reserved the dispensation of mercy to herself, employed clemency toward the culpable; the repose of the state cost no one's blood. The king, adopting sentiments worthy of him, devoted himself to affairs again; he assisted in the councils and wanted, he said, to put himself at the head of his troops; in brief, he commenced to reign. That change had no consequences; drawn away by his penchant or his weakness, he died. We learned of his death almost immediately after learning of his malady. The people, ever extreme, proclaimed loudly that it was the effect of a slow poison that Ufebor had given him. Whatever it was, he was given a magnificent funeral. The princess was carried to the throne by the wishes of the entire nation. Her wisdom and bounty extend everywhere; she is loved, she is respected. Fortunate are people who can love and respect their masters!

"Your sister was the first object of the queen's attention; but, Sire, she believed that she ought not appear at the court yet; she has retired to a city that is in your passage; you can see her there when you return.

"Cimure is not yet married. The greatest lord of Ichionie came to compliment the queen on her accession to the crown. That was only a pretext; the marriage of Algée with the prince was the true motive for that embassy. Times had changed; she told him without any detour that she would have obeyed her brother because she was then a subject, but that, the Princess of Camor having become Queen, could not dispose of her person without the consent of her people, who would be poorly repaid for their zeal and fidelity by submission to foreign domination. 'Monsieur Ambassador,' she added, 'that obstacle does not diminish my esteem for your master; I beg you to assure him of that, and to tell him that I count on living with him in good intelligence.'

"However, in order not to neglect anything, the queen has put herself in a state to anticipate the consequences of that refusal. All was tranquil when she made me depart in order to find you; I have found you, Sire, and I praise the gods for the success of my voyage. I will not stop to repeat to you everything that is being said in Camor, that is not my mission; but I can assure you whatever the queen's designs are in regard to you, they will be obeyed blindly."

Scarcely had he finished speaking than Virtue, quitting the form of the old man, appeared in all her charms. Docility embraced her; Ulibec prostrated himself and adored her.

"Come," she said to him, "I want to present you myself to the Queen of Camor."

They arrived. Algée received Ulibec as a sovereign should—which is to say, without showing too much urgency and without affecting too much coldness. Amour, arrested by the presence of Virtue, retained all decorum, but he lost none of his rights.

As soon as she had assured the happiness of those illustrious lovers, Virtue asked Docility to accompany her, and returned to Funestine. Let us say in a few words what had happened in the Palace of Eventualities.

The princess was occupied in trying to protect herself from the pursuits of the fly fay when Clair-obscur came to introduce Imagination to her. She received them as she received all those who came to render her a visit—which is to say, without looking at either one of them. "Either deliver me from this importunate fly," she said brusquely to the genius, "or I shall throw myself out of the window."

He was afraid that she might keep her word, and made a few attempts to catch her so maladroit that they cost the impatient princess, who threw everything at his head that came to hand, a few bruises. Imagination could not help smiling, but, seeing that the quarrel was becoming heated she made a sign to Clair-obscur to withdraw.

"It's necessary to confess," he said, as he left, "that she's a nasty little creature."

Left alone, Imagination said softly that a bad temper is a frightful thing in a young person. Funestine was intolerant of remonstrations; she wanted to respond arrogantly, but, retained by an invisible power, she stopped, her eyes attached to Imagination, whose majestic and flattering aspect caused her emotions that she had not yet experienced. The fay perceived that, and in order to finish winning her, she laid in wait for the cruel fly, which was continuing to pester her; she seized it, and immediately immolated it.

"Eh! Who are you?" demanded Funestine, in a tone of surprise and gratitude. "You give me advice that doesn't revolt me; you render me attentive, sensible, and begin by rendering me a service that I shall never forget. What god sent you to my aid? Are you not one yourself?"

"I'm Imagination," she said. "I've come to ask for your amity, and to offer you everything that depends on mine."

"You're Imagination?" the princess replied, with chagrin. "You're not my friend, then, and I can never be yours. My fate is to be bizarre and unhappy; I commenced by being prejudiced in your favor without loving you, when I knew who you are. I'm ugly; I only have sad ideas; I can't have others; don't aggravate the woes I suffer by means of the image of those I will suffer in future. I'm only too ingenious in tormenting myself.

"The greatest good that could happen to me is that of not thinking, or not feeling anything; let me, if possible, forget that I horrify others as much as I horrify myself; take the charm of your illusions elsewhere; their sweetness isn't made for an unfortunate who dreads everything and ought not to hope for anything. Born the daughter of a great king, the sight of me rendered him barbaric and he exposed me to wild beasts. Why didn't Clair-obscur leave me to be devoured?

"Clair-obscur, out of cruel pity, snatched me from death. He strives to correct the influence that persecutes me, but his cares and his power are futile; nothing can vanquish the malignity; the gods have exhausted all their anger on me. I'm unjust, nasty, intractable; everything displeases me, everything irritates me. Formosa, for whom I'm destined, is the object of my hatred and I'm the object of his. The sumptuousness of this palace importunes me; I've filled it with my extravagances; every instant of my life is a new disgrace. 'Everything afflicts me, harms me and conspires to harm me.'[66]

"That sincere confession of my faults astonishes you; it astonishes me too. Why have I made it to you, since it will only render me more unhappy? The deceptive calm that has suspended my violence will soon dissipate and augment it. Yes, I sense more sharply than ever that I'm hateful; to complete my woes, I sense that I can't do anything to cease to be. Flee, Imagination, and if it's true that you're sensible to the

---

[66] The quotation is from Jean Racine's tragedy *Phèdre* (1677)

pains of Funestine, send her, for pity's sake, death or stupidity."

Imagination was touched by a discourse that gave evidence less of fury than sorrow. "No," she said to her, wiping away her tears, "you're not as unfortunate as you think; cease to fear me and to despair. Instead of accusing the gods of injustice you should render them thanks. Calm down and don't interrupt me. You have intelligence; that gift alone is worth as much as all of those you lack. Begin to make use of it. Moderate the impetuosity that makes your torment and that of others. Remember, in order to reduce your regrets, that the beauty whose privation puts you in such an ill humor, is a chimera that depends on hazard or opinion. Cease to regard as the sovereign good an advantage that you could not have given yourself and that you could not conserve. But tell me, Funestine, in what does the beauty consist that is the object of all your desires? Confess that you place it entirely in a certain arrangement of the features, in I know not what glamour that struck you in Imaé? You don't have a more distinct idea of it.

"Emerge from error. There is another beauty more precious and more desirable, which one can acquire, and which one never loses. It is inside you; work to develop it; it allows itself to be found when one looks for it; it loves to communicate itself; nothing is necessary to fix it but mildness and simplicity. It elevates the sentiments, it perfects the talents and puts them into the light; it makes the justice of the mind extend to the rectitude of the heart. I can only show you the road that leads to its temple, Virtue will open the sanctuary to you, if you follow her advice; expect everything from the gods and from yourself; I can't reveal the future to you, but I can promise to occupy you with agreeable objects and to direct your views to what can flatter you, as far as they can extend."

This discourse made such a deep impression on Funestine that it was as if she were taken out of herself. One does not pass without agitation from one state to another; unexpected joy affects one as much as dolor; her own was filled with trouble and anxiety; she gazed at Imagination and then turned her eyes away; she sighed, she kissed her hands with transport; she wanted to mark her gratitude to her but could not find terms to express it; her thoughts were confused, resembling fever dreams.

Imagination applauded herself for the movements that her presence excited in Funestine's soul; she saw with pleasure the full extent of her sensibility; when she had enjoyed her triumph sufficiently, she returned to herself. The princess said to her then: "You have commenced my happiness, finish your work; introduce me to this Virtue, of whom I only know the name as yet, but for whom I feel more eager because you have inspired me with tenderness for you."

Imagination praised her impatience, and promised to satisfy her, without telling her the day; she had her views.

The author that I am translating writes at this point: "Fortunate Funestine, you no longer have any sad return to fear; your woes are ended; the calm you are enjoying is only a feeble image of the happiness that the future is preparing for you."

A mysterious dream occupied her all night; she had not yet woken up when Imagination, taking her by the arm, informed her that it was time to go to met Virtue.

"Divine fay," the princess said to her, "I am ready to go with you, but if it is true, as I suspect, that nothing is hidden from you, combine with all the benefits that I have already received from you the complaisance of explaining the meaning of a dream that was too coherent to be merely an illusion.

"Slumber, which I no longer knew, returned as soon as you had quit me. It is said that the ideas of the day are retraced during the night, but nothing similar happened to me. Present as you were in my heart, I had forgotten you. Scarcely was I asleep than I found myself in a valley so profound that my sight could not attain the summits of the mountains that surrounded me. I was walking over flowers that were unknown to me; I have never seen any similar; they perfumed the air and embellished it. I made a garland of them; they lost their colors, and faded as I arranged them, but I felt no less pleasure n adorning myself with them.

"I was on a path that led to a river I could see in the distance; I followed it. A voice I heard behind me shouted: 'Stop, Funestine; you are going to find monsters by which you will be devoured. I offer you a refuge from them.' An involuntary movement made me turn my head. Gods, what did I see? A dragon was pursuing me; its horrible hissing chilled me with fear. A frightful noise augmented it, and I started running away with all my might. I arrived, out of breath, on the river bank. I found a small boat there, into which I threw myself. There was a woman with an equivocal physiognomy in it; I begged her to take me to the other side; the perfidious woman seemed to consent to that, but she enveloped me with almost imperceptible nets, which gripped me so tightly that I could not move.

"She put me back on the shore; she disappeared, and came back followed by a host of monsters of every species, which she animated against me. I thought I was going to be their prey; death seemed inevitable. I waited for it, without lowering myself to beg my enemy, and without a sigh escaping me. The frightful dragon was already opening its mouth to swallow me; I was in that state when a bird with the most beautiful plumage in the world came to peck my bonds. I remained motionless without even thinking of seconding it. It finished breaking them and flew away to a tree. I had a bow and arrows; I made use of them. The dragon was my first victim; all my shots struck home. The monsters were less ardent to attack me, but I emptied my quiver without being able to destroy them.

"The beautiful bird came to my aid; it punctured their eyes with thrusts of its beak; eventually they took flight. I gave my liberator thanks that I strove to make proportionate to the service that it had just rendered me. Instead of responding to me it took me on its wings and transported me in rapid flight on to one of the mountains I mentioned. 'It's there, Funestine,' it said to me, showing me a temple situated on an even higher mountain. 'It's there that you must seek the end of our troubles. I can't take you there.'

"'You can't take me there,' I replied, with a sigh. 'Who will help me, then, to get rid of the thick brambles that surround me? No path is offered to my gaze; I shall perish in this desert.' Alas, I saw it fly away. I sensed all the strangeness and all the rigor of my destiny, which had only delivered me from one danger to expose me to another. My courage weakened; uncertain of what I ought to do, I perceived that I was trailing behind me the remains of my bonds. I got rid of them. My firmness got the upper hand; I surmounted the obstacles.

"I arrived at the enclosing wall of the temple, my face bruised and my hands and feet all bloody. I was suffering from indescribable pains; I was weeping bitterly; I could no longer sustain myself. I lay down under a tree; when its shade had refreshed me, I began to breathe; my strength had returned. I was standing up in order to knock on the door when an admirably beautiful young woman came to stop me. I looked at her with the penetrating expression that marked so clearly the pleasure one is feeling. I found myself so ugly compared with her that I was surprised that she wasn't shocked by my ugliness. I was grateful to her. I was no longer mistress of my heart; it escaped me.

"'Where are you going?' she asked me, in a tone of voice whose softness further augmented the power of her charms.

"'Goddess,' I replied, 'for, if my eyes are not deceiving me, you are a divinity, I'm going into the nearby temple to seek a remedy for the trouble that is agitating me.'

"'Be very careful,' she said, 'the goddess who is worshiped there is a savage prude, difficult of access and vexatious in commerce. You'll only reach her sanctuary after the rudest ordeals; when you get there she'll treat you like a slave; without me you'd commit some imprudence that would have poisoned the rest of your days. Render thanks to your good genius; he's the one who sent me to help you. Come into my palace; you'll find the true happiness there.

"I listened to her with pleasure, but I dared not believe her. I recalled the discourse of the faithful bird; I had too much obligation to it to suspect it of wanting to deceive me; however, I only resisted feebly, and I felt myself being drawn away. A woman from the stranger's retinue, almost as charming as her mistress, offered me an elegant dress; my clothes were in too great a disorder to refuse it. I was ready to put it on when two priestesses came out of the temple. One was wearing a veil, which hid her entirely; the other, of a masculine beauty, showed in her stride a strength above her sex; she had whips armed with iron tips, with which she struck the mistress and servant pitilessly.

"Moved by compassion, I criticized internally such a great inhumanity. Imagine my surprise: those women, whose charms had seduced me, then appeared to me as hideous flesh-less skeletons, whose ugliness still makes me shudder. When they had run away, the priestesses gave me their hands without speaking to me, and introduced me into the enclosure. They moved aside an infinite number of fearful specters that blocked my passage; the specters disappeared, came back, and finally vanished. I entered a pathway so narrow and scabrous that without supernatural aid I would have fallen a thousand times over into the precipices that bordered it to the left and right.

I emerged from it. I arrived without accident at the base of the temple; one climbed up to it by so many steps, and they were so slippery, that I doubted the success of my enterprise. A man lying on the ground augmented my mistrust; sadness and languor were painted on his face. 'Do you hope,' he said to me, in a poorly articulated voice, 'young and feeble as you are, to vanquish the difficulties that have deterred me? You'll succumb to them. Let my example teach you to measure your strength; believe me, turn back.'

"That timid counsel made me pause for a time, but a desire for glory made me go on. I endured so many fatigues and so many contradictions in that difficult march that I thought that I had employed an entire year in it. The door of the temple was closed. I knocked gently; no one responded to me. I redoubled my blows; I didn't see anyone. I armed myself with patience; I invoked the goddess; I combined tears with prayers. Finally, after a long wait, the door opened of its own accord.

"The interior of the temple had as much magnificence as the exterior had simplicity. It was ornamented with large pictures representing allegorical mysteries. I considered them attentively, without being able to penetrate their meaning. An old man sitting on a globe wanted to explain them to me. I didn't listen to him. The sanctuary was offered to my eyes; I ran toward it ardently; but I wasn't yet at the end of my proofs.

"A woman brilliant with light took me by the hand; she took me into a nearby room; my garments were taken off; I was plunged into a tub full of a liquid so strong and spirituous that I could not sustain the effect; a devouring fire consumed me; I thought that an arrow pierced my heart; I lost consciousness. Then you came, and I woke up."

"That dream," said Imagination, "will soon have no more obscurity for you. I shall leave you the pleasure of recognizing it. If, however, a few features of it escape your penetration, Docility will reveal its connections with the situation you are in. She is the person into whose hands I will put you for a few days; she is the one who will introduce you to Virtue."

"What!" said Funestine. "You're going to abandon me, then?"

"You have no further need of me," Imagination replied. "You can support the present, you are hopeful for the future; your anxieties are dissipated, and agreeable objects have taken their place. The story that I have just heard enables me to see all the rectitude of your mind; my power does not extend beyond what I have done for you. I have enabled you to glimpse happiness; you alone can procure it. Adieu, Funestine. When you are happy—which is to say, when you are perfect—don't forget me. Virtue is my friend, the progress she will make in your heart ought not to efface the impressions that I have made in your mind. It is not enough to be virtuous, it is necessary to be amiable; one is only one and the other by means of the good usage that one makes of the mind and the heart."

Then, without waiting for a response, she conducted her to the house that Clair-obscur had prepared for her. It had no sumptuous furniture, and no mirrors; everything there was neat, but simple. Funestine had quit the Palace of Eventualities without repugnance; she felt none at the sight of her new dwelling. Docility came to meet her, and took her to her apartment.

Imagination ran to meet Virtue; the joy of seeing one another again was equal. After the first transports they rendered accounts mutually, one of the success of her voyage, the adventures, misfortunes and happiness of Ulibec and Algée, and the other of the fortunate change in Funestine.

Virtue said to her: "When Docility brings her to me she will occupy me entirely. Let's take advantage of the leisure that we have. You interrupted the story regarding yourself at the most interesting part; I beg you to resume it."

Imagination could not refuse her friend anything. It is her who is going to speak.

"I have told you about my dissipations; I shall tell you about my weaknesses. Fabulous had a brother about whom she never ceased talking to me; she enabled me remark such singular rapports of humor and character between us that, in the time when I suspected her of exaggeration, I felt a violent desire to know him.

"That brother's name is Extreme. He was then bearing arms for the first time with Prince Formosa, rumor of whose exploits have doubtless reached you. They had conceived for one another at first sight the esteem to which superior merit gives birth wherever it is found. Their amity did not last long. As they were marching at the same pace in the career of glory, they passed from emulation to jealousy; it became so intense that they were obliged to separate.

"Extreme came back. Renown had announced him as a prodigy; it was not belied. He appeared like one of those luminous phenomena that everyone rushes to see, and which are the subject of all conversations. The personal graces, the sublimity of intelligence and sentiments, everything that composes the amiable man, the man in fashion: such was Extreme; at least, that was what women said of him, even if they had not seen him. It was a badge of status to know him and to have been to his house; there was no reputation, merit or beauty except at that price. For some time, there was nothing but stratagems and enticements to attract him; he was the terror of husbands and fortunate lovers. The most confident fops dared not appear before him.

"I saw him in one of those tumultuous circles of which persons of my rank can never rid themselves. On his part it was only a ceremonial visit, but he said so many brilliant things, in such a fine manner, that it seemed to me that he was only saying them for me. I was flattered by that; I strove to respond. I don't know whether I succeeded, but I believed that I perceived that the admiration was divided between us. The desire to please is so natural in a young woman that she does not even think of shielding herself from it. We separated prejudiced in one another's favor and impatient to see one another again.

"His sister rendered me an account of his sentiments; I did not hide mine from her. When he found an opportunity to talk to me, he made use of it with a noble assurance that ordinary men do not have. His declaration was too flattering and too delicate to appear offended by it; I did not use with him the refinements of self-esteem that are disguised beneath the exterior of an apparent pride while they are secretly delivering themselves to the pleasure that a triumph causes. I did not affect the tones of anger and scorn that the heart almost always disavows; but I measured my response and my conduct in such a way that amour and duty had no complaint to make.

"I shall pass lightly over the pleasures of a union formed by sympathy, entertained by mystery and augmented by hope.

247

Extreme had sworn an inviolable fidelity to me so many times, and I was so disposed to believe him, that I was about to make use of the absolute power that I have over the mind of my father to engage him to make my happiness is making his own. Alas, my dear Virtue, I was the victim of Amour and perfidy.

"I had demanded of Extreme that he would see me infrequently; I feared the outburst of an overt passion. I had represented myself for so long as indifferent that I did not want people to know, if possible, that I no longer was. He groaned at that constraint; he complained of it tenderly, but he obeyed. I was charmed by his complaisance; I did not read what was in his heart. By what cruel fatality is it necessary that one cannot be in good faith without being betrayed?

"That lover, whom I thought incapable of dissimulation, was deceiving me at the very moment when he appeared to me to be most sincere. I learned of his inconstancy from a man so marvelous that I cannot dispense with giving you an idea of him. His birth is illustrious, his merit above his employments. Old age has fortified his mind without enfeebling his body at all; one can only judge his age by his experience; he is knowledgeable without ostentation, accessible without familiarity, firm without rudeness and sage without bitterness; he is the soul of councils and makes the delight of society. My father, who raised him, regards him as his own; he had seen me born and loved me since my childhood; he cultivated my mind by means of everything he thought capable of embellishing it, and gave me advice on my conduct that would have made my glory and my happiness if I had followed it. I was too lively then to profit from it; only time could enable me to know its price. However, his zeal and his mildness, which augmented one another instead of belying one another, inspired me with the most respectful tenderness for him.

"On day, finding me alone, he said to me: 'Princess, I am going to displease you, but I beg you to sacrifice your resentment to me. I know society too well, and I am too attached to you to be mistaken in what regards you; I shall spare your delicacy, but I will not flatter you. You love Extreme; he knows that you love him. Should that confession escape you? I want to believe that one cannot reason with one's heart; that, at least is how one excuses its weakness; but if one cannot help loving, one can avoid saying so, and above all, one should, when duty does not speak first. The brilliant qualities of Extreme have seduced you, you have thought him worthy of pleasing you, because he does please you. You have committed a fault for which you are being punished; you have touched his vanity, another has touched his heart. At the moment when I am speaking to you, he is at the feet of your rival. Do not demand that I name her; I am reproaching myself for the dolor I am causing you and I do not want to sharpen it.'

"He took a letter from his pocket, which he handed to me, and left me in a state of shock that I cannot describe. Given what I had just heard, I ought to have torn up that letter without reading it, scorned Extreme and labored to cure myself. I took an exactly opposite course; I doubted my misfortune, I read that fatal letter avidly; I wept; I lamented Extreme, and I did not cease to love him.

"I sent for Fabulous and told her about my adventure. I examined all her reactions; I only found surprise there. 'Is it possible,' I asked her, 'that you do not know the person preferred to me, and that you are not partly responsible for betraying me?' She destroyed my suspicions in such an ingenuous manner that I ceased to suspect her, but when she wanted to excuse her brother I interrupted her. 'Look,' I said, 'and see if you can justify this,

"*What! You fear the charms of Imagination?*—this is what the letter said—*You render yourself scant justice; she has wit, she is amusing, but what is all that compared with what you are? I only see her for the sake of propriety and in order to keep our secret. Is it necessary to cease to see her, and to do so with ostentation? Speak, you will be obeyed. I only know of emotion those that you inspire in me. The heart of Extreme is yours. He adores you, and will always adore you.*

249

"That reading redoubled the astonishment and indignation of Fabulous. She criticized her brother; she swore to me that she did not know the name of my rival. She promised me, in order to convince me of her good faith, that she would make every effort to discover it.

"I had no need of her aid; a deceived lover becomes clairvoyant. For some time there had been at the court a young scatterbrain whose character and face made a great deal of noise. She was announced as a great princess; she affected the manners of one and demanded the respect of one. However, no one knew her; she spoke of nothing but her alliances, her pretentions to all the estates in the world, whose sovereigns were, she said, her relatives, or her adorers.

"She only said incredible things; she only related unprecedented adventures, of which she had been the heroine or the witness. She had nothing natural in her intellect, no accuracy in her expression; her tastes were bizarre, her ideas extraordinary, her sentiments excessive. She was prodigal without being liberal; she gave without discernment and refused by caprice; she overwhelmed the ministers with projects that were nothing but ridiculous visions; she invented extravagant fashions every day. Her garments were singular without being stylish; she adorned herself excessively, and never judiciously. Her stature was tall, without the elegance that makes for charm.

"One could say, on looking at her: *there is a well made person*; but one sensed that she left something to be desired; her beauty was striking at first, but had nothing real, and did not stand up to examination. Her features, taken separately, were admirable, but the ensemble did not have the piquant and flattering I-know-not-what that one cannot resist. She had large eyes, the movements of which she could not regulate; she strove to give them an expression of mildness and tenderness, which degenerated into languor or stupidity.

"Her name was Chimera. She had made advances of amity to me, which I had received coldly, because at first sight I felt a secret antipathy for her that I had not taken the trouble to overcome. She made a semblance of not perceiving it, but she was too vindictive to restrain herself. I was told that she was neglecting the respect due to me, that she sometimes praised me in a manner whose ironic tone was a true satire, that at other times she threatened overtly to avenge herself for the insulting scorn I had for her. I was offended by her indiscretion. Extreme entered into my resentment and offered to impose on her; I did not want to involve him in the quarrel and contented myself with having the madwoman told that I was not in a humor to suffer her extravagance.

"She went to too many places for it to be possible for me to avoid her. On one apartment day she came to that of my mother, the queen, more bizarrely clad than she had ever been, but as nothing is so unreasonable that it does not find partisans, people praised the taste and understanding of her attire. After a few vague discourses in which I remarked that she was seeking to provoke me, the conversation fell upon the different characters of minds. I declared myself in favor of those which, sage in their vivacity, attach themselves more to retaining it than giving it free rein; which, circumspect in their thoughts, do not seek to shine at the expense of reason and common sense; which, simple in their expressions avoid with the same care exaggeration and dryness of style; and which, understanding themselves when they write, are understood by all those who read.

"'For myself,' said Chimera, 'I compare them to timid slaves who, able to break their fetters, do not have the strength to want it; scrupulously enclosed within the narrow limits of a cold plausibility or a sad exactitude, the ennui that they inspire spreads over everything that they touch and chills everyone that approaches them. I know others, and they are the only ones I love, who, enemies of constraint, rise up to the marvelous by unknown routes; they launch themselves into noble flight; they abandon themselves boldly to the movements that agitate them; they fear getting lost less than crawling. With them, one senses oneself transported outside oneself, one flies in their wake on the wings of pleasure and admiration.'

"She sustained her opinion by means of reasons so pompous and so subtle, but so strange, that I had difficulty comprehending that one could combine so much aberration with so much intelligence. The rest of the assembly judged her differently; there were some who applauded. Even Fabulous followed the torrent. Her brother gave her praise so delicate, but so excessive, that I took it as a joke; she repaid him with a glance in which there was something other than gratitude. That glance, which revealed the depths of their hearts, did not escape me, and caused me the most intense dolor that I have ever felt.

"I returned to my apartment, I groaned, I shed tears, I experienced the cruelest things, he most opposed emotions; they succeeded one another rapidly; I succumbed under their violence; but my woes were aggravated by the remedies that ought to have soothed them. Reason, chagrin and self-esteem were all futile.

"I thought I saw Extreme, I spoke to him, I made him re-proaches. Soon, I represented him to myself at the feet of my rival; that sight caused a cold poison to flow through my heart that even took away sentiment. An instant later, I reassured myself with Chimera's extravagance; I flattered myself that Extreme's passion for her could only be a temporary error. That idea brought back hope; I was foolish enough and enemy of my glory enough to settle upon it. I carefully avoided the sight of the admirable man I mentioned; I feared the wisdom of his speech and the firmness of his advice. When I was obliged to hear it, I lowered my eyes, I sighed, and I made no reply.

"Fabulous, fearing that I might make a crime out of her brother's infidelity, or perhaps, imitating his inconstancy, had ceased to see me; I had lost her. Extreme and Chimera no longer maintained any reserve, no one was talking about any-thing but their amour; every day they gave themselves to scenes that afflicted me. Decorum did not permit me to appear sensible to it, and I constrained myself; but I only appeared in public when my tears were exhausted.

"That state was too violent to sustain; I fell ill, I was in danger; I saw death at close range, and did not tremble at her aspect; she only had to show herself and I was cured. I was told then that Extreme and Chimera had disappeared suddenly. The languor of the body was communicated to the mind; that last blow, instead of crushing me, rendered me a species of calm, of which I thought myself incapable.

"Novelty, whom I had neglected, wanted to resume her foremost place in my heart; I received her well, but she perceived that everything was indifferent to me. A year passed in that fashion; I heard mention of your charms and your power, and I came to throw myself into your arms; you welcomed my with kindness; your examples and your advice have rendered peace to my heart; you posses it, never weary of reigning there."

Night was beginning to make way...

I am obliged to interrupt this story because the rest of the manuscript is in another hand, and the characters are unknown to me. I presume that the author, anticipating death, was unable to finish it, and according to all appearances, some Indian gymnosophist, older than Homer by a few Olympiads, continued it in order to immortalize it.

I will be told that I am making use here of a bad finesse that returns every day. If that is so, is not imitation a fine thing? Ask any maker of tales who begins to run out of breath, or any publisher who produces supposed works, whether they do not find that innocent artifice useful. Where would the equity be in forbidding me what is permitted to them?

The scholar that I have consulted had just told me that the rest of the manuscript is in the Malabar language; that word makes me fear that the style might resemble the princesses of that name, and that one can do nothing about it.[67] He has reassured me on that article. One can judge by the translation, in which I have changed nothing, whether it is sufficient to understand Malabar to please readers.

---

[67] See the note on the Malabar princesses in the previous story.

PART THREE

Docility treated Funestine kindly in order to gain her confidence. She feared provoking a revolt by untimely instructions. When she had studied her character she had the pleasure of seeing that it was only necessary to show her benevolence in order to make oneself loved by her.

"Princess," she said to her then, "you are entering into a difficult career; it is necessary to rid yourself of your prejudices, triumph over your humor and vanquish your passions. The enterprise is great, but it is not above your strength. As is rare for a person of your rank to be taught what veritable grandeur is; an imperious governess gives them false ideas. They believe that everything is permitted to them, because they only see flatterers around them who deceive them, or slaves who fear them.

"People say a great deal to them about the prerogatives of their birth; they do not tell them that the more elevated it is, the more obligations it imposes on them. Common virtues spoil it; it only admits purified and sublime ones, and only the latter are appropriate to you. Let discretion rule your speech, let sagacity preside over your actions; it is in that fortunate mixture that the solid glory consists that never passes. Be mild, not with the mildness of temperament that degenerates into indolence, but with the active, reflective mildness that is not belied and enables our happiness in enabling that of others. Be compassionate; one gains more hearts with good will than with benefits; it is not so much a refusal that offends us as the manner of the refusal. One cannot always give, but one can always want to, and make it felt that one desires it.

"Have no fear that your affability will make people forget what you are; all those who make themselves loved are respected. Dissimulation is of no use to princes; the enlightened courtier studies them and penetrates it; imaginary faults can sometimes be attributed to them, but their virtues are never disputed when they are real. If you are only virtuous in appearance, you will not acquire the delicate esteem that makes all the charm of life; men fear truth for themselves, but they seek it and adore it elsewhere; if a lie dazzles them, it is only for an instant.

"Without the bounty of the gods, who watch over you, the misunderstood amity of Clair-obscur would doom you; you would only be famous for your faults. The greatest of all is ill-humor, that monster born with us, which, feeble in children, is manifest in cries and tears, but which, having become stronger, rises and escapes like an impetuous torrent that carries ravage and horror everywhere; it is not arrested by reason or duty; the enemy of propriety, it spares no one; it does not listen to advice or threats; it disfigures the finest qualities and renders them hateful; it poisons pleasures, disperses friends, and drives away fortune; everything embitters it and nothing appeases it; everything fights it and nothing destroys it; its fury extends even to insensible things. Don't tell me that yours was the effect of your ugliness; you followed its movement before knowing that you were ugly.

"I know that, by virtue of the power of Imagination, its fits are less frequent and less nasty, but she has only showed you thus far pleasant images on which your mind can dwell agreeably. That calm, even if it is only external is already something, but he most difficult work remains to do. Listen to me, and you can examine afterwards: be careful, above all, of deluding yourself. Mistrust false shame. In order to put yourself in a state to defend yourself against it, I shall teach you to recognize it. It affects the external appearance of modesty; timid, it walks with lowered eyes; slothful, it stops at the slightest obstacle; its extends it advantages so meagerly that it renders itself ridiculous by fearing to appear so; it is so unskillful that it only deceives itself when it imagines that it is deceiving everyone. It has only ever been able to make one dupe, and that is self-esteem, which it blinds by humiliating it and discredits by persuading it that it is only acting in its interests; its cold poison is all the more dangerous because it insinuates itself without violence and numbs all the faculties of the soul. Shrug off its yoke; not to dare to fathom its faults, nor to admit them, or only to admit them while blushing, is to love them, and not to be cured of them.

"I shall pass on to the essential. You have to uproot from your heart harshness, jealousy, hatred and vengeance; it is here, Funestine, that you must no longer look backward; sacrifice yourself with a good grace, your glory and your felicity depend on that sacrifice. Our passions are dear to us because they are born with us, and they are, so to speak, a part of ourselves; it is so natural and so comfortable to deliver ourselves to that which flatters us that one hardly ever bothers to examine the principles and effects of its movements. What it will cost you to combat yours is nothing compared with the price of the advantages that their defeat will procure you.

"Harshness departs from a foundation of pride and scorn that nothing can authorize. The gods are infinitely further above our heads than you are above those of other men; take them as models; they love us and do not scorn us.

"Jealousy is a sentiment that dishonors us all the more so because it forces us to recognize in those of whom we are envious a superiority of talents and enlightenment that we lack; it agitates, torments and afflicts those who feel it, and changes nothing of the merit or the fortune of those who give birth to it; one yields easily to those impressions, one allows them to dominate because one does not render oneself justice; the more one has, the more one wants to have and the more one complains of not having enough; those with the poorest share are always the least unreasonable. That jealousy, the horror of which I am inspiring in you, is so base and so abject that one dare not pronounce its name when one speaks about oneself.

"Hatred is a bizarre monster, which is not appeased either by homages or sacrifices; it persecutes those who serve it, and respects those who scorn it. It is so painful and so shameful to hate that hatred is its own torture and executioner. Do not believe that it needs reasons or pretexts to exercise its fury;

it is a frenzy of caprice or temperament, so is it not the prerogative of petty souls?

"I shall not pause to depict vengeance to you; however horrible the portrait I made for you might be, it would not approach the idea that you ought to have of it. Of all the passions it is the one that degrades the excellence of humanity the most; unfortunately, it is the one that flatters it the most, because it only offers itself as the generous sentiment of a noble heart, incapable of suffering an insult. However gross the illusion might be, it is only too accredited, even among your sex. It is said that the gods reserve it to themselves, but the maxim is impious. The gods do not avenge themselves; vengeance is returning the harm that one has received.

"There are other passions; thanks to the gods, you do not know them yet. Virtue will prevent them from approaching you; I have only told you all these things in order that you will be prepared to receive them. She does not stop at speech; she only wants and only loves actions. If it is the case, which I dare not presume, that my advice will have effaced even the trace of your faults, it will only be a feeble commencement; it is very little not to do harm if one does not do good, and if one does not love to do it. You are troubled, Funestine!"

The princess had listened without impatience; suddenly she seemed gripped by a disturbance that passed from her heart into her eyes and her face. Ill-humor, ready to cede, was making one last effort. How much it costs to destroy the first impressions of habitude! The combat was painful, the victory dubious, but in the end reason got the upper hand.

"Ah!" she cried. "My dream is coming true, and I no longer need to have it explained to me."

"What dream is that?" asked Docility.

"You want to test me," said Funestine. "Nothing is hidden from the immortals. However, I shall obey you. Then she repeated, word for word, the dream that has been described.

"What meaning do you attribute to it?" asked Docility

"It seems to me," he princess went on, "that the profound valley is childhood, to which all objects appear to be mountains; the flowers that fade are amusements; the voice is instruction; the dragon is ill-humor; the river is the passage to a less frivolous estate; the perfidious woman is habitude, who is aided by the passions; the bow and the arrows are books, examples and advice; the bird is Imagination; the temple is that of Virtue. The rest is self-explanatory; the two women, so beautiful in appearance, are voluptuousness and coquetry; the priestesses that strike them with whips are modesty and firmness; the man lying on the ground is discouragement; the specters are prejudices; the steps are proofs; the closed temple door that only opens after a long wait shows that one can only enter it by perseverance; the emblems are the attributes and mysteries of Virtue that only time, symbolized by the old man, can make comprehensible; the ardor that I sensed at the sight of the sanctuary is inspiration; the woman radiant with light is reason; and it is you, divine Docility, who, piercing my heart with an arrow of fire, has purified it in order to render it worthy of Virtue."

Invisibly present at that conversation, the goddess was so touched by Funestine's sentiments that she suddenly showed herself. Less surprised by that prodigy than by the radiance than surrounded her, Funestine threw herself at her knees, clasped them with transport, bathed hem with her tears, sighed, groaned and fell silent.

That eloquent silence had its effect. Virtue lifted her up, embraced her and directed a gaze at her that penetrated all the way to the depths of her heart. From that moment on, the monsters that afflicted it gave way, quivering, to the goddess, who took possession of it. That change was followed by another even more marvelous. Beauty ripped the veil by which it was obfuscated and shone over Funestine's face, reclaiming all its rights there.

The two goddesses thought it appropriate to hide that new metamorphosis from her. They feared that an excessive joy might cause too sudden a revolution in a soul that was not accustomed to such transports. Perhaps they also wanted to wait until she was capable of judging things sanely enough not to regard beauty as the sovereign good. They gave orders to all those who approached her not to mention it to her; they were obeyed.

Funestine fund herself in a calm of mind the mildness of which was communicated to her speech and her actions. On guard against herself, the memory of the past rendered her attentive to the present and timid with regard to the future. Her domestics adored her, her masters were charmed by her grace and her progress; however, they served her poorly and scolded her, in truth, in spite of themselves, but Virtue made use of that to test her. The stupidity of some and the ill humor of others did not disturb her tranquility at all. *I have given them the example*, she said to *herself, they are compensating themselves for my injustice and my indocility; I have no grounds for complaint.*

At the word *injustice* she uttered a profound sigh. *O gods, what have I done? The unfortunate Quart-d'heure and the even more unfortunate Imaé are languishing in an obscure person, and I'm not doing anything to set them at liberty. What will Virtue think of me?*

She saw her enter her room, ran to her and said to her: "Quart-d'heure... Imaé..."

"I've anticipated your intentions," she replied. "They're free. I'll bring them to you, treat them kindly.

"Virtue alone," replied the princess, "could repair the imprudences of Funestine; she repents of them, but without you it would only be a vain repentance. It is for them to pardon me. Let Imaé cease to fear me; I sense that I am disposed to love her; she did not make me sense my ugliness, I would be very unjust to make a crime of her beauty."

Quart-d'heure appeared, trembling. It is not given to all tellers of tales to come out of prison prouder than they went in. He changed occupations sagely; Formosa took charge of his fortune and enriched him without elevating him. As for Imaé, attached to Funestine by sympathy and gratitude, she did not want either to marry or to quit her, to the great regret of Quart-d'heure, and a thousand others who found her as lovely as he did.

A few days later, Virtue came to see Funestine. "The manner in which you have received young Imaé," she said, "causes me to judge that you would not be sorry to see Princess Rêveuse; she is a charming sister who merits your tenderness; I do not oppose what blood and reason authorize; you might love her, and I even recommend it. Imagination has gone to fetch her, and she will soon be here; but let's talk about something else. How do you find your situation?"

"Alas," replied the grateful princess, it is a thousand times milder and more gracious than I deserve, or dared to hope. I only respire—I only exist—since I have known you; before you I did not exist."

"That response," said Virtue, "merits its recompense; I'm no longer thinking about anything but rendering you happy; you are commencing to be by your own efforts, and I do not want exterior things to get in the way of your felicity. Your domestics will be more submissive and more attentive, and your masters will no longer scold you. Continue to love me; you will see that I don't neglect the interests of my friends."

Rêveuse had an excellent depth of character, which only lacked a little vivacity; that did not appear to be a defect to the lovers of indolent beauty who make of languor a fourth Grace. Imagination exercised her benevolence on the princess, communicating to her a few sparks of the divine fire that enlightens and vivifies. Their effect was prompt. Rêveuse came to know herself, and made such good usage of that knowledge that for some time, few princesses in the world would have dared to dispute anything with her.

She was announced; she came in. At the sight of her, Funestine felt a secret emotion, a natural reaction, and pardonable in a young person who believes herself to be ugly and who sees her younger sister displaying before her eyes everything that beauty can have of the most seductive. That involuntary disturbance was only momentary; she had the courage to triumph over it and to run to her sister with open rms. She said things to her do tender and naïve that there might only have been sentiment and no intellect in that reception.

For her part, Rêveuse, obliged to keep quiet about her older sister's charms, the shine of which she could not sustain, appeared nonplussed; she could not reconcile what she saw with the idea she had formed of her; less mistress of her passions than Funestine, she could not forbid her heart a small twinge of jealousy.

How touching she is! What grace she has! she said to herself. *Simply dressed, she owes all her beauty to herself! Why am I not the elder, if being older has so many advantages?*

Funestine noticed her embarrassment, without divining the motive. "My sister," she said, "I frighten you; if my sentiments and your amity do not make you forget that I am ugly, you could not tolerate me." Such an ingenuous kindness made Rêveuse blush at her weakness, but did nothing to dissipate it; she was a young woman, and Virtue had not been her mistress.

Meanwhile, Clair-obscur, anxious about the fate of the Princess of Australia, consulted his mirror. He returned to it several times; he wiped the glass, he turned it in all directions, he rubbed his eyes, but did not find what he was looking for. The same object was presented there obstinately: a perfectly beautiful young woman. That could not be Funestine, and it made him impatient. *It might well be,* he said to himself, *that Imagination and Virtue have rendered her less nasty, but that they have rendered her beautiful surpasses their powers, and I'm not simple enough to believe it.*

In order to get out of his anxiety he set forth for his island, but one of the springs of his chariot broke as he was passing over Cythera. He landed, and while it was being repaired he went for a walk in the gardens. He found Amour there, who was amusing himself sharpening his arrows on a stone stained with the blood of hearts that he had wounded.

"You're at a loose end," the genius said to him. "If you care to take a little trip with me, I'll give you an occupation and I'll show you a palace that might not seem to you to be in bad taste. I love a princess; I intend and want to make her marry my son; she has intelligence but she's indocile; I warn you, too, that she isn't pretty, but I've got it into my head to make her my daughter-in-law. I've gone to a great deal of trouble to render her supportable, but thus far I haven't had a great deal of success. Marvelous things are said about your power; I knew something about that once, but I'm liberated from your pains and pleasures now. Write on one of your arrows the name of Formosa and on another the name of Funestine, and make use of them to wound them mutually.

"Where are they?" asked Amour.

"One is off fighting somewhere; the other is in the Palace of Eventualities. Let's begin with the princess; that's the more urgent. I've put her in the hands of Imagination and Virtue, but you can do more in two minutes than they've done until now."

"In truth, Sire Genius," said Amour, "you can't think so. Pass for Imagination; she's my friend; but Virtue can't stand me; she'll quarrel with me, and I won't endure it; I'll get carried away."

"Good, good," said Clair-obscur. "You can handle her; it's only a matter of fooling her; in any case, we have only to hide what we're doing from her."

"Let's go, then," said Amour. "I won't refuse, but I can foresee the enterprise going badly."

When they arrived at the Palace of Eventualities the genius said: "How do you like all this?"

Amour, less difficult than the fays, seemed content with it.

"Funestine is in the little house you can see in front of us. I'll go make enquiries and come back to give you an account of my discoveries.

He penetrated all the way to the princess's bedroom, but only found Imaé asleep there. The opportunity was favorable; he picked her up. "Quickly, Amour!" he shouted, while running. "Quickly! It's all set. In order to introduce yourself, take the resemblance of this sleeper; she's Funestine's favorite and confidant."

"I'm not fortunate in disguise," Amour replied. "I remember having made a rather thin personage under the features of Ascanius and Eucharis.[68] I even fear greatly for an author who has made me take on the name and features of a certain Aglaure in a comedy he's preparing for the public.[69] No matter; I'm still ready to attempt the adventure. How do you find me?"

"So similar that I'm confusing the true and false Imaé. At least refrain from wounding Funestine for anyone except Formosa, and do your best to give her a little beauty."

Amour introduced himself into the princess's chamber, and saw her come in with Rêveuse; he found them both so beautiful that he thought that neither of them could be Funestine, unless that the genius had deceived him. While he was seeking to clarify the matter, Funestine, mistaking him for Imaé, came to kiss him. Rêveuse caressed him in her turn. The perfidious individual smiled and, wanting to make himself loved, he forgot Formosa and only occupied himself with pleasing them. His uncertainty regarding the choice saved the two sisters.

After that great measure of prudence the genius encountered Virtue, who informed him of what he had done for Funestine.

"When will you take me to see her?" he said.

"Right away," Virtue replied, "but it's necessary to promise me first that you won't show any surprise and that you won't say anything about her beauty."

---

[68] Ascanius [Ascagne in French versions] is the son of Aeneas in Virgil's *Aeneid*. Eucharis is one of Calypso's nymphs in François Fénelon's *Aventures de Télémaque* (1699).
[69] Aglaure, featured in Ovid's *Metamorphoses*, is a central character in Molière's tragicomedy *Psyché* (1671).

"I'll consent to anything you wish," replied Clair-obscur, "but I admit that I don't really understand what you're saying about her beauty. Isn't she ugly?"

"You can judge for yourself," she added. "Follow me."

Funestine received him with an air of nobility and mildness that he did not expect. "I have so many obligations to you," she told him, "that I don't know how to express my gratitude to you; my words would enfeeble its vivacity, only my conduct can enable you to see its full extent; I will be fortunate if it effaces my first imprudences."

The genius, less attentive to that discourse than dazzled by the splendor by which he was struck, remained motionless. It was not the fear of disobliging Virtue that prevented him from speaking, but admiration. He would still have been admiring if the goddess, fearing some indiscretion on his part, had not said to Funestine that her masters were waiting for her. Seeing the false Imaé following her mistress, Clair-obscur made signs of intelligence to her, which she pretended not to understand.

"Are you content with me?" Virtue said when they were alone.

"Content?" he replied. "I'm enthused. To make you see that I'm not ingrate, would you like my island? I'll give it to you, with all it contains. I confess that I didn't believe that you were so skillful. This reeks of prodigy; it's a veritable one. If I knew your secret, I like beautiful women so much there wouldn't be any ugly ones in the world any longer. But is it really possible that Funestine doesn't know what she is? A young woman who is beautiful but doesn't suspect it! There's only her in the world of that species. I'm not opposing your ideas, but it seems to me that that ignorance is depriving her of the greatest pleasure of her life. Will you leave her for long without informing her of your benefits? Will it be my son who will inform her?"

Without replying to hose frivolous questions, Virtue asked him what Prince Formosa was doing.

"He's frankly irresponsible," he told her, "and utterly headstrong. He hasn't wanted my advice or my help. I believe he's attached to a fortified city that he desires to take by storm, and I'm very much afraid that he might be obliged to lift the siege."

"Don't worry," said Virtue. "All will go well. Go and tell him that I beg him, when the city has surrendered, to come and find me at the Palace of Eventualities. It's necessary to make him think of marrying Funestine; if you haven't changed your opinion about the marriage I presume that you'd like me to take care of it."

"With all my heart," replied he genius. "I'll go in search of him, and bring him to you."

He was getting ready to depart when he saw Rêveuse appear. "O gods!" he cried. "What do I see? How feeble chagrin is against such a charming sight! Princess..."

In order to interrupt a discourse that displeased her, Virtue sent Rêveuse to join her sister; she curtseyed and drew away.

"You're very wicked," said Clair-obscur, "to have taken away from me the pleasure of seeing her and talking to her; I felt enough intelligence to please her, and enough amour to touch her.

"I won't make you long reproaches regarding the imprudence of your sentiments," replied Virtue. "You don't doubt that I condemn them, and however little reason you have left, you ought to condemn them yourself. What has the queen done for you to repudiate her? I demand of you that you resume for her the tenderness that she merits; I want you to be reunited; that's the sole price that I put on the services I've rendered you."

Clair-obscur hesitated, but when Virtue wants something strongly she makes herself obeyed. He promised her everything, and did not break his word.

Amour could not make up his mind. His arrows were all in his quiver. *The elder is the more beautiful*, he said to himself, *but Virtue is defending her heart, and I don't like difficul-*

ties. I'd better stick to the younger; it's true that her beauty, striking as it is, doesn't have the charm I'm looking for, which arrests me when I find it. Oh well. I'll only love her for a moment.

In spite of his indecision, his power acted upon the two sisters. Uncertain, irresolute amour is nevertheless amour; its presence is always dangerous. Funestine became distracted, less applied to her exercises, less tranquil. Virtue noticed that change, and was astonished by it. She examined her; she interrogated her. The princess agreed, without excusing herself, that she was experiencing stirrings whose cause she did not know, and that her languor was increasing by the hour.

The false Imaé lent an ear maliciously to that speech. Virtue looked at her; nothing escapes her penetration and she recognized the author of the disorder. She took him apart and said to him: "Did you think you could deceive me with that disguise? Why have you come to interfere with my work? Don't you know that the hearts I protect are not in your jurisdiction? I'll soon render you master of Funestine's, but wait until I call you; you won't gain anything by anticipating my arrangements. Go away, Amour; I won't make you wait; when you establish yourself somewhere, nothing expels you."

"I could dispute the terrain with you," he replied, "but I don't want it to be said that we're never in accord; I cede to you with good grace." While speaking in that fashion he picked up his arrows. He appeared beautiful, even in the eyes of Virtue.

"It's a pity," she said to him, "that you only have the appearance."

"There you go," he went on, "You're always ready to decry me, but I'm not in a mood to get annoyed today. Adieu, remember our conditions. I'm counting on it, because you're not a liar. I'll send you Zephyr. When you need me, give him your orders."

Clair-obscur, intent on his project, was prowling around the Palace of Eventualities. *There's no hurry*, he said to himself, *about going to find my son, and I can always find my wife*

son enough. Let's find out, before leaving, what Amour is do-
ing. I'll be delighted to take Formosa the news that Funestine
is mild, beautiful and sensible.

While he was occupied in reasoning so sanely, Amour
passed in front of him.

"What, victorious already!" he said to him. "I don't suspect you of having quit the game; you've triumphed, since I
see you."

"I suspected," replied Amour, "that you were going to
cause me to make a false step, and that I'd be discovered. Sire
Genius, I wish you good day; I don't believe that we'll be seen
together for a long time." Having said that, he flew away.
Clair-obscur made no reply, and departed in his own direction.

The next day saw a singular example of the inconstancy
of things down here. Rêveuse found herself so changed when
she woke up that she had difficulty recognizing herself. There
were the same eyes, the same features, but there were no longer the same charms. What became of her? Only those who
have been in the same situation can say.

Her beauty was the work of the fays; it ended when they
ceased to exist. The sad princess was afraid to look at herself,
and did not dare show herself. Imagination, Docility, Virtue
and Funestine did everything they could to console her. Did
they reassure her? You might doubt it, as I do.

The fays were nothing less than tranquil. Having become
mortal, their empire was collapsing day by day. The good or
the evil that they had done in the world was so slight that their
existence had hardly been noticed. What a change! What a
reverse! The desire to avenge themselves sometimes drew
them out of the languor into which the dolorous sentiment of
their condition plunged them, but the scant success of their
attempts immediately threw them into a confusion mingled
with despair.

They had tried to introduce themselves into the presence
of Funestine in order to annihilate the designs of Virtue and
Imagination, or at least suspend their effects; far from being

able to enter the inaccessible island, they could not even find it. They cited the two fays at their tribunal, who did not appear, and were demoted. Dissatisfied with a futile vengeance, they turned their fury against Formosa, who triumphed over the obstacles that their malice created with as much facility as if they had not been raised.

In that extremity, what course of action could they take? Only one presented itself, the idea of which filled them with horror: recourse to Clair-obcur! Ask him for peace! What shame! What ignominy! They were too proud to consent to it, and the genius was too irritated to sacrifice his resentment for them.

"Well," said one of them, then, who had a bad cold, the consequences of which she feared, "give me the power to act. I won't betray either the interests or the honor of Faerie. You know that I'm not maladroit. If, at the beginning of our quarrel with Clair-obscur, I had been permitted to respond to him, we wouldn't be reduced to seeking expedients to appease him. This is what I propose. You know Pacific; I have some credit with that genius, he has some with Clair-obscur. I'll ask him to talk to him, and to arrange a reasonable accommodation between us, of which these are the conditions: He'll promise...."

"No, no," said those who were listening, interrupting "If he promises anything, he'll run the risk of being disfavored."

"How quick you are," replied the fay. "He'll promise to dispose us to receive him well if he comes to render us immortality. You can see that I'm not going too far. If, however, Clair-obscur demands some other evidence of benevolence, I don't believe that you're sufficiently enemies of yourselves not to hear him. You're shaking your heads; apparently you're not thinking about what an ugly thing it is to die. In any case, if he employs good grace, as I don't doubt, for he's quick-tempered, but he doesn't hold a grudge, we can, for our part, do something for this Funestine who has such a strong hold on his heart."

The affair, put up for debate, suffered great difficulties, but finally, in spite of the opposition of the most stubborn, the mediation of Pacific was agreed by a majority vote.

He would have liked nothing better than to accept; he knew the easy-going humor of Clair-obscur, who did not have the strength to refuse him anything, but he was lazy and did not like to transplant himself. The fay said so many nice things to him that she eventually persuaded him. He set forth with a good equipage and reached his friend's palace in short stages, at the moment when the latter arrived there with the queen, whom he had picked up on the way.

"You've arrived just in time to share my joy," he said to him. "It's excessive; everything has succeeded beyond my hopes. What an admirable person Virtue is! When you know what she has done for Funestine you'll be amazed. I want to take you there; you won't believe your eyes. Those impertinent fays, who gave themselves airs and defied me, have been completely belied. I learn with pleasure that they'll die in a matter of days. When you see them again, tell them that I'll be content when I've seen the last of them die; but I scorn them too much to talk about them anymore. Let's only think about rejoicing."

"However," Pacific replied, "I'm charged with proposing an accommodation to you on their behalf."

"To me!" said the genius. "Are they mad?"

"On the contrary," replied the negotiator. "I find that they're very sage, since they're trying to regain your amity."

"But I no longer have any passion than to get along well with everyone," said Clair-obscur. "If we've fallen out, it's their fault. They're repenting of it! They want an accommodation! I consent to that all the more willingly because, having no more need of them, it will be without interest on my part. I see that the loss of immortality afflicts them; it's necessary to console them for it. Is that what brings you? You have only to say so; I'll give you satisfaction."

"I confess," replied Pacific, astonished by such a prompt mollification, "that you couldn't give me a greater pleasure."

"Ah, genius," said Clair-obscur, "you've loved someone, or perhaps several. Well, when I've married my son, I'll go to pay them a visit; I promise to rehabilitate those you indicate to me then. You don't count on returning today; we'll sup with the queen, then I'll tell you the story of Funestine and that of Formosa, in order that you can tell it yourself to your good friends."

The supper was long. Clair-obscur was a great talker, and narrated heavily; if metempsychosis occurred among the genii, one could have believed that that one had been a woman and would become a financier. The queen, less patient than Dido, yawned two or three times. Pacific bit his lips until he drew blood in order to avoid doing likewise. Fortunately, the story-teller went to sleep in the middle of a long pause during the most confused part of his story, and his servants put him to bed. Pacific escorted the queen to her room and then went to bed himself.

After twelve hours of peaceful slumber, he took his leave of his host and went back to announce to the fays that peace had been made, but he arrived too late; they were no more.

The conquests of Formosa are not my subject, I fear the declamatory tone too much to go into the details of warfare in a tale of fays. I could, like so many others, have divided my work into several volumes, speaking of plans, marches, campaigns, contributions, sieges and battles, but that reeks of the historian, and I am not one. I could even, by making a poetic effort, have entered into the council of the gods assembled on Olympus in order to deliberate the fate of mortals; one would have seen them arouse that proud conqueror against them and make terror, death and victory march before him, but those sublime images are too elevated for a teller of tales, who is only recommendable by his simplicity.

Let us, however, say something about his expedition against the fays. He had just destroyed the Severambi.[70] Strange things had been said about the mores and politics of that people; he was informed of them; he was horrified by them; and he exterminated them all.

Only Embarces found mercy before the conqueror; he was a young prince about the same age as Formosa; he also had great qualities and views so vast that fortune did not second them. He had just conquered twenty rival kings, and Néodie, one of the most beautiful princesses in the world; he had scarcely savored with her the first fruits of his victory when Bellona snatched him from the arms of Amour.

At the rumor of the rapid exploits of Formosa, Embarces tried to engage the neighboring peoples to join forces for common defense. Fear not allowing any resource to be glimpsed except in slavery, all of them ran. Too weak to resist alone, he threw himself into a fortress that closed the entry to his kingdom. He defended it with a valor that initially excited Formosa's anger, but which soon changed it into esteem and admiration.

Embarces had neglected nothing to make Néodie consent to put herself in security in his capital. "You will be necessary to me there," he said to her. "You will strengthen the fidelity of my subjects, you will be able to send me help, you will conserve a retreat for me, and you will spare yourself the horrors of a siege." Either out of obstinacy or tenderness, she was absolutely determined to share his fortune. The most complaisant woman always reserves the right to do as she wishes.

---

[70] The Utopian novel *The History of the Sevarites, or Severambi*, attributed to the Huguenot Denis Vairasse d'Allais, was first published in English in 1675 before a much expanded and somewhat different French version appeared in four volumes as *L'Histoire des Severambes* (1677-79). Set in Terra Australis, it is a significant precursor of *roman scientifique*.

Every city besieged is taken; the strongest resistance ends like the weakest; sooner or later, one yields to the truth, but one yields. A few days more or less decide the glory or ignominy. Such is the belief; it is the sovereign of the world, it is necessary to respect it.

The prince, reduced to the extremity, assembled his officers; there was only one opinion, which was to perish in the breach. "Sire," said Sevaris, an old soldier whose merit had elevated him, "perhaps we will repel the enemy, perhaps we will be forced. We will do our duty; that is all that we can promise you; we only ask you for one favor, and that is to make the queen leave; her presence would not astonish your courage, but it would alarm our tenderness; you would be prodigal with your own life, but you would tremble for hers. The passion to acquire renders men bold, that to conserve renders them circumspect; often, in spite of oneself, one is a fortunate lover at the moment when one ought only to be a hero. I know a subterranean tunnel that emerges in a wood beyond the besiegers' lines; I know all its detours; if the garrison had been more numerous I would have proposed it to make sorties, but far from being in a state to attack, we are scarcely sufficient to man our ramparts. Confide Néodie to me and I will answer for her with my head; I only ask for ten soldiers to conduct her to Embarcide; I hope that I will be able to return soon enough to die at your side."

The king liked the proposition, but that was not enough; it was necessary to make the queen agree to it; she nearly drove him to despair with her tears and her resistance.

As soon as she has given in, she is disguised; the night is advancing, time is pressing. Sevaris puts her in the middle of her escort; they go down; the darkness and the silence favor them; they emerge from the issue and believe themselves to be out of danger, when, by one of those strokes of fortune so common in war, Formosa, who had been shown the same tunnel, appears, ready to enter it at the head of a hundred men. What can valor do against numbers? Sevaris is killed with two of his companions, most of the others are wounded, and, not knowing whether Néodie is among them, are preparing to flee.

A voice rises up crying: "Save the queen, comrades, and let me sustain the effort of the enemy." Those few words are heard by Formosa, who gives the order to suspend the combat and only take prisoners.

Meanwhile, the unknown man attacked with an astonishing vigor. The destroyer of so many nations was obliged to dispute his life against a simple soldier. They became animated, they dealt terrible blows, their weapons shattered, the blood flowed from all parts of their bodies. Embarces fell, covered in wounds. Who else but Embarces could have held firm against Formosa? There was enough daylight to distinguish objects.

"O Heaven!" cried one of his men. "The king is dead!"

Formosa recognized him, had him carried to his tent, and, without forgetting the state he was in himself, he searched for the queen. Needless haste! She was found expiring beside Sevaris. He helped to lift her up; she scarcely opened her eyes; she asked in a faint voice where the king was; she learned that he was not in danger. "I die content, then," she added, and rendered her last sigh in the arms of those sustaining her.

Embarces was cured; the death of his wife had been hidden from him. "Prince," Formosa said to him, "an enemy worthy of me, arms in hand, has sacred rights over my heart when he is disarmed. It is not me who has vanquished you, but fortune that has betrayed you. I render you your estates. I wish the gods permitted that my amity could render you..."

"Oh, Sire," Embarces interrupted, "You are telling me too much! The queen is no more. What use can your benefits be to an unfortunate who only dreams of being reunited with the one he loves? What is my destiny! The author of all my woes inspires gratitude, and I shall die without hating him."

"No, no," said Formosa. "You will live in order to be loved by me, perhaps to love me yourself. Prince, put the greatest price on the amity that I am asking of you, my heart will find nothing impossible to obtain it."

Formosa was too proud to dissimulate, Embarces too generous to be ingrate; their union became as celebrated as their valor. The idea of the queen became less vivid; it was gradually effaced; the tender Néodie was forgotten. "On the wings of time sadness flies away."[71] Perhaps that new Aeneas did not find his Dido in his passage; but we shall see him consoling himself with Rêveuse, as the first was consoled by Lavinia.

The story of Embarces might seem out of place; it appears less so to me. We authors are bizarre; one gives what he has not promised, another does not give what he has promised; it is necessary for us to let some things pass.

It was at approximately that time that the Thuvarians came to complain to Formosa about the insupportable pride of the Medoncires. The prince did not think that it was in his dignity to enter into a quarrel of such scant importance, which did not trouble the tranquility of his other subjects, and he sent them away.

The story of their dispute has nothing interesting for the reader who hears talk of similar things every day. People are no longer amused nowadays by the bizarre scenes that those two nations gave to the public; they recur too frequently. One sees without astonishment that in spite of the scorn and hatred that each had for the other, they live together, because we know that interest is stronger than antipathy. The Thuvarians can say that the Medoncires have shrugged of their yoke, but no one listens to them because those new helots, in spite of the obscurity of their origin and the baseness of their occupations, take a tone of superiority with their former masters with so much arrogance that no one knows any longer who were the slaves.

---

[71] The quotation is from "La Jeune veuve," a poem by Jean de La Fontaine

The Medoncires, informed that the Thuvarians had asserted their rights in vain, thought they owed thanks to Formosa. They delegated one of their number, who was a summary of the nation in himself. That modern orator, imagining that a passable face was a title of intelligence, presented himself with an air of confidence that surprised Formosa, accustomed to see everyone tremble. His discourse, although sugary, was rather good, thanks to the pen of a Thuvarian who sacrificed the honor of his brethren to the love he had for the daughter of the speech-maker.

The prince listened to him with a sort of pleasure, and was perhaps about to judge in his favor if the imprudent Medoncire "had not presumed to combine inaptly/the praises of a fop with those of a hero."[72] He was sent away without a response. Following the example of their master, the courtiers turned their backs in order not to be surprised making him false caresses. All that was nothing for his self-esteem, proof against disgraces; he was scarcely humiliated by the discourse of Embarces, which he heard distinctly. "That species of man," he said, "only has consistency when they speak about others and have the habit of it."

There only remained one realm for Formosa to conquer, and he could only render himself master of it by traversing the empire of the fays. He delegated Embarces to request passage from them. That step had unfortunate consequences.

The prince departed with a brisk and superb retinue; the marvels that were offered to his sight made an agreeable diversion for his dolor. He was in the land of the fays, that says it all, Many others have talked about it, and I do not want to be a plagiarist.

The rumor spread that Formosa was sending them a ambassador. They assembled and deliberated as to whether they ought to receive him and hear him. Opinion was divided; the

---

[72] The lines are from Nicolas Boileau's satirical poem "Discours au roi."

275

affirmative prevailed, and they reunited to decide that he would not be granted anything before the return of Pacific.

Embarces arrived and requested an audience. He endured a thorny ceremonial before obtained it; he was lodged in a palace so vast, and the apartments of which were so high-ceilinged, that it requires neatly thirty thousand aunes of jonquil damask to furnish them. They quibbled over his prerogatives, over his equipages, over his expenditure, over everything.

Finally, he was given permission; he entered the council chamber and said: "Formosa, master of all the earth, or at least the greater part of it, has sent me to tell you that he leaves you free enjoyment of your estates, I have the power to treat with you, Mesdames, as with sovereigns, and to offer you, on his part, all that can depend on a conqueror of whom laws and obstacles only know him moderation. He only expects of you a slight complaisance, which is to give him passage in order to go against the Apicholes, who do not want to submit. I promise you, word of a prince, that his troops will not cause any disorder on your lands, and will even pay for the water of the rivers if you demand it."

They replied harshly that, it not being permitted to any mortal to enter their empire without their permission, he was fortunate that they did not want to violate the rights of people; that he had doubtless forgotten that all the kings of earth were their subjects, otherwise he would not have had the temerity to assume before them the title of prince; that with regard to the son of Clair-obscur, he was a petty braggart of whose hatred and amity they were equally scornful; that the Apicholes were their allies, and that they would never suffer that he might try to oppress them."

"But have you considered," Embarces said, "that you might irritate Formosa?"

At that speech the ceiling of the hall opened; a frightful monster filled it with sulfur and smoke. The prince, who saw it hurl itself upon him mouth agape put himself on the defensive.

His sword broke in his hand; he called to his men for help, who could not hear him; they were petrified.

"So, Mesdames," he said to them, "you are coming to acts of hostility? Do you think you can intimidate me with vain illusions? You will see that the friend of Formosa does not fear prestiges." Then, uncorking a phial that he took from his pocket, he raised it to the nose of the dragon, which came crawling to lick his feet. After that mark of respect the monster took flight, and the vault closed again. The prince immediately ran to his men, whose different attitudes amused him greatly. Scarcely had they respired the precious elixir than the charm ceased.

The fays, surprised by that event, disappeared one after another. Embarces returned to Formosa and rendered him an account of his commission. "I'm annoyed by this contretemps," he said. "I would have like to have had no quarrel with them, for fear that it might be said in the world that I made war on women; but they are extravagant individuals who ought not to arrest us; we'll get away with enduring a few insults."

The next day the army couriers reported that they had been repelled by a few cavalry units; others said that they had seen troops forming up and retrenching on a hill three leagues from the camp. The princes found such scant plausibility in that story that they wanted to see for themselves what it was.

They started marching at the head of thirty masters. Scarcely had they taken a thousand paces than all of them, except Formosa, who was in the lead, cried: "Sire, you're going to drown us; the river is rapid and appears very deep." He thought they had lost their minds, because he saw nothing but open country ahead of him. By virtue of a prerogative of which he was unaware himself, enchantments, whatever they were, could not change the natural order of things in his eyes. He continued his route; his detachment followed him, astonished to be in the water without getting wet.

Embarces threw a few drops of his elixir into the river: a new prodigy! They found themselves in a vast forest, filed with a prodigious quantity of wolves, the sight of which, and their howls, frightened the horses so much that the troop was carried away by a stampede. The princes would have suffered the same fate had they not jumped promptly to the ground

"What does this panic terror signify?" Formosa asked.

"It's a gallantry on the part of the fays," replied Embarces laughing, "who are sending wolves to devour us."

"Wolves!" said Formosa, almost angrily. "Are you speaking seriously?"

"What, Sire, you don't see wolves, and you don't believe that you're in a wood?"

"No, in truth," said Formosa, "And all these jests are beginning to annoy me."

Embarces understood that Formosa was not subject to enchantments, and Formosa knew that Embarces had the gift of dissipating them.

They decided to return to the camp and make the army march, which the prince would precede in order to destroy the phantoms that presented themselves. It was not a petty occupation, but he carried it out to his honor.

The fays, seeing that their artifices were not succeeding, changed tactics. On the second day they saw in the distance an army that came in good order to form up for battle in a plain. Formosa thought that it was the Apicholes who had come to meet him. He fell upon them. The battle lasted nearly four hours without any sensible advantage.

Formosa, irritated by the stubborn resistance, made one last charge. Embarces seconded him; everything ceded to their efforts. The enemy broke up, the ranks were confused; there was no longer anything but horror and carnage; no one fled, no one wanted to yield, everyone was put to the sword.

The victorious soldiers shivered as they stripped the dead and only found women. And what women! Here the truth ceases to be plausible. The fays, not seeing Pacific return, who always hastened slowly, imagined that he had failed in his negotiations; drawn by a superior force that precipitated them to their ruination, they had made the insensate resolution to disguise themselves in order to oppose Formosa.

Such is the epic of their annihilation. Those who do not know it put them in works every day as existing beings; those who are better informed make vain attempts to resuscitate them, but only substitute abortions and ephemera.

Formosa forbade his historians to mention that expedition; he sensed that it interested his glory. Incredibly, he found the means of being obeyed; and in the secret memoirs that Alexander discovered in the temple of Jupiter Amon, that great event was still unknown.

The Apicholes, too confident of the situation of their country, did not defend the entry; they threw all their troops into fortified places and remained tranquil. Winter was approaching; they did not believe that Formosa would expose his troops to perishing in the impracticable marshes. They were mistaken; their cities were besieged and taken one after another. The last was defended for three months; the Greeks would have spent twenty years in it. It was that siege that Clairobscur had mentioned to Virtue, where he came in search of his son.

He arrived too late. Formosa had departed by another road in order to go to the Palace of Eventualities. He could not help trembling in examining his works and saying to all the genii in the world that he would have failed in it himself.

For some time, Formosa had felt a secret languor mingled with anxiety, which he strove to hide. No matter what efforts he made, he changed so much that those close to him were alarmed.

"I don't know what's happening to me," he said one day to his dear Embarces. "My conquests no longer flatter me, my glory is a burden; I'm no longer the same. Raised in my childhood with a young princess named Funestine, whom I hated, and I thought I had forgotten, her image persecutes me, I'm burning with the desire to see her. In an involuntary movement is pushing me toward the Palace of Eventualities. What god disposes thus of our hearts? Don't imagine that it can be Amour; monsters don't inspire him.

"Let's go," he continued, "to where destiny calls us. Men cannot resist me; I cannot resist the gods. Let's hasten to give the orders necessary to the tranquility of our kingdoms—I say *our* kingdoms because everything is common between friends. When everything is ready, let's depart without saying anything."

The journey was sad; Embarces' joviality could not extract Formosa from his reverie. They arrived at the Palace of Eventualities almost like a lover and his mistress, one of whom is sulking.

The isle being inaccessible, it is easily imaginable, without my saying so, that Virtue had taken possession of them while they slept and introduced them to it by unknown routes.

"Would you believe," Formosa said to his friend, "that my father has made all these marvels for a princess that you will not dare to look at? I don't criticize his idea, but it seems to me that this small building would have sufficed to lodge her. Would you believe, too," he added, "that he wants me to marry her?"

"You, Sire?" replied Embarces. "You were born to destroy monsters, not to live with them. What have you decided?"

"Never to consent to that marriage," said Formosa.

"Why, then, do you want to see her?" responded Embarces. "And when you have seen her, what will you do?"

"I don't know; let's commence by seeing her, and we'll decide afterwards," Formosa continued.

"But what if there is no longer time, sire," said Embarces. "I fear these involuntary impatiences; they're a bad augury for an indifferent heart."

"You're mocking me," said Formosa. "I merit it, but spare me."

"I spare you!" I replied Embarces, laughing. "It's for me. Sire, to make you that plea; perhaps I'll need sparing myself.

Who knows whether I might also find some Funestine, who will give me the desire to love her and please her?"

Formosa was too agitated to continue that conversation. He quit his friend in order to give his orders in the palace, of which he had put himself in possession by right of conquest or propriety; he regulated everything there with the sovereign air that accompanied him in his smallest actions. Surprised not to see Funestine, he asked for news of her.

"Sire," said a man of the species who make a feast out of saying what they know and what they do not, "the princess occupied the crystal apartment, but she was so ugly and malevolent that Clair-obscur has put her in a prison in order to do penance there for the rest of her life."

"She's no longer on the island, then?"

"Pardon me, Sire, it's in that little house that she's imprisoned."

"Can no one enter it?"

"No, Sire, the door is forbidden to all those who present themselves there, but I don't believe that it can be refused to Your Majesty. Would you like me to go and ask?"

"No, I'll go myself."

Embarces laughed at Formosa's questions and the courtier's replies; the former never wearied of interrogating, nor the latter of replying.

Meanwhile, Virtue went to find Funestine; she informed her of the arrival of Formosa and told her to prepare to receive him.

"Your orders are sacred for me," the princess said to her. "Far from resisting them, I would like to be able to anticipate them. My ugliness gives me no pain, I have no fear showing myself to Formosa, but gods, what an object is Funestine for him!"

"What!" said Virtue. "If he wanted to marry you as you are, would you refuse to consent to it?"

"Would you consent to it yourself, Goddess?" asked Funestine.

Without replying, Virtue went into Rêveuse's apartment. "Princess," she said to her, "the loss of a temporary beauty is afflicting you too much. You regard the privation of it as an effect of the wrath of the gods. Disabuse yourself; they destine you for an amiable prince whose happiness you will make, and who will make yours. Soon you will no longer envy the fate of Funestine."

The princes were walking in the garden of the little house; they perceived in the distance two young women coming to meet them.

"Sire," said Embarces to Formosa, indicating the more beautiful of the two to him, "there's an unknown woman who seems to me able to relent your urgency for Funestine. The attention with which you're looking at her makes me suspect that she will not be indifferent to you for long. Have you ever seen anything that resembles those eyes, those features and that grace? But I'm wrong to depict them for you; you've remarked them only too well. Your choice is made, I'm glad of it; it accords with my respect and my amour. The other pleases me; she's less beautiful than her companion; so much the better, her beauty won't remind me of that of Néodie, and I don't want to love anyone who can retrace her image for me."

The princesses advanced, and could not avoid them; they went past them. Formosa, the intrepid Formosa, remained tongue-tied, bowed to them, and dared not approach them. Funestine recognized him, and mistook his disturbance for a sign of scorn. She sighed; self-esteem, stronger than reflection, drew a few tears that filled her eyes.

Rêveuse did not see anything; she was occupied with the unknown man who had looked at her in a manner with which she was content. She believed, and not mistakenly, that he was the prince of whom Virtue had spoken.

"What have I just seen?" said Formosa. "If I can believe the simplicity of her clothing, she's only a servant of Funestine."

"And the other?" replied Embarces. "For whom do you take her? She's at least her maid of honor. It would be amusing if amusing if the master of the world only loved a freed-woman, and that his confidant had chosen better than him.

Formosa was not listening. "I'm doing her wrong," he went on. "I ought to judge by her marvelous beauty, and even more by the impression she has made on my heart, that she was born to command the whole world, since she reigns over me. While he was speaking in that fashion, he was following Funestine with his eyes as she went back into her apartment.

Never has there been a less tranquil night than the one that followed. In order to develop the movements that those four persons experienced, it would be necessary to know all the mechanisms of the heart; it would require more, it would be necessary to have loved.

Formosa adores an unknown woman, but feels, in spite of himself, that his idea cannot drive away that of Funestine, whom he believes that he hates. What bizarrerie of sentiment!

For her part, Funestine is prejudiced in Formosa's favor by the initial esteem that precedes amour; she cannot doubt that he is prejudiced by hatred for her. What a situation!

Rêveuse hopes, Embarces desires. They are not to be lamented; they are no longer interesting.

Formosa, followed by Embarces, went to Funestine's house. The first object he encountered was, once again, his unknown woman.

"Madame," he said to her, in an embarrassed manner, "I have come here to render a visit of propriety; I did not count on..."

"Sire," the princess interrupted, "I sense what the effort you are making is costing you. Funestine is not a sufficiently agreeable object to merit it."

"Oh, Madame," said the prince, who feared what the slightest rumor might have announced to her, "believe..."

"Sire," Funestine interrupted again, "this visit is as dolorous for her as it is for you, however different the reasons might me. Suffer..." She did not have the strength to finish. "O

Virtue!" she cried, as she withdrew. "Is this the last proof to which you will put my heart?"

Formosa found himself alone, and did not know what to do.

Embarces, who had been talking to Rêveuse, came toward him. "Good news, Sire," he said to him. "You have just been conversing with..."

"With whom?" he demanded, precipitately. "Speak, don't let me languish."

"Give me the time to speak," Embarces said. "The person I love is Princess Rêveuse, Funestine's sister, and Funestine is your unknown woman."

"Prince," replied Formosa, "I am in a state in which anyone other than you would not make fun of me with impunity."

"Me, Sire?" said Embarces.

"Let's leave it there," Formosa went on, without giving his friend the time to disabuse him. "You're violating the rights of friendship; don't force me to violate them myself." With that he quit him, and plunged into a wood in order to meditate at liberty.

Virtue, who wanted to conclude the adventure, had sent in quest of the King of Australia. His extreme old age did not permit him to undertake such a long voyage. Clair-obscur, the queen with whom he was reunited, Amour and Hymen had also been summoned.

Amour arrived first. "You can render Funestine sensible," the goddess said to him. "I deliver her heart to you; you will not have the time to make great ravages therein; I am only confiding it to you in order to hand it over to your brother this evening."

She showed herself to Formosa then. "Prince," she said to him, "I am Virtue. While you were making your name celebrated, I was forming a wife worth of you; your eyes have already responded to her charms, Amour and Hymen will answer to you for her heart. That wife is Funestine. I astonish you; you cannot believe, given the idea that you have formed of her, that she is the same person of whom the sight has given birth in you to such a prompt and violent passion. She does not know herself what she is; I wanted to leave you the pleasure, in telling her that you love her, of informing her that she is beautiful. Receive this mirror; enable her to look at herself in it. It is just that you enjoy the fist transports of her surprise, her joy and her gratitude. Go, Prince, don't delay your happiness any longer by the thanks of which I dispense you."

Penetrated by amour, occupied by the most flattering ideas, he flew to Funestine's house.

"Oh, Madame," he said, approaching her, "pardon me if I mistook you for someone other than Funestine..."

"What, Sire!" she said, interrupting him. "Am I even more horrible today than I was yesterday?"

"Say rather," added Formosa, "that you are a thousand times more charming, a thousand times more adorable."

"Is it thus," she said, "that the most generous of all men makes a cruel pleasure out of insulting an unfortunate princess? I know that I am ugly; I say it to anyone who wants to hear me; but Sire, I admit my weakness to you: I do not yet have enough virtue to hear you saying it to me. I ought to be less sensitive, or better able to hide my sensibility, but I am complaining to you now in order never to have to complain to you again."

"This is too much," said Formosa. "You have been left in ignorance too long of what you are. Take this and judge."

Funestine looked at herself. "O gods!" she cried. "What do I see?"

The mirror escaped from her hand and shattered into smithereens.

"Prince," she said, "mirrors are not fortunate with me; I break them out of chagrin or surprise. If it is true that I am such as I have just appeared to myself, it is the work of Virtue; she is the one you ought to thank; she wanted to render me less unworthy of you."

"And she is the one," said the prince, kissing her hands, "who is giving you to me."

"Very good, my children, very good," said Clair-obscur, coming in. "Embrace me. I doubt that you are as glad as I am; I knew, personally, that I would bring this marriage to a conclusion." Addressing Formosa's mother, he said: "Was I wrong, Madame to destine this princess for your son?"

Virtue arrived and said to them: "Prince, everything is ready to unite you. Embarces and Rêveuse are waiting for you in the temple. Live happily, all of you, and never forget me."

When the ceremony was over, Virtue and Imagination took the road back to Thyas. Docility returned to her dear unfortunates.

I do not know whether those goddesses have rendered themselves invisible, but I have not read in any other story that they have since done for anyone else what they had done for Funestine.